A Matter Of Seasons

By Karl B. Koth

Copyright © 2013 by Karl B. Koth
First Edition –March 2013

ISBN
978-1-4602-0887-8 (Hardcover)
978-1-4602-0885-4 (Paperback)
978-1-4602-0886-1 (eBook)

All rights reserved.

No part of this publication may be reproduced in any form, or by any means, electronic or mechanical, including photocopying, recording, or any information browsing, storage, or retrieval system, without permission in writing from the publisher.

Produced by:

FriesenPress
Suite 300 – 852 Fort Street
Victoria, BC, Canada V8W 1H8

www.friesenpress.com

Distributed to the trade by The Ingram Book Company

Dedication

*This book is dedicated to the warm memory of my Mother and Father,
Beryl (nee Campbell) and Bernard Koth*

THIS HISTORICAL NOVEL IS SET IN Jamaica in the early 1970s at the beginning of the PNP's introduction of "democratic socialism." Through richly developed character and realistic colloquial Jamaican "patios," its accurate historical information is effectively interwoven with fictional characters and situations. Throughout, it portrays historical events and societal problems, such as the disparities between rich and poor, and black and white at that time in Jamaica's history.

(Dr. Keith A. P. Sandiford, Professor Emeritus (History), University of Manitoba)

Table of Contents

Dedication iii

Acknowledgements vii

Parting viii

Prologue 1

Book One: Return 7
"Come back Liza, come back gal, water run a me yeye."

Chapter I
Me Ya-So 8

Chapter II
Bruckins 18

Chapter III
Red Stripe, Domino and Justice 31

Chapter IV
Highgate and Banggarang 51

Chapter V
Staff Meeting 62

Chapter VI
Wuk, wuk an' more wuk 73

Chapter VII
Mary Jean 85

Book Two: Work 99
Chicken merry. Hawk a near

Chapter VIII
Stanley's Piglets 100

Chapter IX
Socialism, Race an' Pum-pum 111

Chapter X
Madge 124

Chapter XI
Crime and Custos 134

Chapter XII
Madge Again 146

Book Three: Departure 157
"Wha gone bad a mornin' kyan come good a evenin', Oh."

Chapter XIII
Christmas Dinner 158

Chapter XIV
New Year's Even Nuttin' 169

Chapter XV
James's Plan 177

Chapter XVI
Madge: Nuff, Nuff Na Nuff ... 187

Chapter XVII
Ganja Tragedy 198

Chapter XVIII
Epilogue 209

Author's Note 214

Author's Biography 216

Glossary 218

Acknowledgements

A Big Up to my wife Nina, Angela Koth, Caterina Reitano, Keith Sandiford, Anke Sturm and Diane Vaz, for reading the first draft, making lovely comments, and proffering encouragement. And to Luther Pokrant for his suggestions for the front page design.

Thank you also to Kelly Kwamsoos and Kathie Allen, Author Account Managers, who guided me effortlessly through the publishing process, as well as the other members of the FriesenPress, for their professionalism and kindness throughout.

Parting

'Twas time to go,
The Feeling from frank reality
To myth explored-reverted,
Clanged and thudded againt my inner skull.
My concentration heroically battered,

Strove against countless devils:
(Enemies of love; murderers of feeling),
Won the day, not vanquished, only spent.
A cold hand gripped my heart,

Began to tug.
The flesh refused to give,
Won the battle and pulled back.
My whole refused to part,

Your part remained my whole.
Bruised, the internal flesh lived
Stronger in our rising sun.
(K. B. Koth, unpublished poem, 1979)

Prologue

My name is Norm, Norman Robertson, to be exact, a Canuck, actually from small-town Guelph, Ontario. And I am a friend of Doug Austin's.

I first met Doug when he came to Toronto to do his master's a few years ago. He had been teaching at his old school in Jamaica, Jamaica College, and decided to return for further studies. He was looking for a place to stay and saw my ad for a roommate on the bulletin board of the History Department at the University of Toronto.

Over the three years we shared the apartment I came to know him quite well. He was the first "White" Jamaican I ever met. Didn't even know they existed. But he was such an affable fellow, a West Indian in every sense: lively and dynamic, always ready for a laugh and a beer, with an eye for the girls, and what they called "pum-pum." And why not?

We got along very well. In fact, he was so lively, that he pulled me out to many a West Indian dance together with other friends we made, and I got to see another side of the world: the Caribbean world of Jamaica, but from the perspective of a *very* nationalist, White, Jamaican.

But heck! Let me set you straight. When I first met Doug I couldn't understand a word he was saying. That broad Jamaican patois was not something I had been prepared for in high school. But he would just laugh, slap me on the back, and say, "C'mon mon, yu soon learn' it."

He was not overly tall, about five feet ten inches. And he was handsome, with a mass of unruly dark brown hair and chiseled features. His eyes were a light hazel, and he could use them to fix you with a stare that challenged. But it was the way he walked, no, rather, strode, with a firm purpose, chest flung forward, hips thrust out, undulating slightly in a manner that bespoke of extreme confidence.

Laugh is right. He knew how to laugh. But that was his light side. He had another one. I mean, hell, I never met anyone among my friends from high school or university who had such a broad grasp of history. Maybe it was his time in Germany. You know, during his undergraduate years his father sent him to stay with a friend in Munich. He eventually enrolled in the university there and did a lot of reading, of people we never heard of.

What I'm saying is that Doug had a grasp of history way broader than my measly little undergraduate understanding. But that was good. It led to some great discussions. We would stay up till all hours, especially when he had his West Indian friends over to talk about the past, when there was some rum to drink, and in ways I had never heard of.

Well, let me explain that one a bit. Because coming from a Canadian high school, who hears about subjects like imperialism, slavery, the misdeeds of our own western society to people of the Third World? Get what I mean? That was all new for us. But these guys talked with a passion about their history that made us blink. Who thinks about Canadian history as a problem, eh? You know. It's just there. But for them, for Doug, there was living evidence of all their societies had encountered. They lived it. They were witness to the results in their daily life. They could see it: in the consistent poverty, the lack of education, the kids running around without clothes, or with stomachs sticking out from kwashiorkor. And they were bloody concerned and angry about it.

The first time I got together with Doug and his friends we talked late, late into the night. I mean, they talked. Me and a buddy, we just listened. At one point the talk was so loud, so vehement I thought they were all going to start fighting. It was only later that I learned that this was just natural, the West Indian way. Points were made with logic, but also with volume—the louder the volume, the better the score. These guys sometimes shouted down the damned roof, and more than once neighbours complained. But it was all in good fun. No, not fun. It was damned serious, too. Doug and his friends take on history was simply that the islands had been screwed by slavery and now continued to be exploited and drained by capitalism and imperialism.

Doug felt so strongly because his family had been there for generations. I mean, generations. From what he told me, his original ancestor there, the original Messermann, Jacob, had come to Jamaica in the 1780's and had married a woman of colour, a Mary Austin. Since Mary was coloured, Jacob did not marry her right away, but only after she had given birth to three children, the first of which took her name. This firstborn, James Austin, had later on taken over the estate, brought it back to life when it boasted some 300 slaves, and somehow survived the Emancipation by becoming a lawyer. Leaving the estate in his overseer's hands, he had moved to Montego Bay in the 1840's, established a successful practice, and eventually sold the estate. Later heirs had married "White" producing a blood line—called locally "Jamaica White"—whose appearance belied their true origins. They were inextricably intertwined with the history and, thus, the racial and economic fortunes of the island. These were the beginnings of Doug's family, which had managed to produce enough male children over the next hundred years to ensure the family name. Now they belonged to the opulent, self-satisfied Jamaican upper-class, pretty sure of itself, even now.

Doug didn't know all these details till later, especially the part of his "coloured" ancestor. That was when an intrepid cousin had dug up old records and written a family history. But that wasn't important. He did have generations of ancestors buried there. And he really did know the island's history. I'll give you an example.

When he first moved in with me I was intrigued by the stuff he would cook or brought home to eat. I'd never heard of salt-fish and ackee. Of course I know what cod fish is. Most Canadians do. But the place this had in the history of the island? And the ackee? This was all new to me. Who ever heard of ackee in Canada? A tree. And the tree had such a bloody significance for the island. He knew it down to the minutest detail. Listen to how he explained it to me, in one of his long lectures on island history.

"The ackee tree was brought to Jamaica in 1778 from West Africa as slave owners were looking for cheap sources of food for the slaves. It quickly proliferated and became one of the main sources of important minerals and even protein. Then the ingenious Black slaves had married the fruit with the salted cod coming from Eastern Canada, Newfoundland, and Nova Scotia. This has now become Jamaica's national dish, but not just because of nutrition. When prepared with coconut oil, a hint of Scotch Bonnet pepper, thyme, bacon, or salt pork, it is "raas" delicious.

And the history bound up in that simple tree is astonishing. The quintessential story of British imperialism could be wrought out from a description of the tree's importance to and other connections with Jamaica. From West Africa had come slaves and the tree. The first had grown the cane and harvested the sugar on large plantations, sweating through the long days in the merciless sun. Watchful overseers on horseback waited with ready whips equipped with leather thongs for use on their backs, should the cutting falter. For the cut stalks had to be harvested immediately when they were ready, then hauled off to the factory to be ground on immense rollers, squeezing out the last drop of liquid. Further processing, mainly boiling, then produced the finished product, the muscovado, which was collected, barreled, and shipped off, some to Nova Scotia and Newfoundland.

Eastern Canada supplied the barrel staves used to transport the muscovado and rum back to the east coast and then to Europe via the Atlantic slave trade. Its well-documented Middle Passage demonstrated the depths of the inhumanity of man to man. Then, trade was extended through the Triangular Trade with Europe, and its extension through the Quadrangular trade with the eastern seaboard of Britain's northern empire. One tree: such a history."

See what I mean, eh? Yea. One tree: such a history. Can you tell me the history behind some Canadian tree? No, he was behind it, into it; it just oozed out of him. He was an avid reader of all the great West Indian historians such as H.P. Jacobs, C.L.R. James, W. Adolphe Roberts, Eric Williams, now the prime minister of Trinidad, and Walter Rodney, the radical Marxist from Guyana. And he just lapped it up.

Not that Doug was some kind of fanatic. Oh, no. I mustn't give the wrong impression. He was just as adept at tearing ideas to bits as relating. But he was adamant: imperialism and its handmaiden, capitalism, had destroyed and continued to destroy the potential of the islands. And he was particularly hard on the Yankees. They were the ones providing the modern muscle to continue the destruction and exploitation.

Well, to be frank, here is where our minds met; I could relate to that. Yankee imperialism was a topic we never got tired of discussing. And it gradually came home to me how lucky we Canadians were. After all, we shared race and a continent with them. So we got the better part of a shitty deal. Not so the southern, "coloured" nations. They got roundly screwed.

That was the mood Doug was in as he decided to go back after his MA in History and try to make his own contribution. He was utterly convinced that he personally had to do something. Talking was not enough. So that was when he decided to apply to a government programme recruiting teachers and got the job at St. Mary High School.

Later, when he returned after that long, tragic year, he got in touch and shared my apartment for a while. It was actually only about a year because he then decided to move in with some lady he met down there. But during that time he began to relate his adventure to me. I insisted on taping some of it; it was so rich in information, at times downright funny, too. In fact, it fitted quite well into the oral history direction my doctoral studies were taking.

Then later on I decided it was too good not to write down. There was an historical value to this adventure I thought ought to be preserved. We had already finished our doctorates; I had gone off east to teach, while Doug managed to get a position in British Columbia.

Anyway, enough rambling. Here is Doug's story. You judge for yourself.

Book One: Return

"Come back Liza, come back gal, water run a me yeye."
(Jamaican folk song)

Chapter 1

Me Ya-So

The noise was like a gunshot. It reverberated off the lush, green banks of the roadside and up the low river valley. Doug Austin wrestled with the wheel of his old Morris wagon and managed to come to a stop before he reached the next steep curve. He remained seated for a few moments to gather his thoughts. Suddenly he was interrupted by a voice belonging to a raggedy-looking apparition appearing from nowhere over the top of the bank.

"Hey, man," said the voice, doing its best to imitate an American twang. "Yu back tyre flat. Yu wan' I fix it?"

Doug swung his legs slowly over the edge of the Morris. He got up and stretched, surveying the damage as he did so. The jack was in the back under his knapsack and an assortment of suitcases and bundles of books. He would have to shift all of these before he could change the tyre.

"Hey, man. Yu wan' I help yu?" This time the voice was right beside him. Doug looked down, becoming aware of its owner. He was about eleven years old, cheeks slightly sunken, body thin from lack of nourishment and too much bush tea, but wiry and not unhealthy-looking. The little boy was wearing what had been a khaki school uniform in its better days.

"What kind of help can you give me?" he asked, mischievously.

"Man, I man do anyting," the voice replied. "Yu got dallars?"

Doug's countenance changed from one of amusement to irritation. He realized that he was again being mistaken for an American tourist. He wasn't angry at the little boy. The increasing influx of North American tourists had made Jamaican whites invisible; everywhere he went it had been the same story, and the same tired explanations. Couldn't people tell by his accent that he was Jamaican? Christ, he thought, they spotted it like a flash whenever he was travelling. He had been politely refused so many jobs in Canada because over the phone he sounded Black. Only in his own country was he unrecognized.

"You can help me if yu drop that stupid Yankee accent. Besides," he added, "if yu think I'm an American with a pocket full of dollars you're going to be disappointed. What's your name?" he asked.

"John, sar," the little boy replied, slightly confused.

"All right John, help me change the wheel and I will give you a smalls."

John nodded his acceptance, although Doug could see that he was very confused and still somewhat suspicious. The tyre changed, Doug fished into his pocket for a fifty-cent note and handed it to the boy, "Mind you, don't spend it on cigarettes," he cautioned.

"No sar, I gwine buy some food right now."

"Alright John, God bless."

"Yes sar."

He watched the skinny pair of legs disappearing up the near bank-side on to the path that probably led to a small shop. Doug started the Morris and resumed the clattering trip up the steep, curvy mountain road in the direction of the city. Thoughts crowded in. This is probably the last time he would be on this road. Raas, how time flies. It seemed as if it had only been yesterday that he had returned home, full of enthusiasm and idealism. Now just over a year later, all those feelings had dissolved into one large presentiment of intense sadness, of frustration and disappointment, but above all, of failure.

Down from the winding hill he approached the lower part of the river valley where the road straightened out and the turns became gentler. He almost went to sleep with the monotony. Funny, he thought, it didn't feel at all as if he were leaving. This drive was so much like the weekend trips he used to make into town. He wondered what it would be like to be in another country again—anonymous, completely on one's own, away from family and friends in an alien culture without roots of any kind.

But, it was his choice, one that had to be made. There was no denying that. There was no place for him anymore in Jamaica, at least, not at the present it seemed. That was why he wanted to leave now, and he had felt the mortal blows that produce only bitterness. Better to leave now while beautiful memories assailed his consciousness: the contemplation of a fern, the smell of a bougainvillea, ripening sugar cane, salt sea spray. And friends, old friends and new, especially new ones he had met in the town.

Simple people, sophisticated others, new friends. These he could never forget. How could he? Centuries of grafting had forged a soul that was of this land. It could never belong anywhere else. One could survive, be comfortable, successful even, in another country. But there was that gaping chasm left from roots being torn from one's soil that would never heal.

*****

The plane banked lazily over the blue-green Caribbean, making its turn to land towards Palisadoes. He could see Port Royal through the starboard window. Ft. Charles with its cut-stone ramparts was in brilliant relief. Did Nelson's ghost still walk the deck looking for the French fleet? Across the harbor glistened the white hole in the hill to the east of the cement plant, left after scouring it for gypsum rock. Further up and to the west the green hills gave way to the rise that culminated in the Blue Mountains. He could see Bull Bay clearly, in the old parish of Port Royal. From there the land rose sharply to the escarpment called the Port Royal Mountains. A few more chains inland lay the ruins of Bilderburg. It was built on the edge of the cliff. Its southern portico gave a splendid view of Kingston, the harbor, and distant Port Royal. The view from the old sea-plane terminal east to Hunt's Bay and Salt Pond Hill also displayed the ruins of Morgan's old great house. Morgan (Sir Henry), then lieutenant governor of Jamaica, liked to stand on the hill and survey the scene at Port Royal, which he, himself, former buccaneer, had helped clear of pirates. So long ago, and still so present, Doug mused. History with its long arm and incandescent sweep carried all before it. None could escape.

It was in those years that the island's history had been stamped. Bilderburg, Doug, the Austin family were all part of it. The old great house had presented itself to him years before when he had bested the circuitous, treacherous gravel road from Bull Bay in an old Hillman Minx. He was the first of the living family to have found it after all those years. With a cousin he set out one Sunday afternoon, armed with maps and topographical charts on which the estate was clearly marked. But not until he burst around a corner was he in full view of it.

The gate was padlocked, but since no one seemed around he vaulted the low fence and made up across the pasture to the front of the house overlooking the harbor lands. The portico had extended along the back of the house. Now all that was left were some stumps of rotting wood. It faced a sloping pasture at the end of which were a cluster of mango trees. Beyond these the land rose again, eventually to terminate in the upper peak of the Blue Mountains.

Going around to the front he immediately noticed two small three-pounder cannons, strategically placed as it were, overseeing the escarpment, guarding against unwanted intruders. They were relics of some man-o-war, of the time when the great excursions of empire, the appropriation of golden wealth, the search for sugar lands, had led to that deflowering of innocence, the introduction of slavery that imposed itself like an ugly stain on the New and Old Worlds.

To the side there was an impressive rose garden, whose ruby-red flowers were stubbornly and brilliantly juxtaposed to the decaying wood and stark stone blocks that signaled a mausoleum of only one phase of that venture. The great house must have been impressive in its day, especially if it had been lined with warm Jamaican mahogany, as it was sure to be; but that comfort on the inside masked its sinister purpose. It was from a past he wished had never been, a past of which his family were indelibly masters and victims.

Around the house came a sturdy man of dark complexion, carrying a machete, followed by a mastiff of unrecognizable blood line.

"Good afternoon, sar, me name is James, an' I de headman up here."

"Good afternoon, Mr. James," Doug answered politely. "My name is Douglas Austin, and time ago my ancestors use' to live up here and own dis place. So I just come for a drive and thought I would have a look."

"What family dat, sar."

"Fe dem name Messermann. But dat was a long time ago."

"Yes, sar, me hear a dem. An if you come down wid me, dere is a ole man of dat name. Him can tell yu bout yu family."

Doug accompanied the head-man back to the gate where a little crowd had appeared. A White man up here was something of a rarity and sensation. They were formally introduced. The old man's name was indeed Messermann: his slave name. He was of slight build, and short, very dignified in his Sunday suit with felt hat, which he doffed politely, but without shoes, as was the custom. He must have been eighty if a day, his speech slow but firm and gentle. He could remember the family, he said. He indicated the rose garden, explaining that it had been planted by the first Mrs. Messermann. Down by the mango trees was the family burial, and right beside it the graves of deceased slaves. One family member had died in his eleventh year; poisoned, it was reputed by a Black nanny who carried out a curse on the family.

Doug drove slowly and carefully back to Bull Bay with thoughts racing through his head. He had come visibly close to the horrible slave past of his family's background, had wanted to scream at that history in attempts to erase it, but could not countermand this consummated blood experience. Slave owner and Black ancestor alike dueled in his soul, leaving no respite. It was the microcosmic history of the island. Everyone, Black or White, was conditioned by this pitiless, persevering, historic, encounter. They had all been conditioned one way or another; there was no escape. And they would all have to suffer the march, wherever it took them, whatever the outcome.

*****

Doug stepped through the doorway of the big plane, steadied himself on the railing and took a deep breath. He hadn't smelt that salt air for years—three and one half, to be exact. Now he was filling his lungs with it as if he had been gasping for breath on some operating table and some alert assistant had clapped an oxygen mask to his head. Raas, it felt good, especially after the foul air-conditioning and cabin full of over-perfumed American tourists, with their inane chatter.

He had been rescued just in time by the understanding Jamaican hostess who had smuggled him into a seat in the first class section and had kept his glass filled with Appleton and ice. He sauntered down the long corridor leading to immigration trying hard to look sober. There was a knapsack over his shoulders and a briefcase and small typewriter in his hands. The immigration took less time than he thought, except for one minor incident: the cynical look of the immigration officer who had looked at him and said, "Jamaican?" It was a bit annoying, but he supposed that he would have felt the same way had he been dealing with a bunch of jabbering tourists all day.

As he passed into the customs area he became aware of the confusion with tourists trying to find their bags amid groups of returning Jamaicans arguing and gesticulating furiously. There was a Black, oversized lady returning from the States. She was vociferously trying to convince a skeptical customs officer that a child's panty was really her own bikini. Her logic and the sheer volume of her voice were relentless. The custom's officer had had enough.

"Lady," he bellowed, holding up the little panty for everyone to see, "Go try it on and if it fit yu body come back an' convince me." The look of stupor on her face and the loud laughter of fellow passengers shut her up instantly.

Doug pushed his way to the front of the room, took a Sugar Manufacturer's cocktail out of a waiter's hand in passing, and got his first glimpse of the family he hadn't seen for some time. There they were: his sister Anne, his junior by five years and startlingly pretty, with a mop of dark blonde hair, carefully tied in the back as a ponytail. She had a mischievous look, accented by her pug-nose and twinkling eyes, sporting a golden tan. Anne also seemed to smile with an easy jocularity that made her induce an immediate liking in anyone who met her.

On the other hand, his sister-in-law, Christine, was as serious and guarded as Anne was open. Slightly more corpulent than Anne, still she had a nice figure, kind eyes, and a flock of brunette hair that just hinted at unruliness. She was smiling now that she saw him. What a thrill he felt pushing past the Custom's guards somehow, and then hugs and kisses.

"Raatid! You all look so boonoonoonoos," Doug blurted out.

"But what about you," Anne answered. "Yu in stiff need of a tan. Yu look like a ghost. Can't have anyone calling you whitey in this country."

"Pork, you mean," Christine countered. "That's the latest expression. You'll have to get used to it, if you know what I mean." But it didn't register. It was as if her statement had missed its mark completely.

"Where is everybody?" Doug demanded.

"If yu had told us a little in advance yu were coming they might have been able to get away," Anne said reproachfully. "James is busy at the office, and David has payroll to look after today. Anyway, they all sent to say hi. You'll see everyone when we get home and we have a little something planned for tomorrow."

"Well, that's nice," Doug answered. "I just hope you haven't invited a lot of buttus who are going to bore me with a lot of idiot questions."

Christine looked slightly hurt and also a bit apprehensive, as if she thought Doug was going to pull one of his weird tricks and embarrass everybody. She remembered the time he had appeared at his aunt's Christmas luncheon in a pair of worn-out old shoes and tattered shorts, and had taken his lunch outside to eat with the gardener.

"Now look Doug," Anne said trying to sound jocular, "these people are all your relatives and friends. They don't understand your radicalism. So give them a chance man. All they want to do is say hi and welcome back."

"I suppose so," he answered. But, he thought to himself, the truth is a bit different from that. They'll want to say hi, all right, but actually they will all be so damned curious to see how radical I really am, and what I have to say about Jamaica. Besides, they always gather when any member of the family has accomplished something as if to say, see, our class has achieved again. It really was a reaction caused by fear and constantly having to justify their wealth and ostentatious style of living in a country where over half the children went to bed hungry every night. They had to live vicariously through any of their family who had achieved distinction abroad, as if to say to the hungry, you see, it is not our fault we're rich, it's just that we're better.

The three piled into Christine's big, comfortable Ford, pulled out of the airport and onto the highway leading to Kingston. Doug was soaking up the warm sea air and admiring the sand dunes that he knew so intimately from many amorous excursions.

"People still come and park out here at night?" he enquired

"Not unless you intend to commit suicide," Christine answered. "Anyone who comes out here must have a hole in their head. A young Chinese girl was raped in front of her boyfriend just last week, and both had their throats cut after."

"Well its time the government and our set understood that hunger and lack of jobs lead to crime. Besides, I'm sure that it's only the well-off this happens to."

"Boy, Doug, that shows how long you've been away. The criminals these days respect no one. And the people who catch the most hell are from their own class. It's the poor domestic from Trench Town going home at night who is most likely to have her entire week's wages stolen, and, if she's unlucky she'll get a knife across her face."

Christine's tone was grim now, as if she had already run out of patience. She was tired of having to explain to Doug over the phone and in letters about the situation. She felt he was biased, not only because of lack of knowledge—he had been away for a number of years, at least during the time when things had begun to change for the worse. Besides, she felt that she was having to defend her own status and that of her husband too much.

"Well, there must be an explanation," he answered, unconvinced. "Domestics are usually supporters of the system, and that's why the criminals rip them off."

"But it's not just domestics," Anne added. "Anyone, including children, can be unlucky enough to meet one of the gunmen."

"I suppose you're right," Doug conceded. "But the initial cause is a system that has ripped off and robbed people for so long that some feel there only chance is to turn to crime. The miracle is that there is not more crime or that a Black revolution hasn't started yet."

Anne laughed. "You're such a cuffy. We'll never get a revolution here. Don't you know the average Jamaica Black man is a coward? Point a gun at him and he'll run a mile. Besides, we Jamaicans are so individualistic that we could never get a group together long enough to agree on a plan, much less carry it out."

Doug swung his head back and forth, a glint of anger appearing in his eyes. "Your remarks, Anne, are typical of the kind of verbal racism that abounds here. It's like an un-erasable pattern. It's as if everything you see comes through that prism of privilege that's informed by hundreds of years of slavery."

"I don't understand." Anne looked genuinely confused now and even upset at Doug's chiding tone. He attempted to mellow it. Only, what came out instead was a pontificating lecture.

"You see, my beautiful sister, if you ever took the trouble to read Jamaican history—which is difficult since there have been only a few superficial attempts to portray, let alone teach it—you'd know that there were, throughout the history of slavery, some superbly and brilliantly planned and executed slave uprisings that caught the authorities by surprise. It's only a matter of time before some really radical group decides to build on this tradition and teach their followers these facts. Understanding one's past can do wonders for self-confidence, if that's necessary, since I don't accept your argument about cowardice. And if one couples that with present economic conditions, which I see as getting worse, then we will have the perfect combination for a revolution. The probability is there."

Now it was Christine's turn to look hurt but, above all, bewildered. "I don't understand, Doug. Even if what you say is true, whose side are you on? Are you trying to tell me that you would be on their side? Even if I understand your feelings and your reasoning, don't you see that you would never be accepted? No matter how good you were in trying to help, your colour would always make you suspect in the eyes of a Black man. How would you feel having to accept as an equal the descendant of someone who had been the slave master of your ancestor? Could you ever trust that person?"

"Don't think I haven't thought that out carefully, Chris, darling. But that only makes me more determined to succeed. Besides, I don't agree with you. When people see what I am up to, I will be accepted. Besides don't assume that all Black people here are like that. There are many moderate and sane Black people who only want progressive change, not something radical."

Outside the window were the slums they were passing through on Windward Road with the heaps of refuse, old coconuts, and dark, filthy water running down the gutters and spilling over the clogged drains. There were literally hundreds of children milling about, playing amidst the garbage and filth. Some had carefully patched school uniforms; others, not so lucky, wore only a tattered trouser or skirt. None had on shoes.

It was useless to carry on the argument, he thought to himself. Even though Anne and Christine were intelligent enough to understand his argument, they could never accept the implications. Both lived within the system and were dependent on it. Their loyalties, if not conditioned by time, were related to circumstances. At least they were not hypocrites. Perhaps it was easier for him. He had decided long ago not to go into business, as he had been expected to do, but to become a teacher. That way he would not have to pay lip service to a system that he could not support intellectually or emotionally. Yet, he couldn't abide their stubborn refusal to understand. Why couldn't they see it was incumbent on every person of standing, Black, Brown or White, in Jamaica to start doing something different, to start making a new political contribution, at least to acknowledge that there would have to be change? And there lay the root of the problem. No one in a privileged class is going to give up their advantage so that more is distributed at the bottom. Marx was invincible on that point. It could only happen through a bloody revolution.

It was not as if some hadn't shown the way. There were examples of philanthropy, compassion and genuine concern. But too often these took the form of money handouts—paternalistic gestures. The bourgeois upper class, as a whole, did not see the necessity for social change. They were still too much armed with the tired justifications of the past to see that the present was outrunning them; and that, despite the new Manley government with its rhetoric of change. But here was another problem. Rhetoric and ideology could not eradicate five hundred years of history. For exploitation was as endemic to the social culture of this and many other ex-colonies. But people cannot be convinced and converted overnight.

History had that stubborn way of playing itself out exactly how it wanted. Even "little" people, the poorer folk, had incorporated that language of exploitation, even racism, which touched and imbued all social transactions with special meaning. Change, if it came at all, had to be slow and purposeful. Could it be implemented, grab hold of people's imaginations and psyches in one term of government? Even two?

And what about interference from the outside? Change in the New World always seemed to bring down the wrath of ex-colonial powers. That is what had happened to Cheddi Jagan in Guyana in 1953. Britain robbed him of his electoral victory by sending in troops and suspending the constitution. Then it shunted Guyana back on the "correct" economic path: the path of the Tate and Lyle's, Barclay's Bank, the Demarara Bauxite Company, and the other large corporations. Notwithstanding that this Marxist-oriented politician won two more electoral victories, every obstacle was placed in his path to thwart a less exploitative economic and social system.

It was not only the British. The U.S. was never far behind. After Guyana, it tried to turn back the Cuban Revolution with the Bay of Pigs invasion. Sure, that had failed, but at what cost was Cuba forced to subsist? It seemed the whole western world was intent on maintaining its repressive, capitalist browbeating of colonial and ex-colonial peoples: White against Black, Haves against Havenots. It could be put as simply as that. Economic wealth had to flow from south to north. Black – and

Brown-skinned workers had to subsidize Yankee and Brit. And no one should hate the White man for this continuing outrage? This projection of old slavery in modern form? Doug dreaded to think of the result in a tiny island like Jamaica. His class, his family, his friends should have been the ones taking the lead in forcing change. Yet, he knew this was idealism at its worst. They could not, would not budge. But, if indeed, they refused to change, then heaven help them if a revolution ever came. They would all be massacred.

But he didn't want to worry Anne and Chris with such morbid thoughts. It was his homecoming, and it was supposed to be a happy occasion. He would just have to carry on and work, make his own contribution. It was useless getting into arguments with his family. He had an obligation, and that was all that mattered. And the curious anomaly of his own position did not occur to him. That he was preparing to accept food and drink from people whose way of acquiring these he did not accept, did not yet set up that conscious tension that would eventually tear at the very roots of his own soul.

The car sped past the golf course and the village and began to climb the hill just past the little bridge. Christine was such a good driver; those blasted busses thought they owned the road. As they swung into the long driveway, he waved out the window to Clarence. Old Clarence, who was a fixture now, with the hose contentedly aimed at the gerberas. A relic of their recent plantation past: the faithful old worker. He could see his mother leaning over the verandah rail and his grandfather getting slowly out of the old wicker chair. Doug felt good. He was home.

Chapter II

Bruckins

Doug was still dressing when he heard the first car pull into the driveway. It sounded like his uncle's Buick. Of course, he would have to be the first to arrive. He was probably dying with curiosity. Despite his astonishment, perhaps even apprehension of Doug's views, he had always shown a liking and an interest in him. Possibly he really likes me, but more probably he wants to draft me into the family business, Doug thought. Fat chance; true, he loved salt-fish, but to eat with ackees, not to sell. No, he was not being fair. Uncle Benjamin was a kind, old soul. Not that he was an uncle in the true sense but a distant cousin of Doug's mother. But they had all grown up close together, an extended family. So thinking of Doug's own good came natural to him. Besides, Doug would have been more than a mere asset to the business.

He took out a brightly-coloured, Nigerian, dashiki from the cupboard where Imogene had neatly unpacked all his things, then put it back. Better to wear something a little less likely to jar on already sensitive emotions, he mused. Ah yes, the long cotton Indian shirt that Shanyahan had given him before he went back to Bangla Desh. That would be cool enough but still a bit different.

He made his way downstairs, past the study lined with his father's books, which no one besides himself and Anne had ever stopped to read, and made his way out to the long verandah. Two more cars were pulling in through the gate.

"Well, boy, yu looking fit and healthy as usual." His uncle bounded out of his chair, hand thrust forward.

"Hello, Uncle Ben, nice to see you again. You're not looking so bad yourself." Doug shook hands heartily then leaned over to kiss his Aunt Mae.

The driveway was beginning to fill up, and he walked out to the front, shaking hands and exchanging kisses, in the perfunctory manner honed by years of endless birthdays, anniversaries, Christmas dinners and New Year's Eve dances. They were always the same people.

Coming up the steps was Anne's husband, David, managing director of McCormack and Sons, Ltd. The firm had been started by Uncle Benjamin and consisted of a declining import-export business, a small hardware operation, and a few country properties. The latter were run by David's younger brother, John, although because of the decline of business due to the government's import restrictions, David had begun to spend a lot more time on the properties.

He held out his hand to Doug in his usual jocular and easy manner, "Well, yu ole raas, when was the last time I saw you?"

"Yesterday, as far as I can remember," Doug answered laughing. "I blacked out shortly after the second bottle. I not use' to that amount of raw liquor anymore."

"That's okay," David laughed, "at least yu lef' a good reputation wherever we were." David grinned in a knowing manner. David had picked him up shortly after arrival, and ferried him out quickly to one of their favourite bars. This was the Ferry Inn, an old seventeenth century cut-stone building at that point where the Spanish Town road turned east just past the Fresh River, opposite the huge cotton tree named after the man who had been hanged from its lower branches, Tom Cringle.

The Inn, which was what it had been back then, put up travelers proceeding from Kingston to Spanish Town, the old capital, and to points further into the country. Now it was a fashionable "rum shop," to use the local colloquialism. David's easy ways, not to speak of his love for rum, had made him popular all about the country. Nearly every bar on the way to the various properties counted him as a regular and welcome customer. He knew every barmaid by name, was a good spender, and blended easily with the local scene. Part of this was due to his jocularity and fluent use of Jamaican patois. Another was the way he dressed. He was one of the first to have dropped the almost mandatory jacket and tie in favour of the Caribbean shirt-jack, years before the new government made it almost official.

This evening he was sporting a splendid maroon, silk jacket cut in the Mao style with a high buttoned collar. "Anyway, forget about last night.

Look who's here. Remember her?" A lithe, handsome girl was just stepping out of a Fiat Spider. It was the latest vehicle to be deposited on the lawn, guided in by Clarence and his flashlight.

As she walked up the steps, Doug felt a twinge in his groins. Mary Jean Barrett was a fine looking girl, not beautiful, but comely. Tall, lithe, with long, light brown hair down to her shoulders, and with a skin that took a tan easily, she walked in a confident and pert manner. That she had had a crush on Doug ever since they were childhood friends, everyone knew. That he had ever reciprocated the feelings, no one could say with certainty,

Mary Jean's father had been a close friend and business associate of James Austin. When both her parents were killed in a freak accident in 1953, after their plane crashed off the end of the Palisadoes runway during a cloud burst, the Austins had taken Mary Jean to live with them. She had been Anne's best friend, and, in the meantime, had acquired a firm and invincible love for Doug. The two girls had boarded at St. Hilda's in the country and had taken their A-levels together. Then they had gone to England to do their degrees.

But Mary Jean had come down after her first year and joined the ground staff of Air Jamaica in Kingston. Now she was the office manager. She was intelligent, but in a practical, common-sense way. Doug had often remonstrated with her by letter about not continuing her degree, but without success. Mary Jean had inherited all her father's shares and was fairly well off. She had no desire for a university education or formal learning. Perhaps her only true desire was to get married—to Doug, of course—and settle down to raise a family. As she walked confidently onto the verandah, she was not the only one wondering how the two were going to get along.

Doug strode over to kiss her. She hugged him close, with a look in her eye that revealed all her thoughts. He looked down at her tenderly and said, "It's been too, too long."

"You know I've not found it difficult to wait, but sometimes I wondered if you were going to come back."

Doug didn't answer. He just looked at her deeply, then said, "I have to say hello to a few more people. We'll talk later."

He continued to move around greeting various old friends. At the edge of the verandah he stopped to exchange his empty glass for a fresh Appleton and water, which Clarence, dressed for the occasion in black trousers, white shirt and black bow tie, handed to him. During that moment, Doug let his thoughts drift to the slow, lazy chatter coming from the rest of the verandah. There was no accent in the world that thrilled him as much as the West Indian. It was British English, infused with accents and words from Africa, Spain, France, and a thousand places. It was also laid-back, and, at times, downright slovenly. But it could also be used to express the most hilariously funny situations.

Unfortunately, as lazy as the sounds were, not so the content of some of the thoughts that were being expressed. Doug shuddered when he thought of the rest of the society hearing what was being said here. The women of the upper class still managed little in the way of good conversation. In her famous diary, Lady Nugent had recorded their favourite topics two hundred years before: lazy maids and the latest French perfumes or fashions.

However, the conversation had undergone one slight change in the period. For these ladies were accustomed to having their fashion fancies satisfied by the chic boutiques located at strategic points in St. Andrew. But now with the new government's restrictions on luxury imports, shopping was not quite as interesting. Lately, the most important topic of conversation, judged by the dedicated air of the participants, concerned which shop had quantities of this or that luxury that was already under import ban.

Doug looked up and noticed Anne standing apart from a little group where her husband was the center of attention. Smiling, he walked over to her, "This little surprise is not so little after all"

"Well, what you expected," she replied, "don't you know we still do things in style here?"

He smiled, then decided to change the subject to one which he had been thinking about for some time, "Tell me, Anne, how are things between you and David these days, not that I want to pry, understand?"

She became suddenly serious, so much so that he realized that this was no longer his little sister but a grown woman, with adult problems. At this moment, perhaps they were the kind of problems she would have been better off not having. Moreover, he wasn't to know yet that he had landed squarely on a sore point.

"We understand each other," she replied, "not that that's telling you very much. There really isn't much to tell. David is wrapped up in his work and spends most of the time in the country. I'm not even sure what he does anymore, but he says he is trying to get all the properties into production again. Apparently they have plans but…" She broke off, grimaced before continuing. "Besides, he has the rest of the business to look after. I suppose that what I'm really saying is that we have an ordinary marriage. But it isn't at all satisfying to me, and, because of this, I imagine all sorts of things, like other women and God knows what."

Doug had watched her thoughtfully as she was speaking. He could see that although she was smiling, she was really very unhappy, but he didn't want to pry. He knew that he was the last person to offer advice on marital problems; besides, Anne would come to him first if she wanted to talk about her problems.

Smiling up at him again, she broke through his thoughts. "And what about you now, brother man? We haven't had much of a chance to chat. What exactly are you up to besides chasing gal dem and breaking female hearts?"

"Frankly, there isn't much to tell, darling, except what you already know. I accepted a post at a small secondary school in the country and intend to teach there and get as involved as I possibly can in community affairs."

"But wouldn't it have been better for you to have taught here in town, perhaps at Jamaica College? Surely they would have loved to have an old boy with your academic record as a teacher?"

"Sweet chile, that is exactly the sort of thing I wanted to get away from. In the first place, I think all those private schools should be abolished and turned into public schools. It's time Jamaica started to realize that everybody has a right to be educated to his or her capacity."

"But that wouldn't be fair to all the Old Boys who've spent so much money to keep that school going."

"Anne, that's a myth. The people of this country, all the people, are paying taxes so that a few can get a secondary education. That is not only not fair, it's not even good for the country—all that talent going to waste." Doug was obviously heated, as he approached another of his favourite topics. He could never quite seem to measure his tone with the degree of enlightenment of the person he was talking to. It was as if he expected all his words and arguments to be accepted without query by his friends, and as if it were a personal insult to his integrity that he could not make them understand his thoughts.

"Well, I don't know," his sister countered sincerely. "Education may be fine for some people, but look at all those fellows who were educated on government money. They're all up at the university plotting how to make a revolution. Is that what they were sent there to do? Anyway, that's all politics, and way above my head. I just wish you would realize how you hurt those of us who love you when you talk and act like that."

Doug looked hard at his sister for a moment. Then his face softened. He smiled and chucked her under the chin. "You're right. Anne. Yu don't know one damned thing about politics. But yu asked me what I was going to do and I told you. Let's talk about something more pleasant."

"OK by me," she answered. "There was, in fact, something else. Do you know that one young lady in particular has been burning her heart out over you?"

Doug laughed. "If you mean that beautiful, sexy, athletic, rich, gal, standing over there nursing that gin and tonic and stealing glances over here, then I am well aware."

"Well, are you going to do something about it?"

"Depends on what you mean," he answered, grinning.

"Come nuh," she replied, lapsing into dialect for a moment, "be serious bwoy, you know what I mean."

"If you mean get married serious then forget it, sweet gal." Doug's voice had taken on the hard edge that it assumed when he was getting into a political discussion. "I have no intention of getting hitched right now. Besides, you know me better than most. I'll probably end up marrying someone with similar interests. Where am I going to find that person in this crowd? That means you might have a Black sister-in-law soon."

"If you don't want Mother to have a serious fit, yu better shut up fast," Anne's voice took on a concerned edge now, which it always seemed to develop when she approached such topics with Doug.

But he refused to give up, wishing to pursue the point. "Mother's attitude is clear, but how about yours?" As was usual, his replies usually cut through to the core of the situation without wasting much time on sparring.

Anne's reply betrayed her own ambivalent position. "You know how I love you. You're still my Doug to me, regardless of who you marry."

"But that's exactly what I mean," said Doug. "I'll still be me. But what I want to know from you is this. If I did marry a Black girl, would you treat her as a sister?"

Anne thought for a moment, and then slowly she said. "I can't honestly say I would be pleased, Doug. But you know that we younger people are different from the older ones. Time has worn a lot of the prejudice out of us."

She paused and looked around before continuing. "You know that it would cause a terrible rift in the family. But I would stand behind you."

"Good for you, sis. Anyway I've had enough serious talk for one night. How about a drink? Scotch and water?"

Anne nodded, and Doug drifted away to the bar. By this time the gathering had broken up into several little groups. A few people were over by the bar drinking. Then, there was the serious group of women clustered around two elderly matrons who were carrying on the inevitable conversation.

Out on the terrace, which led away from the verandah, and which consisted of vines intertwined beautifully and completely with the bamboo lattice-work, a few couples were dancing. At the entrance to the terrace stood a small circle of men who were listening to what Doug's brother, James, was saying.

Doug took the glasses from Clarence and looked around for Anne. She had joined the largest group, which was also the loudest, around David. As Doug walked over he sensed that they were talking about him. Were they never going to tire in their attempts to have him change his ideas and to model his life on their choices?

As usual David was in an affable mood. As soon as Doug reached the group David's arm found his shoulder. "Welcome home, Teach," he remarked jocularly. "Hear yu' going up to the great Jamaican bush to bring education to the natives."

Doug grimaced slightly but kept his cool. "As a matter of fact yu heard right. As I mentioned yesterday I am going to teach in the country, in Highgate, to be precise."

"Well, that's nice," David continued. "Just thought I'd ask to make sure you were really serious."

"Why shouldn't I be serious?" Doug was beginning to get testy, but tried not to sound defensive.

"Oh, no special reason," David replied warily. "Except that with your brain and education I can't see you wasting your time at a little country school."

At that moment John McCormack, David's younger brother, joined them. John was a much smaller, and, as far as Doug was concerned, a most unlikeable individual. He was the nearest thing to a racist, redneck, Jamaican that Doug had ever encountered. John managed some of the McCormack properties in the country along with David.

But whereas most people liked David, who was never above taking a bottle of white rum into the fields and drinking with the sugar workers, let alone indulging in his passion for dominoes at any local rum shop, John was a perfect snob. Moreover, unlike his elder brother, he was blessed with very little brains. He chimed in: "Not much money in teaching."

Doug felt the hair at the back of his head begin to bristle. John was not one of his favourite people. His cock-sure, simplistic, right wing views usually came out without any extra thought or subtlety. Either one agreed with him or one didn't. There was no middle ground. So Doug held back his anger. Besides it just wasn't the occasion to let off one of his blasts. And anyway, one could not score points with John. Once more he held himself in check. But he couldn't resist getting in a quick dig. "Not everyone is like you, John. Money isn't the prime target for all people."

"All those I know," John shot back briskly. "You must be the first person I've met who didn't want to make money. Or maybe, you have some other plans?" The last remark was obviously an accusation rather than a question. Stupid bastard, Doug thought, while he tried to think of a way of keeping the contemptuous edge out of his voice. He decided it was time to take the conversation in a different direction

"Didn't you ever hear of service? Service to one's country, service to people? You just can't take from society all the time, John. There comes a point where you have to start putting something back into society to help other people who are less well off."

"People," John snorted. "Do you really think that those people want you to help them? I know; I work with them every day. None of them have any ambition. They don't want to learn anything. They're the laziest bunch of raases I know."

"You would be lazy too if you had to exist on the measly wages that landowners like you pay for damned hard work," Doug answered, beginning to get visibly angry.

David, noticing the possibilities of a very heated argument tried to smooth the talk and reduce the antagonism slightly. "I don't necessarily agree with John, but I think what he is trying to say is that even if they do want to learn you'll never be the right person to teach them."

"What do you mean?" Doug demanded.

"Come on man. Yu been away too long. Things are quite different from when you left. Even if some do appreciate your efforts the vast majority will always view you as a White man and you'll never be accepted. All of us have our little place in this society and as long as we stick to it we'll be O.K. You know that."

There it was again. David had hit on the one argument that really affected Doug deep in his soul. He had heard it so many times abroad when he had tried to explain why he was going back home. Always his answer had been the same. It was his country. He was born there, raised there, and knew no other home. Its soil formed his soul. In Canada, and anywhere else for that matter, he felt like an alien. This little island is where he belonged. He understood the country and the people, he would argue. And he knew his cousins were wrong.

The majority of Jamaicans might not like some Whites because of what they represented and still represent. But when they came to see him out there contributing to the growth of the country, instead of trying to exploit people, when they saw him really making an effort to help, instead of thinking of some lousy profit, then he would be accepted, and on his own terms.

Besides, he would hotly counter, he was not the first person from his class or race who had made contributions to the country either. Now however, he decided against pulling out his old line, taking a lighter tack instead.

"It might take a little while but I'm going to prove you all wrong." The words exploded from his lips, and the expression on his face was vehement. An observant onlooker would have had a hard time figuring out who he was trying to convince, his family or himself. The fact of the matter was that deep inside him there was a twinge of doubt. It had always been there whenever he managed to acknowledge it. But he felt it was a good sign. It would only make him try harder. Success would be his criterion, and he was going to succeed.

Just then Mary Jean walked over to him. She had been standing at the edge of the group listening for a short time. Now she took him by the arm. "Come dance with me Doug. I'm sure you haven't had much practice with reggae." So saying she led him out to the terrace where someone had strung up a pair of loudspeakers. Doug felt a thrill as the sensuous bass sounds wafted over him and attacked his stomach. He began to move easily with the music. He noticed Mary Jean in front of him. He relished the way in which she let the music take hold of her body, moving it effortlessly to the hard beat.

Someone changed the record, and before Doug could realize it Mary Jean was in his arms, pressing close to him as they danced. His annoyance at the ending of the throbbing, pulsating, 'dungle' beat was soon soothed by another animal sensation. He became aware of her breasts pressing against him and her thighs as she moved with him in time. Her hand was already at the back of his neck, and softly, so softly, she drew him in closer, nestling her cheek against his. He let himself go completely and gave in to the lovely warmth that engulfed him, and, after the song had ended they stood together holding each other for a few moments. This, for him, was another station of confusion.

"Music finished, man," someone yelled out teasingly.

"How 'bout a drink," Doug asked?

"If you haven't had enough, I'll join you," Mary Jean answered. Together, still holding hands, they went over to the bar, got two drinks, and went out the far door of the terrace that opened up to the garden. The Jamaican sky was bright with the moon, and the only sounds besides the revelers were the chirping crickets. It was peaceful, beautiful, warm, enveloping, and smelled good besides. There had been an unexpected afternoon rain, which left an aroma made up of the mixtures of the fragrances of wet grass and damp earth, weeds and flowers.

"Doug, you really do want to teach in the country, don't you? I mean, it's not just out of a sense of duty?"

He interrupted her quickly. "No, Mary Jean, not just duty. I really like teaching, but it's more than that."

"That's what I thought," she continued. "I had a feeling back there when you were talking that you were trying to make up for centuries of injustice—that sounds too pompous and I don't mean it that way. It's only that when I look at you talking you seem to be hurt by something. I just can't put my finger on it"

"No, Mary Jean. I like the profession I've chosen. Learning and teaching—I can't even begin to tell the immense satisfaction. That's all I can say really. And I'm thrilled no end about going to live in the country. I always wanted to get to know Jamaica—the other Jamaica—not the urban middle-class one. There is another culture out there that we have only had a foretaste of in Kingston. It's vibrant, it's alive, and it's damned creative. I suppose I also want to get away from the stifling city atmosphere here, the silly round of cocktail parties, the banal conversations. It's hard to explain. Besides, it will be good to breathe the fresh country air again. You must remember how I used to love to go out to the estate and run around with Clarence."

She didn't answer for a while. Then she looked up and asked, "Will I see you at all?" Doug knew exactly what was going through her mind. He didn't know how to answer and took a while before he did. His mind drifted back to that comfortable feeling he had had when they were dancing. But he also knew that he could not succumb to it without compromising his own values and creative existence. Old boys, tennis, parties, clubs—he didn't want to go back to them. Somehow, even though Mary Jean was not the typical brainless, rich daughter, he couldn't see her living the life he was choosing. Not yet, anyway. Yet he didn't want to hurt her.

"I'll probably be back in town quite often for one reason or another. If you like we could go out when I'm in town."

"I'd like that," she answered quickly. "By the way, would you like me to drive you up to Highgate tomorrow? You are leaving for the country right away, aren't you?"

"Yes, I am," he replied, "but I've already made arrangements to get over." He could see the disappointment on her face. "I have four big cases of books to take, and David said he would send one of the vans. But thanks anyway."

Doug didn't tell her that he wanted to ride over in the van. In fact, he was really looking forward to the trip. The driver would be Eustace, who worked for his uncle. Doug had known him since they were boys. He thought of the many stops along the way to Highgate: a Red Stripe lager, patties, and maybe a rousing game of dominoes, spiced with some hearty Jamaican swearing, in some little country shop.

He remembered some years ago another village. With his motorcycle he had ridden up Manning's Hill road, turned east towards Cavaliers, then up past St. Christopher over the winding dirt roads of the Red Hills, and up to Lawrence Tavern, set deep in the upper reaches of the Parish of St. Andrew.

There, feeling thirsty, he had stopped for a Red Stripe. The little shop was hardly that; the one counter was barely ten feet long. The girl behind it shyly offered him a seat on a turned up Red Strip box, then asked him if he wanted to eat something. Since the walls of shelves were practically bare, he asked her what she had to offer.

"Ah can strip some salt fish fe yu, sar, wid some coconut oil, onion, and hard dough bread and tomato." His mouth watering, he was barely able to mumble yes. Over this repast he made yet another experience. Word got around. Soon the little shop had a few extra customers, not to buy anything as much as to look. Hasty introductions were made. And like many country Jamaicans, stories began to be told. Soon the conversation turned to more esoteric things: duppies and demons. Of these there were many varieties.

A favourite demon was Rolling Calf. Said to look like a hog, or again like a calf, it coursed the nights with fiery eyes trailing a chain behind it. Anyone bitten by one would turn into the same. The conversation ran for over an hour. One man had seen duppies climb an ackee tree and walk out on a branch. Yes, no, the chatter went on with a fascinated Doug losing count of the Red Stripe. This was Jamaica; his Jamaica, island of stories, fantasies, imagination. Some were from the deepest parts of Africa, told with a gusto and a heart of belief and conviction that would have been the pride of many a preacher.

But Mary Jean just wouldn't fit into that atmosphere. She belonged to the urban group of Whites who felt more at home in Miami or Toronto than backwoods Jamaica.

"Doug," his mother called to him from the terrace, "your uncle's leaving." He walked back with Mary Jean, glad for the chance to get away. "I'll call you as soon as I get back," he told her gently. He looked at her, trying to conceal his impatience. But she just looked back and he knew that he wasn't doing a very good job of concealing his thoughts. She reached up and kissed him lightly on the cheek. "I think I'll call it a night too. Give me a call when you come in, and don't wait too long." He followed her over to the steps, while she said goodnight to his mother and a few other people. Then she walked down the steps without looking back. He wanted to accompany her to her car but she was already climbing in.

"Well boy, it was nice seeing you again." His uncle held out his hand. "Pity we don't have more time to talk. You know you are welcome in the firm anytime you want. Jus' wanted to let you know. Your mother knows it too. Anyway, a man has to work out his own life the way he thinks best. Jus' thought I'd tell you, though."

Doug knew exactly what his uncle was thinking. A brain like his would be a profitable coup for the firm. It would be a welcome addition to the business. His brother, James, had done well in his association as lawyer representing the firm. Doug could see him over by the terrace talking earnestly with someone Doug did not recognize. The successful lawyer: carrying on the family tradition. James was aware of his own importance and success. No one would have thought he was only five years older than Doug.

James Austin dressed in coat and tie all the year round. Occasionally, like this evening, he would allow himself to put on a cool, long-sleeved shirt. But that was as far as he went. He had no intention of adopting the new mode of dress. Doug couldn't quite figure out whether this was because of his innate conservatism or his dislike for the new government that had introduced the shirt-jack. This symbolic break with the colonial past could not impress James Austin. However, Doug had to admit that his brother was a scrupulously honest person, who had a special, if paternalistic, regard for the poorer folk. He was one of the few lawyers who would take on a case for a poor person without sending a bill afterwards. Yet this approach bespoke of no 'socialism.' Indeed, it evidenced James's arch-conservatism and his aristocratic approach to social affairs. It was strange the way the world ordered its participants.

Both James and Doug had been given the same sample of noblesse oblige upbringing reinforced by his education at secondary school. But while James practiced the philosophy in earnest, it had taken quite a different tack with Doug, who had come to see his task in the world as helping the lower classes achieve the end of their oppression. Actually it was not strange that the two brothers should think differently. They had both grown up during an era of tremendous change. They had both imbibed differing social doctrines that were abundantly and feverishly discussed in front of them. Yet their predilections had been different.

Ah well, Doug thought, he and I live in two different worlds entirely. To each his own. It would not have occurred to Doug at that moment that perhaps he and his brother were not that far apart in their praxis. They only reasoned differently. If that thought had managed to bend his thorough purpose, he might well have changed his plans. But that discussion was furthest from his mind now, consumed as it was with his own perspectives and desires.

After the last guests had departed, he strolled through the garden again and stood there sipping his Appleton. Tomorrow is going to begin a whole new episode in my life, he thought, and I'm looking forward to it. Better to get some sleep now. If he knew anything at all, it was that Eustace would be on time.

He undressed quickly, throwing his clothes on the floor, and lay naked on the bed. Thoughts came and went, none coherent, but images and remembrances from the past: teaching, Mary Jean, his mother and father, John, till at last he drifted off into sleep. The first early morning clouds were beginning to cover the moon.

CHAPTER III

RED STRIPE, DOMINO AND JUSTICE

Doug awoke at the sound of the loud knocking on the door.

"Mass Doug." It was Imogine's voice. "The time way pas' nine and de truck coming at ten. I cook some salt fish an' ackee fo yu."

"Coming, Imogine. Thanks." If there was anything that could get Doug out of bed in a flash it was the thought of a salt fish and ackee breakfast, with boiled green bananas and dumplings. He literally flew into the bathroom emerging five minutes later dressed and ready.

As he was eating, his mother came and sat down beside him. He knew what she wanted to say and wished she would get it over with.

"Mr. Johnston phoned this morning." Her voice betrayed her real thoughts, that she hoped Doug would perhaps change his mind. "I told him you were sleeping."

"Did he say what he wanted?"

"I believe he wanted to know when you were coming. I told him I would ask you to call back." She hesitated a while, watching him devour the plate of food. Then she began.

"Doug, I don't want to interfere but you would make me very happy if you accepted your Uncle Benjamin's offer. You know they would love to have you in the firm. That teaching business does not look very sound to me. There are already so many people doing it. Why must you waste your time?"

Doug chewed slowly on a dumpling as if that almost tasteless glob of flour and water were going to give him sustenance to combat his Mother's insistent argument.

"Mother," he answered slowly, "in the first place teaching is not a waste of time, especially in Jamaica right now, but do we really have to discuss it? I have tried to explain to you any number of times, and I just get the feeling that my words are completely wasted. We don't think in the same terms, and I often feel exasperated in trying to explain." He looked at her as he spoke and saw the blank expression on her face that told him so clearly that he shouldn't even bother trying. Their worlds were so far apart.

His mind drifted to her person, and he realized that despite her fifty plus years she was an extremely attractive woman. Her hair, a rich auburn, told him that she was a real daughter of the Caribbean. Who knew how many different bloods mingled tolerantly in their veins. There were Jewish ancestors, French, Scots, English. And he knew that the light swarthiness of her skin was due to an African great-great-great grandmother. His mother's family had certainly been in Jamaica long enough.

Their slavery past was well known if not exactly remembered. As for ancestors, these were never discussed. One didn't have to. Their family was not arriviste, or "hurry come up," as Jamaicans would say, and therefore there was no need to prove family history. Or, he wondered was it because of the fear that they might have discovered some African ancestor?

The word 'White' for his Mother was not up for discussion. It was a fact, and about facts there could be no discussion. But it gave him an uneasy feeling nevertheless, for he would have liked to have had his existence grounded in the secure knowledge that he wasn't and couldn't lay claim to pure Europeaness.

Her brown hair carefully permed bespoke of a meticulous person who laid great store in outward appearances. He had never known anyone who could keep house better than she. Indeed that was what she had been brought up to do. Born in Portland, on one of the big estates there, she had from her early years been trained in the sacred West Indian art of managing servants and running a household. Only that running a big estate house with armies of family and friends forever coming and going was a little different from running a smaller establishment in the city.

But after she had married James Austin senior, also a scion of an old plantocratic family, but whose family had forsaken country properties generations before, she had had to adapt to the somewhat faster ways of the city and learn to entertain her husband's business friends.

She had certainly responded well to the new demands and had acquired a somewhat enviable reputation as a skilled cocktail hostess. Now that her husband was dead, her life had emptied of almost all meaning. Not having any skills that were useful in a modern, progressing world, she found herself with nothing to do except to help out at some ladies' charity or attend weekly meetings at the Woman's Club. And she did not have the perspicacity to adjust to this new world. Unfortunately, this was the one with which her son was so familiar, and which he lived for. No wonder then that any attempt at conversation or understanding was doomed from the start.

She smiled sadly at him, as if she were hurt and yet embarrassed as if he had said something stupid, or something that didn't quite seem to fit into the conversation. Without missing one single stroke of the fan that was providing a faint whiff of air, she said, "You shouldn't be exasperated with your mother, son. I'm only trying to think of what's best for you."

Doug chewed on, not lifting his eyes from the plate, wishing that the truck would come, giving him an excuse to leave. He did not really want to hurt his mother. At times like this he had no difficulty in remembering scenes from his early childhood, scenes that despite the changes he had undergone in the last few years reminded him of tranquility, of love, of security. He remembered the long afternoons sitting in his mother's room, laboriously trying to finish some silly essay for homework, how she would sit there patiently knitting or sewing something, occasionally ringing for the maid to impart some spontaneous instruction, or perhaps just responding to her training and calling the maid just to remind her that the 'missis' was still there, in case the servants had taken a respite from the hot afternoon sun and were having a break. And she would help him in her soft voice, with a word or a phrase, or perhaps comfort him when his pen flooded all over the clean paper where he was about to write out the finished essay.

He decided that the only way out was to turn on the charm. So he reached out and covered her hand, which was resting lightly on the table, with his saying, "I didn't mean to sound cross, Mother. It's just that I know what I want to do and I mean to get on with it. I am really happy with my decisions, and I want you to understand that." He lifted his hand and stroked her cheek while he looked intently at her.

"Come nuh, don't be so sad. I'm only an hour's drive away." She smiled back at him, and he knew that that touch was really what she had wanted all the time: the reassurance of love. And he thought again how lonely she must be, and of the tremendous changes there had been in her life over the last ten years. For those ten years since independence had spanned the time when Jamaica had really undergone its most rapid transition.

Not likely that she would ever really grasp it all. But then she didn't need to, not if her family, her children, responded at least lovingly. Doug realized this and was wont to do so on occasion. Yet sometimes he did try to articulate things that she had never heard of as he strove to overcome two centuries of cultural inertia with one little gasp of breath.

Then again, her husband's death had been an extreme shock. James Austin senior, barrister at law, had been her helpmate, confidante, partner, lover for many years. He was an extremely devoted husband. Gentle with her always, he loved his wife in a singular way, not common to many Jamaican men. Every day, at about twelve o'clock, he would phone her from the office, regardless of what matter he was engaged in. They would chat for a few minutes. She would tell him about the day's struggles. Softly he would advise, cajole, commiserate—express his love in so many ways. She would return to her duties, making sure he came home to a spotless house. The ineffable was their code, the empathy complete.

As a father he was just as concerned. Too wise to demand from his children, he counseled, demonstrated, led by singular example. A man of taste, avid consumer of philosophy, of matters he was never able to communicate with her, he could rise to the legal challenge as no other. As gentle as he was at home, he was strident, demanding, and relentless when arguing a case, or a point he took personally. Not one to deride points of law, he rose above his calling with a wisdom that many commented had been drawn from a superior grasp of life. At the same time, at home, he could be folksy, use wit and patois with dexterity, and make even the shyest maid relax in his presence. He was missed by his wife. He was missed by his children. Doug could remember the occasions his dad had imparted something special. And then there was the time he taught Doug how to swim, challenging the boy's courage by throwing him in the water of a swimming pool at friend's house on the coast outside Kingston, encouraging Doug to swim, but ready to jump in if the effort failed. His death ten years before had left an obvious void.

As with his father, Doug could muse on the closeness between his mother and himself. The little episodes from childhood resounded. There was the time when she took him shopping, when he had asked her to wear that brown dress with polka dot spots, and just to please him she had. He knew that she lavished more affection on him than either James or Anne, and wondered why. And he also knew that it was the very bonds such as these that kept him from making that total, irrevocable break with the past.

It was all very good to talk about the new Jamaica, but among his best friends, his political buddies from the university, he had always drawn the line when the generalities of class struggle and race swept up the inclusion of family. He could never forget the challenge one of his Black West Indian revolutionary friends had thrown out to him during one of the regular Friday afternoon beer sessions.

"Ah wondah when the shooting start which side yu will be on. I mean, bredda, when yu shootin beside me, and yu blood brother and class opponent comes into yu rifle sights, what yu goin' do?"

And he had always answered with a laugh before launching into a serious debate on class struggle. He was at his intellectual best when so challenged. But he also knew that intellectual resolution and blood reality were two different things, and that question would remain unanswered until it came time to pull the trigger. Not that he liked the thought of violence, but he knew historically at least that a bloodless revolution was a myth. Wasn't it Nietzsche, the German philosopher, who had remarked that all great European revolutions had been born in blood? Sure, he had been speaking about Europe. But the same was true of the world's: the American, French, Russian, Chinese, and Cuban revolutions had been bitter, bloody struggles fought relentlessly to the end, class against class, brother against brother with no quarter asked and none given.

But it was all very good to think of history. What he found difficult to do was to relate this to his here and now. Why should a man like his brother James be automatically pushed to the reactionary side? James was conservative in his lifestyle, that was true, and he was a staunch friend and defender of the free-enterprise system. Moreover, it was because he was sincerely convinced that it was the best for everyone. And on top of it, James had always made his nationalistic position clear, long before it had become fashionable at the Lions and Rotary clubs. He had always maintained that Jamaica would never be able to develop properly if its industries and especially its banks were controlled from external metropolitan centers.

His attacks on the insurance companies and banks had already forced a reluctant government to put restrictions on the movement of capital abroad. In fact the new policy of forcing the insurance companies to keep their premium income in the island had forced two of them to close. One of the immediate results had been the fantastic expansion of the Jamaica Mutual, a move that James enthusiastically greeted.

Doug sighed inwardly. No, it wasn't so simple after all. It was one thing to argue from a clear ideological position. But where was humanity in all this? Ideologies always seemed to imbue leaders with the desire to make everything perfect. So it had been with the French Revolution. Robespierre had lopped off heads in his attempt to cut the "cancer" of privilege out of French society. But was it that simple? Were there not more impediments to reaching a "pure" society? Human nature was one. Although some clever academics were wont to argue that such a thing did not exist. Could they be mistaken? Could the human condition not be rooted firmly in attitudes ingrained over ages, such as the struggle for survival? Could plain greed, for example, be exorcised by the constrictions of ideology? These and other questions were to occupy his mind in the coming months as he embarked on his mission.

"Would you like some more coffee, dear?" His mother's voice yanked him out of the depths of the discussion with himself, and he answered with hasty irritation.

"Yes, thanks."

"Imogene," his mother's voice took on that shrill tone she used when talking to servants.

"Get Mr. Doug some more coffee."

His irritability gave way to a foaming internal anger as he recognized in that voice again the epitome of centuries of injustice against Black people. It was not only the voice of a woman, a lady of privilege, talking to a maid. It was a voice of authority with all the overtones of racial superiority and class privilege. And he wondered why someone like Imogene could ever stand for this oppression. Of course, he knew the answer to that as well. Imogene was as used to accepting oppression as his mother or her class was at practicing it. The irony was that neither would have identified the relationship as oppressive. For both had been equally conditioned by the same centuries of history. And both had equally never been enlightened as to its presence. This historical bond that had conjoined his mother and Imogene, and had made them into a functioning cultural unit, was iron clad.

It was stronger than any bond that Doug would be able to forge with Imogene or someone of her class. He was aware of that. But he was also aware, nay, hopeful, that the very elements that had forged those bonds were now working for a resolution. He was not the only one of his class and background who felt this way. But he was unique in what he was attempting and in the way he was going about it.

For as yet the countervailing forces within the middle and upper classes had produced some interesting phenomena. Some sons and daughters were literally "dropping out." He smiled at himself of the use of that American pseudo-sociological term. Yet, there was no better word for it. Already quite a few sons of so-called "decent" families were living up behind the university, dirty, unkempt, utterly contempt of the bourgeois society that had hatched them. Copying the locks-men they had joined, they were the new phenomenon of the "White Rasta," by now fully versant with Rasta patois. Caricatured from one end of the island to another, they were at best the butt of long curious stares, at worst the targets of intense ridicule.

On the other hand, of serious, dedicated, leftists armed with a dramatic ideology, willing to leave their homes in St. Andrew, rejecting the pathetic Beverly Hills manner, there were too few. No wonder then that Black radicals rejected White West Indians as a class. To be honest it was a valid rejection. He knew this but felt inside that someone had to make the start. Somewhere it all had to begin. It was a terrible responsibility, and even, in some manner of speaking, an anti-historical one, but it had to be accepted.

The blast of a truck horn again impeded his discussion, and he rose swiftly from the table, relieved as well that he could get going. That truck could have been a trumpet call: his own personal Abeng. It was not just the sound of a crusty, impatient truck driver signaling his authority with a melodious swagger-stick. Instead it was a reflex action honed by countless trips to stores and wharves where groups of raggedy little boys stared in awe at the commander of such an imposing a vehicle, and who had to be startled into the reality that the vehicle was heading straight for them, had no intention of stopping, and that they had better jump out of the way.

In a way it was for Doug a reflection of his own impatience to get started, to take up his new life, to begin to do the things he had been contemplating and planning the two years he had been at university completing his master's. It meant an end to the verandah idle chatter, societal dullness, repetitiveness, and conversational mediocrity of last night's party.

With a jump he was up from the table and crossed over into the kitchen from where he could see the driveway. A red, open pick-up was in the process of turning around in the driveway so as to get the back up against the garage door where Doug's four crates of books and belongings had been sitting for a few weeks prior to his arrival.

His mother called to him. "Doug, don't forget to look out for Green Castle estate. You remember I told you. It used to be in the family years ago. I believe you can enter it from the coast road before you turn up to Highgate. We used to go swimming and picknicking there at Jack's Bay. It is fairly secluded so you have to be careful."

"Eustace, you old raas," he yelled out the window.

"Doug", his mother's shocked voice came from the entrance to the kitchen, but he grinned at her, turned back to the window to see the driver turn his black, shiny, handsome face out of the cab, glistening white teeth proudly exposed.

"Ahright ." A hand glided out of the cab and waved a happy salute, curving beautifully through the air before rejoining its owner behind the wheel. Doug spun away from the window and rushed past his mother, who by now was secretly thrilled to see him in the state of animated joviality she much preferred to his serious side, and had replaced her shocked tone with a smile. He gave her a hearty hug and kiss then bounded down the steps leading to the back of the house and the garage and reached the pick-up just as Eustatius George Washington Headley was swinging his legs out of the open cab.

He was about as tall and as old as Doug. Features finely chiseled, a colour a few shades darker than brown, with a fine row of white false teeth and two gold molars on either side. Eustace had a lean, muscular body and was dressed in light pants and green shirt-jack. The two other fellows in the truck, the side men, stayed put, acknowledging the greeting, but preserving the space for their driver.

Eustace held out his hand as Doug approached. "Well, Mass Doug, welcome back. Yu here to stay? How was the trip?" The questions tumbled out in no order as he displayed his pleasure.

Both he and Doug had played together as children when Doug had spent the long holidays on one of his Uncle Ben's estates near Tulloch, in the old district of St. Thomas in Ye Vale. Eustace's father had worked as headman on the estate as far back as Doug could remember and Eustace had not only been schooled at his uncle's expense, it was natural that he would have found a place in the firm. Eustace had been encouraged to go on to secondary school, but unlike his younger sister, who had done very well and was at the Mona Campus, Eustace's priorities had been decided very early. He was content with a steady job that enabled him to carry out his amorous pursuits with some style.

"Yu looking great, Eustace. Must be all that raas liquor an dem pretty gal that keepin' you so healthy."

Eustace laughed. "Sometin' like dat. An wha bout yu. Me hear you going up to Highgate to teach. Why you don' come down to May Pen an mek we have some good time togedda?"

Doug laughed again as he remembered to what Eustace was referring. In the summer after he had left J.C. and was waiting to go up to university, he had worked a short time in his uncle's main office in May Pen. Both of them had kicked up their heels in such a way that his uncle had had to caution them once or twice. There had been no evening that both had not taken the truck up and down through St. Catherine and Clarendon on the prowl. There was not a bar or shop from Old Harbour Bay to Frankfield or from Ferry Inn to Porus that didn't know those two. Any time that truck pulled up, the proprietor could expect a handsome profit at the price of keeping the bar open long after closing hours. And the barmaids were equally receptive to the two "pretty boys."

One of their favourite haunts was the little whore-house just outside May Pen, which served the bauxite workers and the sailors who landed with the bauxite ships at Rocky Point. Here Doug and Eustace had spent many a night for free, only covering the room bill. What they hadn't known was that the prices always went up slightly after their visit to cover expenses, and if it had ever become known the two would have come away with a lot more than just free-love.

Their other spot was Old Harbour Bay with its raucous fish wives and raw fish smell mixed with salt spray. Doug always looked forward to the drive from Old Harbour. The long, straight, flat road was bounded on both sides by waving stalks of sugar cane. Here and there were the occasional fields of cattle: one could make out the hardy Brahmin with its humped back and long horns, or sometimes the fatter Jamaican Hope that had been so successfully bred at the Hope station many years before.

But he especially liked the scene from the little village at the end of the road, with its lonely-looking seventeenth century church, resplendent with bell tower. There the road turned sharply to the east, running parallel to the coast for the few hundred yards until it ended at the edge of a more or less dried-out swamp.

That was a scene of utter desolation: in spots hard-baked earth studded with small crab holes; tiny volcanoes of bubbling mud, oxygen escaping from the bowels of the swamp that was still very much alive despite its haggard appearance. Too, skeletons of mangrove grape waved eerily and solemnly in the torrid sea-breeze. Finally through the little opening in the bush onto somewhat higher ground past the market, and, as if by utter surprise, the 'road' thrust into what could have been a pioneer village draped in a rectangle around a large clay-baked square. It was bordered on the south by the gentle waters of the Caribbean, and, in utter contrast with the swamp, packed with humanity.

Of course, all the people did not live down there, but by about ten each morning some villagers would gather to await the return of the canoe-outboard fishing "fleet." Looking at the faces of the people, Doug had often felt that the whole economy of the village was evident right here. It was at one and the same time commodity market, wholesale and retail store all wrapped up within fifty yards of beach. All the great transactions that were the daily habit of large brokerage houses in London, New York, or Toronto were to be found here in the microcosm. Here loans were made, interest paid, bets taken, mini-fortunes made, and bankruptcies enacted—and all revolving around the sea and the fish.

The fisherman's skill each night meant a fish tea for some protein-starved school child, or a hungry belly the next day. Even the dogs were dependent. Scavengers all, they roamed the beach by instinct at the appointed hour looking for scraps of fish gut. Skillfully avoiding the inevitable kick in lean rib-displaying sides, they kept the carrion John Crow at bay until they had patrolled the entire length of beach.

When Doug and Eustace had found their regular fisherman, they would enquire quietly for Cunny-Buck. It was the peculiar fish found only on the south and southeast coasts of Jamaica. Half turtle, with its triangular body decked with a plate of armour, was the finest roasted meat one could find anywhere, at least as far as Doug was concerned. And although they were in short supply, the fishermen could always find one or two hidden under an old crocus bag and stuffed down behind the rear seat or under the fishing gear. It was not so much a special favour as it was a two-way trade. The fishermen knew that if they had had a bad catch and were in need of some rope or tackle, even a tin of gas, that McCormack and Sons would not hesitate to advance the necessary credit. And they never foreclosed on a fisherman who was having poor luck. Besides, somehow, the bills always got paid. It was perhaps not a sound way of doing business, at least in terms of efficient North America, but it was the Jamaican way, and moreover, it worked. This was the price that Jamaican businessmen, whether the largest hardware house or the smallest Chinese shopkeeper paid for the privilege of making as profit.

It was difficult to assess the origins of the system. Perhaps it was rooted in the simple economics of a poor country with its vast army of seasonally unemployed who more often than not were dependent on the shopkeepers for the tins of milk, or flour or salt fish that were needed to keep wife and pickney alive during Crop-over. Perhaps also it was the realization by the shopkeepers that this was the only way it could work, or maybe it was the relic of African and European feudal societies where cooperation was the rule rather than the exception, before unfettered, brutally efficient "free enterprise" had dislodged humanity in favour of the dollar, as was the case already in Kingston.

They had passed Long Lane, and up through Red Gal Ring. The truck lurched as Eustace flung it into the first sharp corner after the flat almost straight road that led out of Golden Spring. There it paralleled the now-trickling Wag Water River whose substance had been drained off higher up to fill the ever thirsty Hermitage Dam that serviced the growing needs of the bulging capital city, which refused to stop growing.

"Take it easy," Doug remonstrated. "Ah wan get dere in a one piece."

Eustace grinned back, taking his eyes carelessly of the road as the next corner approached. The two side men in the back were hanging on, but used to the driver by now.

"Man, dere is only one so-so way fe drive a vehicle. Foot flat down an' horn at every corner. When the wheels bawling that mean she movin.'"

"At this rate It look like we gwine haf fe stop plenty to make me catch up with me nerves." Doug laughed as he saw a tiny rum shop flash by on the side. "Next bar we come to is time for a Red Stripe."

"Now yu talking," Eustace answered. "Ah was wondering how long it would tek yu to get thirsty."

As they came around the next corner what could not even be described as a village came into view. Hugging the side of the steep cliff were two or three tiny houses, which stood clinging to the side of the grassy hill, as if they had been molded into it. The fronts of the houses rested on long stilts that almost reached down to the street, and as the truck slowed down, Doug could hear music coming from somewhere, not too loud because this was Sunday. Besides being a holy day the not too frequently enforced liquor laws said that 6 p.m. was opening time. Nevertheless, they would be able to get in via a back door, since business had to go on, despite laws, and since thirsty travelers like these had to have their thirsts quenched.

When they got out of the truck, a little dog, which had been sleeping far back under the house where concrete and wood met hillside rock, began to bark. The boy who had been in the back of the truck bent down, picked up a stone, and flung it accurately into the ground in front of the dog. Thinking better of its earlier aggression it took off with a whelp out from under the house and into some bushes at the side.

Eustace walked up to the side of the house, and rapped sharply on the green door with the bright Coca-Cola enamel sign that was hanging on by two rusty nails, a jarring display of urban America, raping the tranquil, beautiful river bank of rural Jamaica.

Hesitatingly, the top half of the door opened and a small apprehensive face topped by a carefully woven head of wooly hair peeked out.

"Open the door, we thirsty." Eustace's voice was authoritarian, but not unkind.

The little face disappeared as quickly as it had come, and they heard a deep, female voice from the innards of the bar call out, "A who dat?"

"Four thirsty man from Kingston, sister." Eustace's tone changed swiftly to jocular as he realized that the little girl was not tending the bar alone.

The half-door swung back again, revealing a woman whose age was hard to tell because of the rolls of fat whose increase every year had refused to allow the skin to crease. She waddled to the door, her enormous breasts, perfectly revealed by the dirty outline on the front of her light coloured dress, came to rest on the top of the bottom half-door.

Her eyes swept swiftly over the ground and came to rest on Doug. Her features immediately turned shy, and she nodded her head slowly as she reached down to undo the latch that held the lower portion of the door.

"Mahnin, sister."

Doug swung the door back and squeezed into the corner behind it as she motioned with her head for them to step inside. The bar was a simple and typical Jamaican rum-shop. It consisted of one room in which there were four aluminum tables with matching chairs and a skittle table in the center of the front wall. Off to one side was the juke-box, turned low because of the Sabbath. Behind this along the back wall was a long wooden counter with a formica top and four heavy bar stools. A door behind the counter led outside to the back. A small glass cupboard was on the far end laden with various sweets, coconut cakes and coconut drops, and a stack of bullas. Behind the counter as well were various iceboxes and shelves stacked with assortments of liquor, beer and cigarettes.

Above the bottles was a picture that looked like a Sacred Heart, and the words "In God we Trust." On both sides of it were large photographs of the Ethiopian Emperor Haile Selassie and Marcus Garvey, and below them an autographed photo of the late Hon. Norman Washington Manley, the present prime minister's father.

The woman had taken up a position behind the bar and was busying herself digging some ice out of one of the boxes. Doug had noticed two men standing over by the far wall, leaning against the bar. The one was short and black, dressed in khaki clothes and water boots, while the other had on dark trousers, a white shirt and tie, topped off with a grey felt hat. On the concrete floor between them lay a short-handled machete on which the mud, gathered from a Sunday morning stint in a yam field, was already turning a light, dry colour from the midday heat. They had nodded a curt greeting, the one dressed in Sunday clothes touching the tip of his hat, the other barely bothering to move his head, just enough to be polite, but with a look of forced indifference, even slight hostility.

"What we drinking?" Doug asked.

Without answering, and confident that he knew what his friend needed, Eustace looked over to the bar and said, "Bring a Q of whites and chaser, sister."

"Which one?"

"Coke," Eustace answered.

"You have any Cola champagne," Doug queried? "Eustace forgetting my habits."

"True, true. But is long time me no see yu," Eustace grinned.

The two men at the corner of the bar were engaged in a heated conversation. Occasionally the words "white man" and "tief" could be heard, amidst much sucking of teeth. The man dressed in the felt hat had his hand around the other's shoulder, as if trying to pacify him.

Then the farmer dressed in the "Iron Man" water boots turned aggressively towards the group. Doug had been sitting with his back to them and noticed nothing. But Eustace did. He quickly interposed himself between the two saying briskly to the man in the felt hat, "Bredda, how de day hot. We can offer unnu a Stripe?"

The man obviously understood the tack and assented rapidly. Turning to the farmer, he said, "Mek we accept the kine offer, nuh? De day really hot."

The farmer was now caught in a dilemma, but from which a back down with a cool Red Stripe posed a sensible way out. The other continued, "Me fren' not only hot, him really angry at people who tief him Friday."

At hearing the word "tief" Doug swung around. "Who tief," he enquired? "Wha' happen?"

"Me dear sar, me fren' work inna small property up de road, cleaning banana walk. Las' Friday when he go fe him pay, de Busha say him nebba cut so much, an' gi him only half wha' he expectin'."

"But dat is raas. How he could do such a ting!" Doug exclaimed loudly. "Either he cut or he don cut it. If he cut it he shoulda get him money."

By this time the farmer had begun to drop his angry look. It changed only slowly, but an expression of doubt and interest began to shade over his face. "A cut it, sar. Plenty witness. But de damn Busha feel him could mek likkle money out a we."

"Lissen," Doug's voice was registering indignant concern at the injustice. "My bredda is a lawyer in town. If yu gi me de particulars I will see what I can do fey yu. Him never charge poor people. Come gi me yu name, an everyting else. Trus' me."

The man in the felt hat was nodding. He took his friend by the arm and counseled taking the offer. Names were exchanged, particulars too.

The barmaid standing behind the counter and listening carefully would only say, "Hmmph. Is so it shoulda go."

True enough, on reaching Highgate Doug contacted his brother, who promised to look into the matter. Actually it took James only two phone calls, and he didn't have to threaten a lawsuit either. Two weeks later, the farmer and two other workers who had also been shortchanged were called to the owner's house amidst apologies and the full wages paid. What they didn't know was that the Busha, the overseer, was given a hefty dressing down for his arbitrary actions. A few weeks later Doug stopped by the same spot to make sure the wages had been paid, to the eternal thanks of the farmer.

This is how it was in Jamaica. If the farmer had worked for one of the larger estates, he might have been protected by one of the big unions. But in a small operation he was at the mercy of an unscrupulous Busha, who often ran things his own way, far from the ken of the owner. This was rural Jamaica. It had been that way for centuries.

The matter having been taken care of, the tension eased. Doug motioned to the two side-men who had taken a seat by themselves over by the door deferentially to come and join them. The boys walked over silently and without changing the expression on their faces took a seat at the table, but in such a way that their chairs were slightly further away from the table than the rest. The drinks poured, they raised glasses, and after a swift thirst-quenching slug Eustace refilled the glasses.

"Well, what is all the news from your side," Doug asked.

"Nuttin much yu know. Same old ting. I still driving around as usual. Mr. Mac say I to try an' do a little selling so I take a few orders here and there every time a deliver." Eustace was silent for a moment as if he were thinking out his answer.

"That's great. But wha 'bout the properties? How they doin?"

"Well, I don't really get up there too much these days. The truck work and the selling keeping me running bout," he tried a little laugh and did not bother to offer any more explanation.

Doug was slightly surprised since Eustace had always made a twice a week run up to the property in Tulloch to deliver feed or some fertilizer, and was often required to make additional trips for some reason. But he did not press the point, thinking that he had been away so long that perhaps he was out of touch with all the new developments in the business; perhaps there were other drivers that looked after that route now. In fact, even in the old days his uncle had found it necessary to take on a second driver when the building season was at its height because Eustace could not look after both areas at the same time. Still, it was obvious Eustace was too embarrassed to reveal the real reasons behind his shift to the hardware run and selling. What was he trying to hide, Doug thought? Strange was this reluctance to open up. The two had been so close in the past, closer than brothers.

"How 'bout some domino? A bet yu a give yu six-love. Dem play domino a Canada all the same? You must be rusty now?" Eustace changed the subject neatly to an area that he knew Doug would not resist.

Doug let out a half-yell, half laugh as he brought both the front legs of his chair back to the ground, swung around and stretched out his hand toward the bosomy woman leaning over the bar.

"Yu have any domino, sister?"

"Yes, saar." The words came out slowly but with a great deal of effort as she shifted slightly on the bar. Her right hand disappeared below the counter and slowly appeared with a worn, discoloured wooden cigar box in which a number of ivory domino pieces reposed. She placed it on the bar beside her as Eustace motioned to one of his sidemen with his head. With that the boy lifted himself out of the chair with two broad hands (made broader by lifting miles of pitch pine lumber off the truck) and sidled over to the bar, his bare feet making a swishing noise as they brushed over the concrete floor, and returned.

Eustace took the box and emptied the contents onto the table, putting the box on the floor. He began to turn the dominoes upside down and mixed them with wide circular sweeps of both hands reminiscent of a truck driver trying to maneuvre his vehicle around a sharp bend, while the others adjusted their chairs closer to the table. Eustace looked around and asked, "How we stay? Same way?"

Doug, who was sitting opposite the younger side-man, answered, " O.K. by me." He smiled across at the boy. "Me 'ope you can play no?".

The boy showing emotion for the first time, as if the mercurial shift to an area of his own familiarity had evaporated his shyness, replied with an open-mouthed smile, balanced both arms carefully on the edge of the table, as if in anticipation of the gunshot that would start the runners off at a hundred-yards dash, hands hanging down as close to the dominoes as was possible without touching them. He passed his tongue quickly over his lips and not bothering with the formality of giving a verbal account of himself, said only, "Me ready, sah."

The domino game was finished with a flurry of slamming, swearing, numerous " me rass" and "rahtids", plus other pungent Jamaican expressions. It was a six-four victory for Eustace and his partner, the summing up of which had required a second Q of white rum. Then the four said their goodbyes and returned to the truck for the rest of the journey.

Eustace was wasting no time, Doug thought as they careened around the narrow bends, almost touching the sides of the hill. Strange, he mused, the totally different architectonics of British and North American road building. While the British engineers who had constructed the Kingston-Castleton route routinely conformed to the hill patterns, North Americans would have blasted through rock and shale, built tunnels and bridges, and thus destroyed the natural landscape. They always planned in a straight line, totally out of synch with nature.

A few miles further on the river valley narrowed as it approached the borders of St. Mary, close to the beautiful botanical gardens at Castleton, and the river channel became deep as the water picked up speed and burst with flaming white foam through the rocky' rapids and miniature gorges. Just past the gardens Eustace braked hard as he noticed the small squat river-stone building that was the local police station, but picked up speed again as they approached the next corner.

Just as the scenery was becoming more desolate, changing from the lush growth of the hills to the more weathered emptiness before the coast, they reached the flat narrow bridge at Grandy Hole, which was a popular mark for the half-way point between the coast and Constant Spring. Straight ahead the river widened.

Eustace roared over the bridge, which was empty, very little traffic being on the road at that hour. Doug, clinging to the door, one elbow sticking out more because of the effect of the rum than for fear of the driver's ability, wondered if the six-inch high, round, concrete mounds at either side of-the bridge were enough to keep any car from careening over the side, but knew they weren't. On the right was a steep cliff at the side of the road, which he knew ended somewhere beyond at a flat piece of ground on which would be a little house or shack.

From here on they were climbing steadily. Every now and again, practically at every corner, there would appear a tiny waterfall dashing past centuries old, carefully smoothed rock, to disappear down the side of the road, only to reappear some hundred feet down, where it would futilely fuel the Wag Water for the last few miles to its estuary on the north coast. Yet, despite the used appearance of the river, it was the only water source for countless families who lived along the river, and who eked out a precarious living on the flat wide banks by growing bananas, a little sugar cane, or even had a small pasture for the odd cow, goat, or pig.

Eventually the road flattened out and they were off the hills.

"Yu wan drive down to the coast, Doug?" Eustace asked.

"No, I think I will have to leave that for another time. Really, I want to get to Highgate as quickly as possible."

"Yu mean yu wan go sleep. Yu kyan tek de whites anymore." Eustace's teasing brought a laugh from his friend.

"Someting like dat," Doug answered. "I want to get settled as soon as possible."

They turned off at Chovey across the one lane metal span bridge from which Doug could see the river as it mixed slowly with the Caribbean, and at once realized the tremendous importance of the river for the local people. On the south side of the bridge a bevy of little raggedy boys were standing in the shallow waters fishing for jonga, or river prawn, a favourite food that was cooked into a soup. Over by the bank among the low trees, one or two boys were waiting patiently with slingshots made from the rubber of some abandoned tire, hands holding the loaded sling taut waiting for some hapless White-wing or Bald Pate to pitch. These two birds were favourite eating, but an empty stomach would make a prey of even the Pitchairy or little Canary, protected species though they were, although no protection in the world should have argued against their natural use by children whose only meal for the day might be the sweat meat from these miniature fowl.

Further downstream women were laying out the weekly wash, utilizing the smooth round rock and the early afternoon sun as bleaching agents to remove the evidence of a week among the soft St. Mary clay or to ready a school uniform for the Monday begin of the school week. They were always careful to do the washing far enough downstream where the water was shallow, and where there were not enough rocks to provide the hiding places and breeding grounds for the jonga.

In any case, Doug thought, soap was in such little use there anyway, the natural elements doing most of the work, that pollution was almost non-existent. He wondered how it would be with so-called "civilization" pressing down, forcing people into the mold and way of life that would support North American business interests.

He thought also about the river, how it was dammed way up at the source to quench the thirst of the parasitical city. But down here, the people who did the hardest work, the people who worked in the banana and cane fields, the people who produced the foreign exchange which the greedy middle and upper classes spent on luxury goods from abroad, like champagne, jewelry, and apples, were denied the sustaining power which would have allowed them to produce more and better crops that would enable them to be lifted out of their shattering poverty.

He thought of the ingenuity of the Jamaican Black man, from whom it had not been possible to rob the centuries of experience of living in a harsh African reality, and who managed to survive on practically nothing, subsidizing his better-off brethren in the city; and he thought of the women who were too poor to buy soap, but who would make sure that their children wore immaculately starched uniforms to school on Monday morning, washed and cleaned not with the products of the metropolis but by nature's hand.

He looked and wondered, his attention riveted on the Great House, now falling into ruin, set on a low hill just on their right side. They passed grove after grove of neatly planted orange trees, the property of the big estate that owned all the best land on the flat around the coast, and which raped the labour of the local people for a few dollars a day, while children scrounged with slingshots for a bit of meat, and while fat ugly North Americans belched their contemptuous obesity in the tourist hotels owned mostly by foreigners. They continued past the orange groves where not five hundred yards from the turn-off, the road bent sharply upwards. Here they began the winding climb towards Highgate.

Past village after village, Doug breathed in the cool air of the upper levels while he continued to stare at the melange of racial mixtures, people walking by the side of the road on the way to or from church, or sitting on a shop piazza out of the way of the direct midday sun. This mixture of colour and race never ceased to fascinate him, especially when he thought back to the monotonous blank hue of a Toronto or Vancouver street.

Only here he was the oddity, not the other way around, a fact that would only manage to slowly penetrate his feeling of comfort which came from being in a familiar setting. Still, everyone was not as mixed as he would have liked. The perfect Asian features of East Indian and Chinese spoke of some reluctance to enter into the racial jazz of the Caribbean. Even so, he knew that mixing was taking place between these two relative newcomers to the Caribbean scene and the dominant African stock.

Soon they approached the top of the hill and the road leveled off as they continued along the top of the ridge that led into Highgate. Here there was a magnificent view right down to the north coast. Here also he noticed the wide spacious homes and beautifully kept gardens of the upper class. He could bet that the colour of the people who owned them was light. Certainly they were all descendants in one way or another of the old plantocracy that had inherited acres of land. More than likely, with the exception of a few dedicated people, these were kept for future value and not for the growing of crops that were sorely needed in the country, which had to import most of its food from abroad. What a crime, he thought, that there were people literally living out of garbage cans in the city while all this beautiful farm land was overgrown with weeds, kept for its future utility value amidst a semi-starving population.

The jolt of the truck as it careened over a rock around the corner by the big new water tank focused his thoughts on the changing scenery. Gone were the palatial homes and inviting gardens, giving way, just past the new supermarket, to the smaller houses, some really only describable as shacks, wood instead of concrete, zinc roofs instead of shingles, and narrow well tread paths instead of gardens. By the animals, the scrawny dogs alone, one could have foretold the change in economics.

Here and there too were a few concrete homes of the slightly better off labouring class, those who had managed by a combination of guile and opportunity to land even a small paying government job, or who had been lucky enough to learn a skill. Still, the break had not been advantageous enough to carry them further up the road where they would have liked to have been. But he imagined that they must have gained some satisfaction from staring across the road at the shacks and even practicing some snobbery.

The road was descending slightly, and he realized that they had reached the summit and would be travelling along the crest of the mountain almost level and straight. Off to the north there were glimpses of the coast and small white dots as the churning sea glided past the reef that almost surrounded the north coast to land quietly on the beach. In places where the reef was not as solid, the full force of the sea slammed against the rocks and beach. This was the hurricane season, and the sea was in constant turmoil from the strong wind currents. Down there somewhere were the cliffs from which the Australian swimmer, Annette Kellerman, had dove into the angry sea, in the twenties or thirties. He couldn't remember exactly the details his mother had recounted as it was before he was born.

Between the road and the next hill the land sloped down sharply to the north and the coast. Here and there small patches of cultivation were visible, studded with rows of banana trees. But at least two thirds of the land was not cultivated, its use limited to feeding the odd cow or goat. Doug wondered why in this bountiful and blessed land people had to starve? But he knew the answer without pausing too long over the question. To the south, inland, where the hills rose even higher towards the mountains that ran east and west across the island, there were here and there the odd red blur signifying the roof of some poor farmer's shack.

For this is where most of the ex-slaves had to turn for a piece of land after abolition. Two or three acres, at the most, unsuited for the growth of sugar cane or banana, the two crops that had been grown capitalistically. Instead, ground provisions were all that a farmer without tools could grow on those steep hillsides, possibly enough to keep children from outright starvation, but woefully inadequate for a decent standard of living. And over to the north, where the land sloped down gently till it reached the coast, was where the descendants of the plantocracy still dominated by virtue of private ownership.

The uncultivated land around the township was probably being reserved for future development. Unfair and unjust, Doug thought, that the best farm land would be divided to serve the financial needs of a well-heeled class of people, while the worst land was reserved for growing food crops. Only a revolution could break with this pattern. It had been too long, too many years; the system that fostered such crazy underutilization of resources was too old and entrenched. And the whole was protected by a series of laws that favoured private property, and was administered by the scions of this class which knew so well how to protect their interests.

Before he had the time to look back, they were entering the outer precincts of the town. Here the houses were closer together. Now the tiny railway station came into view, another anomaly in this place. For while the railway had been built to transport bananas to the wharves at Port Antonio, it was no longer used for this purpose, while small farmers found it difficult to get trucks to transport their produce for the overseas market.

They reached a crossroads, and Eustace made a wide turn back in the opposite direction, which carried them up a steep driveway. Now Doug could see the buildings that must obviously be the school. On the right was what looked like an assembly hall, and in front a two-storied building stretched for thirty yards, classrooms on either side of a stairwell. As they skidded to a stop, a tall, dignified Black man stepped out of a room marked "Office," and made his way towards them smiling. Doug knew that this must be the headmaster.

Chapter IV
Highgate and Banggarang

"Mr. Austin, welcome to St. Mary's. I hope you had a pleasant trip."

"Yes, thank you Mr. Johnston. It is so nice to be here, and I'm dying to get started."

"Before you know it, Mr. Austin, the term will be upon us, and there will be swarms of children here for you to meet. Then, I assure you, you won't have time to turn for the first few days," he said laughing, but in a kind manner that seemed to characterize the man who had to be jocular but forceful and stern as the occasion demanded.

"But first let me get you settled. I have you booked in at a beautiful old house in Fraserwood. There are three other teachers there. You will enjoy both the view and the tranquility. It used to be a Great House, played host to many governors, before being converted into rental units. But the setting is fabulous, with a view to the ocean and a large plot of land behind with coconut, banana and ackee trees. Do you remember ackee?"

"Oh yes," Doug replied. "Up in Toronto there are many stores where we could buy Jamaican produce. Ackee and salt-fish being one of my favourite dishes, I will no doubt scrounge through those trees quickly."

"Very well, sir. Let me guide your pickup to the house, and I will explain a few more things." Mr. Johnston was affable, but Doug could quickly tell that he was used to leading and would brook no nonsense from either staff or students. It was a good feeling to be working for a competent and confident headmaster.

Doug got inside the headmaster's blue Chevrolet, and they started off. The school was not far from the clock tower, which fronted on the empty market. There the road divided, the right fork continuing down towards Port Maria and the north coast highway. But they took the fork to the left, going through the town, and after about a mile, swung right on to a driveway guarded by crotons on either side, arranged deftly along the cut-stone rockery.

To the left before they turned onto the lawn was a huge guinep tree. There were still a few branches with fruit, and Doug thought of immediately beginning a stoning campaign. There is a saying in Jamaica that girls learn to kiss from the pulpy, sweet membrane that covers the seed. If so these must be the sweetest kisses in the world. Better yet, if a girl bites a guinep and finds two seeds inside, the saying goes that she will bear twins first. He smiled to himself.

Mr. Johnston motioned the pick-up to the side of the house as they got out. "Follow me," he said as they entered the house by a long back verandah which separated it from another smaller apartment. As they crossed the verandah, Doug spied the tall ackee tree about half a chain from the house. It was still bearing a few fruit even though the summer was almost over. Some of the pods were already open, displaying the black seed at the end of the yellow arils, which were what would be actually cooked. Doug's mouth began to water as he thought of tomorrow's breakfast.

"Let me show you inside." Mr. Johnston led him through the dining room which backed onto the back verandah, through a corridor to a huge room looking out at the guinep tree. "We thought you would like this room. The one further down is occupied by Dave Crichton, our physical education teacher from Brighton. And here, this smaller room at the back we thought would be ideal for your books. I'm sure you can get some bricks and supplies from the hardware store in town and make a fine library."

Doug noticed there was already an easy chair and small table in the room. With a lamp and some bookshelves it would be a cozy place to read, write, reflect.

"And the kitchen is just off the back verandah. We thought you would take your mid-day meal with us at school, and you could prepare breakfast and supper for yourself," the headmaster added. "Of course, if you would like a maid to prepare those for you and do some washing, I can recommend someone. Oh, by the way, you can walk to school, it is not that far, but we also have three bicycles you are welcome to use. They are parked by the verandah, and the keys to the padlocks are in the kitchen."

"Mr. Johnston, this is great. I already feel at home. And is there a shop nearby?"

"Yes, Mr. Austin, there is a small one for basics just down the hill in the front. Well, I am going to leave you to get settled. But if you need anything else, here is my home phone number. You have the weekend to yourself, but we expect you at ten o'clock Monday morning for the first staff meeting. That will give you time to meet the other teachers. See you then." With that he left.

"Eustace," Doug called, "get the fellows to put those crates on the verandah right here su. An ah know you dying to get goin, so yu can go. Is a long drive to Old Harbour."

"Yes Doug. All de bes'. An if yu come dung we way, mek sure yu let me know before, se we can ordah a whites." Hands given, they were off.

Doug was left on his own. The house was empty as the other teachers were away. He could explore for himself. But the first thing he did before even unpacking was slide down the little hill in the front. There was a small opening in the hedge, and as he looked down he could see a small shop with what was a little bar at the side. He introduced himself at the small shop, where they were only too willing to pour a whites for the new "Teach."

Over the weekend Doug walked down to the town. What happened next was like a whirlwind. The hardware store was a few blocks from the school. On hearing that he was a new teacher, the clerk called the owner, a Mr. Porter, to tell him the news. Porter was a short, rather paunchy individual, light brown in colour, and with a busy, but pleasant looking face. It was Saturday and business was good.

"Ah already hear bout yu. A Jamaican fellow coming back here to teach. Yu could a strike me dead. We so use' to foreigners. But congratulations an' welcome. As yu see here we have everyting except books." And with a hearty laugh he reached out his hand.

The conversation that ensued was quick and businesslike. No transport. Man, I can fix you up in no time. Let me use the phone. You want a vehicle? I have a friend in Port Maria selling used cars. But I don't want a car just a motorbike. Motorcycle, yes man, we can fix you up with that too.

Not an hour later Doug was walking out of a shop in Port Maria with a second-hand, but in good condition Triumph 500cc, a powerful, popular, and handy machine used mainly by the police. He remembered his youth again, with the much smaller Francis Barnett plowing through Above Rocks and beyond into upper St. Andrew. But this machine was different. Here was power to spare. And he thrilled with the feeling as he left Port Maria on the long straight stretch through endless banana walks, until the short, steep, winding climb up to Highgate.

What was strange, invigorating was the way the transaction had been conducted. Porter had driven him down and introduced him. Small chatter led to who are yous. A maid was summoned to bring glasses and a bowl of ice. Rum as usual. Then Doug realized the man he was talking to was brother of an old boy from Jamaica College he faintly remembered. Another phone call, and enough raas this and raas that, and the business was done. Money would change hands later. And the price had been good, hardly 300 Jamaican dollars (about one month of his promised salary). Even the bike's license came with the deal so he could drive it away, as it had not yet been re-registered.

The business had been handled in less than half an hour. That was the best part, for it meant that Doug would not be stuck in town all weekend. Then the right turn came at the clock tower, and he was speeding up Fraserwood to his new "yard."

Saturday afternoon he spent surveying the town. There was actually not much to it, at least in view. The main street, about half a mile long, was the main hub of business. On the right was a small shopping mall. And beyond that was a new government fixture, a farmer's market, to facilitate the agricultural sector by giving small farmers an outlet for their produce. Actually it hid one of the government's intentions, which was to undercut the higglers who were used to going into the country, buying the farmers' produce cheap, and then bringing it back to the towns and markets to sell at a good profit. This new institution would allow the farmers to get the majority of the profits for themselves. About a hundred yards further on was a small bar or rum-shop called the "Pirate's Cove." Then, after a few houses a larger supermarket. Across the street from the market were a service station and garage, and then the hardware store.

The homes along Main Street belonged to the middle or lower middle class. The upper class all lived further down, past the railway station, in a suburban-like setting, with wide spacious lawns, finely groomed and usually tended by some youngster, called a "garden boy."

Of churches the town had a number. There was the typical and stately Anglican church, the queen of them all, but stuck away here and there would be a Bethel church, Church of God, Seventh Day Adventist, and many smaller ones still.

The crown jewel of the town was the new, modern shopping center just to the north of the clock tower. It had literally been dug out of the sloping terrain so as to provide a flat surface for a parking lot. Boutiques, a Bata shoe store, a jewelry shop, and the usual mercantile paraphernalia were displayed as in a North American mall. As yet the mall had not been a success, owing to the small size of the Highgate middle class. But that would come. Even the local law firm had its office there, as if to signify its importance. And banks too were in full display. There was a small branch of the Bank of Nova Scotia at one end, and a tiny Royal Bank at the other.

Canadian banking had controlled British Caribbean finances since the 1880s, so all was in order.

Sunday presented another adventure, but of an entirely different kind. Sunday afternoons in Jamaica are usually a dismal time, at least before the bars open at 6 p.m. The afternoons are sleepy. People return from the beach or church, or both, by about one in the afternoon, have a large dinner that is usually laden with ground provisions such as yams, and the ever-present dish of rice and peas, and then repair for a long nap.

Doug remembered his many trips to Cable Hut on the road to Morant Bay, on many Sundays as a boy with his father and the others. There they would meet cousins and friends, partake in soccer or volleyball, swim, get burnt, and later down a few Red Stripe.

At about four o'clock the radio stations broadcast the obituaries, perhaps the most popular broadcast in the island, then present an hour or two of classical music, the only such broadcast for a week. Yes, classical music only on Sundays. How strange, he thought. At six came the world news from the BBC, and the island seemed to wake up.

This Sunday, Doug waited until after the news, then got on his bike and rode slowly into town, looking for a local rum shop to "grounds". As he turned right on Main Street just past the clock tower, he noticed a little bar on the north side, on the high ground just above the new mall. Outside was a man who had leaned his chair against the wall and was reading. Reading? Raas, this needs to be investigated, thought Doug. He braked hard and swung around, heading back east. He pulled in at the piazza just as the man was getting up to go inside.

"Yeah, man. What fe yu. Yu stop fe a cool down?"

"If yu open, I wouldn' mine a Red Stripe."

"Dat no problem. Ice cold. Now tell me. Nebah see yu before. Yu new in town." There followed the full explanation. "But, whey yu get dat accent from. Yu soun' like a real Jamaican." Another explanation.

Now followed the more substantial chatter, facilitated by the "What were yu readin?" Now the conversation became fluent. One thing led to another. He had been reading a short biography of Marcus Garvey, the first modern Black Jamaican hero. Garvey had awakened the consciousness of many Black Jamaicans in the early years of the century. He was an indefatigable visionary who had even founded a steamship company, called symbolically the Black Star Line, to take Black people back to Africa. It hadn't lasted long, nor had it been financially successful, contrary to the idea, which had resounded across the continent, indeed the African world, in various ways.

From Garvey the conversation flowed into Jamaica's modern problems, the economy, the society, racism, the viability of Socialism as a solution, and, of course, to local politics, and the new Manley government and its prospects. Doug was totally surprised. In a sleepy country town on a Sunday afternoon he had bucked up against a man he could actually exchange ideas with. He thought back to his family and their take on the local situation. Raas, this going to be a good term, he thought, I actually found a man I can talk to.

The next part (after four Red Stripes) was the best, at least as Doug was concerned.

"Well, bredda," Ralston (for that was the rumshop owner's name) continued, "wha' yu gwine do 'bout it? Yu 'ave any plan. Yu join de party?" He was referring to the PNP (People's National Party) that formed the present government. "Yu know what Karl Marx seh! Is not enuff fe analyze an talk, yu haf fe tek action."

Doug was taken aback at first. Then he quickly realized Ralston was right. Still, there was a great feeling of misgiving. He knew things had to change. Jamaica could not go on the same way. Yet he had his doubts about what exactly to do. Marxist theory was all very good in analyzing history, but what about after a revolution? There were no blueprints. And the kind of society organized in the Soviet Union was not to his liking either. Then again, how could anyone expect a government to change the local mentalities drastically in four years, or even eight? These were the questions he wrestled with.

Then there was the other question of race. Already the government was latching onto the remnants of the Black Power movement and using it to try to break the cycle of repression and exploitation: the White world of business, large corporations, the Euro-American world against Black Power. What power? There was none. The only power came from the North, and there was enough of that. Besides, physical power would not be used to hold back a revolution in Jamaica. It wasn't necessary. Soft power, intellectuals, hegemony, exactly as Gramsci had analyzed, held Jamaicans in its grip. First the churches, not exactly a screaming mob of radicals. No sir, no help from that quarter. As for the little Social Action movement of a few foreign priests within the Roman Catholic Church, emboldened by the 1968 Medellin Conference of bishops, it was as ineffective. Words on paper, nothing more. And only viable if people could and cared to read them.

History really held people in its grip. Begin with the first Black slaveholders, the coloured minority who had been satisfied with a few acres of land, enough to create a small class of conservative peasants. These were hardly the grist for a socialist or communist mill. And what about the dominant ideology of centuries: the sanctity of private property, the gospel of individualism. To top it all off, and the most powerful of all, the social practice of slavery: every man for himself. No discipline. Jamaicans had a reputation for indiscipline, to the point of "Me nah wuk fe YU, even hef I starve." How to break this grip that both past and present exercised on the island.

These were Doug's thoughts as he contemplated action. Plagued with doubts, one might say, at the feasibility of achieving change. That these doubts were justified could be seen in the government's own rhetoric. It seemed to be just that, rhetoric. Sure, there had been some positive changes: free school lunches, establishment of a Youth Corps to serve the government's development plans like conscripted soldiers for one year. Then there was the Gun Court, set up with two huge watch towers painted in red, and alongside Mountain View Road for all to see.

This was set up to stem the crime wave that was escalating daily. Ganja and robbery, both accompanied by murder, were the new goals of an underclass that was fed up with poverty. How it had taken over the imaginations of many young people. Children of the age of ten and eleven could be found incarcerated at Up Park Camp, held at the Queen's mercy indefinitely.

The whole island seemed to be caught up in a new hiatus. It was trying to break with the old, but it had great difficulty imagining the new. The government itself was caught in this bind. Manley had said early after his election that his government would be built on no new "isms." But no one believed him. Jamaica was too small to keep secrets. Then had come the introduction of "Democratic Socialism," which was a contradiction in terms if he had ever heard one; a front for the real thing, for all he could surmise. Everyone knew that bauxite shipments were being sent to the Soviet Union. Some people guessed what was in the offing. But no one except a select few knew that the intention was to get the Soviets to undergird and sustain a second Cuba in the Caribbean. But what was wrong with Cuba? It housed the homeless, fed the hungry, expanded education at all levels and provided free dental and medical care. What was wrong with that? Well, they also muzzled free speech. You had to conform to the ideology, at least pay lip service to it. No Jamaican would put up with that.

Especially after the fall of Allende in Chile, the Soviets were interested. But in 1981 came the news that Manley and the government had actually offered Jamaica on a bronze platter, so to speak, to them. The irony was that they had declined the gift. Perhaps they saw the proximity to the United States as an inhibiting factor and would not have wanted to waste time and money. Cuba was already costing them a more than a mite. But Doug was not to know the facts of the Soviet visitation for a while yet. Had he, it would have confirmed some of his own doubts.

Perhaps though, the Soviets saw the average Jamaican as too undisciplined to make good "communists." Undisciplined, indeed! Jamaicans were no more undisciplined than other people, and given a fair wage would work as hard as any other person. But with the pittances that were paid, and the inabilities to find a good job, some even refused what work they were offered, preferring to spend their time 'limin' or lounging against a piazza wall gyrating to the Reggae juke-box music coming from inside. But after all that it was a fact that no Jamaican was going to play "follow el Líder" for too long. That smacked too much of slavery and Big Man rule. No sah, me free to starve. That was the standard slogan. No Communist Party discipline would survive in Jamaica for long.

"Yu kyan expeck me to come here after two or three days an tek action. Man yu jokin. In any case preparation for revolution is a responsible an difficult thing."

"Yes, bredda Doug. Dat is right. But somewhere yu have fi start. Mek I ask yu dis question. We have a small organization here in Highgate, tryin to edicate people. Yu willing to help?"

"Of course," Doug replied. "But don' forget dat teachin is another way of helping prepare people. My students have fi know a likkle bout history, and why and who is de situation. In addition to dat, invite me. I ready to talk." So the stage was set for at least this minor political involvement. He wondered how it would eventually work out as he rode back up to the house to prepare for the Monday meeting.

Two more teachers had arrived, and to one he took an instant dislike. She was a blonde Canadian, Barbara Prescott, who had taken the flat to the back, as Mr. Johnston had said. She had a mousy but prim look about her. Not unattractive, she had, however, an off-putting air, bordering on cold arrogance. She was to teach English, and Doug thought of nothing more unlikely than a Canadian teaching English to Jamaican children. I wonder how she's going to deal with the dialect, the insects, the grass ticks, the heavy morning dew, and the lizards on the walls. Knowing Jamaican humour and its penchant for merciless teasing, the pupils might also just make mincemeat of her in no time. Ah well, we'll see, he thought. But he was already put-off by her opening remarks.

"Hi, I hear you're from Toronto."

"No, I'm Jamaican, but studied and lived dere for a while," he drawled in his broadest patois.

He could see her quizzical look and decided to leave well enough alone and go into his little study, closing the door firmly.

The other teacher was John Patterson, who had taken the little house off to the side and just beyond the crest of the hill. He was a short, round, Black, young-looking man: a young Jamaican returning home from studying in Britain to make his own contribution to the island's development. The only problem was that when he opened his mouth a stream of perfect Oxonian English ensued.

John was likeable enough, Doug thought, at least the first impressions, but his voice clashed so much with his skin colour, and produced such an incongruous effect, that people could not help but make fun of him constantly, from the newly-hired washerwoman to the children at school. Besides, he acted so fenky-fenky, he was almost instantly the laughing stock of the school and the town.

Jamaicans have a quick eye for the incongruous, the out-of-place. And they never let one get away with it. It is almost as if there was a physical birthmark, something stamped indelibly on the skin saying, laugh at me. From one end of the island to the other it would follow one around like a brave hyena, chiseling away here and there with bare teeth, like the bite to the Achilles heel, which was just a foretaste for the jugular.

Jamaican humour was like that. It was relentless, boisterous, raucous, and flew straight to the mark. It was intensely personal. One could comment on a friend's hair, nose, eyeballs, or whatever peculiarity came into view. In Canada it would probably have broken every rule of propriety, not to speak of political correctness. But Jamaicans were used to it. If one had a friend, and didn't do that special bit of teasing every time you met, the other would think there was something wrong. It was expected. Doug had made many a faux pas when he had forgotten himself in Toronto and laced some poor, unsuspecting Canadian with a raucous remark. The result had always been embarrassment, resentment, and hurt looks.

Such was the time he had met with some university friends in Yorkville for a TGIF. One of them showed up in the new style of shorts that were just appearing; it reached just below the knee, not quite shorts and not quite pants, in Doug's estimation. But when he asked his friend jokingly if the shorts were really meant to be long pants but he had run out of money to buy sufficient cloth to bring them down to the shoes, the joke did not really go over very well.

So he had finally given up. Canadian humour did not exist, no use in even trying. But Jamaica? That was something else and all classes participated, regardless the outcome. Now Liz, the woman whom they had collectively engaged to do the laundry, had a mouth and character that could make the hardiest soul wince, if she didn't take a shine to him or her.

On the first day when she had come up to do the laundry, she sat outside in front of a large, aluminium wash basin, chewing on an old cigar, skirt drawn up to hide her crotch in the usual way, Q flask of rum snugly beside her. Her back was against the large water tank, and she was facing the pipe in the back yard.

She had just started to sort the clothes when Patterson walked by on his way to his Minx. He saw her, but perfect Englishman that he was from the inside, he wasn't about to greet a washerwoman the expected Jamaican way.

So she decided to test the waters, take him on so to speak. "But Missa Pattison sar," she called out to him tartly, "How yu wan me do yu drawers, sar? Wash an iron?"

Since Paterson was not about to signify any part of the apparel that carefully covered his body in a derogatory way, he replied rather condescendingly and sarcastically. But whatever or whoever had counseled him to answer Liz like that must have been in need of brain surgery. "I am really not quite sure what you mean by 'drawers' Liz," came the hesitant, soft, but supercilious reply.

"Is wa hide yu batty from the sun, sar," came Liz's limpid reply, followed by a deep raucous laugh. Patterson turned a deep shade of purple, and Doug had to come to the rescue. Patterson rushed off without saying a further word, mumbling some Oxfordese under his breath, but obviously stung by the episode.

After he left, Liz turned to Doug. "So wa do dis likkle raas, Maas Doug? Him nu know say gud mawnin like de res a we? Him too good fe we or wat? But every dawg have his day and every puss him four o'clock (Do not act as if you are better than others, your day will come)."

Patterson should have been glad he had not been regaled by more choice language dredged from the pearly depths of Liz's voluptuously vulgar vocabulary. That was the lucky part, for he, unfortunately, was not to know how soon his very own four o'clock was going to be.

At school the first week, after the children had got used to the new faces, (which they tended to do fairly quickly), the first attack came. Children, especially Jamaicans, seem to have a natural gift for summing people up quickly. So they soon realized that Patterson was someone they were going to have some fun with. On entering the classroom, as he was carefully and neatly arranging his books on the desk and had turned to find some chalk, a hand shot up from one of the fourth formers he was about to try to impart some geography facts to.

The boy got up slowly and respectfully from his seat, almost standing at attention. "Ah would like ask yu a question, sir."

"Of course," said Patterson smiling, fully expecting to be quizzed on his knowledge of West Indian geography obtained by bagging a first before going down from Oxford.

"Ah want to know, sir, if yu get it a'ready?"

No sooner than he was finished and observing Patterson's quizzical but humiliated expression as he struggled with the Jamaican semantics of sexual expression, the class erupted into a howl of disdainful laughter, but the Jamaican way, drawn out, long bursts, and full of contemptuous ridicule.

The laughter was so powerful, assisted by the pounding of desks, and hoots of derision, with enough "raas claat" and "me bumbo" thrown in, that the headmaster, on the second floor had come bounding down the stairs to see what had happened. But Patterson stood there meekly, headmaster on one side, pupils on the other, opening his mouth to say something, unable to voice a reply, that the disgusted headmaster didn't bother to ask for an explanation, but hushed the class with various threats, and with a backward glance at the hapless teacher, strode back to his office.

This was Patterson's initiation. Disaster, first week on the job. And it was to continue until one year later when he could take no more of it and resigned early.

Doug chuckled to himself at the altercation with Liz. Patterson was just not going to get on. He was too locked in his exaggerated Englishman's attitude, a feature of his own Blackness for which he was obviously trying to compensate. Liz and others would see through this immediately. Patterson was going to be history. Such a resilient culture, born through slavery, was not going to permit a 'facety' Black Englishman any quarter. The incident warmed his heart. We would see about the rest.

Chapter V

Staff Meeting

On Monday morning at ten sharp the staff meeting began. The headmaster walked in slowly followed by the senior mistress, Mrs. Madge Cummings. First, they were all introduced by the headmaster and asked to give a short introduction of their backgrounds, country of origin, and academic specialties. There were altogether five expatriates, two Canadians and three Brits; also, there were four Jamaicans returning from overseas and sixteen other staff who had been previously at the school. There was a bit of a hiatus in the group as most of the expatriates would be teaching the upper school. That meant preparing students for the Caribbean fifth form exams and the A-levels, which were still administered by the Cambridge Syndicate. So the exam was based exclusively on the British system, except for the paper in West Indian history, which was set and marked at the Mona campus. Many of the local teachers had no degrees, but had been prepared at local teacher training institutes, such as the very excellent Mico College in Kingston.

The other Canadian, Barry Ritschuk, was a young chap from Ontario whose father owned at least a section of prime wheat land farmed by him and four sons. As well as Barbara Prescott, Barry had been sent out by CUSO, the Canadian University Service Overseas, an organization initiated to foster development in the Commonwealth. He was the new biology teacher.

The three Brits were Dave Crichton, the tall, lanky, laconic physical education teacher, who lived up at Fraserwood with Barbara, John and

Doug; and two young women, Misses Edie and Cameron, who were teaching English and Spanish and French respectively. They both were extremely shy and looked slightly bemused, possibly slightly apprehensive about teaching so far away from home, and having to converse with students whose patios was further from standard English than Eastenders.

Among the Jamaican staff teaching in the upper school there was Madge, the senior mistress who taught geography, the chemistry teacher an older Black man, Ralston Roberts, a physics teacher and fairly recent graduate of UWI at Mona, Lyndon Waters, and Winsome Brown, who taught some Spanish as well as home economics. Both Waters and Brown were shades of brown, attesting to the mixing of races which had taken place over the centuries.

Doug, of course, was the history teacher, responsible mainly for the fifth and sixth forms. He was the only teacher to sport an MA, which he had taken at Toronto and passed with distinction. He had majored in English and French Canadian history, but had had more than a smattering of Latin American courses, especially of the imperial Spanish phase, so he was well placed to teach West Indian history. In any case, he had taught that syllabus previously at his old school, Jamaica College, in Kingston, and was well prepared to take on the fifth and sixth form external examination challenges.

The foreign and returning Jamaican staff must certainly have been idealists because the wages paid by the Ministry of Education were not exactly designed to make anyone rich, and they had all probably taken a cut in pay from wherever they had come. So they were particularly appreciated by local folk, as well as parents and pupils. The scheme, under which they had been recruited, had been inaugurated by the Manley government in an attempt to foment the island's development and featured paid return trips for a two-year contract, exemption from income taxes, and a 20% gratuity paid on completion. Teachers were then paid the regular government scale and were responsible for finding their own accommodations and making their own living arrangements.

After the meeting, and just before lunch, the headmaster quietly asked Doug to join him in his office for a private discussion. He wondered what was coming now. Scarcely here three days and excitement already. He bounded up the stairs, taking them two at a time. At the door, Johnston was waiting for him and motioned him to a chair across from another now occupied by Madge Cummings. She smiled at him. Madge was about his age, of a light brown colour, a little shorter than Doug, slim enough, but with a nicely rounded bottom that merged into a perfect pair of legs. Bosomy, she had a small waist, and it was all topped off with intelligent, humorous eyes and a beautiful, perfectly shaped Afro. He knew from the short chat he had had with her that she was no old-fashioned lady, fully supported the new government and its vision, and, more importantly that she was a kindred spirit. She was married to a parson of the Baptist faith who presided over a small church outside of Port Maria, and they had one child, a boy of ten, who attended St. Mary's with his mother. Her smile put him at ease instantly.

"Mr. Austin, I hope you survived the first staff meeting."

"It was good to see such a qualified and dedicated staff, sir. I'm sure it is going to be a good two years."

"Yes, Mr. Austin. That is exactly what I wanted to talk to you about. We have already encountered a slight problem." Madge Cummings nodded. He continued. "You probably know that the Ministry affords us two senior staff to assist me, who are assigned various administrative duties."

"Yes."

"Well, most unfortunately, the lady who was part of the team working with myself and Mrs. Cummings just became drastically ill. She will not be able to resume her duties in a short time, if at all, and so we are short of important administrative help."

"That is horrible Mr. Johnston," Doug replied, "I do hope her illness is not that serious."

"We pray it is not sir, and she will be undergoing further tests to determine exactly what the doctors must do. But I must get to the point quickly, because hers is an absence we must fill on short notice."

Doug wondered what was coming next, and had some premonition because Madge was leaning forward expectantly in her chair. A quick glance had taken in her cleavage as she leaned forward, producing a reaction that Doug wished hadn't occurred. But the fortuitous moment was flushed from his mind as the head proceeded.

"Mr. Austin, I have had to have a talk with the Ministry outlining the situation, and they have accepted my tentative proposal. As you know senior staff must have at least two years of prior successive teaching in Jamaica to be appointed. I noted on your record that you had previously taught for two years at Jamaica College. The Ministry is willing to forego the successive element, since you also have senior academic qualifications, and I want to ask you whether you would be willing to be nominated for the post. I must tell you first, that since I have to find a replacement for the lady, we are all going to have to pitch in and do some extra teaching. It will only be as long as we need to replace her subject area, but I have two applications that look promising. On a happier note, senior staff is paid three increments extra in recognition of their position."

"Thank you very much Mr. Johnston, for this confidence. You know I have not done much administrative work, so may I ask what is involved?"

"Primarily, the duties are timetabling, scheduling, seeing that the teachers are facilitated in whatever way possible, in organizing and running the house games in conjunction with the phys. ed. staff, and discipline."

"I think I would be up to most of that, except the timetabling. Honestly I have never tried my hand at it."

"Thank you for being honest, sir. Mrs. Cummings is an expert at timetabling," at which time Madge burst into laughter, only to be joined by Johnston who chuckled and continued, "and I am sure she will show you the ropes." Timetabling was a task no one liked doing.

"Then it is set then, unless you have any other questions?" And seeing Doug nod, and the appreciative look on Madge's face, he added, "So, I will make the announcement at lunch."

Their meeting being over, the three went down the steps, walked over to the assembly hall, where the headmaster motioned Madge and Doug to take their seats. Doug felt elated, though he didn't show it. Christ, he thought, the first day on the job and a promotion. Recognition, acceptance, trust—what the raas was John McCormack trying to say a few days ago? Johnston was Black. Madge was Black. Neither had shown any hesitation in recognizing his qualifications, commitment. Was he going mad? Or had he just been given a senior position in a secondary school? He felt good. The sweat began to come as he realized that he was in—inside the system, accepted for what he was and wanted to do, despite colour, despite history. The rest would depend solely on him. And he was ready.

Jamaica in the 1970s was as formal a place as when Doug had been himself in school. Headmaster and senior staff usually ate at a separate table. Staff addressed each other by Mr., Mrs., and Miss. Familiarities were frowned on. Everyone knew his or her place. Language was formal so as to set a good example. Staff did not use patois in the staff room in case they might be overheard by pupils passing by outside. Indeed, patois was considered a mark of ignorance, and well-educated, intelligent people used it only on special occasions, or when they were with special friends, as a mark of intimacy. It was even stricter with swearing.

Young Barry Ritschuk had fallen afoul of these strong cultural traditions the first few days of school. The staff room was considered a place for work. Each teacher had an ample desk on which to prepare lesson plans, do marking, or read quietly. It was universally accepted that one spoke in hushed tones, if at all, and certainly no one ever, ever swore. But Barry, like so many Canadians his age, was used to using the words 'shit' and 'fuck' as liberally as if he had invented them. Plus, his entrance into the staff room was usually accompanied by throwing his books down with a loud clatter, while he flounced into his chair, stretching out his feet on the desk. Yet, he was affable, easy-going, the kind of young man that did not seem to have come with preconceptions. He was already on friendly terms with some of the staff, indicated his curiosity of Jamaican flora and fauna, and liked to take the occasional beer in town in a relaxed atmosphere. He would be well liked and accepted.

This was Doug's first "administrative" assignment. The ladies on staff complained, and the headmaster asked Doug to have a word with Barry. So, he dredged up his best diplomatic tone and explained encouragingly to the young Canuck that Jamaicans considered swearing a sin; moreover it was punishable by law, loudness was disturbing and disrespectful of others, and putting one's feet on the desk was a piece of rudeness reserved for crude North Americans but not condoned in Jamaica. But he said it so smoothly and with such camaraderie that Barry took it in good spirits and "changed his ways."

At lunch, in contrast to the existing, more formal, hierarchical manner, the headmaster sat down at a table with some staff, Madge doing the same at another table. Doug, noticing the pattern, did the same at a third. Good, he thought, the school leadership was trying to practice the spirit of the government's drive for democracy and equality. He liked the atmosphere the headmaster was trying to create.

Now, the formalities, especially the saying of grace being over, and with the headmaster's announcement of Doug's appointment, which was greeted by quiet applause, they all sat down to lunch together in the assembly hall, courtesy of the school. There was conversation, shy at first, as new teachers tried to get to know each other, and barraged older teachers with questions, or exchanged cultural lore about their individual countries. Obviously, the expatriates were curious about the lunch. It was served hot and steamy as usual, with the flavours filling the room. Miss Prescott and the English gals especially picked at this and that. He noticed young Barry nyammin' away as if the food might disappear.

For the lunch was good solid Jamaican food. Doug wished he had had a Red Stripe to wash it down with instead of insipid lemonade, but proceeded to nyam away. Some fried chicken, rice and peas, fried plantain, a piece of yellow yam, and a boiled green banana all efficiently bathed in an ample sauce lightly seasoned with Scotch Bonnet peppers. Then Doug said his goodbyes. The next few days were for preparation. Teachers would be working furiously on the one Gestetner producing notes and exercises for the next week when the pupils showed up.

For Doug, however, the first task was to meet with Madge over the timetable. She beckoned him to follow her.

"Maas Doug," she called out, using the familiar servant greeting as comradely parody. "I will meet you upstairs with all the stuff which will keep us for a few hours."

So saying she departed to get sheets and paper, files etc., while he wandered through the upstairs looking at the various classrooms. The school had been carefully laid out to catch the prevailing winds coming off the coast. There were two parallel constructions, joined by a covered walkway. But since the land sloped, the northern block did not shield the wind, nor hamper the view of the coast. Lower down behind it was an expanse of land, not huge, on which bananas, the staple export of the parish, were growing. These were used to prepare lunches in the school, as boiled bananas and rice and peas were favourite starches.

Working with Madge at this tedious but necessary task proved better than he had expected. There were more than a few points of intellectual contact with this intelligent, broad-minded, and tolerant woman. Doug had to wrench his gaze away from her cleavage as she leant over the tables, two of which had been pushed together to contain the large sheets used for time-tabling. And he was lured by her efficient but versatile mind that could multi-task so quickly, moving from a short discussion of Max Weber to how many history slots there needed to be, and what Mr. X's or Miss Y's teaching strengths were.

He noticed though that there was no talk of family, her domestic scene. He knew that she and her family lived in Port Maria where they rented a small house, that there was one child, a dog, a cat and three chickens in the yard. But as to husband, his church, job, congregation, likes and dislikes, there was no disclosure. He thought it odd, since Jamaican women were naturally garrulous, especially about family.

But he didn't miss it, not being inclined anyway to useless chatter about trivialities. And they were agreed on one thing: Jamaica had to change. So there followed endless discussion, which seemingly had no closure, about whether Manley was doing or not doing right, and the difficulties of overcoming centuries of racism and imperialism. On those topics they were together, and the one supplied the other with perspectives that rather than arguing or disagreeing, provided only new dimensions to explore.

They got through the task in about three hours. It was a quarter to four. Doug felt good that they had worked together seamlessly. His only little problem was that he couldn't get his eyes off her ample bosom, waiting for every opportunity when she reached over the tables to feast his eyes on what he was coming to see might be an impossible dream. And he liked how she finished the day, with a smart salute accompanied by a throaty chuckle, which was another stimulant that had him sitting down quickly to avoid utter embarrassment. Then she departed with a familiar and colloquial, "Enuff nuh, time to go home." He started to help her clean up.

"Don bodder yuself. I just cartin' all the paper downstairs. See yu tomorrow."

After placing a few books and papers in his bike's side pocket, Doug mounted the big Triumph, brought it to life with a roar, and rode slowly down the hill, as one could not see oncoming traffic. Then he swung out onto Main Street. Clouds had been gathering all afternoon intimating some shower activity, and as he approached the "Cove" rain began to fall with intensity. Parking the bike quickly by the curb, he leapt for cover.

The rain came down viciously hard and intense. People scurried from all sides to find the nearest shop overhang or to ram themselves against a building under the protection of the eaves. Doug managed to reach the shelter of the "Cove." The bar itself was jammed. Even so he would not have wanted to be inside that mouldy, humid bar, thick with clouds of smoke and sweat. Outside he huddled close to the wall, sharing the small space as best he could. Here amidst one of nature's fierce showers, humanity took a respite from egregious competition and united itself. No matter how crowded the piazza, there was always room for one more.

He watched as the rain drops fell into the little watery craters creating a momentary splash, then mingled with the quick natural streams which fought their way around the building to lower ground. Fifteen minutes or so from now, when the "cloud burst" stopped, it would all revert. The sun would again parch the smooth soil. Here and there a banana peel or an old tin can, temporarily obscured, would signal the recurrence. Peace and normality would descend again. People would venture out and take up their business as if they had never been interrupted.

One man, in particular, he noticed detaching himself from the crowd and ambling out into the middle of the road. Since school had not started yet there were no rushing busses coming down from the clock tower. This was Boysie. One fellow shouted out to him teasingly, "Boysie, mine de bus dem."

Boysie continued sauntering down the road, threw back his head, and sucked his teeth at the miscreant passer-by. Doug couldn't understand what it was all about, so he turned and went inside the bar to enquire. The afternoon was hot so it was a good excuse to order a few Red Stripes and relax after the long day, and listen to a good tale or two.

Highgate is the center of the banana industry for that part of the island. Bypassed by the coast road connecting the other two towns, and, therefore, somewhat isolated, it had acquired a reputation for breeding eccentrics. Of all its well-known citizens, however, no one quite stood out as did Boysie Williams.

Where Boysie had come from was a mystery. He had arrived in the town some years before and had earned the reputation as one of Highgate's most interesting drunks. He was about five feet five in his bare feet, with a well-built, muscular body, shiny, healthy-looking ebony complexion and a bald head around which grew a patch of thin hair. Boysie's official territory was on the piazza just outside and a little to the left of the entrance of the Pirate's Cove. He would stand there for hours with both eyes shut, apparently asleep. No conclusion could have been more wrong. At the sound of footsteps Boysie's eyes would spring open, taking on an alert, expectant look as his mind went to work.

Boysie's main problem in this world was who was going to quench his never-ending thirst that morning, afternoon, or night. His wants were really that simple. He lived with his mangy-looking dog underneath Miss Vi's old house on Main Street, just across from the garage. Food was always available in return for a little work, and drinks were usually on the town. The particular dilemma of perpetual thirst Boysie had solved by utilizing his natural talents as an actor. Depending on his impending victim, Boysie would contort his body into a convincing spastic pose. What stranger could possibly resist such a perfect extortion and not drop a few coins into his outstretched hand? This tranquil and satisfying existence, however, was marred occasionally by Boysie's great character flaw. Every now and again he needed to play a practical joke on an unsuspecting person.

Boysie's joking was an innate part of his nature. But it had not really started until the first incident with the bus. One has to say the first incident because it was the first, but by no means the last. Boysie's other trait was the he could never leave well enough alone. But his best joke concerned the incident with the bus.

It had all started the previous year. Boysie had been drinking heavily one afternoon at the Cove. About four o'clock when the buses were coming through for the afternoon school run, he had staggered out on to Main Street. Unfortunately, he had been hit by one of the country buses. His injuries had not been serious and had it not been for the local MP, a lawyer McPherson, Boysie would still have been in his usual penurious position in life. However, McPherson had decided to intervene on Boysie's behalf. He had sued the bus company and won. Furthermore, the judge had stipulated, on hearing about Boysie's character and circumstances, that the settlement be held in trust and a small sum given to Boysie each week by McPherson. This way Boysie would have sufficient funds to live on for a long time. But he would not, the judge reasoned, be able to drink out the proceeds in a few months perpetrating much mischief at the same time.

The judge was wrong. He underestimated Boysie's craftiness. Since he needed very little to live on, Boysie decided to save up his weekly allowance so that he could have a really good "drunk up" from time to time. One week in particular saw Boysie well off. He had taken some work in one of the small banana properties near Highgate. Boysie was an expert cleaner.

That is to say he could wade into a banana patch and clean out unwanted suckers from around the banana plants like no other worker.

That Friday Boysie was at the Pirate's Cove particularly early. By four o'clock that afternoon he was well on his way to complete inebriation. As he heard the first bus draw up beside the clock tower and gear down for the short stretch down the incline of Main Street, Boysie was seen to stand up straight. When the bus was a few hundred yards away, Boysie slowly staggered out of the bar and fell down, right in the path of the bus. The screaming of brakes was heard as the bus came to a halt a few feet from Boysie's apparently lifeless body. The bus driver was livid. But before he could get to the source of his wrath, three men appeared and carried Boysie off to the side of the road amidst the most fearful cussin' anyone could remember.

Far from being seriously admonished, Boysie became an instant celebrity. On Saturday mornings, especially on market day, Boysie could be seen in the Cove entertaining all who could afford to hear about his adventure. In time, however, even the most admiring disciples tend to become weary of the same story. Boysie's sources of drinks slowly began to dry up. This was serious and something had to be done.

Thus it was that one Friday afternoon a few months later Boysie realized that he already knew just how to make the world work best for him. An hour or so at the Cove had strengthened his resolve. As the clock struck four and Boysie heard the first bus gear down by the clock tower, he sauntered slowly—but with a stagger that would have convinced innocent bystanders that he was drunk—into the middle of the road and collapsed. His head was pointed straight up as if he was asleep. The bus came slowly down Main Street. Boysie waited for the tell-tale squeal of the brakes. The bus drew nearer. Suddenly he heard the roar of the engine as the driver shifted gear. The whine switched to a lower register. Bosie's eyes flew open. This could only mean one thing. The bus driver was coming through.

Still, Boysie's pride would not allow him to turn his head to make sure. No brakes were heard. People began to pour out of the bar and the shops. The bus was about two hundred yards away but picked up speed rapidly. People began to shout.

"Run Boysie," shouted the barmaid. "Him comin' tru."

Still, Boysie did not budge. People ventured on to the street and waved frantically at the bus. For those who were close enough to see him, the driver was leaning grimly over the steering wheel, gripping it firmly with both hands. There was a determined, vicious look on his face. It was the same driver Boysie had stopped a few months before. The conductor, who had climbed up on the roof of the bus to throw down the baggage and had remained up there for the short run to the bottom of the hill, was banging on the roof with one hand while trying to steady himself with the other. Finally he stopped. He needed both hands to hold for the inevitable bump which might throw him off.

By now Boysie was getting anxious. The bus was less than a hundred yards away. The barmaid was going mad. Tears began to stream down her face as she screamed at Boysie. By now, the angle between Boysie, the inn and the bus was becoming a straight line as Boysie disappeared from her view. Boysie began to react. He realized the bus was not going to stop. His legs began to flail like a wheel as he tried to get up. His feet impatiently slapped the road under him. He turned his head and saw the conductor on the top of the bus leaning down with his mouth hanging open, too scared to shout. Eventually, Boysie's feet connected properly with the street. They came down hard and he went flying backwards just as the front wheels of the bus were almost on top of him.

He went back with such force that he left the street altogether and landed head first in the drainage ditch which carried away water and refuse during the heavy rain showers. That drain was always muddy and filthy.

Once the bus had gone past, the people at the Cove could see once more. But where was Boysie? No one moved. They were all in state of shock. The odd person who could still think envisaged Boysie crumpled under the left fender. But then, slowly, a figure emerged from the ditch and out came Boysie covered from head to foot in slime and with a rotten orange peel sticking from under his shirt collar. Ever so slowly he straightened up and with his hands hanging stiffly at his sides he walked from the street in the direction of Miss Vi's house, accompanied by hoots of laughter from both sides of the street.

The story was too good to be true. But the barmaid had told it with such sincerity that Doug had to accept it. Besides the other patrons in the bar were nodding their heads in unison. Fact was, Boysie did display a few dollars every Saturday when Mr. McPherson came through to visit his constituency. So at least that part was true. But there had been so many witnesses at the second incident that the chances were it had really taken place. In any case, Boysie was not as confident as he had been after the first encounter. That was proof enough. And he NEVER played that trick again.

As Doug carefully and slowly made his way up Fraserwood, since he didn't want to cause an "incident" after a few Red Stripe, he thought with relish about the story, about the mixture of fantasy and reality that made storytelling such an art in a country where it was absolutely essential, the art of decoding the written word not yet having captured sufficient adherents. And Jamaican storytelling was the best of all: from the official tales of poet and folk-writer Louise Bennett, "Auntie Lou" to the ever present Anancy stories that every child knew and loved and lived.

He thought back to his pre-teen years, when his mother had hired a gardener who just happened to be the "Shepherd" of the local Pocomania cult. Slater would be weeding a bed at the side of the house. Doug would approach gingerly. Slater would look up, "How yu stay, Maas Doug?"

He knew what was coming. Doug knew how to ask in the right way. And since they couldn't tell Anancy stories in daylight, the two would creep under the house, and Slater would regale the eager boy with tales of Bredda Tigger, Bredda Tacooma, Anancy and the other animals. He couldn't get enough of them, especially since Anancy, the trickster spider, was supposed to symbolize the Jamaican, the eternal "jinal". Slater, for his part, didn't resist either, since the cool under the house was a welcome relief from the hot sun.

But Anancy had a way. One never knew exactly what he was up to. Even now, Anancy was busy in his web plotting, planning, weaving new skeins and threads of future becomings, encounters, all the better to trap unsuspecting, confident little flies, especially those who were feeling good, lucky, prosperous, and satisfied in some way.

Chapter VI

Wuk, wuk an' more wuk

The first few weeks went by so quickly he couldn't recall what had happened. There had been first, the organization of the A-level students. Doug was teaching both the history syllabus and the general paper. The second was an essential part of the preparation for higher studies. Nothing like it existed in North America, and it was the essential part of the British requirements for acceptance to higher education, that students should be equipped with a liberal amount of general knowledge. And being so, it was difficult to teach, because it meant organizing not only readings from many different areas including general science, but teaching students how to reason and think across a broad philosophical spectrum introduced by picking contemporary topics and reading widely. The topics themselves ranged from as far afield as architecture to contemporary politics. And so it was quite demanding on the students, who were required to do a lot of general reading. On the other hand, it was perhaps the most engaging and interesting course to teach. And Doug relished the thought of preparing assignments and lectures on such a wide variety of topics.

The history curriculum was narrower. The school had already picked Tudor England as the sixth form topic. And the text had already been ordered: G. R. Elton's, *Britain under the Tudors*, a standard and comprehensive work. For the fourth and fifth forms it was straight West Indian history, beginning with Columbus's voyages, conquest and exploitation that eventually led to the Spanish Empire. Doug had taught this history curriculum earlier and was familiar with the syllabus. He relished the thought of challenging students away from the traditional notion of Columbus as "discoverer" to that of facilitator of the first great environmental, not to speak of biological and racial disaster in the hemisphere. How to explain that not greatness and human magnanimity but rampant profit and greed had been the underlying motives in that colossal adventure?

The real challenge would be the students. How would he lure them away from orthodox ways of understanding the history of the islands, to more acute, radical and iconoclastic modes of interpretation? How to connect present poverty with structures of conveyance linked to slavery? And how, indeed, to do this without falling prey to the new catchy "ideology" of Black versus White? But how to move minds anyway, to free up creative instincts that had been suppressed? How to loosen the Victorian brackets that still circumscribed Jamaican thought while at the same time imparting some historical truths? These were going to be the enduring pedagogical problematic. And all that in an atmosphere that regarded rote memorization as the preferred teaching method.

This rigidity of teaching and thinking appeared early in the term as he was trying to engage one of the fourth forms in a bit of brain teasing. "Imagine," he said, "that you are Columbus. Now, this man had no idea of what he was going to encounter in his voyages. He sets out from Palos in Spain and starts sailing west, thinking he would end up in Japan or China. Try to imagine sailing west from Europe. What continent then blocks your way to China?"

There was utter silence. No hands went up. He tried it again, reformulating the question. Still there was no response. He tried yet another way. By this time he had noticed the headmaster drifting by the door, obviously on one of his missions to check how staff was teaching and dealing with students. Doug's glum and serious look perturbed the pupils. He felt his adrenalin rising. He questioned his motives, his methods, while striving to keep that quick anger inherited from his mother under control. How could they not get it? It was so obvious. He began to feel sweat forming under his arms and at his waist.

The children were expecting the worst: an outburst, sarcasm, or a raised voice declaiming magisterially how stupid they were. A dead dawg would have more brains than all o' you, they were expecting. But no retort came. Instead the teacher strode around the room, hand appearing to shave the very stubble from his keen chin, as if trying to dig into his head for a solution that would help all of them. He remained deep in thought. Suddenly he looked up as if hit by a premonition. He would try a different tack.

"I want one of you who can draw to come up to the blackboard."

Finally, he had asked for a volunteer artist. It seemed to break the tension. Many hands went up. He picked a boy at the rear of the classroom who had quick, intelligent eyes. He came to the blackboard where Doug asked him to draw as best he could an outline of Europe and Africa on the right side. This was done fairly easily, and actually it was a better outline than he had expected. Then he picked a second student. This time he motioned to the left of the blackboard and asked for an outline of India, China, and Japan. The outcome was not quite as good as the first in view of the increased difficulty of the task and a few pupils tittered. Still, it was a brave rendering. To relax them he tried some humour. He walked up and down the rows smiling, but looking intently at various students.

"If any one o' yu can do better, please come up." Everyone laughed.

Then he asked a third to indicate the possible route Columbus might have taken. This time the student stopped and drew the outline of a little island in between the two, Cuba. Instantly hands went into the air. "Please sir, please sir?"

Doug was only happy to please. One student asked if the island was Jamaica. No, another responded, it was Cuba. Excitement was building. No. Columbus had actually first landed on Watling Island which was near Cuba, not Cuba itself. The little gal must have been listening to some history lesson in junior secondary school. She was a product of some intrepid, dedicated, under-paid teacher.

"Yes," Doug replied. "Very good. And what continent does Cuba and Jamaica, and Watling Island belong to?" More hands went up until finally someone yelled "America."

Slowly, lights began to go on. What was the first question? It had taken him close to thirty minutes to get at the point. But he had gotten there. Shifting the mode of reasoning was not going to be easy. But these children were not stupid, and even eager to respond, at least some of them. No, it wasn't going to be easy, he supposed.

Yet he consoled himself that he had actually got to his goal without getting angry, using sarcasm, belittling anyone, or giving the answer himself. His Socratic technique had worked. The students had got the answer themselves, but he had provided only a process of reasoning. Would it work eventually? Would there be time to mould new ways of thinking and simultaneously impart a curricular object? And what, he wondered did the headmaster think about his methodology, for he knew Johnston had been listening around the corner? That was part of his job.

Yet this project and new methods had to be successful. Not that he could do it all himself, but only in his quiet little corner. Jamaica just had to incorporate new ways of thinking, as the government was desperately trying to convey. To reason thus was to escape the trap of moving from one barbarism into another. But how to change a psychology honed by centuries of other methods and precepts? How to escape the trap that slavery and subsequent imperialism had set, not by replacing them with another system of repression, but transcending the brutalities that must appear were one not to move forward into a more enlightened state. This little lesson had been a microcosm of the difficulties that lay ahead not only for these pupils but for the island itself.

And for him, personally, the only answer, the only way forward was to throw himself headlong into the abyss of work, of reason, of imparting history, of fomenting enlightenment, attacking myth and promoting curiosity and questioning. A daunting task if ever there was one. But he was determined not to stint himself and to take on as much as he could in order to realize his personal goals. His own, personal life would have to sit quietly in the background, awaiting its moment of completion.

For the next few weeks then, Doug threw himself at work as if time itself were running out in the universe. They had no time. He had no time. One of the first things he did after organizing his classes and teaching assignments was to figure out a way of involving himself in the community. In fact, he did not have to do much figuring as he was literally dragged into the maelstrom of the government's feverish plans to continue trying to transform and develop the island.

As it happened, during one lunch time in the staff room talk turned to the government's initiative of the previous year to begin making a dent in the country's serious literacy problem. Doug listened intently to the criticism, the usual Jamaica labrish about the government's "faults," incompetence, lack of interest ,and so on. He decided immediately that here was an area he could make a mark in.

So he immediately entered the conversation. Why not form a committee in the school to start a literacy programme? It was a perfect place to meet given the empty classrooms in the evening, and besides, look at the talent among the staff. Talk went back and forth. There were the usual nays and yeas. Some felt it wouldn't work. People were not interested in literacy because there were no jobs after training. People had to have a goal, see a positive outcome.

From the other side came the counter. What if jobs came and people needed to be able to read and write? What then? Doug decided on a different approach. Why not start, at least try, and then see what happened. Winsome said she would give a couple hours in the evening. Slowly, more came around to the idea, saying they would help. The infection spread. Doug suggested they form a small committee and offered to do the necessary work to get started. Someone asked him if he would agree to be chair of the committee. He said yes. Finally a group was identified, "elected," and Doug was told to proceed. He would start contacting the government department to check on materials.

The next day the committee met after school to make plans. It decided to start a blitz campaign around the town, by running off posters on the school Gestetner and pasting them on every lamp post in and around town. Barry offered to take care of one stretch of road. Barbara Prescott offered her services as a teacher, saying that she had had some experience with literacy in Canada and would be willing to help any of the volunteer teachers prepare lessons and material. Hmm, Doug thought. I probably misjudged her. He reconsidered his earlier impression of Barbara for hers was an appreciated gesture. But it was so hard to tell with her as she showed so little emotion. Some of the Jamaican staff also offered, although for most, by now with families and small children, a few hours a week away in the evenings took precious time from family matters.

Anyway they were off and running. The posters appeared promptly, and word of mouth, always a good source of news in Jamaica, did the rest. The first Monday there were about thirty people. But it quickly grew and, at one point it had ninety. There were the serious, such as the lineman from the telephone company, a good technician. But without full literacy he would never be promoted. There were teenagers who somehow had fallen through the cracks in the school system, or for one or another reason had not completed school and wanted to continue. And there were a few older people, including one gentleman of advanced age, such as Mr. McKee who had his own special reasons for wanting to be literate, as we shall see.

That Friday, Doug, who had wangled the afternoon off, sped into Kingston, leaving the Cavalier water filter plant on his left, past St. Andrew's Club, Mico College, Wolmers Secondary school, and down into the southern end of the Race Course, as it was called from earlier days when it was the first Jamaican race track. He was prepared for a runaround, an endless stream of under-burdened civil servants trooping off to the lavatory with their towels on an arm or a shoulder. So, he was very surprised when he found that there had been an entire section "liberated" as it were, from the rest of the Ministry, and dedicated entirely to the literacy campaign.

Yes, we have heard about you, but No we cannot give any materials without authorization. How to get them then? Well, they would have to be requested from the man in charge of the campaign for your area. His name? And where was his office? Promises. If he put his name to a letter you could pick up the materials immediately. Doug had not even known that there was an agent in charge of the campaign in St. Mary, so he was taken aback. But he took the information gratefully and headed back, not quite empty-handed as he was given some sample materials for various levels to begin with.

On the way back, he stopped briefly at his brother's house on Long Lane to say hello to his mother who had not seen him in a few weeks.

"But what a nice surprise, son. I didn't know you were coming down this way?"

"I didn't know either Mama, but it so happened I needed some stuff from the Ministry. So on my way back I thought I'd stop over."

"What kind of stuff?"

"Well we've started a literacy class up at the school and need some materials, since it seems to be quite popular and in demand."

"Who's running it?" she wondered.

"Guess," but she already knew the answer.

"But mind you don't take on too much, Doug." He flinched as he knew what was probably coming next, but neither did he want to get into an argument and possibly hurt his mother.

Instead he rose quickly looking pointedly at his watch. "I have to get back. Just wanted to see how you were."

"Don't run away yet, son. You haven't even spent five minutes with me. Besides, there are messages."

"Messages for me?"

"Mary Jean has phoned three times since you left. Of course she always asked for Anne. But I know what she was thinking. Why don't you give her a call?" His mother was an ace at matchmaking. But this was more than that. She loved MJ as her own daughter. MJ was the perfect match for Doug. She was from a good family, level-headed and not as idealistic as her son. She would calm his inveterate social activism by providing him with a family which he would then be responsible for. Perhaps then Doug would consider his future, enter his uncle's business, and settle down, giving up his crazy ideas. But she also had her doubts. She had known him from a baby, but didn't understand what influence his father, nor the university, for that matter, had had on him.

She did not know how accurate her doubts were. The thought of entering a family business, any business, would most likely have caused him to retch. His formation had been so different from that practical world of account books, imported salt fish, milk production and hardware goods. That world hardly existed in his mind. His father had seen to that. A self-educated man despite his law degree, the older Austin had arranged for Doug to spend some time in Germany. Living in the house of his father's old, enlightened and cultured friend Reinhart Sieger, Doug had been introduced to another world.

Sieger was a Bavarian businessman, owner of a factory producing parts for the auto industry. Married to a Jewess, he had left Germany in the thirties, aware of the danger to his wife. He had chosen England, where he had met James Austin while the latter was practicing at the Inns. When the war broke out Sieger and his wife were both interned as enemy aliens, but due to Austin's constant petitions were finally released. The friendship, earlier consummated had received a final seal, as it were.

Sieger took Doug under his wing, treating him as a son. He pulled strings so that Doug could enter Munich University, study German and history at the same time. In his second year there Doug had managed to enroll in the series of lectures by one of Germany's leading historians and humanists, Prof. Hans Schnabel. That professor's reputation was legend since he had continued to lecture even while bombs were falling around him in the city at the end of World War Two. His lectures on Liberalism had been a source of comfort to many people during the brutal days of the Nazi dictatorship. Liberalism was a viable antidote to the obtuse musings and goals of Nazi pseudo-economics, not to speak of its anti-Semitism. And so many people, afraid themselves to speak out, revered the aging professor for his dogged, unflagging persistence against the tyranny. His lecture halls were consistently full, a fact that must have induced the Gestapo to use caution in handling him. And despite promises, cajoling and outright threats, he never joined the NSDAP, (the Nazi party), a fact which was well known.

Doug remembered his indulgent German experience with a feeling of intense gratification to both his father as well as to Sieger, who had lodged Doug in his spacious house in Graefelfing, the wealthiest suburb just on the outskirts of Munich. There he had spent many a night with the gentle, benevolent, and humanist, Sieger, discussing history and philosophy. He encouraged Doug to make use of his voluminous library, which had miraculously survived both Nazi dullards and equally destructive bombs.

And Doug was especially appreciative of Sieger's humanistic insights into Christianity, his comparisons of Thomas More and Dietrich Bonhoeffer, the compassionate pastor of the Lutheran Church imprisoned by the Nazis and murdered just as Russian troops began to encircle Berlin at the end of the war.

These had been good years, and had cemented Doug's intention of pursuing an academic profession where he could ponder and contemplate the lofty and enduring problems of humanity. But there was another side to Doug. This was his impatience merely to imbibe and discuss the written work, without accompanying it with deeds and actions, and humanitarian succour.

So, how could one sell salt-fish with Scriabin, Katchaturian, Chopin and Mahler in one's mind? The *Ode to Joy*'s promise of humanity would not be constructed with hardware materials, but only through trying to understand the contemplations of a Horkheimer, Adorno, and Marcuse and taking actions to implement these ideas. And all by hard work, of course.

Those first two thinkers specifically impinged on his thoughts about Jamaica. He had read the reissue of their seminal 1944 *Dialectic of Enlightenment* a couple of years before returning, and it had scored. This was what Jamaica needed. It was better than Marx, who offered a way out only through the materiality of harsh change (although many would argue differently).

Affecting the spirit was the way to effect real change. How had one come so far from Enlightenment ideas in the European world? But that was one world, Jamaica another. It had never had Enlightenment. The colonial regime had failed miserably, no, not failed. It never intended to develop the island, preferring to keep it for the hundred and thirty odd years after slavery as an agricultural production unit within the empire. Here was the material problem, which it was also necessary to address simultaneously.

So what a massive task the government was saddled with. To develop meant creating jobs and building a solid manufacturing base, so as not to be dependent on the vagaries of agricultural propensities in the metropolitan world. But how to do this with pressures from multi-nationals like the bauxite companies, even the sugar companies, not to speak of their control of the tourist industry? How the raas did one combat all that power, he mused. But I need to get back.

To please his mother, he decided to make the call and risk the transaction. Getting hold of MJ was easy. But responding to the why don't you stay was harder. "Suppose we make a definite date a few weeks from now. That will give me time to settle into a routine and manage all the things I've started. Then we could spend the weekend together, I promise. You come up one Friday afternoon and we will have the weekend to ourselves, maybe even go to Ocho Rios."

MJ was not just keen but delighted. That sounded like a great plan even a good portent. An entire weekend with Doug somewhere quiet was a dream she had entertained for quite some time. Besides, it would be really the first time they would have seen each other in ages, without a bunch of nosy people staring at them. Her mind flew into planning mode immediately. Leave the office early for Highgate; hairdresser the previous day; clothes, bathing suit, a little present for Doug, and someone to watch the office in the late afternoon.

As her mind roamed over the plans and accoutrements of her visit, Doug was already speeding up into Golden Spring and getting ready for the winding stretch across the mountains. In little over forty-five minutes he was plowing past the railway station and onto Main Street.

The school was already deserted. He continued up Main Street stopping at the "Cove" for a Red Stripe or two. Barry was in the bar chatting with a couple of local people. The talk was about politics and turned to the literacy venture that was making a name for itself in the area. A couple of regulars congratulated Doug on starting the class. One man remarked on the sincerity of the government for bringing young Canadians like Barry to help with education.

The tone was jocular, but spiced with tales of what was happening in the banana industry. Banana production was up but there was a serious problem that no one knew how to solve. The more bananas, the more nematode worms seemed to appear. Barry said he had no idea how to combat it. He recounted tales from his father and grandfather about the Great Depression, about how they had suffered during the great dust bowl. It seemed as if just as people were getting ahead nature would send some blight to remind humanity of its own fragile existence. One man remarked that God always wanted to make sure we didn't get too confident. Then he would send a plague and put us back in place.

The next week started with the feverish activity of trying to copy materials for the literacy programme. Doug managed to ride to Port Maria and have a chat with the campaign director. He told of the success of the class and begged for materials. Promises were made. "By next week we will have a van drop off some supplies for you." The promise was kept. The government meant business. It realized the importance to many people of these efforts.

Little did it know, nor could it know, of the miniscule personal triumphs that just the recognition of letters and words could bring forth. Such was the case of one of the oldest "students" motivated by factors no government could have discerned. If they, if Doug had only known what was going on in the head of this quiet, unassuming old man, whose best years were behind him, but who carried within him that indomitable spirit of perseverance, and the patience to overcome obstacles with integrity and pride. How would they have understood that intense desire to be able to read his beloved King James Bible replete with its poetic spirituality and translucent life's messages?

The Tuesday class was about to begin on one of those hot, sultry, September afternoons. Highgate's Main Street was still full of school children in their dull, starched uniforms, stragglers waiting on the six o'clock bus to Annotto Bay and points further.

Here and there were a few tired men gathered for an after-work chat before wandering off to wash down sugar fibre and brown clay with a "whites."

It was windy, this afternoon, old Rufus McKee thought, as he ambled down Main Street in the direction of the high school. Wonder how many people here tonight? Old Rufus, the oldest member of the literacy class was also one of the most persistent students. He had been coming now for almost two years, but now with renewed vigour since the new government had begun its reading campaign.

Already he could write the alphabet and recognize the odd word in the newspaper. And what a surprise it had been for Mae, his companion for thirty years, when two Sundays ago he had swiftly corrected her during the routine Bible reading before the mid-day meal.

Not that Mae could read. But over the years she had so deftly learned to recite a few psalms by heart and follow the words with her finger, so that most people thought she could. Until that Sunday when Rufus, always too awed by Mae's skill to do anything but nod a reluctant "amen," caught her finger at "and" when in fact she was saying "at."

What a delicious brawl it had caused. Mae was speechless for the few seconds it took to gather her wits. But that silence stood no comparison with the furious class of language that burst shatteringly on the peaceful Sunday yard. The neighbours couldn't stop talking about it for a week. And the conspicuous absence of Mae's face around the yard for the next few days only underscored Rufus's discovery.

Yes, Rufus thought, it was about time she learn her place. This literacy thing was a good thing after all. It mek a man feel like a real man. He chuckled softly to himself as he passed the little beauty shop on the right.

Looking up he saw Doug standing by the stone parapet, waiting to welcome students as they walked up the driveway. Rufus got to thinking again. Wonder why that man bother with all of we. The government says this literacy thing supposed to be voluntary. That mean teacher don' get pay. Then I wonder why him do it? From I was born I never see somebody do something for nothing. Only parson sometime, but everybody know that the church collection have a funny way of getting lost inside his pocket. So that wasn't really voluntary.

Rufus's mood changed from indignation to serenity as he thought to himself: anyway, why worry? Only hope him never ask me for no money otherwise me might have to cuss him.

"Evening, Mr. McKee."

"Good night, Teach," Rufus answered.

"Go right up to the classroom. John-John is there with Mr. Redford," Doug smiled. Clive Redford was a volunteer from the community who worked in a local government office. He had been helping with the literacy campaign for a long time and seemed never to lose his motivation.

That means only two of us in that class this evening again, Rufus thought. And that mean I have to sit beside that idiot boy from Cromwellland. John-John was not the brightest of persons but he had a blind ambition to better himself. Only problem was, Rufus decided, those young boys always dreamt the impossible. It was one thing that John-John wanted to learn to read and write. Nothing wrong with that. But he never wanted to stop there. Just imagine! He intended to get a job in Kingston. One where he could wear a nice white shirt and tie like teacher. And then he would "trust" a car and come tearing up to Highgate to pose to all the young girls. John-John was really stupid. At the rate he was going he would never reach anyway.

Rufus entered the classroom quietly, said good evening to Mr. Redford and sat down determinedly beside John-John, making sure to give him a quick little bounce, just to remind him.

He took out his exercise book from his back pocket and the reader, "The Morgans" and tried to look studious. Mr. Redford finished with John-John, turned to Rufus and began examining his homework. He made a few corrections and gave Rufus some new words to work on.

An hour and a half later they all tiredly said their good-nights and started off. Another evening gone thought Rufus, but it had been a good session. What was that new word he learnt tonight—progress? He could hardly remember what teacher had said: something about time moving on, and change, and better years ahead. Hard work too. That was it. Teacher said that hard work made things move ahead faster. Well, he was moving now. It had taken him seventy years, and he was getting somewhere. Any man that could get the better of Mae in an argument after thirty years was moving ahead. Progressing, yes that was what teacher had meant. He was progressing.

Rufus stumbled on past the clock tower and glanced inside the market. He could just make out a few shapes in the back near the door to the butcher stalls. It looked as if they were trying to play a ring game. Funny how times change, Rufus thought. In my time that was how all children amused themselves. Not like those tall-haired, idlers up the street who were jiving to a reggae tune in front of the bar. He turned down towards the 'Burial Ground' his pace quickening as he passed the graves. He could hardly make out the little kerosene lamp Mae had put out on the front steps for him.

The sun had long set. Except for the little crowd of usual spongers waiting to "lend" fifty cents from someone for the movies, Main Street was almost empty. Another, two hours and the streets of Highgate would be deserted in preparation for another day. Yes, time moved slowly, thought

Rufus, as he got ready for bed. But still, it moved. After all, one hundred and thirty-nine years was not a long time.

The literacy classes needed monitoring and some supervision. That took some work, but it did not deplete Doug's seemingly endless energy bank. At the request of the Extramural Department of the University of the West Indies, he had also taken on the job of teaching the A-level curriculum to a small group of teachers in Buff Bay, some miles away.

On Wednesday afternoon, about an hour after school was out, he started out on the twenty-mile journey, which he hoped to cover in half an hour. He would come out to the east of Grey's Inn estate house, then along the coast road to Annotto Bay. The first time he took the trip he remembered breaking out onto the flat stretch that would take him into the town, past the sugar cane fields on his right, and the copra plant on the left. He could smell the mixture of sweet cane, coconut and salt from the sea. It was a delicious flavor that he recognized immediately. He slowed the bike down to a crawl as he savoured the intoxicating aromas of two of Jamaica's important exports. This is what it meant to be home. Here was the sea, the earth, and its products that had mixed the island in his blood and made it so much a part of him.

A few minutes later he turned right at the Esso station in Buff Bay and looked around for the junior secondary school where the class would be held. Soon he saw his students coming into the room. They were five pretty young ladies, various shades of brown, teachers at the school, trying to upgrade themselves to take advantage of a meager salarial increment. When they saw him they began to blush and smile and whisper among themselves. He didn't quite know what to do, not being immediately aware of the reasons for their whispers. Then it dawned on him. He was medium to tall, about five feet ten inches, handsome, with curly dark brown hair, and a well-educated young, eligible White Jamaican. And when he opened his mouth and regaled them with a little patois, the whispering increased.

"Well, Mr. Austin, where yu from?" The first question to break the ice. "Then yu really is Jamaican like the university told us?" He liked and abhorred at one and the same time the implications of the affirmation. But he was going to have no trouble with this group. The only small problem was the taller gal, with light brown skin and almost straight hair, who seemed the more intelligent of the group, certainly the more talkative, and whose intense stares (she sat right at the front of the class, under his nose so to speak), and alluring smell of powder, cheap perfume, and scented soap, made his body demand a meeting. And so the classes started.

Chapter VII
Mary Jean

THESE WERE HIS FIRST SOJOURNS INTO the practical life he had been thirsting for, and dreaming of, before applying for the teaching job and boarding the plane from the north. They constituted his personal paradisial world. Far away from the overpowering smell of salt-fish, not close enough to the commanding sounds of Beethoven and Mahler, but mediated by the strident tones of a Peter Tosh calling for spiritual, material and personal renewal from the four and a half centuries of oppression. And aided by a government that was sympathetic, aware of the historical and psychological resistances, the international pressures and relentless supremacy of dollar profits, but who was attempting, not always coherently, to break the vicious, dehumanizing cycle of dominance.

These were his sojourns. At the moment they were his life, a life that he thought he would dedicate himself to. In doing so, however, he found, at times, that he had taken on too much: there were his classes, the literacy campaign, the A-level classes at Buff Bay, and then others as we shall see. So, some evenings he was so exhausted that he could not sleep. Then he would get on his bike wend his way down the hill to the coast road and entre the dirt road going along the little bays of the coast. The Green Castle estate was just to the left. He would stop at the little fenced off beach used by the owners, slip out of his clothes and lie naked on the sand trying to relax and compose himself in the dark.

There, the lazy sounds of little fish eating and splashing in the shallow water, the thirsty frog coming down for a drink, croaking for its mate, the crickets forever chirping in the grass, the mournful lowing of the cows. These and the sound of the waves breaking on the reef lulled the concerns of the day out of his mind. The occasional puff of wind, the cool air, caressed his tired body as the moon drew, as with her gravitational magnet, lesson plans, teaching notes, preparatory speeches, and other mundane matters from his overcrowded mind. After an hour or two he was replenished. He felt refreshed. He could return home to sleep.

Because of the exertions that were managing to overtake and steal his energy he decided to give himself a break and extricate a weekend from the flurry all round him. So he thought of Mary Jean. He really needed and wanted to see her again, to continue their conversations or try to initiate another, a more compelling one. That next Friday afternoon as the bell rang, Doug picked up his books and made his way down the steps to the staff room. Thank God for the end of this day, he thought. Since it was Friday all the students were anxious to get home after another trying week at school. No one wanted to do any work on a Friday afternoon, and it was sheer hell just trying to keep the class quiet.

But his thoughts weren't on school as he hurried back to the staff room. After two months of working his ass off, he was glad for the recreation that the weekend was going to bring. Mary Jean had telephoned him during the week and suggested that they get together. He recalled his earlier promise to her, felt guilty, apologized, told her how happy he would be to see her where they could have two days just to be together. Besides, he told her honestly, you will be such a nice change from all my usual activities. He was honestly glad for the interruption from thinking about literacy classes, 4 H Clubs, local politics, besides all the other things he was involved in.

He bounded through the door and literally threw his books onto the desk. He reached down to the rucksack and made as if to throw one or two books in it, thought better of it and emptied the contents onto his desk. No marking, no lesson preparation, no exercises for the Buff Bay group, no, not this weekend. He was going to be free to devote himself to MJ, which should be his own recreation as well. Madge had just wandered into the staffroom after dealing with some students, spied him and came over.

"Looks as if you're in a hurry this afternoon," she taunted good-naturedly. "You must have an important meeting."

"To be frank, Madge, I'm expecting a friend from town, and so I intend to take a break this weekend."

"Good idea because you have been going like mad ever since term started. I really don't know how you do it. Just watching you mek me tired." She yelled at a lackadaisical boy who was lounging half inside the doorway of the staffroom. Then, turning back to Doug her face took on a serious expression.

"I don't know if you are aware of it, but people around here really appreciate what you have been doing. I don't think anyone has showed this much interest for a long time. Tell me what's your big secret? Where yu get all that extra energy from?" The sincere smile showed her deep acceptance and admiration for her colleague. Then she turned serious again, putting one hand on Doug's arm and squeezing it gently. The touch was warm and inviting. "Anyway, you know how I feel. Sometimes it's good to get a break from the pace and take a weekend off. Then yu come back fresh for new tasks."

"Thanks Madge," he answered. "I'm glad you said that. I really feel in need of a little break. And if things work out that way this weekend, it's going to be pretty relaxing. See you Monday, and get a little rest yourself. Don't spend the whole weekend cleaning house, man."

Madge sucked her teeth at his mild remonstrance, squeezed his arm again knowingly, and gave him a look that said more than her words a few minutes before. She went back to her desk busying herself with some marking, but looked up just as he was leaving. There was a strange, wistful look on her face.

Doug swung the empty rucksack across his shoulders, said his good-byes, and strode out through the little throng of students gathered at the door. One or two came over to chat about the bike as he swung his legs over the Triumph. Then he glanced briefly up to the balcony where he always seemed to get a few barely audible comments from the would-be radicals of the upper school. He smiled to himself as he brought the powerful machine to life wondering if they really understood what it meant to be a "capitalist," a word they liked to fling glibly at anyone from outside their narrow world. But as he maneuvered slowly past the schoolchildren on their way to the bus-stop his mind raced back to Mary Jean and her impending arrival.

As he approached the road, one of his favourite students quickly adopted an A-90 motorcycle position and yelled "Jesaas" as he swung out onto the road. A few chains up Highgate's Main Street he pulled over to the Pirates Cove where Boysie was leaning against the door, his eyes half-closed, his body moving lazily with the music coming from the juke box just inside the little bar.

As Boysie heard the sound of the engine gearing down, his eyes opened really quickly and his body straightened up into a posture of expectancy. Doug switched off the engine and pulled off his helmet.

"Boysie I wan' ask you do me a little favour. You going to be aroun' here long?"

Doug waited a few moments for his question to register, since Boysie's sense of time was a lot different from the average Jamaican. In fact time had no meaning at all for him. But Doug knew that whatever he promised to do would be done, if for no other reason than Boysie knew well how to quench his infinite thirst.

"Well Teach, I don' really have nuttin doin' right now." The word "Teach" came out effortlessly, but it still made Doug feel slightly uncomfortable. Try as he might, he could never get Boysie to call him by his first name, and in fact had given up.

"Listen Boysie, I expecting a young lady from town. She should pass through here 'bout four o'clock that is in about half an hour time, unnerstan'?"

"Yes teach, me know." This was Boysie's standard answer when he was completely at sea. "But wha' u wan' me fe do, sar?"

Doug grinned as he answered. "I want you park you ass right here so, an wait. She, gwine stop ya so an ask de way up to de house. I wan you jump in the car an ride up an show de way. Unnerstan'?"

"Yes, teach, but how I to know is who she?"

Doug grinned again as Boysie's natural curiosity took on the appearance of intelligence. "She drivin' one a dem sport car. It no have no roof. An' she know to stop right here so. All you have fe do is stan' up here an wait. Right?"

"Right Teach, even ef de bildin bun dung, me na move. But boss," Boysie's tone adopted the tenor of servility that Doug hated, and he broke into the conversation.

"When you come up to de house, I will give you someting."

"But boss," Boysie's voice now took on the seriousness of blackmail, "de day hot an I dying fe a cold Red Stripe." He smiled, at Doug as he said it, knowing he was going to win the point.

"O.K," Doug answered laughing, "Here is two dollar. Just mek sure you drink dat beer out ya so, and keep yu rass out a dat bar. An' buy a Q flask for me to tek up to Clem."

"Yes boss, yes Teach," Boysie bowed with mock servility, doubled over with a big guffaw, slapped one bare foot on the pavement, pirouetted, and in an instant had bounded into the bar slapping the dollar bill on the counter as he startled the bar maid out of her afternoon snooze with a loud "serve."

Doug started the bike just as the barrage of cussin' tore the air, stuffed the Q of rum in his pocket, slipped the machine into gear, bounced off the sidewalk, and roared up toward the clock tower. There he slowed down as he passed the market. The Friday market was getting into full swing for the weekend and the bus stop was crowded with people. There were higglers unloading great big hampers of produce, shoppers jostling to get a look at the goods on display; here and there was a mother looking for a pair of cheap shoes for a school-age son, there a Rasta peddling some clay flower-pots in an aggressive and independent way. Further on up the street there was a constant flow of people to and from the back of the market trying to make some deal with a butcher for a piece of stew, or depending on economic status for a length of tripe or a piece of cows head to boil a soup, maybe the only protein a family would have for the week.

Doug's thoughts always turned sorrowful as he watched the scene of raggedy children searching the market refuse for a bit of cow skin that had mistakenly found its way there. He noticed another group of older boys or men watching everything with an eagle eye, too hungry not to watch the shoppers with resentful looks. Yet, they were too proud to do more than hurl the occasional insult across the street while gyrating slowly to the music coming from the juke-box inside a shop.

But the frustrating thought hit him again that there was nothing he could do about it at least in the immediate present and he gunned the big engine and sped on up to Fraserwood. As he bounced over the rocky driveway and made the turn up to the big house, he waved to Clement, the watchman, who had taken the shortcut up the side of the hill and who had stopped to catch his breath.

He parked the bike by the kitchen window, took off his helmet and waited for Clem to get up to him. "Wha' happen, Clem?" he called out.

Clem quickened his pace slightly as he broke into a wide toothless grin, an expression of sheer love for this young man. Clem was light skinned, seventy years old if he was a day. Yet he still managed to find himself down to one of the banana walks every day where he worked as a cleaner. His two skills made him one of the most sought after workers in the area. Not only could he clean out a "banana walk" of weeds like nobody else, but he was particularly adept at preparing clean suckers, which was so important in an area that was constantly wet and therefore favourable for the nematode worms that attacked the banana plant.

"How yu do boss?" Clem grinned and broke into laughter. "How yu come so early? Me never see you dis early before."

"Just decided to relax this weekend, Clem. There is a young lady coming up from Kingston. She supposed to reach here 'bout four or four thirty. She is a' ole frien' an' I don't see her for a long time."

Clem with the same grin on his face was obviously pleased. For some time now he had been counseling the younger man to tek it easy. "Right bass man, right Mass Doug, is time you have likkle enjoyment. Is not good fe a man like yu wuk him head so hard. Head wuk will kill yu if you don' tek it easy an' rest. Time yu get likkle pleasure."

He slapped his hand on his leg as if to emphasize his words while he broke out again into a low, toothless chuckle. Doug could tell immediately when the old man was contented. He never ceased to be surprised at Clem's ability to switch from servant to uncle or adviser without crossing the threshold of his estate. Yet, Clem was never obsequious. Rather he was like the well trained English butler who knew exactly when to offer conciliar encouragement, and furthermore how to go about it.

And Doug, for his part, soaked it all up. For not only was he interested in the infinite wisdom that was a product both of Clem's age and experience, but he was fascinated by Clem who seemed to be able to reproduce an older Jamaica that Doug only knew from history books. Yes, Clem belonged in that plantocratic past where he would have played exactly the same role as he was playing in Doug's life now: that of confidante, adviser, and sometimes even teacher. He prided himself on his brown skin. One of his favourite expressions was, "Me nah no nayga." And from the fact that he had been to school and could read and write, he considered himself another notch above the average citizen.

Even though Doug had tried to convince him that his metropolitan racism was no good, still old Clem stuck to his guns, until Doug was forced to give up. He would never be able to explain the new Jamaica to Clem. This old man was already conditioned by centuries of history that nobody or nothing was going to erase. His was an uncomplicated, an antiquated world that no longer existed. And perhaps he was able to relive a bit of it through Doug's presence here in this equally antiquated and partially rotten old plantation relic of a house that had played host to some of Jamaica's English governors in its time.

Still the friendship was deep and rewarding for both. Many a night Doug would set up his hammock on the back-verandah share a flask of "whites" with Clem while he listened to stories of old Jamaica. Clem could answer any question that Doug threw at him and was well versed in the mores of the bush as well as the little towns. On his part, he was excited that he had found someone like Doug to listen to his stories. He knew the history of the town, the people who had lived and died there, and certainly who was who, or wanted to be it.

"I'm going to take a quick bath. If she should arrive in the meantime, please help her park and show her into the living-room."

"Right Mass Doug, me we do jus dat. Yu gwane. Everyting tek care of."

"Thanks Clem. By the way, here is a little something for you," he said, pulling the flask of white rum out of his rucksack.

With that he made his way into the house, impatiently throwing the rucksack into his little study. He flung off his clothes, grabbed a bathrobe, and literally ran into the bathroom, where he switched on the heater and tap at the same time, not remembering that he had left the heater on that morning.

As he jumped into the barely filled tub he heard a car plowing up the drive and swore under his breath as he applied soap and water furiously. He could hear the sound of Mary Jean's voice talking to Clem. After a while he heard the tell-tale squeak of the back verandah gate as Clem showed her into the house through the study. He heard them enter the living room and Clem opening the doors to the large, wide, front verandah. He could hear Mary Jean's ecstatic, "Oh how beautiful," and Clem's answer of "Yes, missis." He hurried into the bedroom dressing as fast as he could and dragged a comb through his wet hair. He turned to go out into the passage but reversed his steps, taking up a position opposite the mirror again. A few more strokes of the comb and he was ready.

He turned out into the passage that separated the bedrooms from the rest of the house and swung into the living room. He could see Mary Jean at the edge of the verandah admiring the beautiful view that swept past the Highgate market with its red roof, right on down to where the calm Caribbean merged with the shore.

She heard him coming and spun around, her eyes lighting up with a joy and ardour that spoke of yearning. Doug had forgotten how attractive she was, and he felt that same surge of emotion as his eyes embraced her. In that short moment he managed to take in her shapely figure, which she had obviously exposed as much as she dared to entice him. She was dressed in white shorts and a sleeveless blouse, with her long hair pulled back by the simplest of clasps, and he noticed how tanned and healthy she looked. He hadn't felt that their meeting would be so emotional but as their bodies met and her lips sought his, his lungs sucked in air as the blood raced to his temple while he kissed her deeply. He felt her pushing at his shoulders and realized that he must have been crushing the breath from her body, released her quickly as she stood back smiling up at him.

"Wow, I didn't expect that kind of reception, not that I mind," Mary Jean's voice was teasing and sincere at the same time.

"Hope I didn't hurt you. I sort of got carried away," he answered.

She smiled and said softly, "Then get carried away again," as she pulled his face down to hers.

Doug waited on the wide verandah until MJ had finished dressing. Eventually she came out, dressed, this time in a cool, chiffon skirt, which billowed as she walked. Hand in hand they descended the stone steps and walked slowly towards the back where the little car was parked. Doug took the wheel, eased down the driveway, took the turn onto Fraserwood with his horn and eventually turned at the clock tower down the road leading to Port Maria.

MJ sat quietly beside him, her hand on his leg, hair blowing straight back in the wind that came over the windshield. She felt serene, perfect and comfortable. It was a scene she had imagined as permanent without having to expend much thought on the subject. If only she could be sure Doug would come to love her even if not right away. She needed his conviction, his assessment—he had something she felt she missed in herself and could not tell what. It was an emptiness that was completely removed when she was with him. His absence had driven her almost crazy. Yet it was even worse being in Kingston with him in the country only an hour and a bit away. Every morning when she drove from her house to her office in New Kingston she had thought of this moment. Yet, she had not bothered him, instead waiting patiently until he settled in and felt the need for her. Her recent phone call had been opportune, indeed.

At the same time she hoped she could give him something in return. Did he want children, a happy home, a dutiful wife? She wasn't sure, but she knew they looked good together. Yes, perhaps they were even the perfect couple. After all, the ingredients were there. They came from the same background, had similar tastes and liked each other. What was lacking she couldn't put her finger on. Certainly they had more than many of their friends who were now married and fairly happy as well. She looked across at him, at the strength of his hands on the wheel, the swift sure cut of his jaw – she was happy.

Doug turned quickly as they rounded the corner into Port Maria, glanced at her then shifted his gaze out to the little island off shore where she knew he was thinking of fishing snapper and other good sea food. Doug glanced back at her trying to fit her into his mind, into this Jamaican feeling he garnered from the concordia of smells—coconut, sea weed and salt water—surely MJ was his woman. Together they would love and produce more generations of Austins to continue the heritage left for them.

Yet, he feared that was the kind of heritage he rejected and MJ would never be able to fit into his conceptions. Life with her would be the continuation of an historical lie, a dredging up of the past but one which ended in the present. How could MJ enter this new Jamaican consciousness? She never understood him when he spoke of politics or the new man, the West Indian, void of the realities and conformities of the past: ready only to build anew. She couldn't understand his desire to consummate his thoughts realistically. Probably she could never be his wife. But, who could? He wondered where he would find the woman to share his synthesis of new and old and whether if he married into another race there might not be just the reversal of ethnic emphasis. He wondered how and whether he would ever marry.

For the moment, however, his thoughts reverted to the sensual, willing woman beside him, and he felt the twinge of recollected happiness that might have been. But, it was a dead happiness, from another age, another consciousness, which, however, lived side by side within him, as egg and sperm newly come together, now the same, but already changed in their conviction and ancestral being.

They flew past Port Maria, onto the beautiful small hotel "Casa Maria" overlooking the bay, where they had dinner. Holding hands, sharing a bottle of wine, the setting was idyllic. The hotel was not crowded, and they had the patio to themselves. From the piano bar there was light music. Surrounded by bougainvillea and hibiscus, with the evening turning slowly from grey to black, they danced slowly to the music. Doug requested some Jamaican Mento and Calypso and was obliged. *Come Back Liza* segued into *Linstead Market* . He noticed how effortlessly MJ careened with his body, in step all the way, feeling the music in their sinews, working the history of their veins. MJ followed effortlessly, the Caribbean beat as much a part of them as it was of the sea, the land, the nature. The medley over, they paused, just holding each other lightly till the next tune. The pianist decided on a really slow piece: *Begin the Beguine*. This time Doug drew MJ closer to him, without resistance. He crooked her right arm up against his shoulder, but she detached it, slipping it around his neck. He could feel her stiff nipples pressing through his shirt and the warm spot that nestled against his right leg.

They returned after dark. The lights were out. The other two teachers must have been away for the weekend, Barbara probably in Kingston with other Canadian friends, Dave, who knows where? They entered the house together—no arrangements had been made, neither discussed. MJ seemed to know what was coming.

She was not hesitant as Doug guided her gently towards the bed. They removed their clothes. She grasped him passionately; hers had been a longing of years. As he moved into her he was dimly aware of the sound of the sea not far away. That same sea that had borne and nurtured them all, the sea that surrounded them, visited with the land in its own way. It crashed with thunder against the cliffs, entering the small caves and inlets again and again. It stormed through the openings until it filled every last crevice with its playful tongue, forcing the last bubbles out of every opening. At last, spent and satiated, it almost silently withdrew, to rest, to wait, as if contemplating the next unity anew, then to move again against every opening, reaffirming its life, repeating the cycle of the world.

On the Saturday morning MJ got up first. She threw on a light robe and went out to the kitchen. When Doug finally got up, it was to the smell of coffee brewing, and salt fish and ackee on the stove. Liz had made this for Doug as a special treat before she left on Friday. He must remember to thank her, the evidence, the long pole with the metal hook leaning against the tree by the verandah.

After breakfast they decided to go down to the Green Castle estate, where Doug was wont to go to relax at night after a busy day. MJ wanted to go on the bike, so they packed a light bag with towels and some beach clothes. They slipped easily through town and down the hill to the coast. A quick left turn, then an immediate right and they were on the dirt road entering Green Castle estate.

Doug stopped at the entrance to point out the structure of the plantation to MJ. Up on the hill were the two smaller houses, one for the overseer the other probably for an engineer or carpenters, the only skilled labour on the estate. Down by the road, in almost perfect condition were a series of barrack-like buildings, still in fair condition. They didn't look as if they were in use. Doug explained that these had been the slave quarters up to 1838 when slavery and apprenticeship had finally been abolished. MJ had never seen such an estate, especially one in such pristine condition of preservation. But, more when slavery and apprenticeship had finally been abolished.

Doug navigated slowly around the rocks and potholes of the dirt road until they came around the hill to the north side. There the land fell off sharply for a few hundred yards where it met the coast. Most of it was now used as pasture, and there were dairy cows everywhere quietly grazing. On the north slope of the hill they could see the ruins of an old round windmill, and up behind it, the outlines of the Great House. Doug passed the turn-off to the house, continued on into Long Bay. There, as the road passed close to the beach, there was a palisade of bamboo poles and wire fencing off the beach. On the left side of the road were the ruins of various buildings. One was fairly large, but there were two others off to the side beyond the road. His mother had told him that the bigger building had been a Great House in former times, and the smaller ones the kitchens. In the eighteenth and early nineteenth centuries, it was the custom for kitchens to be built apart from the house, not only because smells were considered unseemly, but because of the danger of fire.

They went through the gate and out onto the tiny beach. It was protected by the reef, which was barely a hundred yards offshore. But it was still fairly rocky, and really only for use as a private spot to sunbathe. Swimming was out of the question due to the rocks and the infestation of sea-eggs with their spiny bristles that entered the skin so easily then broke off causing infection and excruciating pain. They held hands as they wandered back out to the bike. Doug led her over to the ruins where one or two cows were chewing slowly on what must have been a drawing room floor, now only covered with grass and mounds of cow dung.

Holding her hand his mind drifted to the past, to a house full of his mother's ancestors, to slaves scurrying back and forth carrying food from the kitchen, or attending to someone's needs. In such moments he felt filled with history, but a history that bound him to this soil with an unremitting atavism, which one could never shake off. He was the master, they were the slaves. A great abyss divided them—the historical, the social, the political. Could it be vanquished? Where and when would these divisions meet their Waterloo? Was he expecting too much, too soon? These and other questions nagged at him constantly, even as he strove to extirpate their very manifestations from the present, even from his mind.

They mounted and drove on. About a mile down the road they entered the turn off to Strawberry Fields. This was an innovative tourist experience: small tent cottages just off from a small, beautiful beach, the entire operation run and managed by a group of Rastafarians. The idea was to get as close to the natural surroundings as possible, the opposite of a hotel experience. They stopped by what looked like an open-walled dining area with a bar just beyond. Doug asked MJ to wait for him on the bike while he went inside. She saw him greet the Rasta behind the bar. Obviously the two knew each other as the greeting was jocular and affable. Two Red Stripes appeared across the counter, and something else that looked like a little packet. Money changed hands.

They took off again, Doug explaining that he knew a little spot further on. True to his word, a few hundred yards down the road they pulled into a small, secluded cove. It was perfectly hidden from the road, and consisted of a small beach, ringed on the side by cliffs that rose about ten feet above the little area. Doug induced her to strip, and naked they entered the water, which fell off rapidly as the cove was deep. He held her and kissed her, and they lounged for a few moments before he beckoned her back to the beach. While they lay with their bodies exposed to the sun, he took a little packet from his pocket and proceeded to roll what looked like a cigarette. But the moment he lit it, by its pungent unmistakable odour, she knew what it was. But her trust of him was now almost second nature.

She could remember an incident which happened in her childhood, shortly after she had come to live with the Austin's. Doug and she were playing hide and seek with Anne. James, the elder brother, was off somewhere. They ran around the big house, hiding in ferns, in trees, under the house, around corners. Suddenly Doug turned a corner and almost knocked her over. Instead of running, however, he planted a kiss right on her lips. She gave a muffled sound, tore her head away, and ran for all she was worth, heart pounding furiously. He followed, striving to catch up, until in her fury she ran for the mango tree and was up in no time. He climbed after her meaning to repeat the kiss. But something, the desperate look on her face must have made him pause. He stopped, on a lower branch. They were both panting furiously from the run; perhaps from something else. He stood there just looking at her ruefully, and as if to say, ok I won't do it again. He reached out his hand slowly to her. After a little hesitation she took it, not quite sure what he would do. But he only held it tightly for a few moments, saying nothing, and began to climb back down the tree.

She allowed him to put the joint in her mouth, after showing her how to inhale, and hold her breath. The hot, drafts of the "…weed, who art so lovely fair and smell'st so sweet" entered their lungs and began to course through their veins. The effects began to drum against their temples, to effuse the senses. MJ turned over onto her right arm to look at Doug, but he pulled her naked body down on him for a long, deep kiss. She drew her knees up on the sand, straddled him, allowing him to enter her wet, throbbing area easily. This time her climax was a scream, as he dove deep into her body, releasing both their tensions easily, but prolonged by the effects of the weed.

"My God," she said, "I had no idea." He smiled and hugged her more, while their bodies resumed a less fervent state. They washed the sand off, dressed slowly and rode back in silence. MJ rested her head on his back, while her arms tightly encircled his waist. Hers was a complete abandon. They returned slowly to Highgate.

That afternoon they napped, showered, and got ready for another adventure. This time Doug drove straight through Port Maria, passing the restaurant they had dined at on Friday, nursing the Spider skillfully towards Oracabessa. MJ had no idea what Doug had in mind, but she was not disappointed. Close to Murdock's Beach, friends of his had a cottage a stone's throw from the water. It was guarded by a watchman, and fully equipped. He turned off the road just past Galina and entered the driveway. MJ was stunned: the quiet, the peace, the water and perfect beach only a few yards away. They settled in then continued into Oracabessa to buy a few groceries for breakfast and lunch.

That evening they repeated the ritual of Friday: dinner overlooking the sea, music at a local tourist hotel, dancing, and back to the cabin. They sat for hours on the little verandah sipping Appleton and tried to converse. But lovemaking was one thing, a discourse another.

MJ tried gently to ease the conversation on the track that interested her most. "Now that you've had a chance to settle down, Dougy, have you any more idea what you are going to do?"

He was not expecting this turn, although he should have. So he answered rather brusquely but teasingly; "I'm not sure what you mean darling, since I *am* doing." The ontological signifier was over-emphasized.

"OK, Yes. But are you saying you want to continue teaching at St. Mary's? Or do you have some other goals in mind." Her tone was measured, even though a bit hurt by his response. For his part there was the sudden realization that he would have to be a bit more explanatory, less strident perhaps, and a lot more patient.

"In general, sweet gal, I want to be in an academic profession. Maybe St. Mary's won't be the answer, but something along these lines I am comfortable in and really love. I had thought about getting a PhD. and moving onto a professorship in a university. I don't know. In a way I'm exploring myself here. You know, I dreamt so hard about coming back. There is so much to know about Jamaica that I only glimpsed when I was growing up: the folktales, the folkways, the use of language. Man, I tell yu I could spend years studying this stuff. I would love to give yu a more precise answer, but if I am honest, that is where me stay."

She laughed, giving him a playful jab in the ribs. "I wish I could tell yu honestly I know what yu talkin' bout, Dougy. But no man. Is too deep for me." They both grinned.

What he couldn't know that what was at the back of her mind was a quite different proposition. For MJ could agree with him about being comfortable in one's task. She could even vaguely understand his obsession with learning. Learning about Jamaica, well, she wasn't too sure about that one. It didn't make too much sense.

The problem with Doug, from her perspective, was that he would never make enough money to support a family in a way they were all used to. At least that's what it sounded like. Worse, he wasn't even concerned about it. And really, that last thought was MJ's major interest now. She loved Doug, but wanted a family with him—to share Christmases with all the family, her children and the others, and to continue life as usual.

But, since she had gone as far enough as she could for one conversation, she invited him into the water in the dark, where they made love on the beach again. Later Sunday evening she returned to Kingston.

Book Two: Work

Chicken merry. Hawk a near.

(Jamaican proverb)

Be vigilant as danger can be found in unexpected places.

Chapter VIII

Stanley's Piglets

One afternoon, a tall, older, Black man, grey strands already peeking out of a full head of neatly trimmed hair, showed up at the school just as everyone was leaving. He asked for Doug. This person was 'Drowsy' Mullings, local organizer for the PNP in the constituency. He was called Drowsy for his propensity to speak with his eyes almost shut, and, as Doug would learn, to seem to drift off into sleep while even standing upright. But he was one of the key people in the local party organization, a veteran of many political campaigns and the bridge between constituency and party members. Drowsy organized meetings and made sure that the words and the philosophy, but also the directives, of the People's National Party, got down to the grass roots. He was not a paid member of the party bureaucracy, but had a small government job which allowed him movement and freedom to organize.

His mission was simple. He had heard about Doug first from the man who owned the bar by the clock-tower, but word had also got around of Doug's ideas, his work habits, and general manner of behavior. In other words, he was a natural recruit in the party's drive to reeducate. Would Doug be willing to give a talk, a lecture to some members of the constituency association? Of course, he answered, indicating both pleasure and agreement at the invitation.

That Thursday he set off at 7 o'clock for a small elementary school on the outskirts of the new plaza. The meeting was already underway. Drowsy was speaking about party membership, the responsibility of paying membership fees on time, as well as some other practical matters, including the possible chance to meet with the elected MP for the constituency.

    He introduced Doug in a fairly formal way, stressing he was Jamaican, come back from abroad to help Jamaica, was senior teacher at the high school, his leadership role in the literacy campaign, and many others. Doug was even a bit embarrassed. As he got up to speak, he was feeling slightly edgy, skeptical that he would be able to connect with this group on their level. This was going to be more difficult than the pupils at school since all were very simple working people, with at most a grade five or six elementary school experience. In no sense were they the working class, the proletariat that Marx had written about, the purveyors of revolution. Instead they represented the under-class, the lumpen-proletariat, the ones who would be carried along by revolution, the *sans-culottes*: cane cutters, banana walk workers, domestic servants, perhaps a small shop-keeper. Doug realized he would have to draw on some hidden talents, transposing ideas into a vernacular that could be readily understood.

    He started off speaking about the government's attempt to change the direction of Jamaica. Then he began to outline the difficulties and the sources of impediment. Several times he was applauded by clapping, at others by the odd "amen." As he talked, as he realized that they were really listening and understanding, he went deeper. He felt fresh, keen, emboldened. Feeling the response of the small crowd who apparently liked what he was saying, he felt a strange empowerment, as if there were new blood coursing through his body, a drug of some kind, an aphrodisiac that gave to his message an added poignancy.

    He launched into the topic of imperialism, at once identifying this as the source of Jamaica's plight. Then he waded into an attack on Yankee imperialism, reminding his audience that only a few months ago, on September 11th, the elected president of Chile had been overthrown in a bloody coup. He reminded his audience of what followed: General Pinochet's brutality, his hunt for socialists, unionists, those people even remotely connected with the socialist government. He spared no adjectives in his description of the lurid brutality, the disappeared, the tortured, the exiled. And for what, he asked? His voice had risen.

    Now he thumped the little desk in front of him as his voice fell to an almost whisper as he gave his answer: for profit, for gain, stealing from the Black working classes so that one could live above them, look down on them, condemn their little children to an empty belly, deprive them of education with which they could better their lives.

    When he was finished, while he was still wiping his face to remove the sweat engendered by his emotional lecture, there was first a moment of silence. Then people stood up rapidly and applauded with a fervor that made even Drowsy open his waning eyes. One woman came out of the audience took his face in her hands and, with tears in her eyes, blessed him, saying she had never heard such true word, such powerful talk. The sweat continued to pour off him. The back of his shirt was soaked as if he had just walked through a downpour. He couldn't even remember what he had said. Was it at all important? How had he allowed himself to get so carried away, to allow the anger against all imperialism to take hold of him, to transform him into another potential Robespierre, an attitude he rejected with his reasoned mind? Yet, it had felt good. He had relished the reaction of the little crowd. For a moment he had felt the power emanating from his position as demagogue.

But he would have to learn how to mute his own anger, explain the actions of imperialism with sophistication, be more objective. He would have to remember that there were always two sides to imperialism. The ruled played a part as well, through docility, acceptance, even connivance. And Black people too, had played their own part in their own domination. Wasn't it true that African leaders had allowed the Europeans into their countries, capturing the slaves that were shipped abroad, until Africa's demography had been so depleted that the Europeans had been able to enter at will. Even Jamaica had its historical examples of Black assistance of imperialism. There had been Black and Brown slave owners. The Maroons had kept their separate existence because of their willingness to help the British recapture slaves. Was it not a Maroon regiment from Portland that had assisted the Crown to put down the Morant Bay Rebellion? On November 13, 1865, 300 Maroons marched past Rockfort and on into Kingston. They were given an official and rousing welcome. A national holiday was declared and they were officially praised and thanked by the governor, sitting down himself with them to a sumptuous meal.

No, it was not easy to explain. And one could get people all riled up by emphasizing this and leaving out that. He would have to watch his words. In particular, he would need to be more sensitive and balanced in his evocation of the race factor. Not that he was thinking of himself. But it would be so easy to turn the whole question into a Black versus White problem. Sure the North, home of the imperialist nations was largely White, and the South, in general was home to the Black and Brown exploited peoples of the world. What about Jamaica itself? Manley, leader of the PNP and prime minister was not Black. He had a White mother. And the later leader of the opposition, of the Jamaica Labour Party, Edward Seaga, was of Lebanese origin. Raas, he would have to watch his tongue.

But Drowsy was ecstatic. He had found a new speaker. That was important. A new speaker would draw people out to a meeting. But a new and powerful speaker, who knew what he was talking about, who knew history, and who could grab an audience as if by the scruff of their throats, could draw people to meetings, which meant more collection money to strengthen the constituency association.

From that evening on, Doug was not without invitations. Other small groups all over St. Mary vied for his occasional presence at their meetings. Prospect, Richmond, Lucky Hill, Annotto Bay, Port Maria and Oracabessa were all put on his itinerary. And everywhere he went, news of his dedication and reputation preceded him. It all added to the hectic pace that had now become regularity in Doug's life.

But the stress was beginning to take its effect. Lately he had added two more responsibilities to his activities. On learning that there was a dormant 4-H Club in the school, he decided to get involved. First, he met with the students, and decided that they were keen to have someone help them. Next, he asked the headmaster if they could use part of the land the school was on to grow some vegetables. These, he argued, could be used to support the school canteen that provided free lunches for the students. The headmaster thought it was a great idea.

The only little problem was that the land was quite uneven and sloped precipitously towards the north. One student came up with the idea of terracing. The only problem with that was where to get a machine to do the job. Here the headmaster's connections were the key. He knew the farm manager down at the government agricultural station in Richmond, a few miles away. The machine was promised.

One afternoon after school, the pick-up arrived with the machine, and a technician to instruct in its use. That turned out to be a very popular move, since the pupils, as part of their weekly 4-H meeting, were given instructions in the use of the machine and in terracing. So, terraces with a total area of perhaps one square chain were constructed on the sunniest side of the slope. The pupils made plans for tomatoes, peppers, cucumbers, and other vegetables. Some were donated by the agricultural station, and various seeds were donated by members of the school board.

Doug's organization of the venture was much appreciated. It provided a healthy outlet for the energies of the pupils as well as making use of the land to provide nutrition. All round, it was exactly the kind of venture the government approved of. The spirit of sharing, of voluntary labour, harnessed to an educational project was a perfect microcosm of the government's envisioned developmental goals.

His keen eyes noticed one thing, however, which was disturbing. If one took a measure of the background of the students who were members of, and participated in the physical activities of the club, they were almost all from the middle class. The parents of these students were either middle farmers, or had some successful small business. Children from the working class, however, stood by and watched, or sucked their teeth in derision at the labours of the clubbites. Doug pondered at this phenomenon. He should have known. This was not a matter of colour but of class.

It was the middle class that was educated to have initiative. The whole history of capitalism was geared to serving, to sponsoring the welfare of this class. They knew for what they were or would be working. It might be sad for some that the others did not see it that way. But they too were right. This was one of the lessons of slavery. Why work hard, show industry, initiative and imagination if someone else was going to collect the rewards. Slaves used tremendous imagination to sabotage the work of the plantation. And in that context their conclusions were quite correct and understandable. The pity was that those negative attitudes had carried over into modern society. Not only was agricultural work considered a drudgery in itself with very little reward, it was also reminiscent of slavery days.

And so agriculture, which could be so productive in a country where there were no frosts to worry about, and where two plantings a year was possible, was neglected. Food had to be actually imported into Jamaica. What a waste when there was land and labour, which, properly utilized, could have fed almost everyone.

Someone had to breach this cycle of colonial outcome. How to affect psychology without changing the material basis? This was one of Marx's fundamental points. Culture and psychology were a reflection of the material conditions of production. And who was going to provide the jobs, the increased salaries and wages, and the well-being of people? Who would ensure that all children went to school on a full stomach when the material life of the island was controlled from outside? The irony of it all was that to break the cycle, Jamaicans would have to become productive in the very area they considered beneath their historical dignity.

And to add to the difficulties of any government trying to change those assumptions, the actual heights of the economy were in the hands of those who were there to exploit, not change the situation: the bauxite companies, the tourist industry, and the sugar and banana companies.

These and other ideas coursed through Doug's mind as he left the meeting. Being not only thirsty but tired he decided to stop for a few Red Stripe and some food at the other restaurant-bar on the left side of the clock tower. This one served a good assortment of Jamaican food and he felt hungry.

So he sat at one of the little tables, ordered a Red Stripe, and for dinner some mackerel cooked in coconut oil called "mackerel and run dung" with boiled green bananas and rice. As he was packing it away lustily, a man in a kind of Stetson walked over to him.

"Are you de teacher from St. Mary High?" he asked. "My name is Stanley Dawkins. Yu mine if I join yu?"

"Of course not," Doug replied, "sit down and join me. What yu would like?" He motioned to the waitress.

"Bring me a Dragon Stout, nuh. I hear people talkin' about yu," Stanley continued.

"I hope is nuttin bad." They both laughed.

"No Teach."

"Stanley my name is Doug. When I leave that driveway in the evening I don' wan hear nuttin bout teach." They laughed again. Stanley was obviously an even-keeled fellow with a confident sense of humour.

There followed an hour of good chatter and laughing. Stanley, while not exactly appearing to be well-read, was well-informed about many topics, but especially politics. When he revealed to Doug later that he was completely illiterate, Doug was taken aback. Not only did the man talk intelligently, he had great powers of observation, far beyond that of some people Doug knew. And it seemed that the friendship would go further.

They finished their beers and Doug gave him a ride home. Stanley lived with his wife on a small half-acre plot just down the hill and a few hundred yards north of Doug's quarters. The house was small, with a detached kitchen made just of zinc sheets, tied together at the back. Over on the side was Stanley's pride, a concrete, absolutely clean and well-kept piggery in which there were two sows and about ten piglets. Another six and a half acres were up in the hills between Highgate and Cromwellland.

This had been the result of a land reform by the previous government, the Jamaica Labour Party. This was interesting, because even though the JLP was supposed to be the "capitalist" party, both it and the PNP had their roots in labour movements, and held strong attractions for "the little man." The land reform was evidence that the JLP took this aspect of their programme seriously. Stanley must have been a supporter of the party. But he had settled in and taken to farming as evidenced by the piggery. Up in the hills he grew vegetables for sale locally and in the market. With this he had managed to educate two sons, one as a plumber the other as a carpenter, both working now in Kingston. Anyway, Doug promised to visit him soon and continue their conversations. Stanley said, "Why not come up dere tomorrow after school, and mek me show you de operation?" Doug agreed.

The next day he headed up to Stanley's house. The latter was just getting out a small tractor, with a tiny engine which could be harnessed to either a cart or a plough, and together they let it pull them up the hill, which took over half-an-hour. Doug was amazed at what could be grown on such a small acreage. But he was also startled at the conditions. Vegetables need constant water, and of this, except for the haphazard rain, there was none. Stanley had to depend on this rain, and to get the young tomatoes going, he had had to carry up a tin of water on the tiny cart. Literally cupfuls of water were doled out to each little plant to keep them alive for a few days and allow the roots to penetrate.

After this work they settled back to enjoy the contents of the Q-flask Doug had brought along. He listened fascinated by Stanley's stories of government land reform, but also about the difficulties: there was no water; money had to be set aside for seeds and young plants; the pig feed came from a government store which was subsidized by the government. He was also astonished at Stanley's deft use of English. Somewhere, someone, probably his mother, must have read the King James Bible to him because his choice of words and vocabulary revealed a depth of linguistic dexterity, as well as an understanding of human nature.

Then he noticed a two inch water pipe that seemed to emerge from underground, cross just by the mango tree they were under, only to disappear down the hill. It was a two inch pipe. Stanley saw Doug's amazement and before anything was said began to laugh. "Don' you know that is fe me likkle savior?"

"But what yu talking 'bout? That is not a water pipe?" Doug questioned, incredulous.

"Yes man, yu wouldn' believe say dat is de pipe wha' feed whole o' Highgate wid water. Everybody whey use water, fe shower or kitchen depen' on dat dere pipe."

"So what yu say is dat water just run right past your land, an yu kyan use it."

"Me nevah say dat. Watch." Stanley bent down, indicating a joint in the pipe that connected two parts of it just on the other side of the mango tree, on the down slope. He reached in his pocket and took out a small wrench. Carefully he looked around to make sure no one was watching from the bush, then began slacking off the large nut. After a few turns Doug heard a hissing sound because the small pipe was under enormous pressure, and drops began to emerge. Then he saw that Stanley had dug a little channel, the outlines of which were only just obvious, that ran straight down to the tomato plants. Rass, the man was ingenious, Doug thought.

"Only problem is if dey catch me, is big fine. An dey have dese fellars from the Water Commission patrolling down the pipe through the bush. Yu nevah know when one a dem gwine appear. But a know one o' de fellars, an sometime he tell me when dey patrolling. How de rass yu tink I survive inna dese conditions? An ah kyan do it too often, only when time really dry. Afterwards I cover up de channel because it leave water mark fe days."

Doug had never really experienced conditions that many people lived under in the island and the sheer ingenuity it took to actually just survive. The little incident heightened both his intent and his frustration. But more was to come which would make him angry.

They argued back and forth about politics. Stanley was not a socialist and did not approve of the PNP's experiment, Democratic Socialism. Government cannot just give to people. People have to earn what they receive. The problem as he saw it was that Jamaica needed to do more for people with agriculture; but people needed to understan' the importance of growing food. Jamaica mus' feed itself first, and not import things which could grow here. The problem though was that people did not want to "dutty dey hands" in the soil. Look at his two sons. Neither wanted to stay on the land; they wanted to earn more money in Kingston.

Yes, Doug countered, but for people to stay on the land they must be able to earn a decent living. Stanley said his living had been decent. He was able to send his children to school, buy books, and put decent shirt on their backs. Of course, there wasn't enough to buy big car, but was that necessary?

Really, there was not much disagreement between their two positions. Doug knew that the cycle of adverse psychology, exactly what Stanley was arguing, had to be broken, so that people would work the land without hesitation, and contribute to the common good. Jamaica would have to get hold of its major industries like bauxite and tourism, and use those profits to stimulate other sectors.

Stanley felt the only problem with that was that government would become corrupt and mash up any business it tried to run. Second problem was ownership. If government owned everything, why would people work hard? Jamaicans had that mentality. Either they had to work for themselves or they would refuse to work. Working for government seemed too close to slavery time when you had to do what the big boss say. And he could predict that if Manley carried this socialism further it would eventually result in ruin. He himself could see the fruits of his labour, but if you took that away from him, why he should bust his ass to work for everybody? It made no sense to him, and was sure to fail.

But Stanley was in for a shock, since his argument did not take in the external factors that affected the small farmer. It was these very external factors which made Jamaica so vulnerable, and which a government was powerless to control unless it had more say in overall development, a plan which Manley was trying to push with his idea of Democratic Socialism.

Just as Doug and Stanley were embarking on a fruitful friendship the shocks came. Simultaneously, hog farmers like Stanley were caught in a stranglehold. In October because of the Arab-Israeli war, Saudi Arabia, by agreement put a blockade on oil shipments, which sent the price of fuel skyrocketing. Overnight the price Jamaicans paid at the pump almost doubled. But the effects were to ripple through the economy in other ways.

Even the previous JLP government had tried to help hog production by subsidizing the price of pig feed. Because of the response by small farmers hog production had increased. To maintain the herd at a reasonable level, government had begun cutting back the feed subsidy. The hardest hit was the smaller farmer like Stanley. In addition, the price of feed had begun to rise dramatically because of late harvesting of soya in the USA and their promise of fulfilling a large order of soya from the Soviet Union. Now because of the oil hike the price of feed was to rise even more and so the government felt forced to eliminate the subsidy entirely.

One afternoon soon after, as Doug rode up to Stanley's house, he found him and his wife, Norma, sitting outside with utterly glum looks on their faces. The government had just announced the complete removal of the subsidy. Even as Jamaica was continuing to have to import hog parts, which could have been supplied by the local farmers, it was putting these out of production. There simply was not enough money to go around.

Stanley and his wife were faced with the prospect of slaughtering their entire herd and suffering the attendant loss of income. "What fe do, Doug? I jus kyan afford to keep dem. Dey have fi go. Tomorrow I tekkin dem to de pen fe slaughter. Piglets an' all."

Doug had no idea how to help. The problem was huge. For now small farmers like Stanley would suffer. Middle size farmers, with more property could at least grow bananas, using the skin to supplement the feed. But Stanley had no such land to spare. The problem of agricultural development was huge. This government had begun experimenting with soya and corn production. But the results would not come in time to help farmers like Stanley.

This was a perfect example of the kind of problems the island faced. For this reason, the Manley government was trying to rethink policy, especially in regards to agriculture. And the issue of animal feed was typical. It showed exactly why the island's mentality had to change. The previous government had been faced with the same problem and had decided on a different policy, but one whose chickens were now coming home to roost. Faced with the question of animal feed years before, the JLP government had argued thus: why try to stimulate corn and soya production in Jamaica when we can buy these cheaper from the farmers of Iowa. From a purely financial point of view the argument was sound. But viewed over the long term, it made no sense at all. Sure, growing corn in Jamaica might be more expensive, but it would utilize unused land, provide employment, and at the same time, keep valuable foreign exchange in the island.

Doug recovered these thoughts as he rode slowly home. That was why things had to change. It was not going to be easy. And where would the money come from. Yes, here was the other problem and Manley's ideas were absolutely correct. Jamaica should be paid more for its valuable bauxite. Instead it was in the hands of these multi-nationals, who could switch production wherever they wanted, control the prices as they saw fit, and force a small nation like Jamaica to its knees.

"Yes, Stanley, if we didn't have to suffer from these raas imperialists, if we all worked together, life might be different. This might not have happened."

"No Doug. The problem is Black man. We too use to carry down each odder. Everytime a Black man see him bredda prosper, him mus' do something like Anancy to screw him. Dat is my feelin'."

"But what yu talking 'bout? Is not Black man causing you problems. Di problem come from tings we kyan control. Is the White man world, the imperialism, the capitalists that put every block in de way for small island to prosper. Dey squeeze every las' cent out o' we hand. Dat is why we kyan get anywhere."

"Listen Doug. I respeck how yu feel. But look at me. I get dis land from JLP, and dis likkle pig farm. An' who come an ruin it? Don' is PNP government? Dey call demself socialist, but all dey doin' is chop up small man so dey can drive dem big car. Don' is PNP cut de subsidy?"

This last statement stopped Doug. There was more than an element of truth. It was not pretty. The government was creating large land schemes in other parishes which would benefit their own supporters. The realization of what was happening struck Doug with such force he was forced to stop talking and ponder for a moment. He had not had the time, nor the inclination, with his busy schedule, to really analyze the situation. Democratic Socialism was all very good. But was it being put into practice? Doug began to feel that he had been looking merely at the ideology, the ideal, the vision, while disregarding the concrete reality.

In its 1973-74 budget estimates, the government had envisaged bringing 50,000 acres of largely idle land into production. This was part of its policy thrust which had (correctly, Doug believed) targeted agriculture as the key to development. Under a programme called Project Food Farms, about half this land would be farmed by the government itself. Individual farms would be set up across the island. The rest of the land would then be leased out under strict conditions, to small farmers who had already proven their skills. Conditions? Yes, these would entail setting up cooperatives. He thought he saw through the plan.

Stanley was being sacrificed. Sure, he was a small farmer. But he was also a "capitalist." The whole drift suddenly made sense. Stanley would be seen by the ideologues of the government, (of whom there were quite a few from the far Left), as a Kulak. And what had been the fate of Kulaks in the Soviet Union in the nineteen thirties? In many cases, yes, in hundreds of thousands, if not millions, Stalin had had them dispatched with a bullet to the head. For the first time since coming back, now that stark reality had leveled a strong blow at his idealism, Doug was really confused. So what he was really fighting, working, yes, even slaving for, he reasoned, was the supremacy of one group of little people against another. Class warfare yes, but even more so, party warfare. Same old story. But, could his analysis be right? Surely what Manley had said in his many speeches, his evocation of humanity, his stress on democracy as the essential condition for achieving development with justice and fairness, surely these principles were inclusive. If so, why did little people like Stanley and his wife have to suffer?

But Stanley's voice broke into his own private bewilderment.

"Listen Doug. Yu know if a man kyan mek a livin' honestly, him force to mek it anodder way."

'What yu talkin' 'bout Stanley?"

"Yu tink al dose fellow Manley putting in de Gun Court wouldn' unnerstan' me. Yu tink all a dem waitin' fe government give out 6 acre here and 10 dere. Dey up in de bush tekking care a fe dem pickney."

"How."

"Yu didn' hear 'bout that airstrip de government fine up in de Dry Harbour Mountains? How de raas dem get such a huge bulldozer up deh, nobaddy know. But is only fe one purpose. Dem building airstrip wid it, an' yu know fe what?"

"What?"

"Ganja, of course. If dis government don' solve de problem of unemployment an' poverty, an what dey is doin' to people like us, yu watch out. Yu know how much pickney in a dis island go to bed feed wid ganja money?"

Doug didn't know. But it made sense in a bizarre way. Unfortunately other things were beginning to make sense as well. They were about to crowd into his imagination and tell him, yes, possibilities existed, but what if? And what if the what-ifs were stronger than the possibilities? In early 1973, the *Daily Gleaner* had trumpeted "Never Before so Many Bright Prospects." Would they come to pass?

CHAPTER IX

Socialism, Race an' Pum-pum

THIS LAST INCIDENT LEFT DOUG WITH a bad taste in his mouth. It was such a shock, seeing the reality first hand, unadorned with phrases of ideological hopes and visions. His own reasoning as to the march of events was frightening. Even more so was Stanley's horrendously disturbing and pessimistic solution. Economics was a great problem for the government. But people could not wait. They had waited too long, chained to the hegemonic soothings of the system, bolstered by an unremitting message of slumber promoted by the Christian churches: "pull yourself up by the bootstraps;" "the Christian awaits his rewards in heaven." For too long people had waited for "trickle-down economics" to work. Well, the wealth not only had not trickled down, it was still trickling up.

"Black man time come," was the new slogan. People's desperation could be seen in a recent incident when an Esso tanker laden with kerosene oil had overturned at Ocho Rios. Despite the pleas of the driver and the presence of the Constabulary, people had descended on it in minutes, carrying every available pot or pan. In no time at all the tanker had been completely emptied.

But woe to Jamaica if economic hardship meant that ganja and other drugs were to become the panacea for the many. That would be the end of Jamaica. Once easy money began to flow, it would take over completely.

Like a vicious, untreatable cancer, it would spread rapidly, sweeping all good intentions and pious ideologies aside. Yet, it had not completely appeared. None the less Stanley's conclusions were disturbing. There were signs that some people could not wait. The crime wave was taking over. Small talk of connections to international crime was now in the daily news.

This led the Prime Minister to declare all-out war on crime. "Anti-Crime Muscleflex" screamed the Gleaner headline. Roadblocks were to become a permanent feature. Motorists would have to carry driver's licenses as identification and a special gun court was to be set up. There was also to be a clamp down on the issuing of firearms licenses. But would it help? Manley had said that they had evidence of increasing affiliations with international gangsters. Hard drugs, cocaine, heroin and 'speed' were coming into view. These were alarming developments. Doug, in the grip of an idealism born of his own sense of duty, of dedication, of willingness to address historical wrongs, had never factored this into his analysis.

Now there were other issues to contend with, which were beginning to appear as well. That issue was the race card. It was, indeed, a conflicted one. In order to ensure continued development or "progress" the PNP had to enlist the help of Jamaica's middle and upper classes. In racial terms, these were the Brown and White (including Jews) part of the culture. Not always, because there were Black businessmen, some who had made substantial amounts of money, not to speak of the Chinese, Lebanese and East Indians, who had produced their own groups of business leaders. But they were, in Marxist terms, the traditional bourgeoisie, and they shared the principles of property and capitalism regardless of colour.

At the other end of the scale were the masses, almost all uniformly Black or East Indian. Sure this uniformity had its exceptions, but in general it was so. Black was at the bottom. And for the government to appeal to this part of the society, what was more natural than to "sweeten" the ideology of socialism with a unifying factor, with something much more identifiable, in other words, Blackness. How could it change the psychology of the nation, how could it cut through the ambient hegemonic structures, without addressing this historical issue? It was forced by the power of its own logic to identify Jamaica's problems emanating from the enduring imperialism. And that meant, in simple minds at least, pitting White, Chinese, Jews, and Lebanese against Blacks.

Already in the sixties Black Power had made its appearance. Dr. Walter Rodney, a Guyanese, had appeared in the History department on the Mona campus preaching his doctrines of Marxism interpreted through a racial dialectic. Rodney had been a brilliant speaker, not only a brilliant academic. He could visit the most remote little bar in some part of the Jamaican bush and almost immediately gather groups of people around him who would listen avidly to his words and doctrine. Rodney's public lectures on the campus were always overflowing.

His message was simple, but underscored with solid historical analysis: Imperialism had destroyed Africa; Black people were the victims of the White Man's greed. Jamaica was only an extension of this argument. The island had inherited all the problems of this brutal, exploitative past, and continued on the same path. Current politicians, and these included Alexander Bustamante (erstwhile founder and leader of the JLP), and Norman Washington Manley, also erstwhile leader of the PNP, were by association, their successors. These men were the sellouts to the White man, and were untrustworthy.

Rodney's lecture had been so compelling that they had caused riots on the campus in 1968. He himself was declared *persona non grata* shortly after, returning to Guyana. But the message of Black Power, allied to the movement in the United States, invoking the memories of Marcus Garvey, and bolstered by the Rastafarian movement with their denunciation of "Babylon" had caught on. When a government in the sixties had tried to combat Jamaica's enduring problems with measures for population control, signs had appeared almost immediately on every vacant wall in and around Kingston: "Birth Control wan Kill Black Man." The campaign was a flat disaster.

Shortly after, a new four-page paper appeared on the streets of Kingston. "Abeng" as it was called, sold for only sixpence (Jamaica had not yet converted to the dollar), and was unabashedly anti-imperialist, anti-White, Anti-Jewish,-anti-Syrian, and anti – anyone associated with those it identified as the bourgeoisie. It was pro-Black, pro-Black Power, supported the Black Panthers, Eldridge Cleaver, the anti-imperialist struggle going on in Guinea Bissau, which was trying to throw out the Portuguese colonizers, and operated under the slogan "Black Man Time Come: Beware Black Traitors."

"Abeng" was allied with the New World Group, a Caribbean intellectual movement which had functioning groups in Jamaica, Trinidad, Puerto Rico and Montreal, Canada. This movement was dedicating itself to discussing, analyzing, and suggesting solutions to a variety of problems from unemployment to the problem of language in their societies. Intellectual yes, but at the same time, it was clear that the analysis blamed imperialism, and government's inabilities to meet this challenge head on for many of the problems confronting the people of the Caribbean.

By 1972 when the Manley government had attained power, these assaults from underneath were at the same time supporting the PNP's attack on imperialism, while criticizing it for not going further and faster. And it was producing this curious outcome: if the solution to the economic problem was socialism, or wiping out the bourgeois approach to "development," that solution also had to pit Black against White, not only to mobilize the support of the masses, but because the source of this imperialism was from the White countries. And that proved to be part of Doug's dilemma as he had noticed in his lectures to the small political constituency groups. He himself could not recount the history of imperialism without recognizing and stressing that historically, at least, and in general, it had been White Europeans against the Black and Coloured races of the world. It was all beautifully encapsulated in Bob Marley's reggae hit, released that year, "Stand Up For Your Rights."

But there was a second problem as well. This was the problem of psychology, not to speak of the endearing one of socialism itself. How to stand up? How to awaken the spirit of initiative, rather than destructiveness that had been one of the most enduring of slavery? How to instill in the masses that if they were not going to rely on capitalists to produce wealth, they would have to do it themselves? In other words, Manley was faced with a two-fold problem: the first was making socialism, or the doctrine of sharing, work; the second was engendering a mentality of innovation and imagination in creating wealth. Mammouth tasks, Doug thought, even if they could be tackled one at a time.

In fact, the government's attempts to address these problems had already produced one humorous, if politically chastening incident. The previous government in its wisdom had bought the sugar holdings of both the United Fruit Company and the West Indies Sugar Company. Now the Manley government was going to try an experiment in both national psychology and cooperative management.

It decided to issue shares of one estate to the workers. These would then be the new owners of the estate. It was reasoned by the government in its wisdom, that once the workers owned the estate, pride in ownership would produce exemplary Stakhanovites who would increase and streamline production for their own benefit. Unfortunately the government had reckoned without the innate folk wisdom of, mainly, the cane cutters.

A few months after handing out the glossy certificates of ownership in an impressive ceremony, attended by all the lords and ladies of the government, and accompanied by masterful self-congratulatory speeches by the Prime Minister, the Minister of Agriculture and any Minister who felt capable of bringing hands together to applaud the scepter-bearing savants of the cabinet, some lowly clerk in the Ministry of Agriculture noticed that production had stopped at the estate.

A hasty phone call to the estate office and factory produced the unexpected and un-reassuring confirmation that, indeed, production of sugar had ceased because, in fact, there was no cane to be ground. The workers had stopped cutting. Amazement and dismay panicked the Ministry into sending out at least three carloads of bureaucrats to enquire into this outrageous set of circumstances. No one had heard about a strike. There had been no reports of violence, of problems, nothing.

The shirt-jack wearing civil servants meekly called a meeting of the estate workers to enquire into the circumstances. The results were startling. It took them first, two days to get everyone to agree to a general meeting of the company. To cut a long story short, the cane cutters, a formidable group not used to smart talk from anyone, had elected as their spokesman a tall, gaunt, senior who was missing his entire row of front teeth, had been working as a cutter since he could remember, and was as used to being a part of meetings as he was at having tea with the Governor General.

So when the Chief Agricultural Officer opened the meeting "Busha" Joseph (even though he wasn't a Busha) got up and asked the man whether he could ask a question. It was simple. They all wanted to know why the meeting was called at such short notice, and what it was supposed to be about. He spoke politely but firmly, accompanied by much nodding of heads, his hands tightly gripped on the shaft of the machete they were used to carrying around as a mark of station.

The civil servant in question explained as equally politely but firmly that the Ministry had taken note of the fact that production had stopped; that no cane was being cut. It had been left in the fields, was ready, losing water content every day, which would seriously affect the amount of sugar product to be obtained.

"Yes," replied Busha Joseph. They had noticed that too, and were wondering what the Ministry was going to do about it.

The civil servant was taken aback. He couldn't understand Joseph's reasoning. In fact, it took him a while, after conferring with his lieutenants to address the main question directly.

"Mr. Joseph," he began tenderly, "the Ministry is upset that sugar cutting has ceased. And we don't understand that after transferring the ownership of the estate to you, that yu would stop working."

Joseph, on his part shook his head. A murmur was heard as he conferred with his own lieutenants. He cleared his throat and rose again to speak.

"Sar," he started, "don' is true dat at dat ceremony government hold here a few weeks ago yu give us de ownership?"

"Yes, that is true."

"But boss, if we de owners now, yu should fine somebaddy else fe cut de sugar cane. When me ever see owner down in de field wielding machete, chopping cane in a de hot sun?" There was nodding all around.

Finally the point settled on the little group resplendently arrayed around the head table. You could have heard a pin drop in the room. Looks of utter incomprehension appeared on the faces of the Kingston delegation, as one person looked at the other, while no one ventured to speak. No one, but no one had envisioned this type of Jamaican reasoning. They should have known better. It was so implacably simple. I am now the boss, so you find somebody else to cut cane. Give us a white shirt, and when we get pay we will buy a car and drive around like owners. After all, the world must go round the right way. Boss is boss; worker is worker. Jamaicans reasoned the Jamaican way. But the government had not reckoned with that approach.

Still the problems that had recently indicated their presence, which would mount in intensity as the government tried to implement its policies, did not impede the pace of Doug's activities. If anything they made him more convinced of the need for selfless dedication, strengthening his own resoluteness. As his not unimpressive literacy class continued to function, he was invited to join the parish committee, which met bi-monthly in Port Maria, the capital.

This led to an incident that sorely tested his patience. One Wednesday the committee was visited by a representative of the National Literacy Campaign from Kingston. Lebert Watson was a young graduate teacher who had joined the campaign as an organizer and motivator. He also occasionally gave instructions on teaching methods and materials used in the campaign. His eyes burned with enthusiasm, and he also had a reputation for utmost dedication, which fuelled the fiery speeches he sometimes regaled willing listeners with. To put it another way, his interpretation of history differed not one iota from Doug's own. But his emphases caused some embarrassment in the room and personally to Doug.

Every person on that committee knew Doug's reputation, his nationalism, his commitment to Jamaica. He and the committee were one, he had never felt anything less, in fact, never even gave it a thought.

But, curiously, the half an hour "history" lesson that Lebert delivered in his ambition to rouse the committee to more dedication and action caused a rift in the group which was unexpected. Doug saw two of the younger female members glancing furtively at him. Before half the talk had ensued, Doug counted the word "White" fifteen times. Each of those times it was inextricable from the condemnation of imperialism which was at the root of the developmental problems they all knew so much about. The problem was evident. How to fix the national problems, how to proceed with development, how to awaken people without these simple lessons of history? It had been Doug's only problem. That had been attenuated because he worked in a relatively small area where everyone knew him, his work his love for the country. Even in Highgate he had had to endure some illiterate foolish boy yelling "Pork" when he walked past the hardware store up Main Street. At those times it was brought home to him what it must have felt like to be called "Nigger" or "Boy," as was still the custom in some parts of the American south. Only that the other wrong was little comfort.

Sure, on the national level, in fact one or two towns further down the road where no one knew him, he was just another White man. He was a sign, a signal, a tocsin of what had to be fixed. It was basically the problem of racism in general. It was so easy to stigmatize an abstraction, to over-generalize, to produce hatreds, because the abstractions were reduced to a few derogatory characteristics: Jews are money grubbers; the Irish are drunks; Blacks are lazy; Indians are thieves; Whites are demons. One could write books about stereotyping. But bring two human beings together, face to face, where each presented the other with an ineffable humanity, and stereotypes would disappear. Instead two human beings would look straight through the "problem" of colour, of race and just see each other as people struggling to make sufficient money to send children to some extra lessons, put food on the table, or just plain exist. There was only one way to counter racism: mix it up. Remove barriers to marriage and stigmas of "family purity," provide public institutions where people were forced to mix and learn from each other, such as a public education system.

Just that intention a previous JLP government had had when it constructed St. Mary High School in 1962, one of the first acts of the newly independent nation. The very first government High School was built in the neglected countryside. Until 1962 all the secondary high schools in Jamaica had been private and privileged seats of the middle and upper classes. But that had been only ten years ago, and miracles could not happen overnight.

Still, the presence or absence of colour, its peculiar habit to be effaced by proximity, but only by proximity, was a lesson he learned the hard way just as they were approaching the end of term, and getting ready for the pre-Christmas school and national exams.

Drowsy had enlisted his help in preparing for the annual Christmas picnic they staged for the youth arm of the party. Doug had decided to give up his Triumph, which he replaced with a Morris station wagon. With all his extra activities he needed the space. So he had offered to drive the dead goat down to the picnic site. Early on Saturday they packed goat and supplies in the back, which he drove down to the beach. Others had promised to bring things back up to Highgate, so all he had to do was drive down, unpack, and bring the wagon back to the town.

An annual event, this outing, they would prepare and cook a goat slowly over an immense fire on the beach. First there was the drinking of that peppery hot soup made from the other goat parts like the head, but especially the testicles, called Mannish water. Jamaicans believed this soup had supernatural qualities, especially that it contained overdoses of ready-to-impart sexual energy. So it was a must. Then would come the savoury meat served with rice and peas (a standard Jamaican dish), boiled green bananas and salad, and gravy.

Next there would be an official part of the celebration consisting of speeches by the elders, the younger leaders, and anyone else who was invited to say something. Prizes and little gifts would be handed out for extra good work done by some youngster. The best part of the evening, the part, in fact, all the young people eagerly waited for was the skits and poetry recitations followed by a few ring games (which the older folk had to teach the younger ones, since ring games were long out of style), and generous libations of blasting Reggae music, dancing and "fun-fun" lovemaking.

Doug was introduced as "Teacher" again, plus a number of other appellations, all congratulatory, approving, esteemed and endorsing. Some of the young people knew him from the high school and gathered around approvingly, some with obvious affection, for he strove to treat each pupil with that special concern the good teacher has for his students, a concern that goes beyond mere teaching knowledge, but encompasses the true meaning of an education that elicits from each pupil the best she or he can deliver to the world and themselves.

He felt good. His words of congratulations to the recipients were received warmly, and he spoke of others, the ones who only gave of themselves without thought of award or recognition: the true backbone of any nation, the salt of the earth. After he spoke, a few pupils drifted up to shake hands and to say their thanks. The smell of the goat had become overpowering, stomachs were straining with patience, the music lulled and beckoned all at once.

He had drifted apart from the main scene, wandering towards the beach when he felt the presence of some one. This person took his arm. "Mister Doug," she ventured, "my name is Joyce Brown. Good night."

"Hello Joyce. Yu know my name, but is just Doug."

She laughed. "I like how yu talk. Mus' be much brains inna dat head." Joyce's voice was familiar but teasing at the same time. Patois was not her regular fare.

He looked penetratingly at her. She was about five foot four, utterly slim, with short straight hair that showed some mixture of East Indian and Black, with a narrow waist, but topped with fine outstanding breasts. Her coal black eyes bored into him as he struggled to contain his composure.

"Doug," she continued, "I want to sleep with you."

"What? Yu mad, yu crazy, yu drunk, nuh?" This was too much, too unexpected.

"I look drunk? Yu tink I mad?" She laughed an alluring short laugh, throaty and hoarse, as if she knew what she was saying.

Doug didn't know what to answer. And at that very moment he could hear one of the leaders of the youth group calling to him. "Mass Doug, goat ready. Cum eat." It was Mrs. Thompson from Richmond, one of the major organizers of the PNP Youth in the area. She was Black, as Black as anyone could be, a beautiful, deep, ebony colour, broad, with a girth that floated usually about her merry soul, quick as lightening with speech, and utterly committed to the PNP programme, understanding with her deep folk wisdom more than many could fathom. "Come sit here opposite me." She had already cleared a spot on the picnic table, laid some knives and forks, and there was a steaming mug of Mannish water waiting.

Joyce had heard the exchange. But she was not about to let him go. She took him by the arm and piloted him over to the table. Mrs. Thompson saw her coming, and quickly, in a gesture of sensitive politeness, or perhaps not to cross Doug, laid a second place by his side.

"Doug what yu drinkin? An yu young lady." Mrs. Thompson was suspicious but did not let it show too much.

"Gi me a 'whites' and Cola Champagne if yu have one Thelma. Tanks. Wha' yu would like Joyce?" He made hurried introductions. Mrs. Thompson inquired who she was and was surprised that she was the daughter of the man who ran the small Public Works department in Port Maria. Joyce's father was Black, her mother, East Indian, and both were well known PNP members.

That eased the situation slightly, as Mrs. Thompson's own daughter had had her eyes on Doug for some time and sat at another picnic table disapprovingly, cutting her eye whenever she could at this new apparition in her territory, so to speak. Doug was completely unaware at what was taking place under his eyes. Joyce ate with one arm on his shoulder, claiming her prize, so that her taut breasts could touch his right arm as he swallowed down the Mannish water with absolute relish. Sometimes her eyes would stay fixed on his face; at others she would take her hand down, lightly brush it against his leg, making sure to reach over to the other leg, making contact as her hand glided over the animal inside his pants that was surely straining to get loose. He was sure she had no bra on. But here was not the place. He remained as aloof as he could be, since the main action, anyway, was occurring under the table. But she knew. The tell-tale response. She was a woman who knew what she wanted, and when.

Thelma had had a few "whites" during all the ceremonies, and was ready for a good chat with Doug, whose views she always seemed eager to hear.

The conversation wafted back over some government business. Drowsy sat at one end of the table, eyes almost closed, but every now and again entering with some comment that showed his ideological inclinations.

"Doug wha' yu tink 'bout Chile. Yu don tink is a blasted crime wha de US and de Chile military commit?" Thelma Thompson was leaning with both elbows on the picnic table, her plate pushed aside, both breasts covering the ample place setting.

"Yu know, this was de mos' cynical, murderous, an sneaky intervention I ever hear 'bout." Doug waxed into one of his lectures, call it a tirade. "This is exactly wha happen when poor people try to help themselves. Then, the damn Yankee White man come down with his fury and weapon dem, to screw everyone. Profit! Money! Greed! Dat is de only ting dey know." He slapped his hand on the table as he spoke. Drowsy, startled out of his perpetual but inconsistent slumber, could only murmur "True wud. True wud."

That was not the end of the talk, however, as Thelma took up the baton. "Is wah yu an I an' de government always talking 'bout, trying to eddicate people. Imperialism. Dem use gun an tank fe fight poor people who only want a likkle smalls. Is a shame an' a criminal business."

"Yu know, all a dis experience tell we one ting. De only way out is one big blasted revolution. That will wipe away all dis injustice." Thelma was warming to her theme, the "whites" helping along an already quivering mind.

Doug continued eating, not wishing to further enrage her thoughts. But he didn't need to.

Thelma's good nature had already given way to the conclusions she was forced to reach, born of a deep-felt indignation and sense of historical injustices. "Dere is only one soso way. Revolution mus en' all a dat injustice. We mus' tek up machete and go up de hill an kill all a dem White bastard dat keep we in a oppression. Revolution mus come to help we. What is on top mus' fall to de bottom. What is at de bottom now mus rise to de top. Black man time come." She ended her fiery outburst by slamming her fist so hard on the table that it stirred Drowsy into muttering another "Amen."

All the time it took for this tirade to end she had been looking at Doug. But she was not talking at him but with him. He had not been included in the White but the Black. Strange? No, it was exactly what he had been musing before. White was not a skin colour here, it was something abstract, synonymous with capitalist, with exploiter, with wickedness. He was no longer White, but belonged. He belonged because he was obviously against repression, against exploitation, and supported Black struggles for revolution, for liberation from an oppression of centuries. Thelma obviously considered him Black.

But that precisely posed another dilemma. White and Black are manifest colours. Inexorably the simple mind would interpret it as such. The syllogism was obvious. Here in Highgate, to the people he worked with and helped, Doug was a savior, a fighter on the right side, an indefatigable warrior for the just cause. But what about even Port Maria, Oracabessa, Ocho Rios, St. Ann's Bay, Falmouth and beyond. Who knew him? If revolution were really to come, it would take only one, swift, powerful, machete stroke to end it all, and by someone not looking past his colour but right at it. Raas, was there no way out?

But the rum was beginning to work his head too. Rather than fight it through here, which was useless anyway, he would have to subject himself and his ideas to some rigorous examination. Then he felt a light tugging at his arm. "It getting late. Mek we go nuh?" Joyce was whispering calmly into his ear. They got up said their goodbyes and made their way to the Morris and the short trip home.

Entering the house from the back verandah, Joyce stopped, looking around the spacious dining room and the living room beyond. Through the glass doors she could see the wide front verandah and led the way to it. Most likely she had never seen such a view, and stood looking out over the verandah wall at the sea beyond, past the red-roofed market down to Robins Bay. Doug walked up behind her and put his hands around her waist. She leaned her head back, touching his shoulder, then moved his hands firmly up her midriff until they were on her breasts. Slowly, she removed her top. There was no bra, as he had thought. She turned around, unbuttoned his shirt with dexterity, and pulled his face down to hers for a long kiss. Her firm breasts pressed into him and he could feel his swelling. She sat back and raised herself on the parapet. Slowly, while kissing him she undid his trousers, kicking them down to the floor with her legs.

Then she leaned back, and just as imperceptibly, drew up her skirt. It would only register for a split second with him that she had on no panties either. Then she drew him into her, leaning back to give him entry but pulling him firmly with her hands on his buttocks. He heard her moan and felt the shudder coursing through her body, and knew she had come.

Heavy breathing followed with her tucked firmly against his chest then slowly, ever so slowly, she pushed him back, away and out of her. He was still pulsating, not yet satisfied, but allowed her her way. Then she slid down off the parapet, turned around, put one hand on the wall, and with the other, lifted her skirt up past her hips. He understood, still heady from drink and her eroticism. Then he entered her from behind, fulfilling his shaft in her wet space, as she encouraged him to come. He did so, with a muffled roar, which must have carried past the hill and down into the interstices of the valley below.

Slowly she straightened up, allowing him to slip out, loosened her skirt letting it fall, and stood still against him, both in their full nakedness, panting from their togethered encounter. They kissed, long and deep, until their lust had been momentarily consumed. Then she reached down, picked up their clothes which had by now been strewn over a circumference of a few feet, and motioned to him.

They reentered the house. Doug locked the front door and guided her in the dark towards the bedroom. He turned on a reading lamp over the bed, and she arranged their clothes neatly on a chair. He took her by the hand, and together they made their way towards the bathroom. There they showered together and got ready for bed.

They got into the bed without a murmur, without conversation and settled down to sleep. But of sleep there was little. All night, it seemed, she kept his penis in her hand. No sooner did he stir than they became active. It was like holding a lightning rod in one's hand. She sensed immediately when he was ready and rehearsed with him every position imaginable, some he had not even dreamed of. It was a passionate, easy play of a kind that was intended to satiate even the toughest participant. Her orgasms were easy and plentiful. He had not encountered this before. Such an un-embarrassed, easy, artless, determined sexuality; it elicited from him an intense erotic fomentation, a true tempering such as he had never experienced.

Towards morning he was lying turned on his right side behind her; her small, slim body was perfectly spooned with his. One hand cupped her large breast. He began to stir again, but this time she didn't move. Instead she raised her left leg slightly, and reaching through her legs used her hand to guide him swiftly into her. The moaning began, and this time both came passionately after only a few thrusts. Then they drifted off into sleep, as the first rays were beginning to illuminate the guinep tree.

They must have slept soundly for the next two hours. When Doug awoke it was already light. He got up quietly, went to the bathroom, and after, started to make some coffee in the kitchen. After a few minutes, she appeared. She stood looking, almost emotionless, at him. Instead, with full, bright eyes she asked "Yu like it last night?"

"Yes, You?"

"Yu couldn't tell?"

"Yes, I think so."

"Me enjoy yu very much. Ah like yu style."

He wasn't sure what she meant, and tried to make further conversation. But she had no idea of politics. It bored her, for her answers were short and noncommittal. As to the government, the situation, the possibilities, his conversation with Thelma. She didn't know. Closure. He did not press her.

Together they ate some fried eggs and left over ackee and salt-fish he heated up. Then she said, "Yu can give me a lift down to Port Maria?"

"Of course. Yu want to go now?"

"Yes Doug. Me frien' waitin' for me. Ah don' wan' she worry too much."

"Aw right. Let's go then." And with that they went outside to the station wagon, got in, and drove off.

The half hour ride to Port Maria went quickly. She motioned with her hand where he was to turn, then had him stop down the road a bit from a small house. She got off slowly saying, "Tanks for a lovely evenin'."

"I going to see yu again?"

"If you want yu can drop by an ask for me. Ask for me frien' Betty."

A week later one afternoon after school he dropped by the house after delivering some papers to the literacy office. Betty was there.

"Hi Betty. Joyce not here?"

She hesitated before answering, a little shyly at first. "No Doug. She gone."

"Gone. What yu mean gone?"

"Jus dat. She gone. Yesterday she decide to leave an go Mo Bay."

"Montego Bay? But I thought she had family aroun' here."

"True. But she gone Mo Bay, looking for work. Yu might buck her up if yu passin dat way."

Doug thought for a moment. Montego Bay. The tourist hotels. No, Joyce was not going to work as a maid cleaning a hotel. She must have other plans. He tried one more time in Port Maria to get some news of her whereabouts. But no one had any address nor had they heard from her. He did not see her again.

Chapter X

Madge

THE CHRISTMAS HOLIDAYS WERE APPROACHING. SO were end of term exams. The pupils were getting restless from the excitement of Christmas, but also from the nervousness exams always cause.

Already Main Street was crisscrossed with glittering tinsel banners, posters of Santa Claus and the reindeer, angels, cherubins and seraphims, signs of Christmas trees, coloured lights and all the other paraphernalia associated with Christmas. Of course, it was all for show, advertising the need to spend. The stores in the plaza were full of the latest toys, Barbie dolls, automatic weapons, space suits, all the presents children would need to advance their idea of a proper "moral" life. It was understood that only those with enough cash were going to fill Christmas stocking and gifts from Santa. Most of the children in the area would not even have a tree. Many didn't even have proper food. A Christmas dinner was only a dream. But there would be presents for the lucky few. The others could only watch or concentrate on going to church where they would be told to be patient, that they would reap their rewards in heaven.

Down at St. Mary's, teachers were putting the last spit and polish on courses, revising, quizzing, cajoling, admonishing, all to ensure that pupils shone at the end of term exams. In the fifth and sixth forms there was heated activity as preparations were made for the A – and O-level exams set by the University of Cambridge syndicate. Children needed certain subject passes to enable them to enter the university at Mona, or, indeed, to go abroad in order to further their chosen careers. Even the fourth forms were involved as they would sit internal exams modeled after the one they would sit for the following year. The mood was tense, though mitigated somewhat by the festive Christmas air.

Madge and Doug settled in one afternoon to draw up the school exam timetable, a somewhat lighter task than the previous September. They resumed their efforts over the course of a few afternoons after school in one of the upstairs classroom, where they would be guaranteed some quiet, amidst the cooling sea-breeze that wafted up from the coast as the sun continued its afternoon descent.

Madge looked tired. Managing family, looking after their child, the daily trips from Port Maria, sometimes in the bus when her husband needed the car, all left their mark. Doug, too, was frazzled. Now that the Buff Bay class had closed for the term, the literacy classes running themselves, and the vegetables merrily producing for the school lunch programme, he had some extra time. This he spent giving voluntary extra lessons after school for the weeks leading to the exams.

The exam timetable did not take much time. The only problem really was organizing the invigilation, who, what, when. But that was not a hard task. It seemed solved to their satisfaction as they went over the assignments one more time, just to be sure.

"Yu look tired, Doug. Wukkin' too hard?"

He laughed. "Not really, but I think everything indicates the holidays will be a good time to rest."

She looked at him quizzically. "I'm sure there's more goin' on than you want to tell me. Yu sure yu not havin' girlfrien' problems?" Smiling, she knew her teasing would bring a response.

But Doug only laughed. "Well to be honest, that is not a problem yet."

Her eyes flickered at the "yet," waiting for more. Now she was determined to probe.

"When las' yu saw her?"

"Yu remember the time she came up for the weekend? That was in October. Well, I went into Kingston sometime in November. That's about it." He sighed and looked a bit sheepish.

"Hmm," came the response. "An what young lady goin' satisfy with that?"

"I really never gave it much thought, but...."

Madge broke him off in mid-sentence. "So what yu really telling her is that all the res' of you doings more important, right?"

Doug looked slightly embarrassed. "No, that is not quite the story. The truth is I'm not really sure."

"Sure about what?"

"That she is the one."

"A-oah." Now Madge broke into some broad patois. "Is pu-dong we talkin' bout'. Don' mek me laugh. Yu and dat pretty gal mek fo each other. Wha' happen? But wait. Sorry Doug is none o' my business, right?"

"No, it's o.k. Madge. She is a nice, nice sistah. But dat's de problem. Sister." He said it with emphasis, pronouncing the word properly. "I just don't feel she is the right one for me. She doesn't understand. Her goals are completely different. We don't have any points of contact, shared values, especially about Jamaica."

"But she is Jamaican just like you! What yu mean about values? Don' she want the same kind o' progress an' change yu always talk about?"

"It's not that, Madge. Of course she does. But I don' think she understands what it is. I don' think she feels where we have to go. To put it plainly, I don' think there is any empathy."

"But Doug, in life yu can' have everything. Yu have to mek some compromise."

"Like you?" Now he had her on the defensive. Madge blushed and didn't answer.

"Yu never talk to me 'bout your marriage. I know yu not happy. But yu never mention Duncan; nor anything about being the wife of a pastor." He was hitting harder than he had meant to. But there was an effect, which told him he had struck a sensitive chord.

"No, is true. But I chose dis life. I know it not easy, but it could have its compensations."

"And it doesn't?"

She avoided the direct question. He was hitting too close to veracity. Could he expect her to be candid? His eyes slid again down the front of her blouse, which was closed to the top. The cleavage was hidden from view today, but not her legs. She had chosen a skirt which sat just above the knees, not quite mini, not quite full.

She was also sitting beside him so they could reach over and push the counters they used across the big chart. Whenever she leaned forwards, the skirt rode high up her hips, although she constantly endeavoured to pull it forward. None the less, his eyes found their mark and he felt that secret warmth flowing within, which he knew had one inclination. If only. The worst part was that they sat there easily agreeing, working, empathizing, as if one. There was little embarrassment, but an ease in asking and responding to questions, even of a personal nature.

"You know, Doug," she continued as if ready for the occasion for candidness, "that is not all. Yu can't imagine."

"Imagine what, Madge? Tell me."

"Yu know when I got married I was in love with Duncan. He was tall, handsome, was moving into a good career, and I never thought further."

"We never do," he ventured.

"Yes, I never expected that with time all those things that are hidden deep inside a man would suddenly come out. To be truthful, I don' wan' make it soun' as if is just him. Me too."

"You mean you began to grow in different ways?"

"Not just that. Things began to bother him I never dream of."

"Like what?"

"Well, for instance, I went to St. Andrews, your sister school. And that was because my father had two shilling to rub together. Doug only went to elementary school, finished sixth standard, then went to Mico College, and from there to Baptist seminary. He was a good student, and earned everything he got. But I was the one from the class that could afford a private secondary school. That difference now seems to bother him."

Doug was a bit unprepared for the disclosure. He hadn't quite figured out the insidiousness and pervasiveness of class, its effects at the personal level. Sure, he was aware of the big picture that between the erstwhile scion of the plantocracy such as he himself, and the bottom reaches of the society there was a huge gulf. But now it was brought home to him of the other gradations within the society and the debilitating effects and divisions that class awareness could engender.

"Yu mean he feels inferior to you?"

"Something like that. I don' know how deep it is, but he refuses to talk about it. Every now and again he comes out with some little quip, which comes from the depths."

"Raas." She slapped him lightly on the hand laughing. "Yu talkin' to a lady, yu know?"

"Sorry," he grinned. Then spontaneously took her hand in his. She grasped it tightly as if not even thinking of what it was she was doing. Then when the warmth and electricity began to flow, withdrew it hastily, her face turning a deep red. Doug looked down. He was also blushing.

"But it's not only that." She was quick to broach another topic to get away from the moment.

She began running one finger up and down her right arm, looking at him with an expression of chagrin, one side of her mouth turned up. It took him a while to catch on and respond.

"If I think is what yu tellin' me, I'm flabbergasted. No, nuttin' go so." He had uttered the last with amazement.

Das right," she nodded. "Yu got it."

He could almost not get the words across his lips. "Yu tellin' me that both o' yu have racial problems?"

She could only sit and look back at him with the same expression of chagrin. "Don' we both Black? Don' we both born and grow up here? Don' we both eat the same food, sing the same song? Don' both we blood in Michael?" Now the tears were coming. Doug got up, bent down, and put his arms fully around her, holding her as she sobbed the full extent of her pain. She responded by laying her head lightly against his chest and putting her arms around his waist as the sobs racked her body. He didn't know what to do next. So he just held her until she was finished.

She took a small handkerchief from her pocket and began dabbing her nose.

"Hole on." Doug ran downstairs quickly and just as quickly reappeared with a box of tissues that had been on his desk. No one was in the staff room at that hour, so no one saw him. She continued her recovering, began looking fresh and open-eyed as if the catharsis had long been coming.

"Sorry Doug."

"Nuttin to be sorry 'bout, Sis. Everybody has their problems. But I am really surprised. Really. An I thought I was the only one."

"Only one of what? What yu talking 'bout? Tell me."

"O.K. I have an idea Madge. Yu have yu car, right? Duncan expecting yu early this evening?"

"No. An I sent Michael home with a friend. Why?"

"Why yu don' come up Fraserwood, have a cup of tea, calm yuself and we can talk some more? I have lots to talk about."

"So, in other words," she broke into senior mistress mode but mockingly, "we goin continue the timetable session on yu verandah."

He grinned. "Right. Come."

When they got up to the house dusk was well entering its last phase. Doug showed Madge through the house first. She remarked that it was the first time she had been inside it.

"But yu livin' like backra, Maas Doug," she couldn't stop teasing him. "But what a lovely view. Yu mus spen' a lot of time here."

"Time? Yu mus, be jokin'. Come we go in de kitchen an finish up."

Madge followed him to the kitchen, spread the big chart on the long table, and so they began to put the finishing touches on the exam timetable. Just then the door to the back flat opened, and Barbara Prescott came out with some laundry to hang by the back verandah.

Doug called to her. "Barb, would you like a cup of tea or a Stripe? We just finishing some work." Barbara came over, sat down, and exchanged a few words of shop talk with Madge.

Good, thought Doug, a chaperone. No fast-fast mouth could put any meaning into this encounter, nor impute any bad motives.

"No thanks. You know I don't drink beer, besides I just had dinner, so see you later." With that Barbara sauntered off, checking her laundry and going back inside her flat. Doug noticed the door was left open. Well, that could have been to let some of the cool evening air in or…? Good, he thought.

Finally satisfied with their product, he ushered Madge, the tea, and his Red Stripe out to the front verandah, where they sat for a final chat before she had to depart.

"Madge, yu know, what yu said about you and Duncan really surprised me. I can't imagine that the problems of race go so deep."

Madged sucked her teeth. "How long yu been here anyway. Yu should know by now race is the most serious component in the social fabric of the Caribbean. How could you imagine that after slavery, after all the class and race divisions that we could ever be easy about race?"

"I have to admit," he said. "I never thought it through so keenly. Recently I have come to see it, of course, but that you would be affected by it, too, I would never have imagined."

"What yu mean by 'recently'?"

"Well actually, there have been a few incidents lately that I never told anyone about. I'm not talking about the occasional yard boy yelling "pork" when I walk past Porter's, but ones which have made me think very deeply recently."

"Like what? Say more."

He started. "Yu remember that literacy meeting I attended in Port Maria? Well, the word 'White' was used so often, and in a derogatory sense, that I was actually embarrassed. Then the fellow who was holding the meeting came up to me afterward to apologize personally to me. It made things even worse."

"The fact that he apologized quietly?" She was quick to discern his drift.

"Yes. Why apologize at all if you don't do it openly in front of everyone. But that was only the indicator of the problem, Madge, because, if he had apologized openly, it would have given the lie to his entire thesis."

"But isn't that part of message, I mean, I talkin' now 'bout imperialism, in general, part of his message the destruction caused by the White world, and slavery?"

"Yes, sis. But the worst part was I agree with him. I could have given the speech myself."

"So yu hate yu own skin, bredda man. Tell me is so." She was teasing again. But this time she reached out, took his hand, and neither withdrew from the simple flow of energy which announced a connection of some spirit.

The discussion continued for at least an hour. Doug explained his second eye-opener at the beach with Thelma Thompson.

"How could she have looked straight at me and talked about killing White people?"

"The reason is yu too Black," Madge couldn't help another friendly dig.

"But this is madness. How to have a revolution in a society which is so damned complicated? Erasing class is one thing, but trying to solve the problems of race is another. And the two are so intertwined it befuddles rational thinking. Besides the whole problem is deeper than I thought. Now that I know this I am even more baffled."

Now Madge leaned forward to his chair. Somewhere she had unbuttoned the top button either for more comfort or to let in a little air. But the effect on Doug was symptomatic. He felt that warmth begin to rise, as his temples began to pound. But she brought him to his senses rapidly.

"Who the hell yu tink yu is to try solve the world's problems, even little Jamaica's, in a short time? Yu think human nature easy?"

This last bit sharpened his attention. "Wha' human nature? Yu think everything is fixed? That is because of your biblical upbringing. Nothing is fixed, it can all be changed."

"I didn' say no, Maas Doug," she replied bitingly. He knew a blast was coming. But he was not quite expecting it to be so strong.

She leaned forward even more, looking him intently in the eye. "Yu might be able to change human nature, but it tek time. Human beings don' change fast. Besides, yu know from history, an yu is a history man, how difficult it is to change from one mentality to another. Yu think Jamaica go change overnight? Yu think Manley have a chance even if he wins another term? Yu think four years can effect change? Come on now!"

"Yu right Madge. I know all that. But still we have to try. We at least have to plant the seed, and expect some growth: maybe not now, but sometime in the future."

"Planting seeds is one thing. Yu first have to know about the soil, the weather, the rainfall. And still it might come out wrong."

"Yu right Madge. It was just what I was thinking right after Thelma Thompson was talking. Besides there is another question entirely."

"What?"

"My own responsibility, especially to those I love: my family and friends. I can't simply think of revolution when I know that people I love are going to be slaughtered, because they happen to be on the wrong side of history. To do that I would have to be a fanatic."

"And that is the las' thing you are, Mr. Doug Austin. Besides," and now she leaned forward again, looking straight at him, her face not a foot away, "other people love yu an' don' wan' to see yu come to no harm."

It took a while for him to understand what she was saying. She was still looking at him intently and closely, watching to see if her remarks had registered. Suddenly he reached around and drew her mouth to his. She was startled at first, not expecting his reaction, and his muscles relaxed as she gave in to the kiss, which was long and arduous.

His other hand reached for her breast, covered it, their feelings now emulsified. But she drew back slowly, disengaging her mouth, taking his hand gently, moving it off her breast.

"No, Doug. Not now, not here." She pulled back, smiled at him, recognizing what they now knew, but were too overcome to acknowledge earlier.

"I'm sorry, Madge, I didn't mean to…"

"Yes yu did. An' did I tell yu I didn' like it? Come, but yu mus' have patience."

He understood intuitively. Another fork in the road had appeared. He had no idea what was coming. But they got up slowly.

"Is time. I have to get home. Thanks for the tea." She re-buttoned her blouse, looking at him with a twinkle in her eye, pulled down her skirt, and made for the door. She turned once more, saying nothing, just putting her hand on the lapel of his shirt, just by his nipple. It was not meant to be an erotic gesture, but he could not contain himself.

Just inside the door he pulled her against him, luxuriating in her warmth, her breasts against him, the warm spot between her legs now nestled against his throbbing member, and went as so to kiss her again.

"No. I must go." And with that she turned towards the back.

Barbara's door was still open. Doug escorted her to the car and opened the door. He made sure to give it a little extra bang as she got in. He watched the taillights descend behind the guinep tree and down the drive, heard her turn down Fraserwood, making for the clock tower. He turned and went inside. The moon had come over past the ackee tree and now stood almost perfectly overhead. He heard a rustling in the guinep tree as swallows and canaries settled down for the dark, for the night.

He walked back inside slowly, bathed in sweat, locking the back door behind him, and went straight to the bed, not even pausing for his nightly toiletries. That night his sleep was fitful. He tossed and turned. There were new thoughts, there had been new encounters, new emotions to contemplate. It was not going to be easy. The dream did not help.

He began to see shapes emerging from a thicket. At first he could not make them out. They wore blackened hoods and were carrying "sore toes" as if they were going fishing. Some were carrying machetes. He realized that one of the men in front was he. He couldn't see their faces, nor was there any clue as to their furtiveness.

As they broke out of the bush, a wailing and drumming seeming to come from nowhere overwhelmed them. They had become part of a group of Jonkanoo dancing down a street. The lead dancer was dressed in a tight-fitting doublet and carried a massive long pole as mark of authority. He was crowned with a headdress resembling an estate, or Great House. A group of chanting, singing women danced behind him, and all was accompanied by loud drumming and shrieking.

Suddenly Doug felt himself pushed out to the front. He was propelled past the leader, who began to poke him with his staff, forcing Doug to break into a run. His running became swifter, directionless, sweat from fear producing the effect he was running for his life. He found himself at the corner of Barbican road where it meets Hope Road. The turn to the left which would have taken him past Jamaica College was blocked by police. It wasn't certain if the group were going to cross over to Old Hope road so he decided to turn right and head down Hope road. Already he could hear the sounds of the drums receding in the distance behind him.

Someone called to him from a house on the right. It was a friendly Chinese face, but he wasn't sure. The man was joined by his wife who kept calling and beckoning to him. He slowed down and went over, glad that the ordeal was over. It was Mr. Chiang the Chinese grocer from Constant Spring where his brother's household did the weekly shopping.

His heart was still pounding from the run as they opened the gate and ushered him inside. It seems they were in a small covered, latticed porch, looking out onto the driveway and the road. They invited him to sit down. Very politely and kindly they then brought out food and coffee. There were his favourite salt-fish and ackee, boiled bananas, and this time, some cassava cakes called bammy. Thirsty and hungry from the rum and the adventure he wasted no time. The food disappeared to the smiling approval of the old couple. He finished, helping himself to more coffee. The whole atmosphere, meanwhile, while friendly, dripped with a haunting eeriness that he could not fathom.

When he was finished the old couple beckoned him once more. He followed them, this time down a long corridor that ended with steps going down to a huge room. It was lit by low-slung, Chinese lanterns which gave off an eerie glow. Moreover, it was filled with people. He did not know what he had got himself into, but knew somehow that he needed to be there.

As he walked down the stairs two older aunties, sisters of his mother, Aunt Joyce and Aunt Alice, greeted him with smiles. His mother was standing over to the left. He could recognize no one else but knew they were all family and friends. He felt their presence, was reassured, began to breathe more easily then started to take in the furnishings of the room. There was not much. All the guests were standing against the walls as if waiting for some ritual or ceremony.

Curiously, right in front of him but closer to the opposite wall there was a kind of table, or even an altar. It was covered with a white, linen table cloth, and had three candles, one at each end, and one in the middle. Was there a cross in the middle, too? He wasn't sure.

At the left side of the table a man was standing. He was tall, had very long black hair which reached to his waist and was dressed in a priest's robe which stretched down to his feet. There were buttons down the front. His face was kindly, but stern and official.

They were all beckoning to him to move forward. Now he could make out a small box, or was it a cradle resting on the floor just in front of the altar? They were becoming insistent. The man in black nodded his assent and Doug stepped forward to look.

He walked slowly, with the dignity that seemed to be required and approached the box. Then he noticed that it was draped with satin lace and was not a box at all, but really a cradle. It was festively decked out as if to honour whatever was inside.

He stepped closer, trying to see, but had to bend down close to make out what was in it. He stared at it. Then he went almost faint, felt the blood rush to his head to compensate, while he broke out into a cold sweat.

He was looking at an apparition of himself as a baby. From baby pictures he had no doubt who was lying there. What he had been witnessing, in fact, was his own christening. He slowly straightened up to the applause of the wind whistling and fighting its way through the guinep tree. Now he found he was sitting upright in bed up at Fraserwood bathed in sweat, with the alarm bell ringing his six-thirty wake-up call.

CHAPTER XI
CRIME AND CUSTOS

CHRISTMAS IS A SEASON ALL OVER the Christian world to make merry, especially to celebrate the birth of Christ. It is a time of rejoicing for some and a time of ringing one's hands with glee at the approaching Season of Profit. For others, however, it is a time to watch other people have a good time, while one goes hungry. It is almost as if the season had been invented as a mockery at those with next to nothing.

Can one wonder then, that it was also the season of crime? The mockery, the insults of gaudy Christmas displays must have been an invitation no one could resist. "Buy, buy" was the message the merchants and shopkeepers broadcast shrilly through TV, radio and newspapers. But what if one couldn't? What if one had to scrape and scrounge to just find a little salt fish to feed a child, or to buy a tin of milk for a baby?

Yet, the problem was not solely that of Christmas. Jamaica's economy had been hard hit by the oil crisis. GDP was not keeping up with the population increase, but efforts to keep that under control had invoked a serious backlash. Then on October 16, Tropical Storm Gilda hit Jamaica. Not a full force hurricane, its winds managed to reach one hundred mph, but the rain bands accompanying it caused serious mudslides across the island, especially the western parishes, and claimed the lives of six people. It was the natural disaster least desired, as it put an additional strain on a government scrambling to find the resources to govern.

The Cuban government was among the first to send aid, with its practiced generosity. Condensed milk, rice, sugar, milk powder, spaghetti, even shoes were donated by them. This gift was graciously acknowledged by the government when the Prime Minister and the Minister of State paid an official visit to the vessel, the SS. Topaz Islands. The gift was generous. But so were the gratuitous rumours that followed, and which were the opening salvo in a campaign to besmirch Manley and Democratic Socialism: *Cuba and Jamaica—marching as one; Manley really introducing Communism; Not long now.* A picture of Manley and his Minister of State, Dudley Thompson, having a drink aboard the vessel with the captain and other Cubans was displayed across the front page of the *Daily Gleaner*. Now the rumour mill got into full swing. On a small island such as Jamaica that is almost inevitable. But who knows what other, perhaps, foreign, coals were flung into that fire.

Jamaicans also still remembered an incident from December, 1970, when squads of armed police had carried out an helicopter-assisted raid in the hills just north of Grant's Pen, St. Thomas. There they had uncovered a camp used for military training. They had earlier received reports from local citizens that military training was taking place in the hills, and later a number of other camps were found. No one was captured, and the affair seemed to have lost interest for the news boys. But it still stuck in people's minds, creating unease and speculation.

Despite a promised increase in bauxite revenues and some increase in tourists, the government could not make ends meet. Income was not sufficient to keep pace. There was massive unemployment in the island, which, and despite government emergency programmes such as "bushing" bank-sides and culverts of major roadways, was not a long term solution. Unemployment was not unexpected, but it had been growing. It had even been estimated back in 1970, when the PNP were in opposition that the rate would reach twenty or twenty-five percent.

How do people survive when there is no work? The answer is simple, not rocket science. If you hungry you either beg or tief—finish. Crime, especially petty larceny, was increasing. And thieves devised ingenious methods with which to ply their trade. Men would crouch down running through the long line of cars snaking their way into Kingston each morning, reach into an open window, and steal a hand-bag. This was then transferred quickly to an accomplice on a small motor-bike, and off they went. No one could follow.

To counter the crime wave, the Gun Court had been set up and was in full operation. But the murder rate was continuing to push up to 30 per 100,000 citizens. People spoke of the politicians arming supporters, and indeed, there was some evidence that both political parties were at fault. But it was also believed that the political gangs, especially in places such as Trench Town and Jones Town in Kingston were morphing into structures which had other than political aims. Ganja was being sold as never before, and ganja exports were on the rise.

And the robbers and gunmen were becoming bolder and bolder. Nothing was safe. Residents of St. Andrew living in the more affluent areas of Norwood, Jack's Hill, and Cherry Gardens were already taking the precaution of installing iron grills all around their house. James Austin had had the entire stairwell leading to the upstairs bedrooms surrounded by iron grill, with a heavy gate, which was then padlocked when they all went to bed. Imagine what might have happened if the downstairs caught fire, while the family were locked upstairs. Middle class men, if they could, began buying firearms to protect their families.

In Highgate and other parishes except St. James, things were more tranquil. But even there people were nervous and afraid. In late November, for example, a small post office in Albert Town, Trelawney was broken into. Letters and parcels were stolen, one supposed, in the search for Christmas money being sent from Jamaicans overseas to their relatives. Gunmen were now coming up from Kingston, marauding small towns, threatening peaceful citizens, and, in some cases murdering them. The newspapers, the *Jamaica Daily Gleaner* and the *Jamaica Daily News*, not to speak of the afternoon scandal paper, *The Star*, were full of unexaggerated reports of murders, shootings, gang warfare and robberies.

Doug had not seen fit to take any precautions. He only locked the doors at night, although these could easily have been forced without much effort. Still more he slept with the huge bedroom windows open, to take advantage of the cool air and Jamaican night sounds. Characteristically, he enjoyed hearing the wind keening through the branches of the guinep tree, and the birds as they ruffled their feathers in the attempt to keep warm. Other sounds too, a distant cow mooing, the barks of several dogs disturbed by unfamiliar sounds, the crickets constant chirping, frogs with their anxious mating calls, these all lulled him into the sleep needed to counter his fervid efforts during the days leading to the Christmas holidays.

Then, in the second week of December, Highgate was afforded its own special drama. It was dragged, as it were, into the machinations of the capital scene, unwillingly, because the country areas liked to think of themselves as peaceful, as not completely "corrupted" as was Kingston and parts of St. Andrew.

One Friday morning this peacefulness was shattered when a group of four gunmen rode up from Kingston on their motorcycles intent on committing a major robbery. After all, country people were "country bumpkins" or stupid bwai, in other words easy targets.

The occasion was the weekly paying of wages to the workers in the banana walks. Highgate was still a simple, fairly sleepy agricultural area.

One of its major industries were bananas, shipped from Oracabessa, which was the town just west of Port Maria. Every Friday, the local Banana Board office would prepare the pay lists for the various workers, cutters, tallymen, and cleaners, divide up the money into little packets slipped into small envelopes with every worker's name on it. This bundle was then put into one or two shoe boxes, fastened to the back of a bicycle and the bookkeeper would ride out unsuspectingly to the banana walks and pay the workers. No one had ever been robbed so it was considered a safe and normal practice.

That Friday morning the bookkeeper set out as usual. When he reached Fraserwood, on the road to Dean's Pen, and just past the house where Doug lived, he had to dismount as the climb was too steep for the bicycle. Pushing his way slowly up the winding road, he stopped occasionally to wipe the sweat from his face as the sun was getting hotter. Then he was suddenly accosted by the four men. Two of them had pistols, one a machete and the other a club. Not only did they demand and get the two shoe boxes, they beat up the poor bookkeeper in a most brutal manner and left him on the road. A passing motorist happened to see him; people picked him up to take him into Highgate Clinic, and called the police.

Before police could arrive in any force, however, the villagers and small farmers of the adjoining area, as well as the banana workers had heard about the incident. They poured out of home and field with every available weapon, machete, or club they could find, and began scouring the fields in the direction the gun men were supposed to have taken off to.

Somehow they became organized, and fanning out in long lines began beating the bush, examining every mango and other trees, in a systematic effort to find the miscreants. They headed north feeling that the gunmen were going to cross the area north and west of Highgate, cut across Cromwellland and so link up with the road going to Unrhumney and Harmony Hall onto Whitehall where they would link up with the A3 going to Port Maria. They were right.

About a mile north of Fraserwood a party of men came upon the hapless outlaws, who, tired from pushing their motorcycles up-hill an down dale in the hot sun, had stopped to take a rest under a huge mango tree. What followed was an exercise in civic solidarity and justice that warned future gunmen to stay far away from the Highgate area for decades to come.

Word had now gone out that the gunmen had been found. The first villagers to find them surprised them, and the gun men opened fire, killing one of them. But as soon as the six bullets were expended from each pistol, and before they had time to reload the rest of the villagers were upon them.

The anger not only at the theft but at the death of one of their own produced such a fury that the crowd beat the four men mercilessly. The anger was so great that machetes were produced and two of the robbers were chopped to bits and died almost instantly. One of them managed to escape in the melee but was caught by other villagers and brought back. By this time the police had arrived in force to take charge and prevent the villagers from administering any further spontaneous justice. Of the two men left, one was so severely beaten that he survived for only half an hour. The other was taken to the clinic placed under arrest and carried back to Kingston.

The shoe boxes were found in the saddle bag of one of the bikes and eventually returned to the Banana Board, where the wages were properly distributed. Not one cent had gone missing. Village justice, ordinary Jamaican views of right and wrong had been upheld. So clear was the situation, and with the island-wide support it engendered, that none of the villagers were prosecuted. No attempt was made to find out actually who had done the "chopping." That would, in itself, have caused a revolution.

But it was fully broadcast island-wide. Even before the incident was over a JBC television crew had arrived, interviewing some of the villagers, who were able to vent their feelings on national television. The best part was that ever since that day, gunmen and would-be gunmen gave Highgate a wide berth in their comings and goings.

In the staff room at St. Mary's, a radio had been installed from mid-day so as to catch the news of the theft. Everyone sat still listening. It could have been a test cricket match against MCC. And at the news of robbers being found by early afternoon, loud cheers and hurrahs broke the air of the normally placid staff area.

"See what I tell yu?" Madge was the first to break the silence. "People justice. That is what we need in dis island. What a bruckins."

"If we could only produce this at the national level," ventured Winsome Brown.

"Don't forget that those men were killed in cold blood. Is that the kind of justice yu want for this island?" Ralston Roberts was not going to allow reason to escape easily.

"Mr. Roberts." Madge's voice took on a shrill note. "Are you saying that we should allow ourselves to be robbed and murdered? These men committed a serious wrong. That was poor people money."

"I don't deny that," the serious, patient Roberts continued, "but justice demands that they be apprehended and brought to trial. Is lynch justice what yu want here?"

Doug decided to enter the discussion. "No, Mr. Roberts. Lynch justice is not called for. But in the circumstances, and I mean the circumstances of poverty and want, something happened which made people so angry they took the law into their own hands. We may not want to make this a general principle, but we mus' admit they got the buss-ass they deserved."

"Yes, entirely," said Madge.

"I only don't want us to start thinking in Jamaica that we can deal with crime, with these things in this way. If so we will be finished as a civilized country. That's all." Mr. Roberts spoke slowly, and his words did have some effect on calming the euphoria in the classroom.

"Well," said Winsome, "that is all true. But I glad they get lick. At least it will be a lesson to others not to come up here and carry out them dirty tricks."

Doug and Madge looked at each other as she said this and went over to a corner of the classroom to finish their discussion. Doug, however, was interrupted by the secretary who came in telling him that there was a phone call for him.

"Mr. Austin," the voice said. "This is Custos' Dorokhov's secretary. The Custos asked me if he could invite you over for a drink soon."

"Tell him yes, miss. I could come next week. I'm giving some extra lessons on Monday afternoon, so after that would be fine."

"Thank you, sir. I will tell him."

He went back to the classroom deep in thought. Why the hell did the old raas want to see him?

"Madge, guess wha' happen? Custos Borokhov jus' called and invite me to have a drink with him next week. Wha' goin' on?"

"Why yu askin' me? Don' all yu White folk have fe drink rum or scotch wid each other now an' again?" She gave him a mock look of seriousness and censure.

"But what he wan' talk 'bout?" Doug was earnestly agitated.

"I guess he gwine tell yu how him know yu modda. An' how de family connect." Madge rolled her eyes and wouldn't let up.

He couldn't help laughing. "Awright. If it is jus' that, o.k. But I bet yu is something different."

"I not bettin yu. Yu right, for once." Now the teasing tone reappeared. It was so good. It showed an ineffable bonding that had occurred ever so slowly over the term and seemed to deepen as time elapsed.

Ever since the incident at the house where he had kissed her something had changed in their relationship. Before, there had been easy banter and a cool way of working together. Now, whenever they entered the staff room their eyes eagerly sought the corner where the other sat. Were one present, furtive but evocative looks would be exchanged, even if they lasted only a few seconds. Everything was avoided to make it seem that here no love affair was underway. For in fact, there was none, at least in the literal sense.

They never had lunch together, nor left school at the same time. Yet, each felt in her or his own heart that something was brewing.

It expressed itself in strange ways. At meetings they would know instantly what position the other was going to take and while not giving immediate or obvious support, managed to agree intuitively and turn conversations around to their way of seeing an issue. From the perspective of all others, they were the perfect team. Never was there any attempt to squash an opposing point of view. Instead, each patiently explained reasoning and opinion without seeming to want to impose. And their support of each other was so imperceptible that no one could have guessed that, in fact, there were two hearts beating here as one.

Madge and Doug, too, were not unaware of what was occurring. They felt their mutual attraction. That had been obvious. But how this played out in the presence of the staff and the headmaster was not theirs to analyze yet.

In the meantime Doug prepared himself for the coming encounter with the Custos. Friday after school he had stopped at the Cove for a few Stripes. Stanley was there with a few friends. "Stanley, yu ole so an' so. Ah don' see you fe a while. Wha' 'appen?"

"Busy, Doug, busy. Ah manage to get a likkle wuk down past Clonmel in one of the banana walk." He was smiling and obviously relieved as well as pleased.

"Dat is a good ting. Stanley. Is likely enough to mek up for the pigs?"

"Not exactly. But we nah go starve. Come join we." He made a seat at the bar. The conversation was lively. Stanley was in a good mood, much relieved by having been taken on as a cleaner. It was likely to be steady, at least steadier than the vagaries caused by the government's agricultural policies, which were dictated by its having to go cap in hand to the IMF. That was good news.

On Monday afternoon, after he finished with some extra lessons for the sixth form A-level pupils, Doug dragged the comb through his hair and headed off down the road, in the opposite direction from the clock tower. The country busses were still coming through, as usual at a higher speed than recommended.

The Custos lived down in Clonmel, a suburb of Highgate about a mile and a half away. There most of the well-to-do people lived in spacious, modern homes surrounded by luxurious lawns bordered with bougainvilleas, hibiscus and other beautiful plants, not to speak of orchids. Poinsettias, called Christmas flower in Jamaica, were in full bloom along the hedges.

Doug thought of the meaning of the word Custos. It dated back to the late seventeenth century. Actually the full term was *Custos Rotulorum*, an office out of English history, the holder of which was chief magistrate of a county. In Jamaica the Custos had become the royal representative in each parish, and reported to the governor general. It was more a representative than an administrative post. What was most interesting, however, was that even ten years after independence, the Custodes were usually chosen from the White or high Brown bourgeoisie or plantocracy. It went without saying, he mused, that they represented the "system," the most conservative sectors and classes. It was going to be an interesting meeting.

As he pulled into the driveway he saw the Custos's wife, Mary Ellen, getting up from the far side of the verandah and walking over to the steps. They were an interesting family with an unusual ancestral mix. She was the daughter of a fairly well-off family of the plantocracy, which had sold their properties aeons ago and had started an insurance firm.

The Custos himself was only first generation Jamaican. His name was Dorokhov, indicating Russian ancestry. Actually, his father Anatole had left the Crimea, where his own father had extensive holdings, in 1905 after the First Russian Revolution. He had been able to emigrate to the United States. When Anatole graduated from agricultural college he had spotted an advertisement for an estate manager in a New York paper. The estate was in Jamaica. He was instantly accepted and left the US, never to return.

Anatole remained in Jamaica, eventually using some of the family fortune he had taken with him to New York, to buy a banana property. He married the daughter, descendant of a former Haitian elite family, a Bagnol-Fournier, who had emigrated from that island many decades before during the Haitian Revolution. Allan Dorokhov was the result.

The father had remained in the Crimea looking after the estates. Then, when the Bolshevik Revolution and the subsequent civil war occurred after 1917, he had become an officer in the White Army. After the Bolsheviks landed at Yalta he had decided to flee. Captured, unfortunately, the old man and two other sons were executed shortly after. Anatole remained bitter and disillusioned after this tragic event. And so he instilled in his son a family hatred of anything called "revolution," in addition to harbouring an instant aversion for any label to which the adjective "socialist" was attached.

Allan grew up in that atmosphere. His early childhood was replete with tales of the Crimea, as well as his father's privileged life as a member of the Russian gentry. But he had been educated in Jamaica, graduating from Munroe College, whence he began to manage his father's properties, which by this time, were not inconsiderable. And although the Russian and White Haitian arch-conservatism, punctuated by a nostalgia for Russian serfdom and the Haitian slave past, had been tempered by some genuine British liberalism, the Custos was not anything if not conservative, nay, reactionary, in his political views.

Doug stepped onto the steps and was greeted by Mary Ellen. He could see the Custos getting up to greet him out of the corner of his eyes.

"Mr. Austin, how do you do?" She smiled cordially but used the more formal English greeting.

" Mrs. Dorokhov. I'm very pleased to meet you."

The Custos had now appeared at her side. "My boy, welcome to our little house. I've been meaning to invite you over for some time. At last you are here. Please come this way." He led the way to the side of the verandah. It was nicely covered with a vine, blocking out the hot, descending sunlight. It was also cosy. There was a small portable, mahogany, bar with the usual bucket of ice. Bottles of Whisky, Gin and Rum nestled together beside it. The Custos motioned him into a chair. Facing him through the open drawing room doors was a huge portrait of Pushkin. Off to the right was one of Count Leo Tolstoy. Off to the side he could spy other framed pictures of Russian writers. He thought he could make out Turgenev and Dostoyevsky. I wonder if he knows Pushkin had a Black grandfather, Doug mused.

Doug sat down as indicated. The atmosphere was cordial. Still, while the atmosphere was not uncomfortable, there was an air of expectancy that he couldn't put his finger on. It was as if the polite reception masked expectancies that each knew could not and would not be realized. Perhaps these would even emanate as firm and unpleasant disagreements. Doug was on his guard.

"You have a lovely verandah with a perfect view," he offered.

The Custos laughed. "Yes, we bought this house a few years ago after I gave over the management of the property to my son. It serves us very well. Anyway, thanks for the compliment. What can I offer you to drink?"

"I think I will have an Appleton and water, sir. Thanks."

"Why don't you pour one yourself. You know how much you take."

The drinks were poured, Mary Ellen contenting herself with a short gin and tonic. The Custos helped himself to a Glenfiddich but refrained from adding ice.

Mary Ellen actually opened the conversation. "Did you know that I knew your mother quite well? We used to meet at dances down at Marymount." Marymount was an old estate house that had been converted into a Catholic boarding school for girls. It was quite an expensive private school.

"Yes, mama did tell me about Marymount when she heard I was coming done here. And there were many stories of her living in Port Maria when my grandfather was managing the Oracabessa shipping installation."

"Yes, but that is a long time ago," she added, looking of into the distance as if the memories were still as sharp as when she had experienced them.

"But tell us about yourself," the Custos interrupted, eager to find out what Doug was up to. "You are teaching at St. Mary's or running the literacy programme?"

"Actually I am trying to do both. I teach as well as organize and help the campaign any way I can."

"That must be a lot of work. Don't you get exhausted?" The Custos was trying to edge towards Doug's activities, but in a very slow and roundabout way. He was not being exactly canny, but careful.

"Yes, it is a bit tiring, but I think the cause is a good one." Doug was now trying consciously to push the conversation forward and get it all over with. He would have much preferred to have been in the bar with Stanley, or out at one of the meetings with the party members, instead of sitting in this overly comfortable setting having polite and useless conversation.

In any case, the Custos took the bait. "Do you really think," he said, looking intently at Doug, while his wife sucked in some air as if she knew what was coming, "that the campaign will do any good?"

But Doug decided to answer diplomatically for a change. "Literacy campaigns have been run before, by other governments, but halfheartedly, Custos. Now a government has decided to take it seriously. But to answer your question directly, yes, not only do I think it can succeed, but it must."

"Why must?"

"Because if we do not advance the educational possibilities of this island now, it might be too late."

"Too late? I don't understand. Too late for what?"

"I really think, Custos, that education is a prerequisite for development. There are too many Jamaicans living in poverty. And one sensible way to begin to attack that situation is through education, of which literacy is a part."

"But do you really think that our lazy Jamaicans want to develop? Want to learn to read and write?"

"I really do not know of any people, anywhere, Custos, who want to remain in poverty and not benefit from development." Now he was getting testy.

"No, no. But Jamaicans are different. You know that. Do you think we can overcome laziness, slothful attitudes, their reluctance to work? You know it used to be, and still is hell to get anyone to do an honest day's work on the farms. No one wants to work."

"I don't agree with you, sir. It is not a matter of wanting to work. Jamaicans who go abroad are considered excellent workers. But who wants to work for the insulting pittances people are paid here?"

Now the matter was coming out into the open. They discussed the matter back and forth, leaving little unturned, as they disagreed about every basic point. It was an old story. Jamaicans were lazy. Government was wasting its time trying to give people land, trying to get the many to work. The only way Jamaicans would work is if you paid them a lot of money, and who could come up with such sums. Already they were stretched to the limit with the wages. And the blasted unions were always telling people to ask and demand for more wages. The university—now there was the hotbed of revolution. Jamaica began going downhill ever since the damned Mona campus had been established.

However, this was the milder of the problems troubling the Custos. As the whiskey settled in (he was on his third drink) he warmed to his topic. What was really troubling him was this damned Democratic Socialism. And what did Doug think about that.

"I believe that co-operation, in general, is a better system than market competition."

"I can't believe you think that. This island would have gotten nowhere if it had not been for capitalism."

But Doug would not accept the bait. He was not going to be sucked into a political argument about parties, but neither could he avoid clarifying his own conclusions.

"In my opinion, Custos, that system has been around as long as I can remember, and it has not solved the problem of poverty in this island. Don't you think it is time to try something else?" But it was the wrong thing to say.

The Custos moved to the edge of his chair, his eye fixed sharply on Doug, He looked as if he were ready to pounce on some prey. "And what is the something else, eh? This stupid Democratic Socialism that the government is trying to foist on us. Isn't it just a front for communism? Look at all this new cooperation with Cuba. And then these various programmes, especially that National Service. I don't want to see my little grand-daughter in some camp with a whole lot of Black and Brown people."

Now the gloves were off. The full force, not only of his economic beliefs, but his social ones as well, was now on the table. And the social ones contained the same racist ideas that had caused his mother's family to flee Haiti. Unfortunately they were shared by not a few members of the White and Brown middle classes. Doug could see no way out of the discussion. There was simply nothing to talk about. They both disagreed so fundamentally that a discussion was only going to be abrasive and perfunctory. The Custos did not intend that there be a discussion. His ideas were fixed. They had been fixed decades or centuries ago. And they were not going to change. Change? The very concept smacked of revolution and was therefore to be condemned. Revolution was a most bloody and horrible thing.

Yes, Doug thought to himself. Revolution is horrible in some of its manifestations. But those people who argued that Jamaica could, and should not change were likely to be overtaken, surprised, buffeted by forces they would never understand. And who knew what the outcome would then be.

He said his polite goodbyes and left.

Chapter XII
Madge Again

A FEW DAYS AFTER THE MEETING with the Custos, the Christmas term came to an end. The last few days had been taken up with marking exams for the lower school, and the fourth forms. The fifth and sixth forms had been writing their Cambridge O and A-level exams in the school auditorium, which doubled as cafeteria and assembly hall.

Madge and Doug had hardly had any time to speak to each other as both were busy with wrapping up the term and trying to gear their minds to the holidays. Doug used what spare time he had to go up to Stanley's house and help him up in his field when he wasn't in the banana walk. Time began to seem more flexible now, and Doug was putting together his plans for the coming festivities. There were a number of books he wanted to read and had not had time for during the term. That was going to be difficult enough, given the heady pace of Christmas activities, the lunches and dances and cocktail parties.

On Friday afternoon, the school having been dismissed, the headmaster laid on a lunch for the staff. As usual thank yous were said, mini-gifts, which had been organized by Madge, were distributed to each teacher. Doug barely had time to speak to his friend.

"When yu leavin?" she asked.

"Probably tomorrow afternoon. I have to pack yet, and don't want to rush."

"Yu going to be with family all the Season?"

"Yes. You?"

"The same. Duncan's parents will have us over on Christmas Day for the usual. Otherwise I was just thinking of relaxing, doing some reading. Nutten much."

"When will I see you again?"

"When yu get back, of course, stupid bwai." She was grinning at him for asking the question. Both knew what was behind it.

Doug said his goodbyes, shook hands with Madge, while giving her hand a slight squeeze, which she reciprocated, and left. That Friday evening he stopped in the little bar, remaining until closing. The chatter was again on politics, Democratic Socialism, the worsening economy, and the future. There was no deep pessimism. After all, it was Christmas time. But there were no optimistic outbursts either, not even from staunch PNP supporters. Doug left shortly after midnight and went home, falling into bed for a good night's sleep.

That was not so easy, though. He thought about the discussion with the Custos, Madge, the impending Christmas festivities that he did not exactly abhor but was not looking forward to, Mary Jean, and then Madge again. Finally he fell asleep.

At around nine-thirty Saturday morning he was awakened by the sound of a car coming up the driveway. Barbara Prescott and Dave Crichton had already left Friday evening to be with their various compatriots in Kingston. Patterson had not moved out of his apartment yet but was living in the house of his prospective parents-in-law having taken up with a pretty lady who worked in one of the banks and to whom he had become engaged.

Doug roused himself and looked out the window. He could see Madge just getting out of her Hillman Minx. She was dressed in white three-quarter length slacks and had on a short blue blouse that did not cover her midriff where the elastic ended, and had on a pair of low open sandals. He could see her beautiful, painted toes. She waved to him. "Go get yu clothes on."

Doug rushed to the bathroom after telling her to go through to the living room. He completed his toilet had a quick shower and emerged a few minutes later, hair still wet and dripping. "Madge, what the hell yu doin here?"

"Yu wan' I leave?" She was standing with arms akimbo, looking at him with a forward, aggressive look that told him she was going nowhere. They both laughed.

"Let me make some tea or coffee. Yu always gi a man such nice surprise?"

"No bredda Doug. Jus count yuself lucky."

"I'm to consider myself flattered," he concluded with a mock bow.

"I goin' flatten yu head wid dis book if you don' mek me some tea."

With that they went out into the kitchen where Doug busied himself with some pots and pans. Madge, meanwhile, had gone out to the car, returning with a couple of small packages. She set them carefully on the table before sitting down. Doug finished brewing the tea and sat down beside her.

"What on earth is in those packages?" he asked curiously.

Madge busied herself removing various layers of wrapping paper, until two little packages emerged wrapped in Christmas paper. "These are your Christmas presents, to be opened not before Christmas Day and to be put under your Christmas tree." She cocked her head guilefully, and with a real Anancy look said, "I am assuming yu White folk have Christmas tree dis time a year?"

"Madge, what the hell, yu sweet woman. I wasn't expecting gifts from yu." He got up went over to her and kissed her full on the lips. This time she did not resist.

"Thank yu. But now I'm embarrassed because I did not think we would exchange presents."

"Who said anything about exchange? Just take them an' don give me any mout."

"Madge, I swear to r…."

She cut him off. "Don' cuss no bad words in my presence, yu hear." This last was delivered with a smile.

"But Madge, yu didn' have to."

"I know. But feelings is feelings. I wanted to."

Doug looked at her. "Let's take the tea on the front verandah. Can you stay a bit?"

"Why not? I have all day. I told the family I was coming up to Highgate to do some work and some Christmas shopping."

"A little white lie?" Doug was now the one to be confused. He had not expected her and was beginning to wonder why she had decided to come.

"No. I don' lie. Is true. But the time is me own to do wid as I like. Just a little freedom after a hard term's work. Besides is time yu an I had a little time to labrish."

"Yu right. Nothing like a little freedom. It feels good that I don't have to go anywhere, do anything at least for a while. And I'm also rewarded with the company of a fit woman today."

"Boy, yu have to tek life when it come, yu know. Sometimes things work out for the good." They were flirting now. Easily they shifted into a familiar banter, the one testing the other, seeing how far they could go, before the other became serious.

Madge was the first to move on the conversation. "Doug, how did yu meeting with his lordship go? Yu know who I mean?"

"Yes," he laughed. "Yu mean the man who would single handedly carry us all back to the eighteenth century."

"Something like that. Tell me. Did yu have a big fight?"

"No, not really. I didn't let it get that far. But the man is seriously out of step with time and history."

"Tell more"

"Well, you know, he even questions the literacy campaign. Can't get it out of his head that education is no use, that Jamaicans will never progress. You know the whole story already. Same old shibboleths."

"Yu mean the man is seriously backward."

"Worse than that. The whole thrust of the government is wrong. Socialism. Communism, where would we all end up, and so on. Like Cuba."

"Well, is he wrong? What do you think about where the country is going? Now really, and honestly?"

"Sweetheart, I haven't stopped to think about it. And maybe I should. Those two incidents I told you about really shook me up."

"Granted. But the question is where is Jamaica going? Do you think Manley and Democratic Socialism are going to succeed in turning this country around?"

She was leaning forward again, with the intent of taking the conversation to another level. She had one arm on the chair, and her breasts on the arm strained to jump out of their halter and come right at him. He could see the faint outline of the bra under her blouse. It aroused him. But he decided to resist his impulse and to stay with the conversation.

"Listen. Jamaica has tried the other system for decades, especially before independence. And even the JLP government had to recognize that for the island to progress government had to play a major role."

"Awright, but what yu saying?"

"Look. Wasn't it the JLP that nationalized the two big sugar companies? Wasn't it the JLP that realized the importance of education? We can't take it from Edwin Allen, even though many people make fun of him, that his vision about the junior secondary school was correct."

Allen, the Minister of Education in the previous JLP government had managed to convince CIDA, the arm of Canada's foreign aid, to fund the building of junior secondary schools throughout the island. The purpose of these had been to catch those pupils who had not got a free place in the eleven-plus exams, give them more specific training, and then funnel them into the secondary schools at the fourth form level. Canada had funded fifty junior secondary schools. Forty-eight had been built. The other two could not be accounted for: they were the victims of either waste or corruption, no one ever found out. But Allen's vision had been correct. More children were being carried into the secondary stream. This was a remarkable success.

"O.K. Yu right bout Allen. But what is your argument?"

"My argument is simply that even the capitalist JLP saw the need for government to take a leading role in Jamaica's development. Manley is just carrying this programme forward and more consequently."

"Awright. So far so good! But what about Democratic Socialism? I'm not concerned about the first, but many people are becoming upset about the second, for no other reason that we don't know where it is heading."

"I think people are reading too much into it. Socialism means, I think, because I am no soothsayer, that government has to enter the economy more rigorously than before, because the problems of poverty just won't go away."

"That may be all very well and good. But people are upset because they are beginning to believe that Manley wants to make us into a second Cuba. How do you feel about that?"

"Frankly, I have those worries too. Cuba is not a shining example of freedom in our sense, even though the propaganda claims it as such. Neither is the Soviet Union. And the Cuban economy only exists at that level because of Soviet subsidies. But what anyway is freedom? Cubans are fed, housed, given medical care, education based on merit? Those are not things to be laughed at. And look at their cultural achievements in ballet, music, art?"

"Agreed. But Jamaicans will never put up with someone telling them what to think. And what about Manley's intentions?"

"That is not easy to grasp. From a purely idealistic point of view one has to admit though, that two serious problems in Cuba which have plagued the Caribbean for centuries have been taken care of."

"Which ones?"

"Racism and abject poverty."

"Agreed, but they have only been taken care of Doug, because of the subsidies. If Cuba had no subsidies, I'm sure that the race problem would still exist, because Blacks would be exploited again so as to subsidize the rest."

"I'm not that sure. But don't you think it takes that kind of system to break people's psychology?"

"That is my dilemma, Doug. Does it take such repression to change people's thinking?"

"But is there really repression? I mean, people who have never seen a doctor or a dentist in their life, now get medical attention, without any discrimination. Children get to go to the best schools based on merit. Is that such a bad system? Is that repression?"

"No, of course not. But people are still repressed, Doug. They cannot read what they want. They cannot express themselves differently from the government's policies. They can't travel freely. And there is considerable pressure on them to give up their faith."

"Well, I think the rumours about pressure on churches are false. But you are right. It is a fact that Marxism and Marxists consider religion 'the opium of the people.'"

"And yu know what that means to me an' to many Jamaicans."

Doug laughed now, deciding that the serious conversation had gone far enough. He was going to tease Madge. "So I kyan get yu to give up de notion of God."

Madge sucked her teeth. "Doug yu crazy?"

"No. Yu know I don' have much in the way of faith."

"Well, I'm not goin' try to convince yu. But one a dese days, we goin' have it out on that subjeck."

"Sweet gal, I am ready. Nothing in my brain is fixed. Yu might even convince me. Besides, yu know there are elements of Christianity I readily accept: some others, of course, not."

"Yu know, what I like about yu is that you're not a dogmatist."

"Like you and yu Christian friends." They both laughed as they knew he had won that round.

"Anyway, there is a book I wanted to lend you some time ago. It slipped my mind, but let's go into the study and I will try to find it."

They got up, Doug taking Madge's hand to help her out of the low, wooden, armchair. Together they walked to the back of the house to his little study. Madge had never been there before. Doug pulled a book off the shelf and handed it to her. It was a copy of Jean-Francois Revel's recently published work, *Without Marx or Jesus*.

"I picked this up in September in the little book shop in Manor Plaza. I also found it highly interesting, not because I agree necessarily with him, but because he is a very provocative writer."

"What is his argument?"

"Basically that in what Che Guevara calls 'the belly of the beast,' that in the America that is the centre of racism, imperialism, conformity and vulgarity, that the real revolution, the one against the crude impositions of technology, will eventually take place. And for a Frenchman, with all their starchy, smug assumptions about the United States to make such a claim is something else. Take it, you will enjoy it."

"I never heard of him."

"Still, he is a well-known philosophical junky who takes a delight in forcing people to see things from another perspective. He is adamant, of course, that neither Cuba nor the Soviet Union will produce the kind of social freedom which is necessary."

"Doug, you know one of the things I love about you is the way your mind moves. You don't seem to get paralyzed by ideologies, but are constantly moving, looking for new perspectives."

"Madge, you are a boonoonoonos. Here, you might try reading that in conjunction with something closer to home. This is called a "revolutionary" bestseller. You know that radical Roman Catholic priest, Daniel Berrigan. Here is his *Quotations from Chairman Jesus*."

She took the book from him, turning it over in her hands. They were standing side by side, close enough so that he could see the pages and read with her. It was the sort of book he knew she would devour.

Then she looked up at him. "Thank you." This, however, was no ordinary thank you. It was a thanks born of that intense feeling that tells a man and a woman that something has occurred between them that defies explanation. They did not understand it. For it is not given to simple comprehension.

Science cannot explain the chemistry that draws people together, especially men and women. Researchers only know it exists. There is also that other thing, that special force, that locks two human beings into moments of closeness, that overcomes rationality, that affronts convention, that yells and screams at all the traditions and rituals of the world so that they must abandon their steely grip in the name of that one word: love.

So it was that Doug had no idea what to do next. But he slipped his hand around her waist, and bent down to kiss her on the lips. They parted to take him in, without resistance this time again. They remained locked in that one kiss for what seemed like hours. It had only been minutes. Madge put the book gently on the desk, turned to face him fully, her arms encircling him to press their bodies closer together.

They parted momentarily. "Doug?"

"Yes Madge."

She drew his face down to her again. Now the fever of passion had risen. He put his hand under her short blouse and undid the straps of her bra. Then he slid them around to the front in order to encompass her breasts. There was no resistance, only a shudder of feeling. Together they went back out of the study, and turned into the corridor that led to his bedroom.

There was no talk as he slowly raised the blouse above her head and removed the bra. She unbuttoned his shirt. They removed the rest of their clothes without talking and lay down on the bed he had left an hour before.

Outside the wind was picking up, yawing crazily through the guinep tree. Somewhere in the trees behind the house an owl uttered a shriek.

They finished their lovemaking and lay back, the sweat and the exertions causing the bed sheets to look as if they had come out wet from the laundry. For Doug could not recall such satisfaction. People fit together or they do not. It seemed to him that the very forms of their bodies had been matched somewhere and moulded so that the fit would be perfect, as if they had been carved out by some Greek or Aymara stonemason fresh from fitting together the columns of the Parthenon or Machu Picchu. Nor had their lovemaking been difficult. Both intuitively knew what the other needed or liked. Not that there had been analysis. They had both climaxed together effortlessly.

For the next moments there was silence. Madge picked up her arm to move it across him and suddenly drew it back, as if to hide her armpit. He knew why. He picked it up, turned over to put his head by her neck and said, "Don't. I like it."

She blushed slightly then stroked his head. "Yu know this was not why I came up here."

"Yu could have fooled me," he teased.

She gave him a playful tap on the chest, and turned to sit up, facing him. Her eyes were bright, her features open, expectant. He now saw that her breasts were indeed firm and round, not having lost their tautness even though she had suckled a child. Her purple nipples stood out and venerated, as with a badge of the erotic, her entire pose.

"You don't have to say anything, Madge."

"Yu mean yu don' want to talk?"

"No. Just that we don't need a *post mortem* right now."

"Even if I need one?"

"If you do, I'm here. Want to talk?"

"What the hell happen to us? How this could happen?" She was trying to confront her guilt feelings, yet, at the same time recognize that both of them had given in to something which was natural, which was wanted, and which was beautiful besides.

"I'm not sure what to answer." He was meditative. "I only know that something very powerful has been taking hold of both of us."

"Doug, you know me. I'm not the kin' o' person to shub blame on other person. But tell me, true, true, did you set out to seduce me?"

He frowned. "Madge, if you think I wasn't attracted to you from the start, then nothing else in this world is true. But honestly, I respect that you are married."

"Awright! That rules one thing out, for which I would have been partly to blame anyway."

"So then you explain what happened."

"Not easy. I not sure I understand yet." She gave the bed a little thump as she said it as if to emphasize to herself that she was right.

"Madge. Let's face facts. Ever since I set face on you in that first staff meeting, and then the meeting with the head, I felt comfortable in your presence."

"Same here."

"And after that, I don't know. There are few people I feel comfortable with, whose company I really want to share, and less few I even want to talk to. The things that matter to me, don't interest ninety-nine point nine percent of humanity. But with you, I feel easy and we always seem to end up with a good conversation."

"Maybe you are on the right track."

"I don't know that I am. But some powerful force seems to have brought us together."

"That was what I was hoping you would say. It was not just lust, or my pretty face, or jus' pum-pum." She made a face at him as if to reinforce the message.

"I am pretty sure it is much more than just lust. No, I don't want to disturb the beauty of our actions by attributing them to lust. Of course, if that's what they were, then we'll find out pretty quickly. Lust usually has a way of disappearing after one or two encounters."

"A-oha. So yu expecting more encounters wid me." Now it was his turn to blush. She laughed and tussled his hair.

"I have to think about it, sweet chile. I don't want to compromise your situation. On the other hand how are we going to keep apart after this?"

"That was my point, although I left it unsaid. Yu want to see me again, then?"

"You know I do. You think I could forget this morning?"

"I didn' think so. But jus' wanted to mek sure."

"Can I ask you a question?"

"Do you and Ducan still. You know what I mean?"

"You mean my wifely duties. Very seldom. But sometimes he feel frisky, so I jus open my legs."

"How horrible."

"Frankly, yes. But what is more horrible is that we never talk. About nothing." Here she drew up her hand and closed thumb and index finger together, while wearing a grim smile that closed the issue.

"So I suppose we just wait and see."

"Let's get over Christmas first. There is a new year coming. Who knows what will happen." She had moved so that she was propped up on one arm, the other free to course through his hair or caress his chest.

He pulled her down on top of him and began kissing her again slowly, deliberately, she feeling for the thing that would join them together in another bout of love-making. This time it was not the blind passion. Rather there was the studied rhythm and appeal of the warmth of those who move together in a confidence that their bodies belong because their souls are at peace.

"I really have to go."

"I know. So do I, eventually, although I am dreading the round of perpetual shit, sorry, banal, talk and cocktails."

"Did'n' I tell yu not to swear." But her rebuke was mild, and her hands caressed within a different mode.

They showered together, for the first time. She looked fully into his face as she washed it. Madge dressed, looking hurriedly at her watch.

"Will yu call me at home over the season if you can?"

"I will try. You know I can't use the phone at home. He checks the bills. Anyway they are paid for by the parish. But we'll see. Give me your brother's number."

So doing, they went slowly out to the car, Madge entering with a very forlorn look. It would, after all, be two weeks before they were back at school again. A long time for lovers: a longer time for soul mates. She drove slowly down the driveway, easing back to wave at him through the window. He stood there waving until he heard the car turn left down Fraserwood.

Doug entered the house slowly and deep in thought. Now life was complicated, he thought. True, he had been dying to jump into Madge's pants since that day they did the timetabling together. But this was different. This was a lust, if lust it was, which could never be satiated by a mere sexual encounter. This lust demanded much, much more. Of that he was sure.

There is no accounting for human behavior. We are such complex beings that the little that psychologists tell us is really very little, indeed.

His packing was dilatory. He could hardly think of what to take. The books he wanted to read had already been isolated and placed on a table. That part was easy. The clothes came next. He knew that he would have to rent or buy dinner clothes in Kingston. He had none. But the rest of the stuff he finally just flung into a small suitcase, onto which he piled the books.

On the way back he drove so slowly that every other car seemed to be passing, for he was deep in thought. His mind returned to the conversation he had had with the Custos. Could he have had a point? Not about the racism, mark you, that was nonsense, not even worthy of discussion. But about Jamaica's possibilities and the Manley government's capability of solving them? There were some nagging doubts. Even Madge had questioned the outcome, although she had not quite expressed it that way.

And what about Madge herself? He couldn't shake the feeling that some line had been crossed, which would not be crossed over again in the opposite direction. What about the future? There were enormous decisions to make which would disrupt the families of both. He could feel the fire storm already. There would be hurt, disappointment, chagrin. Was it worth it? Should the venture be undertaken? These and other thoughts kept swarming his mind even as he passed Castleton Gardens in the direction of Golden Spring. But now he was navigating the hairpin curve at Red Gal Ring, then down Long Lane. He was home.

Book Three: Departure

"Wha gone bad a mornin' kyan come good a evenin', Oh."

(Line from the Jamaican Rock Steady song "Everything Crash" by Leonard 'Jack Sparrow' Dillon)

CHAPTER XIII

Christmas Dinner

As Doug pulled into the driveway off Long Lane, he could see his mother leaning over the verandah railing, waiting for him. She had obviously been taking tea there. Christine and the children were not there. Probably they were at one of their endless extra-lessons: piano, flute, dance.

The garden was lush with the luxurious growth of Christmas flowers, the poinsettias that bordered perfectly the far side of the lawn. The grass had been freshly mowed, and with the cool breeze beginning to come up from the sea, the smell was overpowering. Everywhere was neatness, order and floral beauty.

"Mama, how are you?"

"Son, I've been waiting here for you. So nice you are back home."

"You know mama, I was trying to pack this morning and didn't know what to throw in. So, sorry I'm a little late."

"How was the teaching?"

"Well, it was hectic with all my activity, but very rewarding. I think we may have done quite well at this year's A-level, but of course it will be sometime before we know."

"That's nice, dear. Would you like some tea?"

"Where are James and Jennifer?"

"Oh, they will soon be home. I think it's the last day for their piano lessons, but they should soon be home."

As soon she had said it, Christine's Ford appeared in the driveway. Both children were waving furiously at their uncle. "Uncle Doug, Uncle Doug," rang out as they burst up the steps. "We didn't know you were coming so soon. Are you going to take us to Morgan's Harbour?"

Morgan's Harbour Beach Club was a private club, built near one of the sixteenth century walls in Port Royal, which had survived the devastating 1692 earthquake. In its heyday the port, built at the end of the sandy spit known as the Palisadoes, sported four well equipped fortresses plus Morgan's Line, a battery of sixteen guns named after the old buccaneer, and future lieutenant-governor of the island. In that same sixteenth century the city had the enviable reputation of being the "richest and wickedest in Christendom."

Now it was a shadow of its former self. All that was left was Ft. Charles, the place where Nelson and Rodney had watched for the French fleet, a nineteenth century Royal Navy hospital, and a remnant of the old city, including a narrow lane called Admiral's Walk. The beach club was built on the northern side of the sand spit. In fact, the bar hung over the water's edge and waves lapped under the loosely laid planks that were the terrace. It afforded a magnificent view of Kingston beyond, and Long and Dallas Mountains, the precursors, as it were, of the majestic Blue Mountain range off to the north east.

"Depends" he said teasingly. "Only if you are good."

"We will, we will. And you promised, too."

"O.K. Let's wait till after Christmas when Robert and Susan are here. Then we can all go."

"'Ray, ray," they shouted to their mother, running inside to tell Christine.

Morgan's Harbour, Port Royal. Doug's mind reverted to a pleasurable incident many years before. One of his dreams as a boy was to enter Port Royal by night, from the sea, just as the admirals had done, centuries earlier. One evening an older uncle had invited him out for a night of fishing in the harbor. Fishing, naturally, was not just fishing. Yes, they were going to try to catch fish. But his uncle was a natural storyteller (a disappearing breed), and a consummate drinker besides.

So they took off one Friday, reaching one of the easy boat launches on the harbor side of the Palisadoes but up at the eastern end, away from Kingston. With them was his uncle's friend, known only as Major, since that is what he had been in the war. Major was also an accomplished rum man. The boat was launched off the back of the trailer hitched to his Ford without mishap. It only remained to get all the tackle, cold beer, rum, sandwiches inside. That took no time.

"Doug, I'm pushing off, you start the engine."

Doug yanked the chord, and the seventy-five horsepower Merlin sprang to life. They headed out into the harbor. "Not too far, Doug, I hear king-fish biting close to shore tonight."

King-fish were really the cream of all the fish. But many would have argued it had disappeared from the harbour decades ago, due to the increasing pollution caused by vessels dumping their waste, uncontrolled, into the harbor. Doug eased back and prepared to throw the anchor overboard. The launch settled swiftly in the calm harbor. Only the faint sounds from shore, the occasional car passing, could be heard. Now and again a fish would break water and dive back precipitously. Otherwise, only muffled sounds from the shore could be heard.

Rum was poured. Major preferred Red Stripe. They settled down to fish and to wait. Uncle Johnny began one of his interminable but interesting recounts of the "old days," his life as a salesman for this or that company which carried him all across the island. It was good, for the fish were obviously not interested. It was now seven o'clock. One or two flounders were caught, then a red snapper. But of king-fish there was not one. The night was going to be long. They settled in. More rum was poured. Now Major was tired of drinking Stripe, and favoured Appleton. Doug dosed off.

"Chrise, I have one, " Uncle Johnny roared, as he got up swinging, almost overturning Doug into the scuppers. "Get the blasted gaff." Uncle Johnny's voice was serious as both Major and Doug dived into the lockers, one on either side of the rocking boat.

"Hurry, raas, I don' wan' lose him."

Doug finally found the gaff, under some line in the port locker, and brought it up.

"Steady. The bitch fightin."

Slowly Johnny reeled in the fish, carefully, not trying too quickly so that it would cut the hook out of its mouth, and brought the fish alongside. Doug deftly leaned down, Major was well away now up by the wheel, not wanting to be landed together with a biting king-fish. Doug leaned down, gave a deft slash with the hook, and caught the fish right in the gullet, bringing it up sharply and over the gun-whale onto the deck, where it remained writhing until a swift blow to the head stunned it.

"Nice job, Maas Doug. A knew yu wouldn' let me down." Johnny was obviously pleased. "Look at this raas. At least four pound o' king-fish. Boy we goin' cook some raas fish-tea tomorrow." He laughed, pleased, exhilarated as if that landing of his king-fish should have silenced every critic and harbor fisherman for decades. "Yu see what I tell yu! Those damn' eediots don' know a raas what they talking." He sucked his teeth for emphasis. "Where's the ice. Put him in the locker, mek sure plenty ice top o' him."

No question. The feat meant another round. This time, though, it meant two. And by this time they had drifted, despite the anchor which they must have been dragging, a little closer to shore. That meant starting the engine and moving out once again into the harbor. They moved away safely, dropped the anchor again, and settled down to enjoy rum, stories, and the idea of the king-fish now neatly stowed in the locker with ice to keep it company.

Before anyone could have realized, they heard a blast from a ship down the harbor. All three looked at their watches at the same time. "No raas," Johnny exclaimed. "Midnight blow. Wha' yu wan do now?"

The question was addressed to the other two, but mainly Doug, so he responded. "Uncle Johnny, how far we are from Port Royal?"

"Is a likkle lick down the harbor yu know. Why?"

"Well ever since I was a boy, I've always wanted to enter Port Royal by sea. I don' know why. Maybe is jus' history. But since we here, if yu have time?" Doug's voice was not exactly pleading, but one could tell this was a solid wish.

"Major, yu have anyting' against us going down and rousin' the bar? Maybe they still open."

"Not me Johnny. Yu know I open to any adventure. Let's go."

"Doug, I will start the engine, yu raise the anchor, and sit up in the bow. We have to be careful of the buoys out here, and mek sure we find the channel."

"Yes, Uncle Johnny, forward."

And with that the bow anchor was raised, stowed in the locker, and they were off, gingerly at first, but in the direction of Port Royal. Doug was sitting on the bow with legs dangling over the side. Uncle John was at the tiller, and Major was "navigating." A few minutes out Doug shouted that he could see the buoys. Uncle John said nothing at first. Then, "What buoys. There is only one."

"No," answered Doug. "There are two I can see them clearly. About twenty feet apart. They must be marking the channel."

Uncle John did not reply. Instead, he slowed the boat to a crawl and bellowed, "Jus' watch them carefully and tell me what yu see."

Doug remained silent. Then he answered, somewhat incredulously. "Look like they getting closer together. " Uncle John cut the power to idle, and let the boat drift.

"Oh raas, Uncle John, hard to starboard, is only one buoy. Quick."

John swung the tiller over just in time as they glided by the single buoy not two feet away.

"Yu drunken raas. Was only one buoy. Liquor mek yu see two. Now we in the channel." He and Major broke out laughing as he opened the throttle. Doug was not ready for this and the force pushed him back right up to the windscreen, but so that he almost lost his grip and fell off. "Teach yu to learn how to drink rum, boy." Uncle John was not about to let up.

A half an hour later they could see the lights of the small dock used by fishermen. John cut the engine, and they drifted in quietly, sliding into a berth at the side. Major held the wharf while the other two staggered off. "Well, at least we are here. Yu dream come true Doug." John clapped Doug on the back as they took off for the little bar that was at the end of Admiral's Walk. Major hobbled behind them. The bar was of red brick, built Tudor style with wooden cross ribbing indicating its age, and a few yards at the end of Admiral's Walk, which was actually a narrow lane bordered by a high, cut-stone fence. They entered the bar, roused the barmaid, and began ordering.

Just then a man ran into the bar shouting, "Yu forget to tie up yu launch. She drifting out to harbor."

Doug ran out as fast as could, John bringing up the rear, Major ambled along as best he could. Sure enough the boat was drifting out to harbor just past the end of the dock. Luckily a fishing canoe with outboard was just then pulling into the dock with three men who saw what was happening. One man reached up and grabbed the bow line, towing their boat back in. A hefty discussion followed about the merits of drinking rum at sea. Nevertheless, and although a bit chastened, they made their way back to the bar after tying the boat securely to the dock, fishermen in tow, to resume the nights revelry.

At about one-thirty a crew of cameramen and reporters from the JBC (Jamaica Broadcasting Corporation) who had been doing some filming at Ft. Charles, found their way to the bar. There were three young, pretty girls with them, either reporters or hangers-on. So now the night was in full swing. Doug was able to pass the evening in the company of the ghosts of Byron, Blake, Collingwood, Rodney and Nelson, plus the assembled company of other live souls, and so got his wish. The bar served Mannish water, curry goat and bananas, all which helped to mitigate, at the very least, the effects of the Appleton.

About six o'clock when the sun was just rising over the Blue Mountains, they decided to call it quits and end the night. The water was dead calm. Not a breeze was stirring. And this time, without the aid of the navigator-in-chief, they were able to make their way back up the harbor, attach the boat, and return home.

"Doug," Christine's shrill voice called from inside, "I hear you taking us to Morgan's Harbour after Christmas." Her voice pulled him back from his historic adventure as James came running out from inside the house. "Uncle Doug, Uncle Doug, telephone."

I wonder who that could be, he thought. But it was Mary Jean's voice that greeted him from the other end. "Doug, how are you? You're back."

"Yes, M.J. Almost just got in. How are you?"

"Well, better now that you are here. Listen, I have to work late tonight, so I can't come over. But what if we do the rounds tomorrow evening?"

"Sounds great, M.J. What do you have in mind?"

"Tell you tomorrow. Why not drop over at about six?"

"Fine. Looking forward to it."

At six sharp Doug was ringing the bell at her townhouse, just as she opened the door. He entered and was greeted by a big hug. Mary Jean's face was ecstatic, flushed, expectant after all these weeks of not seeing him. "You looking good, man."

She was dressed in a pair of black, tight slacks and was sporting a loose-fitting green blouse, which contrasted nicely with her hair. Her earrings were long and stylish, and she was wearing heels, which brought her almost up to Doug's height. She pushed her arm through his and led him inside. The table was laid graciously, with two candles throwing off a cozy light as they sat down to a light supper she had thrown together. A bottle of red Chianti was off to the side.

After dinner she suggested they take a ride into town to Parade, to see the Christmas stalls and take in the atmosphere. He agreed, and they set off in his car, rather than her open Spider, just to be safer. They drove down Constant Spring, across Sandy Gully and reached Half Way Tree slowly, admiring the display of coloured lights that had been strung up from the clock tower to the four corners of the road, attached to various buildings.

They continued past Holy Cross on their right, and Westbrook Preparatory School where they had both attended before going on to secondary school. At Slipe Road Doug drove a little faster, as the area to the right, Jones Town, was not without its problem, being the hangout for some gunmen. Slipe Road opens into Orange Street. There they already could see the lights from Victoria Park. Doug eased into a parking spot just south of Orange Street, onto the premises of N.A. Taylor and Son where he had worked as a Floor Walker quite a few Christmases ago to earn some pocket money. They got out and walked down to South Parade, the southern border of the park, where most of the stalls were arrayed with their splendid lights and colourful displays of toys, kitchen wares, even furniture, and arts and crafts. Reggae, Ska and Rock Steady music blared into the cacophony of shouts, queries, arguments, and laughter.

"I wonder how many Christmases more we'll be able to walk down here."

"Hard to tell, sweetheart, this country is moving so fast, and I'm not sure in a good direction."

"You think you'll be able to stay, Doug?" But he didn't answer, instead guided them over to a stall. 'I want to get some trinkets for the kids. Any suggestions?"

She hadn't. "Let's look." They strolled around the various stalls, hand in hand, looking at the various displays till they came to one that seemed to be purely arts and crafts from the country.

"Hey, I like this. Maybe I can find something here." He spied some hats in one corner, all emblazoned with some saying or pithy thought, as was the custom. They would be perfect for the boys.

He bought two straw hats, peasant, country style, round but ending in stands of un-plaited straw each with different slogans, for James and Robert. One said "Mambo Boy," the other, "Dred Locks." For the girls he bought two bamboo fans covered with crepe paper and pretty designs. M.J. looked on and laughed. "Robert will like that. Perfect. He is already trying to grow his hair long, at least while Anne doesn't notice." She approved. Doug's addiction to his nieces and nephews vied for space with his other dedication to politics.

Doug did not stay the night at M.J.'s. Perhaps no one would have looked askance if he had. It was as natural for his family to imagine them together as for the rain to fall. But he didn't want to compromise her. Besides, there was that other nagging vision that seemed to float in and out of his system, giving him no chance to forget. It was the image of Madge that last day, sitting on his bed, talking to him as calmly as if they had been having an affair for ages. It was that feeling that nagged continuously that made him forego a night of pleasurable experiences with M.J. and return to his brother's.

The next night M.J. had asked him to accompany her to the Terra Nova hotel to meet some American travel agent. This was business for the airline, and M.J. was the hostess. He arrived promptly at her house wearing a smart two-piece, dark blue, shirt-jack outfit. He could tell from M.J's. admiring glances that it was appropriate. She was decked out in a long, loose fitting gown, decorated with flowers and colours Nigerian style, the halter enclosing her neck, with a low décolletage. Her hair was drawn back to expose exquisite earrings with an African motif.

Two men were waiting for her in the hotel, and her assistants from the office were just arriving. Introductions were made. Doug noticed the travel agent in question had a southern US drawl and was smoking a large Havana. The waiter came over.

"Can I offer you a Bourbon?" the southerner asked. "The best liquor in the world."

"No, thank you. I'll have an Appleton Reserve, the best drink but none in the world." It was his way of countering the rudeness and braggadocio of the American, there to show off and put little island people in their place. But the brash Yankee, (Yankee despite being a southerner, and with none of the South's graciousness), was engaging the wrong person. He felt Mary Jean's foot pressing against his, as if to say "please."

The pleasantries taken care of, the business progressed languidly, M.J's assistants taking care of most of the details. It ranged through marketing of the airline in the visitor's city, to discounts, deals which the travel agency could secure for a certain number of visitors. Doug was silent, listening and admiring M.J's skillful handling of the negotiations, the quiet way in which she presented the airline's policies, the astute and diplomatic manner in which she parried the visitor's attempts to squeeze more out of them. He noticed the man seemed impressed although a bit annoyed he had not been able to extract more concessions out of this woman. Arrangements were made to conclude the paperwork the next day at the office and so they rose to say good night.

The visitor stuck out his hand to Doug. "Well boy, nice meetin' ya. If you ever drop by Atlanta give me a shout."

"You were told earlier my name is Doug. " He wasn't going to let that one pass and could hear M.J. sucking in her breath expecting the worst.

"Well, you know Doug in the States…." But Doug cut him off before he could finish.

"You are not in the States. This is Jamaica, you may have noticed," the sarcasm was hardly disguised, moreover, it was reinforced by the look he shot out.

The other just stared, one supposes, not being used to being so thoroughly put in his place. His partner, however, walked quickly around to Doug, put out his hand smiling, "Don't mind him. He's hardly civilized yet, but he didn't mean any offense. I'll apologize for both of us."

This broke the ice. Doug took his hand, eased the anger from his face, and said, "No offense taken. It was nice meeting you." He could hear Mary Jean breathing more easily, at his side anyway, to try to calm him even further. She knew his temper, not to speak of his national instincts. But the good part of his temper was that it was as quick to fall as it was to rise. And he did not bear grudges, another positive side of his character. Still, the poor waiter was standing aside with an almost white face, if that was possible: he did not know Doug.

"You know, sweet boy," she said as she snuggled beside him on the seat, "Yu had me going there for a while. I frighten so I nearly fene." She broke into patois to reinforce her state. "I thought yu was going' lick out his brains."

"I'm not sure he has any. But, in any case is about time those bastards learnt. They're so arrogant, those idiot Yankees, and need taking down a peg or two. They think they own the whole effing world and can do as they want. Everywhere they go they cause trouble. Eventually everyone learns to dislike them. And if you don't give them what they want, they send in their Marines or their CIA to take it. They have one conception of the world and expect everyone else to follow. It is Imperialism at its worst, and reduced to idiocy. At the base of it I despise the way they commercialize everything. Nothing is sacrosanct to them except money. If I didn't have to meet any of the stupid raases it would be too much, too soon."

Mary Jean was not up to a discussion about imperialism. Yet, she supported him instinctively. "Well, I can't say I wanted a bust up. But, you know, I'm glad. The little bastard thought he was going to walk over us easily. Now he'll think twice. Besides, he is the one who needs the contract."

Then she laughed. "Did yu see the waiter's face? Looked like he was goin' wet his pants."

The incident was minor. It had not gone badly. M.J., in any case, was on Doug's side in this one. And it had produced a moment of laughter later. Still, it was a deeper problem that would need to be approached again. For the moment it could nestle in the safety of Christmas and in the memory of times past.

They drove home, Doug intending to stay with her this time. They drew up some chairs on the little balcony overlooking the centre of the condominium, opened a bottle of white Chablis, held hands, watched the stars, and chatted. About nothing important, mind you, just about Christmas, the impending dinner with family, a party on Boxing Day, on other minor concerns. Already it was after mid-night, and they slept soundly till morning.

Christmas Day dawned with the usual bustle. Presents were opened early Christmas morning. M.J. was there so she and Doug could exchange gifts. The children as usual were the centre of attention. Soon David and Anne arrived and the children had their cousins, Robert and Susan. Feverish preparations were going on in the kitchen as ham then turkey, were readied for the feast.

Doug, M.J. and David were outside on the lawn refereeing a game of backyard cricket. James junior was sporting a new pair of leg-guards, showing off his batting skills as Doug bowled underhand at him. Several times he hit the ball so squarely that it raced along the ground to the fence while he yelled "Four." By this time, Uncle Benjamin had arrived. So had John with his girl-friend, Shirley, a country girl, White, but not from a very prominent family. Her speech was naturally slow and raw, as they liked to describe it, with a semblance at least of refinement. Her ideas matched John to a tee. They were a perfect couple.

"Children," grandma called from the verandah, "time to wash up for dinner." James hurriedly shed his leg-guards, carefully taking them with him as they ran inside.

"Doug, time for an Appleton before they serve?"

"I'm with you."

They went back to the verandah where the liquor trolley had been placed, together with a bucket of ice. "What you having M.J., Shirley?" Doug called out.

Shirley said she wished for aerated water, M.J. a gin and tonic. Drinks prepared they sat back for the few minutes before lunch. James joined them, so did Anne. Christine was busy inside helping to get things ready.

"Hear yu wanted tek on a Yankeeman," John, as usual, was going to try to needle Doug, get him funkified. Doug looked over at M.J. as if to ask, why did you have to tell him? Then he realized she had probably told Anne, who had told David, who had passed it on to John. There were few secrets in that family.

"The little bastard got what was coming to him," Doug said quietly. M.J. came over to stand beside him. But John continued, Shirley taking on a smug look on her face, "Don't you know Yankeeman is our fren'. We need him. We have to treat him wid respect."

But Doug wasn't taking the bait. Quietly he looked at John, batting his eyes a few times before he spoke, as calm as before. "You can befriend whoever you want John. As for respect, I doubt if by bending over backwards for those idiots you even know what the word respect means."

David intervened before anything more could be said. He knew his brother and his somewhat imbecilic views. "Stand down John. Doug was right. The bugger had it coming. I would have done the same thing."

Now Shirley was the one to look somewhat crestfallen. She had been expecting her boyfriend, with his big mouth to triumph. Tiny mind that she was, she confused volume with veracity. And that David did not support his brother seemed to her a mighty negation of family privilege.

But they were all saved any further nastiness when they heard the bell from inside summoning them for the Christmas luncheon. There was no special seating order, but grandfather was at one end of the table, James at the other. He said the grace, a fairly well-known Anglican invocation. Then they settled in to eat. "Doug, if you have time during the holidays, why don't we get together for a chat."

"Sure" Doug answered. "What did you have in mind?"

"Perhaps we can have lunch together at the Courtleigh Manor, next week before you go back?"

"That sounds nice. You buying?" They laughed.

Doug was sitting between M.J. on his right and his sister. Across the table from them were James junior and Robert. Now the two maids appeared with trays of ham, turkey, rice and peas, fried plantain, yellow yam, cream of corn, asparagus, with all the sauces and condiments to round out a great feast. All were passed around as expectant stomachs strained to keep their patience.

Conversation was minimal, but Doug heard his Uncle Benjamin explaining to his mother how the properties were doing, what was growing where, who had died, who was getting old, and all the gossip from the country.

Then the meal was topped off with the traditional lighting of the plum pudding, one of the few real leftovers from the English colonial past, but hallowed in every Jamaican home. Plum pudding had to be properly prepared. Around July it would begin. Fruit, currents and raisins were kept soaking in rum, which was changed frequently. After months of marinating it was then prepared and finally, steamed. When it appeared on the table, it was then bathed in more rum, leaving a small bit of liquid in the platter, and then lit. If it burned well, that meant it had been properly prepared.

In any case, it was the final flourish to the day's celebration. Most people trooped off shortly after the meal, or sat around for a port or brandy, before retiring for a long nap. His grandfather had long withdrawn, tired from the company and ritual. But the luncheon was the fitting finale for an important family occasion and ritualized togetherness, and few would have missed it.

Chapter XIV
New Year's Even Nuttin'

Christmas was over and now was a little time for relaxation. The Boxing Day party had been at one of M.J's friend's house. Doug had been thoroughly bored, but for her sake had put on a respectable front. There was no gainsaying, though, that he had not had his patience so thoroughly stretched at that party. There had been a few fellows he remembered from school. They were all in business. The topics of conversation he could have written on the back of a cigarette carton: the unions, the government's anti-crime policy which was not working, the restrictions on foreign exchange, the laziness of Jamaica workers, and more of the same. The saviour was that the next day was a working day, so they left fairly early.

The next day M.J. was back at work. Doug busied himself with some earned moments of pure reading. In the morning he usually took a beach chair out under the mango tree, equipped himself with a small cooler into which he had put some Red Stripe, and settled down to a morning's reading. About ten in the morning he was settling down to a difficult passage in Herbert Marcuse's, *One Dimensional Man*, which had come out almost a decade earlier, when he heard his mother call him to the telephone.

He got up slowly and went inside. It was Madge.

"What a nice surprise. Wha' happen? Yu enjoy yu Christmas?"

"Yu know damn well how it go." Madge sounded sad. "I missed yu."

Doug sensed his mother was quietly listening somewhere, so he did not want to let on too much, to be too explicit. She would suspect anything at the drop of a hat.

"Madge, me too, but I can't talk now," he whispered.

"I understand. I borrow this phone too, so is not a long call. Anyway jus wanted to tell yu that, and wish yu a good time."

"I will soon be back. School is going to be in another week and a half."

"I know what you mean. Yu don' have to say it. Anyway, have a good time an' don' drink so much rum."

"My feelings exactly." He did not want to say more. "And you enjoy the rest of yours, too. See you when I get back. Is there anything yu would like me to do for you down here?"

"No, Maas Doug, Thanks, anyway. See yu soon." And with that she hung up.

"Who was that, Doug?" His mother could not contain herself for curiosity.

"Oh, just a colleague from school asking how my Christmas was." He chucked her under the chin as he passed to undermine any thoughts or suspicions. Not that he would have been successful.

That Saturday he spent with M.J. They had both decided to spend the day together, but separately doing things that had been put off. M.J. was at the hairdresser and manicurist getting ready for the New Year's Eve ball. Doug had gone downtown to Sangster's Book Store to check out its latest arrivals. Later they arranged to meet at the Courtleigh Manor hotel for lunch.

On Sunday was the day of the promised outing for the children. They all piled into their various vehicles, the children hopping in with Doug and M.J. for the ride. For them it was a thrill. Uncle Doug was a hit, as he was always doing something different and goofy, at least in their eyes. So when he suddenly stopped on the Palisadoes, got out to wait for the other cars, and began acting like a traffic cop, they thought this was the mostest, doubling up with laughter at the way he signalled their fathers to pass him.

Eventually they all reached. The club was in full swing, the pool was full, not to speak of the bar. M.J. saw friends who were there. Doug knew a few people. Of course, the rest of the family, too, recognized this or that cousin who had come for a dip and a drink. For the children it was always a treat, since the setting was exclusive, away from crowds, private, but within the confines of this little place that seemed to speak so much of the past. For James and Jennifer it was an especial treat as their father was not one to appear at too many family get-togethers. Work seemed to consume him, and Christine bore most of the burden of being father and mother.

Doug stuck close to M.J., or to put it another way, she stuck close to him. The conversation was as banal as at the cocktail party. He couldn't understand. How could people live in this mental vacuum their entire lives? Did the great questions of civilization mean nothing to them? How could one not be captivated, emboldened, nourished by the profound questions of literature, of philosophy, of history? Did the achievements of humanity mean so little? Was humanity reducible only to the questions of commerce, of buying and selling salt-fish, of the stock market? How could a human being live isolated from the poetry of existence, the splendid meaning of language, the discussions of morality? It was too much for him. And before he got into another meaningless, reductive argument, he would rather withdraw into his mental shell, seeking only human contact with the few kindred spirits he managed to encounter.

And here was another problem. M.J. clove to him as if she felt herself to be his Platonic sundering. He felt otherwise. It was pleasant, even comfortable being in M.J's presence. She knew instinctually what he wanted, how he would act; born of many years contact as children she could anticipate his every move. What she couldn't do, however, was share his thoughts, his mind, the commitment to knowledge, his love of ideas.

It was sad, a dilemma, he thought. In every other way perfect for him, yet in these, the essential interstices of his soul there was no resonance. Their hearts did not beat like one. She would never understand what bore him aloft, what stars guided his noetic meanderings, the whiff of poetic meanings which made his heart quicken, the joy of reaching a *Vernunft* , that "which passeth all understanding," a moment of salutary peace.

"Uncle Doug." It was Jennifer calling. This little girl who needed no water wings, whom he had taught to swim at five, who appeared in the water as a nymph, wanted to play water polo. And she was a whiz. Neither James nor Robert could out-maneuver her. As for Susan, she was forever trying to catch up.

Jennifer could bob like a turtle, dive swiftly and come up grabbing the ball from her brother and cousin as if she were a phantom suddenly shimmering. Then she was gone, ball bobbing gaily in front as she punched it to the goal. And Doug loved to see her swim, challenging her more and more, forcing her to exert more energy. M.J. too, took part. She was an agile swimmer; with her light, lithe body and long arms, she could almost outpace Doug.

James, David, Christine and Anne sat back on their deck chairs lazily sipping daiquiris or rum punch, happy that the children were being so entertained. John and Shirley had not joined them, preferring to go with a younger crowd to Cable Hut.

"Doug," James called, rising from his chair to go to the bar at the moment when the children had stopped to rest from their strenuous mock-polo. Doug joined him at the bar and ordered a Stripe. "When we going to get together, brother man?"

"I thought maybe the second, the day after the one we all usually rest. I mean, I don't expect you to be up to it." He gave Doug a playful shove at the shoulder. "But don't fret, is nothing serious."

"Is a long time we two didn' sit down an labrish." Doug grinned. "Looking forward to it. Jus' don' twis' up me mind too much." They both laughed, finishing their drinks.

Now a little band had appeared. There were three of them, in bright Caribbean shirts, and with an instrument that was going out of style. There was a guitarist and a horn player. The horn was a local weed instrument, somewhat like a clarinet. But the man in the middle, he was the bass player; but there was no bass in the usual sense. There were no strings. Instead the player sat on a box, and plucked three metal rods tuned to the diaphonic. The length of each rod determined the key: a piece of Jamaican ingenuity, Doug thought, now being pushed aside by the electronic instruments which he hated.

And they were good. This setting, it seemed, was the place to bring out some old Jamaican Mento. Then they were soon into some more recent tunes. "My Pussin" was a favourite from the sixties which had been under erstwhile ban by the governor, for its obviously suggestive lyrics. Jennifer was gyrating to the music which took hold of her body naturally. She even knew some of the lyrics, especially the title, which made everyone erupt in suppressed giggles.

Susan stuck by her mother, ever the lady, too shy to follow her cousin out onto the terrace. The song was followed by another "rudie" one, "Two sapodilla and a nine inch banana. Wha she want, wha she want?" Robert was taken by the tune and was bopping next to his cousin. After mouthing the title a few times, he shouted across to his mother. "Mama yu ever see a nine inch banana?" Everyone doubled up with laughter as Anne tried to figure out an answer. Robert stopped dancing, aware that he had caused some mirth, but not knowing why?

"No, Robert I've never seen one." That made them laugh even harder, while Anne worked at trying to hide a mounting blush.

"But do they exist?"

Doug, who was holding M.J's hand tightly, couldn't restrain himself. "Of course you can find them, Rob, and they thick as well. At least two inches across." Laughter broke out again, and now it was Anne's turn, as she flashed him a swift dirty look.

"Why don't you bring your clothes over New Year's Eve and dress at my place? I'll make a little supper, we can dress and go."

"Sounds awright sweets, but time is going and I haven't really cracked any of the books I brought. Suppose I bring some over an' read on yu balcony, and we can see from there." Actually it was a good idea. M.J's place would be quiet, no children running about, and the balcony was comfortable and quiet.

"We can stock up on Red Stripe so yu won' have to go to the shop." The suggestion was great. After breakfast he packed his tuxedo, a few things and made the short trip to her house. They would be seeing the others later, anyway.

As for his mother, he felt a bit guilty, but, she assured him, nothing pleased her more than that he would be spending the day with M.J. He knew what she meant.

The day continued as planned. He reached for the Marcuse, eager again to move his mind back to his familiar haunts. The balcony was, indeed, the perfect place for a read. The breeze rustling through the huge ficus tree, which blocked the sounds of traffic, summoned him to an immersion in the critical ontology of materialism.

M.J. busied herself with some work, dismissed her maid early after making sure the house was so clean one could eat off the floor. For her, it was the perfect setting. Her man doing exactly what made him happy, a quiet household with just the two of them, at least for now. Domestic bliss with Doug was at least ensured for the next two days. She was happy and could think of no greater contentment.

But she asked nothing about his reading. That was his affair. She would never disturb him in his private realm. She wouldn't think to try to participate in his world, to intervene with discussion or question, or even to show interest. It never occurred to her that that intervention would have warmed his heart, would have forged those necessary, ineffable, connections of profundity he sought in a woman.

How wrong she was to believe that the crucible of the bonds of emotion did not involve the mind as well as the heart. And had she even known, what could she have done about it? For hers was a practical world, removed eternally from the circles of wisdom in which he chose to ruminate. There was no empathy in that regard between them. They were as far away the one from the other, as heaven is from hell. And she did not understand. It is doubtful she ever would.

After supper they lingered a while. She enticed him into the bathroom where they showered together and made love. Slightly fatigued, at least feeling languid they then dressed at a leisurely pace, also not wanting to be the first to arrive.

The dance was at the Royal Jamaica Yacht Club, recently removed near to the old Sea Plane terminal. The old club had been actually founded by Doug's grandfather, his brother, and other well-to-do Jamaicans. He could remember previous dances at the old place, tables decked with white cloths, buckets of ice surrounded by the usual four bottles: whiskey, rum, vodka and gin. Tickets covered everything. There was no need for calculating individual bills. The graciousness of an age passed, of opulence, of privilege, of command.

Doug was resplendent in his newly acquired tux, with the white tropical-style dinner jacket to top it off. M.J. had on a new black gown, with sequins on the halter top, setting off perfectly her deep, athletic tan. They could have been a couple from a fashion magazine, as they took their places at the table with the others, who had arrived a few minutes before. Doug and M.J. sat beside each other and opposite David and Anne. John was at the other end of the table, a good arrangement.

The other couples, too, were all dressed in dinner jackets and long gowns, some of the latest fashions. The club had not been "White" only for a while. There were new people of a brown hue and some Blacks, but all of the upper crust, the bourgeoisie, the well-healed, the "I-have-made-it" set. And the method of maintaining racial cum money purity in the clubs, the feature of "black-balling" those who were not desired, for one or another reason, had been displaced by a more liberal racial politics.

"Well, yu in for some good jump up?" David was always next to Doug on the dance floor. And the music was good. The club had engaged a versatile band that brought good sound their way from Swing to Ska and Rock Steady. The evening was young so they started off easily with some foxtrots, but would wind up the tempo as the evening wore on.

"This is the first time we all together for years," said Christine. M.J. edged closer to Doug.

"Yu don' know how I missed it. There are places in Toronto, but the spirit isn't the same. Besides," he grinned, "I missed all of you."

So you should stay, you ole raas," David was quick to remind him. M.J. edged even closer.

"So Doug? What you think now that yu have been here a few months?" John was itching to get his teeth in. But David, as usual headed him off. "This is not the evening for politics. Leave him alone. Besides he hasn't been here long enough."

"Even so," said Doug, in one of his less provocable moods, (who knows why), "this is a' evening for dancing and whatever else" He could feel M.J.'s breathing. Besides, she wanted something else tonight.

The band struck up a lively swing, and he squired her to the floor, where they moved effortlessly into the beat, putting on a show for many.

M.J. knew his every move, his sudden tacks and uncommon footwork. He guided her with one finger on her back, looking at her keenly through the rhythm. And she never missed a step, anticipating and melding with her love, whatever dip and tuck the music made.

"Those two are a perfect match," Christine ventured.

'Are you sure, Christine? I agree the two look like mongoose and fowl. But the mongoose goin' really eat the chicken, or let it fly 'way?" Anne was not as convinced. She knew Doug, his moods, his thoughts. She was not sure they were a perfect match at all.

"We all think they getting it on," said James, more sceptical yet, but not unkindly, because of his experiences in the world, "But looks are not the whole story."

"I would bet anyone, from how the two of them just fitting there together, that something good bound to happen." David thought he knew Doug the best. The two had been more than distant cousins, almost brothers. They had practically lived together during their younger years. At least every summer until he left JC, Doug had gone down to Bog Walk and spent the glorious holidays getting into trouble with David.

They would order horses in the morning, ride hell for leather as far as they could go, then trot down to the river, the tributary of the Rio Cobre, where it widens just below Tulloch. There they would tether and water the horses, strip, and jump into the river. Sometimes there would be young Black girls washing clothes in the river. They would engage them in conversation, David always the most precocious, Doug more reserved. There was one girl that David liked in particular. At times the two would disappear in the bushes, emerging a few minutes later with sweat pouring out of each. Doug knew why but they never discussed it.

Sometimes they would sit on the wide front veranda of the big house, Doug's aunt in Kingston, his uncle at the estate factory. Only the maids were at home, but usually in the back doing laundry or cleaning. Then they found their twenty-two rifles, sat down in some old chair, loaded, took aim at some distant zinc-roofed house and fired. It took a while, but the unmistakeable ping on the roof signalled a hit. Then there would be paroxysms of laughter. Those summer holidays always disappeared as quickly as they had come. But the bond between them remained.

"I don' want to put my goat mout' on it. Anyway, I know how M.J. feels. But Doug? It's trying to know how Anancy thinking." Anne was sceptical. She knew her brother, perhaps not in the comradely way that David did, but was spiritually closer to him.

"You comparing our brother to a spider?" James asked.

"Only in the sense his ideas are not easy to see. Doug is not thinking like the rest of us."

"Anyway did you talk to him at all David," asked James.

"Yes," Christine chimed in. "You two were always so close. Have you seen him since he came. Has he been down to Old Harbour or out to Tulloch?"

"Not really, we been really busy with the properties," David answered.

Anne looked embarrassed. "No, we haven't been able to invite him yet. Those two so busy I don' know what the hell is going on." She laughed in that peculiar way that said something. It was expected David would have wanted Doug there, if not just to visit, but to roust about up and down St. Catherine. The others were about to pry into this strange situation but Doug and M.J. were just coming back to the table.

"Don't you all feel like dancing. Yu mean yu just goin' sit here and drink?"

"Us old married people not as agile as you Doug," Christine allowed.

"Go weh! How old yu really is to dance?" Doug was adamant. "Come. Is a nice calypso blowing through the air. Come join us."

They all rose, and once again a family was joining on the dance floor, making the issue of blood confirm, using the space to indicate their generations of connection. It felt natural. It felt good.

Chapter XV

James's Plan

New Year's Day was uneventful. Doug had stayed with M.J. after the dance. They slept late, getting up slowly, without plans. Later that day they dressed and drove out to Cable Hut beach. There were only a few hardy souls about, some children cavorting in the big waves, a few solemn souls, probably hung over from the night's sojourn, sipping Red Stripe. They lay on the beach for a while, regaining equilibrium after the hectic dancing.

"When you plan to go back, sweet boy?"

"Oh, well, James wanted to chat. So I told him tomorrow would be a great time. I think we'll just have lunch at Courtleigh, or something like that. Anyway it's close to his office."

"This just a brotherly catch-up, or something more serious."

"Yu know. I'm not even sure. I think more than likely the first. We'll see."

"Let's get going. The sun's really blistering, especially after last night. My place is cooler, and the balcony inviting."

"An yu have nuff-nuff RedStripe?"

"Possibly some patties too. Come"

"Lead the way."

The day was really hot and the balcony a welcome relief. It was better than air-conditioning which he couldn't stand either. A swift, warm, breeze, a tree full of birds and lizards, a lounge chair, an engaging book, a Red Stripe in hand—where else was paradise? Paradise for M.J. was coming to join him, to look at his intense features as he read, the ruffled brow rippling with thoughts as they came and went, deepening now with the profundity of a thought, relaxing again as he skimmed lighter passages.

"What are you reading so intensely?" She decided to engage.

"*One Dimensional Man*, a work by a German-American scholar and independent Marxist."

"Are you a marxist, Doug?"

"What does that mean to you sweet girl?"

"Well, aren't Marxists communists?"

"Depends what you mean by communists?"

"Oh Doug, is it so complicated?"

"I'm afraid so. But only because lay people use the word "communist" so loosely. Unless you say exactly what you're talking about how can one understand you. I mean, scholars spend ages refining language so one will know what they intend to mean."

"But what is the ordinary person to do? We can't spend the entire day reading, learning these things."

"I didn't say it was easy. But to answer your question, yes, one could, if one wanted to. The problem is no one cares. Interest in the world and its problems are always reduced to the question of immediate survival. I understand it. But I don't like the outcome."

"What's the outcome?"

"Many things, sweetheart. But one of them is insufferably boring people."

"Thanks a million. Like me?"

"I didn't mean that, you know it."

"But still. Be frank. Does that lack of conversation between us affect our relationship?" Then immediately she countered, "Sorry. I didn't want to put you on the spot. It is just..." Here she broke off, looked out over the balcony with a look of helplessness he had never seen before in this very dynamic, positive, and self-assured woman.

Suddenly he felt the weight of truth that should have dawned on him before. M.J. had been so ecstatic the night of the dance. She had been radiant, and now, in his mind, she appeared then to have been expectant. Had she been waiting for the moment of question, amidst the moon, the calm waters of the harbour, the evocative music and the presence of family? Was that what this all had been building towards? And he had been utterly oblivious, not only to her but the entire family's expectations. Sure he knew his mother's expectations but had not taken her seriously. He was not to know the answer yet, though, for at that moment the shrill ring of the telephone interrupted them.

M. J. rose to answer it. He settled back relieved hoping he could postpone the inevitable for a while. Then he heard M.J. gasp and say, "Oh my God."

He jumped up stashing the bottle on the table as he hurried inside. M.J. was standing with the phone in her hand with a horrified yet sad look on her face. "Come, it's Christine. Granddad Cameron."

Christine's voice was sombre as she recounted for him the details of the last hours. Granddad had retired after lunch as usual for his afternoon nap. At about four, Imogene carried his tea in on a tray. He was lying on the bed, his head fallen beside the pillow, saliva slowly dripping from his mouth, eyes wide open.

She had called James who ran to the room. Granddad Cameron must have suffered a fatal heart attack. He was dead.

Doug quickly changed, M.J. striding beside him as he ran to the car. As they drove up Long Lane they could hear the siren of an ambulance. They drove in just as it burst through the gates. The paramedics hurried out and into the room. But there was nothing to be done. Granddad had been dead already an hour. James thanked them, took control. He phoned Morris's Funeral home in Half Way Tree, with whom his grandfather had a contract for his burial. In less than half an hour they arrived.

He tried to comfort his mother. She was weeping. Not that they hadn't expected it. After all grandfather Cameron was eighty-eight. He had lived a long and fruitful life, bringing up a family, converting landholdings into lucrative businesses and ensuring them a prosperous future. Now he was gone.

As James spoke with the attendants from the funeral home Doug tried to reach his Uncle Benjamin and David. The first was easier to find, and drove up soon after. It was more difficult to find Anne and David. Yes, the estate house had a telephone, but sometimes it was hell to get through, if they were at home. Luckily he was able to reach Anne. David was out on the estate somewhere with John, doing whatever they were doing there. She wasn't sure when they would be back.

In any case the arrangements were made relatively easily. Morris's would take care of everything; phoning the church, placing the announcement, and arranging the entire ceremony. It was set for two days after the death. The wake would be held at Long Lane. At six o'clock, right after the evening BBC news, the funeral announcement was made, together with those of the other deceased that day. A more formal announcement, agreed upon by James and Doug was published in the Daily Gleaner the next day.

The next days were filled with the legal aspects of the death, which James took care of deftly, and with the preparations for the wake. Doug worked with his brother as best he could. Now there was no time to spend with Mary Jean. For in addition to the formalities there were the other necessities of spending time with his mother, and with trying to explain the difficult topic of death to the children.

The funeral went off as planned. A communion service was said at Half Way Tree parish church. It was a lavish affair as granddad Cameron was well known throughout the island, and well loved by many. He had been a generous businessman, gracious at all times, a gentleman of the old school and not the type of card-shark newcomer associated with the Yankee way of doing business.

The church was packed. In the front row the family (M.J sat beside Doug) and in between him and James, their mother. Various other family members and friends took up the benches behind them, and many a workman who had been dependent on Douglas Cameron, or who had been helped in time of need was there with wife and family in tow. With considerable chagrin Anne and David arrived late, John behind them, taking their appropriate positions in the family pew. Anne glanced across at Doug, a look of consternation on her face. It was as if she was dismayed, upset at circumstances other than her grandfather's death. Doug dismissed these for the moment.

The service was long and formal, the eulogy brilliant. Doug had written it himself. The long years of service to the country, not in an official capacity, but through his innovations as a farmer and his acuity in business were noted. So were his characteristics of kindness, benevolence, and simplicity especially to those whose station was beneath his own, whose luck in life had been an unfortunate draw. No opulent office was the centre of his business, no plush leather chairs and expensive cognacs to puncture an important business deal. His was a simple philosophy. You make money to give children and grandchildren a better life. With what is left, and in his case it was not insignificant, one had the important responsibility to ensure that no one he dealt with, who worked for him, should find themselves or their children hungry.

Those lessons he had imbibed. They were the ones he passed on. That spirit of giving back to the society that had borne them one and all was passed on to his children. Part of Doug's own makeup had been forged in this atmosphere, amply seconded by the work, the deeds, and the humanistic precepts of his father.

It was significant that the family honoured this tradition: among the pallbearers, James, Doug, David and John, were one or two cousins, but also the last remaining overseers of the properties in Portland. And they too were invited to the wake with their wives. It was a fitting passing.

"Brotherman, this was unexpected. Yu think yu will have time tomorrow for our chat?"

"I have two more days, so why not. Is it convenient for you?"

"I'll make it so. What about a long lunch tomorrow at the Courtleigh?"

"Good, see you there at twelve-thirty?"

"Perfect. Now we haf' to mix wid folks. Tomorrow."

James had picked a perfect spot for lunch. It was off to the side of the pool area, far enough away from other tables so that no one could hear them. The big umbrella gave shade from the broiling mid-day sun. It was quiet, since business had not yet picked up speed after the holidays, and there were few visitors. He was already at the table when Doug arrived. They settled down to a long, leisurely lunch.

"When last we had a quiet moment to ourselves?" he asked.

" You know? I was just thinking the same thing. But I frighten to tell yu. It was two Christmas' ago, when I was back for the season. "

"Too damn seldom, if yu ask me."

"Yu took the thought right outa me head." He and James had always enjoyed, at least after they had outgrown their brotherly rivalry, a closeness despite having different ideas on almost everything. The one thing they both agreed on was the importance of family, of maintaining those bonds of conviviality, of family solidarity, of quiet clan-like adherence, which imparted that special feeling of comfort, especially to the children.

"So, tell me ole man, how yu gettin' on? How the school and all the work?"

"Yu know, in a nutshell everything is going fine in that department. The school is a good place to work, the headmaster keeps a firm but lively hand, and the staff is good. We all seem to get along without any problems. Yu know how sometimes one or two people in a group always stirring up trouble? Not there. It's a pleasant atmosphere to work in. One or two of the teachers not quite up to standard, but it doesn't seem to make a difference."

"Good to know. But what about yu other work. I hear yu bussin' yu ass."

Doug laughed. "I took on a lot at the beginning—literacy, Extra-mural work, Clubs. But I think next term will be a little easier. For one thing the literacy seems to have lost its attraction. We have a smaller group of about twenty. So that means less work for me."

"Yu think it's workin'?"

"Hard to tell. I don't have the picture for the whole island. But I wouldn't be surprised if the programme collapses soon."

"Why so?"

"Because, as I always arguin' with the people, literacy is a good thing in itself. Yu an' I know that. But for the little man, what is the point in learning how to read and write if it not goin' to improve yu life. What I mean is that if a fella can't see a better job, or more money, why bother?"

This argument he had pushed continuously at meetings, especially when there were politicians around. But he knew as well that solving this problem was unlikely in the short run, certainly not in that economic climate where the government was running here, and running there, like a chicken with its head chopped off, trying to find money to balance the budget.

"I agree with you completely. And in my experience, when I meet with the higher uppers, there is gloom and doom. Manley has good intentions, but how he goin' implement them, how he going' turn Jamaican around, is anybody's guess. This problem not goin' solve in one term in office. Is exactly what bothering me."

"Me too. Slowly I beginning to see it. The problems are immense: the economic, the social, the educational, and all connected. Try to solve one, an' the other one knockin' at the door. There is another one that nobody dare talk about yet."

"Which?"

"The racial."

"Hmm. True no' raas. But tell me how yu reach that conclusion."

"Is a long story. There were some incidents along the way that have been opening my eyes."

"Such as?"

Doug then related the two incidents that had initially scared him, first the one at the literacy meeting, then the other at the beach. He was still trying to figure them out, he said, but getting nowhere. Either they were transient phenomena, or they were buried in such a deep way in the Jamaican psyche, that a quick fix was out of the question. How these would play themselves out was anyone's guess. It worried him too, this conflation of Blackness with Revolution. It seemed almost fascist. But he knew better. Here was a confrontation with history which could not be gainsaid.

The shrill tones of Abeng, of the Daily Courier, of the Worker's Party, even some sections of the PNP itself all spoke that same language, even if their general ideological alignment was not precise.

"Of course all these papers are mainly concerned with White as in white imperialist. They not necessarily talking about us, but push come to shove yu think some little man goin' think about those distinctions when he have a machete in his hand?"

"I been having the same thoughts. They really worry me. Never have I seen the island in a worse state. Almost as if it is moving towards something, who the hell knows what kind of bangarang."

"James, I was schooled in history and politics, those strange conjunctions of circumstances, almost like the onset of a disease, the pre-symptoms, if you like. And that is exactly how I feel. History has a way of catching up with itself. As if the problems of yesteryear have to be cauterized in some way. As if a cathartic moment has to be introduced to free one from the shackles of the past, to allow one to move on. I don't know. But something is working under the surface here that is going to explode. I mean, I am, we are too late. It has to play itself out to its own rhythm."

"Coming from you that is some admission. I thought you were hell bent on promoting some such catharsis in the guise of a revolution?"

"I was. At least I was thinking that way theoretically. How else can Jamaica get past its current problems? I remember one of Jefferson's faintly recalled sayings: that a society has to undergo a bloody revolution every twenty years or so, in order to cleanse itself."

"So we have to trundle out the guillotine every now and again to cut out the cancer, at least according to Robespierre and St. Juste?"

'Precisely ole cock, and that's the part I don' see myself playing. Is one thing to theorize it, but the reality is horrible to contemplate."

James was sitting up in his chair. He took a sip of his Red Stripe, then settled back, with a more than sombre look, as if he were thinking seriously, or getting ready to come out with some profundity.

"Listen, I have something to share with you, and to get an honest opinion."

"Shoot."

"When you talk about revolution, don' yu mean something like a movement of people from the bottom, stirring things, pushing the top raases into action?"

"Yes, at least that is the general theory."

"Well suppose I told you that that is not the way it is thought about with our powers that be?"

"I'm not sure I understand."

"Well, let me be more explicit. The story I am getting from the top, an' please don' ask me for sources, is that that revolution is being planned at the Cabinet level."

"Manley?"

"Not just him. All the major fellows. But the way they dooin' it is interesting, and frightening at the same time."

"Gwan, nuh. Me head bussin' right now."

"Hol' on to yu horses. The idea from the top is to set up another Cuba here."

"But how? I don' think Jamaca man ready for that yet."

"That is precisely the point. They either have already, or are intending to invite the Russians to take a look."

"Raas. That is heavy stuff."

"Not just heavy. Total. They intend to invite the Soviets to set up another Cuba. Think of the strategic possibilities. With Jamaica there would now be two islands, side by side, and possibly a third if you count Grenada. And maybe this would even affect the Dominican Republic, which has had a semi-revolutionary, Marxist movement for years. At least there is an undercurrent there."

"For the Soviets that would be a major coup. But you think the Yankees would allow it? That would put them in almost the same position as the Soviets in Europe: hostile forces right on their doorstep. And that would drive them through the wall. It could produce another Bay of Pigs confrontation."

"Exactly my meaning. But I don' wan' at any cost to be around here with my little family if an' when that happen."

"I kyan' lie to you that I not thinking the same. But is such a fuckin' dilemma. I really love my work. I really love wake up in the morning an' see that blasted guinep tree. The children in the school are great. Even the teachers. Everybody workin' hard to make something good out of a bad situation. How the hell to leave them?"

"That I kyan' answer for yu. Yu know me. This island in my blood. Generations of us fertilize this soil. But I have two little pickney dem to think of. An' they come first."

"What yu tellin' me, James? Yu already made up yu mind?"

"That is what I wanted to talk to you about. I was going to tell you, even though I was still hesitatin'. But something happen a few days ago change my mind quick, quick."

"You mean Granddad?"

"I was afraid of trying to pull up roots an' force him to leave. But now he is gone, it will be easier. Mother won't be so hard to convince. Besides, yu there already. Is a matter of joining family, not breakin' it up more."

"What yu mean, I there already?"

"Doug, yu can fool me. We grow up together. I know how you think. I knew with your intelligence it would only be a matter of time when the idealism would be tempered by your own observed reality." James was talking now like the effective and brilliant barrister that he was.

"But what about you? How yu goin' pull up stakes an' leave?"

"What I didn' tell yu was that I've been working on it for a while."

"How?"

"Well, you know I have certain contacts in Toronto. After all I did part of my law work there. I have in mind joining a firm there that deals with the Commonwealth. My experience in Commonwealth law, especially the commercial aspects, will be welcomed by that firm. I've been offered a partnership if and when I make the move."

"Jesus H and raas Christ. Yu really mek my head spin. So yu been doin' this all along, quietly?

"Yes."

"An' what does Christine think?"

"I haven't told her, but I know how fearful she is of the situation here, an' she would probably welcome the chance to leave."

"Yu goin' tell her now?"

"I wanted to talk with you first. Yes. Now is a good time. Besides there is something I haven't discussed with anyone."

"What's that?"

"It's about Uncle Ben's properties."

"I don' follow."

"That's because yu haven't been around. Anyway, didn't yu notice the embarrassed way Anne has been acting?"

"Where?"

"All around. They were late for the funeral. That is unlike Anne and David. Let me ask yu this. Yu an' David used to be so close. Right?"

"Correct."

"When last did he invite yu over to Old Harbour, or to spend a weekend up in Tulloch?"

"Well they haven't. But I never thought about it because I was so busy."

"But I find it strange. And there are other signs, too."

"Signs?" Now it was Doug's turn to register dismay and disbelief.

"I didn't think much until a few weeks ago. Eustace came in to town with some papers for me to sign. So I had a chat with him. How were the properties, that kind of stuff? But he had no answer. Apparently he refuses to go up to Tulloch anymore. You remember he used to take up the extra cattle feed supplements in the truck?"

"Yes."

"Well he told Uncle Ben he not goin' up there anymore."

"I remember now, when I first came and he was driving me up to Highgate. He said the same thing, then quickly changed the subject. So what yu gettin' at, James. What yu think happening?"

"I can't put my finger on it, but something different is happening up there. Yu know, they reduced the dairy side. I can see it from the documents. But still money is coming in."

"Backside! That could only mean one thing if yu right. An' I don' even want to say it."

"Yes, brother, bad business. But yu see, that has made me even more determined to make some decisions."

The discussion had taken a strange turn. He had not expected his brother to reach such radical conclusions. James was not one to undertake sudden, irrevocable turns with his life. It had to take some earth-shattering events to make him contemplate a departure from his steady way of life. Possibly the rumours from his acquaintances had done it. They were based on their connections to the secret world of the Cabinet. That was telling. And that Doug was reaching similar conclusions based on his experiences added fuel to their imaginings.

The second point of the conversation was even more shocking. That James had taken the trouble to share it meant he needed to get it off his chest. For the two, if their conjectures were correct, it would be a shattering blow to the family. Sister, first cousins, and children caught in a web which could have furious consequences: it was unthinkable. Yet, there was no certainty. And what if their suspicions were right?

Still Doug was not ready for an absolute decision. He had a lot to think through. There was still time for a decision. But now he decided on a preventive measure, a Plan B, as it were, in case he also had to decide for a quick departure, to leave the blessed work he thought he had cut out for himself. It would not be easy.

That evening, before returning to Highgate, he phoned some friends in Toronto, including a professor who had been impressed with his MA. He would apply to do a doctorate in September. It was just a precaution. Why waste time? He could always put it off another year, if he decided to stay. In any case it would ensure him an entry into the world he craved, which was already a part of him, the one he enjoyed most. It was time to rethink, to reengage. He did not discuss it with M.J. And he could not know how prescient his thoughts were.

In the evening he went to see her. There was not much conversation, instead, a rather strained atmosphere which made it awkward to talk. He said goodbye. It might be for a while, he said. The next morning found him again on the road for Highgate and his other life.

Chapter XVI

Madge: Nuff, Nuff Na Nuff

Doug drove past Castleton gardens encumbered with so many thoughts he did not know where to begin. Ideas, considerations, musings, they all invaded his mind as he drove past the beautiful, lush, scenery of the depleted river. The drive into Highgate and up to Fraserwood seemed an endless toil. He was eager to get back to his more familiar surroundings, his study, and the school.

Arriving at school early on Monday morning, he went straight to his desk to plan the day. His papers had been carefully and neatly pushed to one side. There, in the front of the desk was a small plant with card attached. It was a sympathy card from Madge. She must have been in on the weekend and left it there. Her words were terse, but imbued with the feelings that flew out at him. She had written simply, "It is at times like these that one's true friends can be the only comfort. Madge."

The headmaster drove in shortly after and came straight to the staff room. Extended hand, he offered his and the staff's condolences.

"The family greatly appreciates the wreath you and the staff sent, Mr. Johnston. It was very thoughtful of you."

"There is not much else one can do on these occasions, unfortunately, Mr Austin. Life gives us this sadness among its many pleasures. Death is a part of what we experience daily. Still, it is always a shock. But I understand that your grandfather had a good innings."

"Yes sir, he accomplished a lot in life, and we think of him as always being a good man, a friend to all those he came in contact with. You know there were not a few of the people who had worked for him at the funeral."

Doug was proud of his grandfather. He was proud that this man had lived the principles that he professed, that he had tried to pass them on to his children and their offspring. Yes, no one could gainsay his personal, his human record. It was one to hold up to the world, especially the modern world of ruthless capitalism. In a sense it was so ironic; the very principles of socialism that Doug had felt in his bones, was trying to live by, these had been inherited from his grandfather, a scion of that other system, of properties, of business, of class.

"But yu busy in yu head this morning, Maas Doug." Madge had entered the staff room and made straight for his desk. She did not restrain herself as she enveloped him with her arms in a tight hug.

"Thanks for your card and flowers, and your tender words. So true. And so very you." He looked deep into her eyes. But the embrace had to be over as other staff was beginning to arrive.

The next few days were busy with settling down to the new Easter term, (as it was still called after its English progenitor). There were the results of the Christmas exams to compare. Doug and Madge sat together after school as usual, comparing results, drawing up statistical charts to see how this year's pupils had done compared with those of past years. The results were not outstanding, despite some really good pupils, but they compared favourably with past years, and were even marginally better. The head and the School Board could be satisfied.

One afternoon that week, since Michael was sick at home and Madge did not have to return right away, she came up to the house. Barbara and Dave Crichton were there, of course. It was mid-week. The former had seen Madge arrive, but had withdrawn to her little apartment. So no thought of satisfying amorous urges. They chose to sit on the front veranda.

"So how yu holidays went?"

"Yu know. In general well, except for the last few days. And I had a good talk with James. We haven't done that for a long time."

"Anything else?" Madge's question had that edge that indicated curiosity.

Doug smiled. "Yu mean M.J.?" Now he was forcing her to declare herself.

"Of course I mean M.J. How yu men dem so fool-fool?" She laughed.

"Well, to be truthful, it was nice, but nothing more. M.J. is getting a bit more, let me say, probing. Of course, she wants something more than jus' galfrien' – boyfriend.'

"An cow los' in a pasture?"

Now it was his turn to laugh. There was nothing like the comfort of patois. It bespoke an easy familiarity that allowed the splatter of words to be directed at the objects of syntax. But also this folk tongue managed to get at the truth swiftly, if sometimes a little brutally.

"The truth is I don' think cow coming home."

"Hmm. Yu sure 'bout that."

"Is anyone, any man, ever so sure?"

"Some, yes. Mine have one way, one direction, one thought, one goal. I could go on."

"But it's not that simple for me."

"Doug what happen here....."

He cut her off. "....going to happen again."

She looked at him, mouth pursed, before breaking into a grin. She reached over and took his hand, got up, and headed for the back.

But he took her through the study, which wall of books blocked the view to Barbara's entrance, spun her around, and reached for her lips with his. Her response was not just enthusiastic. The passion of the embrace told them that the three weeks apart had been too much. More was needed.

But the weekend came with the arrival of an unexpected visitor: M.J. She had decided that it was time to show her hand, her intentions, invoke her desires as the pledge she wanted from him. She arrived shortly after school was over, only to catch him as he was walking out the door. Just before leaving he was able to see the frown on Madge's raised brow, which contrasted with the puckered nose and lips half-twisted at one corner in a questioning smile. His stomach turned over twice as it fluttered close to his guts.

M.J. came at him right away as they entered the house. "Well, are you surprised?"

"Nicely surprised. Wasn't expecting you. What's going on?"

"Nothing much. Just thought I would surprise you. After all the excitement of the last few weeks, it would be nice to be alone."

He couldn't answer her that he had not been expecting a visit, nor that he had made other plans. But he wasn't about to be ungracious. "Let's go down to Strawberry Fields tomorrow. We could picnic."

M.J. wasn't about to argue with that one. The Saturday morning they set off for the same little bay they had sought on an earlier outing. It was deserted as usual. So they stripped. M.J. had brought snorkels and fins; Doug's were always in the back of the wagon. So they spent the better part of the morning enjoying the black stone cliffs extending far under the water, and the teaming panorama of undisturbed fish life. It was all so peaceful, so natural, so cyclical, like the sun and its endless return. Nothing seemed to change. It appeared as if aeons would come and go, but the water would wash endlessly against the cliffs, fish would spawn, the young would thrive. No seasons disturbed this peaceful array of life's forces, competing only in their private, perpetual cycles.

Dougy," she retrieved his thoughts to their presence. "Yu know why I came up?"

"Yu mean it was not just to see me?" he quipped provocatively.

She gave him a playful slap. "Of course it was because I missed you, yu big baboon. But more than that."

"Bamboozle me with explanation." He was in one of his prescient moods. Women love to lie as they get to truth. The problem was that men had a way of usually never understanding their convolutions. This time though, it seemed as if Doug had been sharpened by the circumstance of his own contradictions, and was even expecting M.J. to take the tack he knew she was on.

"Yu know I loved your grandfather."

"Of course you did. You were like his own granddaughter to him."

"Yes. And now he is gone I feel that emptiness too. Is it just that we have to replace death with life, to make ourselves more secure and comfortable?"

Now she was stretching him out. The bait was cast. She had thrown the line out to test his reactions. Not that this was an intellectual exercise on her part; not as if James were arguing a point with a witness, throwing out hook and consciously waiting for the bite to reel in the line. No, from M.J. this was almost instinctual. She could not have analyzed her own question any more than she could have mitigated the effect of its thrust.

"I don't know," he answered carefully. "Life goes on. We have to continue with our own lives." Thrust and parry. But she was not going to let him off so easily.

"Doesn't death make you want to replace it with new life," she asked. "Isn't it as though each of us must return what was taken away?"

But Doug wasn't sure what to answer. The only thing he was certain about was that M.J. was not usually given to philosophizing. Besides, he sort of knew what she was hinting at. And he resisted the bait as long as he could. But she was relentless.

"Think of the fish we just saw. One gets eaten, but it has already spawned, and its replacement appears: life following death. Isn't that the way it is?"

He was trapped. There was no evading a positive reply. He knew now where she was heading. But he decided to play the fool a while longer. "I know that one fish comes after another. But what has that got to do with granddad?"

M.J. sighed. It wasn't working at the moment. "Never mind. I can't explain." No, she had not given up. It was the woman's way. Never try frontal assaults, but go around to the side, mark the weak defences, and when the enemy has settled down to some security of respite, attack. Besides, if brain doesn't work there is always pum-pum. One or the other will wear a man down.

She lay back on the towel, put her hand across his chest, and flung one leg over his naked body. He was caught off guard. The caresses resounded throughout his carefully guarded system. His passion in another direction took over. He did not want to make love. But no one had said anything about love. His response was physical, born of another longing. But who could have known. She took it at face value.

The rest of the weekend passed without much conversation. M.J. did not know how to continue, or, perhaps, thought it best not to. Saturday evening they sat on the terrace of one of the hotels hardly saying a word. It was pleasant, but that was it. Doug did not want to make love in the evening. After lunch on Sunday she decided to leave, to prepare for the week ahead, which, she said was going to be busy.

"Are you coming in soon?"

"Not sure. Lots to do over here. Besides, I didn't exactly get all the reading done I wanted over the Christmas." He tried to make light of it laughing as he spoke. But she knew differently, at least in her heart. This was not going to be easy for her. And at the moment she was not sure what to do, how to approach him, how to ascertain his real feelings, to put closure on her troubling doubts.

Doug did try to spend the rest of the Sunday reading. But M. J.'s troubled departure worried him. It had come on him stealthily over the Christmas holidays, as it wormed its way into his consciousness. He did not love her as she wanted, as she expected, as he had thought he might. He was not going to love her either; nor could he compromise. And he would have to, sooner or later, confide his feelings in her. How to do it without hurting her? He knew she had lived for the day when he would ask her to marry him, through the years in which he had been at university: waiting, hoping. But he would have to tell her somehow, knowing it would hurt, but allowing her to open her life to other possibilities.

Again his dilemma appeared. Was he sure? Was his connection with Madge rooted with possibilities, or was it just a passing fancy. Was there real love developing between them despite the difficulties they would face? Better to be certain, not precipitate. Better not to end up hurting two people, destroying life junctures for all concerned.

He would have to careful, restrained. Could he be? The next weekend brought him a partial answer. As luck would have it Barbara and Dave were away again in Kingston with their respective compatriots. Madge had arranged to come up the Saturday to spend part of the day.

He heard her car come up the drive at about eleven o'clock. It was a cloudy, rainy morning, promising a shower in the afternoon.

"Well, yu alone this weekend again?"

'How yu knew anyway?'

"I heard Barbara and Dave talking in the staff room. They were pretty clear."

"So are yu busy, or yu have a little time for me?"

"What yu think? I look like Anancy who run way from promise?"

She sucked her teeth, gave him a little smile, and went straight for his lips. It was a long one.

"Yu know, last weekend I was really jealous."

"Jealous of what?"

"Cho man. Don' play eediot wid me. Yu know what. In any case I know yu didn' know she was coming."

"Right. I was surprised. She usually not that aggressive."

"Aoah. So she was aggressive; please explain."

"Yu know it wasn' dat way I mean it. Jus' that she usually call first. Anyway, the weekend was not exactly successful."

"I won' ask yu no more." Madge knew she had won, that she had been in his thoughts, and decided not to press the point. Besides, she was not exactly in a position to make demands, act the aggrieved lover.

"Let's go on the veranda. Tea? Stripe? Rum?" He needled her. She laughed.

"Tea. As usual. Lead the way, nuh."

But the veranda was too cool. Drizzle was coming down and blowing in the sides. Clouds had formed, and it looked like a good old cloudburst. They went back inside to the study, a natural place for them. The closeness of the armchairs, the shelves of books, Madge's sweet powdered smell, his obvious intent absorption in her presence, her attraction to him, all provided the atmosphere with a heady aura.

"Doug I want to ask yu a question. What was it that gave yu the impetus to return? I mean yu had a life that was successful, forward-looking, pregnant with possibilities. Why give it up to return to this cauldron?"

He paused for a while without answering. "I'm not sure I can give a good answer, or an honest one. It was more a feeling, a desire, a compulsion."

"Go on, don't stop. I not goin' let yu off the hook so easy." They laughed, as she stretched out her hand to take his.

"It is really hard to explain, Madge. Yu know how much I love my family, and family in general. It was as if all this time in Canada I was doing something that was completely outside my heart. Merely living. There was no special feeling to it, like I was going through motions. But there was no connection."

"What is it really like living in a place yu don' have roots in?"

"Is like a lizard without a tail. Yu jus' go through motions every day. But you are still a stranger. Nothing feels real."

"Like what?"

"Smells, for example. Have you ever smelt Jamaica?"

"No, now that yu mention it, no. Wha' de backside yu talkin' 'bout? I not usually sniffing about? What it smell like to yu?"

"Listen, from I wake in the morning, the smell of Khus-Khus grass attack me. Goin' down the road to Annotto Bay, the smell of coconut, of sweet sugar molasses, the burnt cane. All of these are like, well, painted onto the soul. You breathe free when you smell them. In Canada there are no similar references."

"Is that it, then, smells? Nature?"

"No. Language is another. When I open my mouth up there I have to be careful what I'm saying. The whole thing is different. People don' understand the same humour. I don' hear that deep, belly laugh when I pop a joke. As for joke, them people hardly ever laugh. You practically have to write it out on a piece of cardboard an' hold it up to their eyes."

"Yu not exaggerating. Everybody is like that?"

"Practically. In my experience. Even the fellows I fool aroun' with. If two or three West Indians in a group with Canadians, when everything finish, and we go for a rum together, we always talking 'bout how dis one, or dat one stupid."

"As bad as that?"

"Worse. Folk wisdom like we have here, usually does not hit anyone in industrial society. That is lost. It gone."

"So yu decide to come back because it was home." She began to probe deeper, not satisfied with the answers, which did not sound sufficiently compelling to her.

"No there were other factors."

"Like what?"

"Duty, commitment, love of country, that sort of thing." Now he was a bit embarrassed. So she went about it a different way.

"Doug I just don' believe yu left a promising career in Canada just because of language, jokeyfying, social customs, folk wisdom, and all of that stupidness. There is something deeper. I been watchin' yu. Coming back is one thing. Throwing yuself into work like yu do, is something else. Is some deeper kind of meaning yu work out for yuself. Correct me if I wrong, an' beg pardon for digging."

"Pardon? Yu don' have to beg pardon for nuttin', Miss Madge." But as he laughed, she knew that she was going to have to dig harder.

"A man like yu don' simply act out of them simple, back yard motive. An' is not jus' rungles. Something else workin' in yu system. I sure of it. But—as I said. I don' want to pry."

She looked at him softly, but with a great deal of understanding that was pouring out, desiring to probe the mystery, to share what she thought made this man in front of her tick. But for now it would have to be a subtle approach.

"Tell me, did yu ever have cause—and I know yu don' like religion—but did yu ever read any of those thinkers like Buber, like Bonhoeffer, like Niemoeller, those men who decided to give of their love no matter what?"

She saw him breathe in deeply. Not knowing it, probing only, she had struck a chord. He reached back behind him on the self and pulled out a book.

"You mentioned Bonhoeffer, Dietrich Bonhoeffer. Have you read this?" He showed her Bonhoeffer's *The Way to Freedom*?

"What yu mean, have I read it? He was one of my main spiritual mentors at theological college."

"I didn't know you had studied for the ministry."

"No, I didn' tell you. That was where Duncan and I finally got together. But then I decided a ministry was not for me and went on to finish my BA."

"Holy shite. Sorry." He covered his mouth, as if to expiate the swearing. "You know, Madge, when I was in Germany staying with Mr. Sieger I came across those works in his library, and he encouraged me to read Bonhoeffer's prison diary and more. But you're right. I am not very taken with religion but this man, and he is not the only one, impressed me with his courage, of his commitment to good in that horrible time of evil. How he could stay on an even keel while in prison awaiting trial and possible execution, how he could be impelled by that simple faith—it is nothing short of impressive."

"And so you read more, and deeper in his philosophy."

"Yes, I was impressed by his willingness to suffer for his convictions, but above all by his call to action, that it is by bold actions taken selflessly that we really attain what he called the 'kingdom of heaven.'"

"I was right. There is more to you than disliking a few cuffee Canadians."

"Come on! There are good Canadians, too: warm, tolerant, compassionate. But yes, I thought his message and admonitions were too powerful to ignore. His actions, his willingness to act in the face of all that perdition, put all to shame who do not try to emulate."

Madge leaned back as he warmed to the topic. She listened closely, carefully to his reasoning, noting all the time the sincerity, the intenseness of his emotions.

He got up. Grinned. "Madge sorry. I get very—well—carried away sometimes."

"Sorry. Sorry for what. I look fenky?"

"An' I'm thirsty. Time for a lager."

They rose together and went out into the kitchen where Doug opened a Stripe, offering it to her. She laughed and shook her head. Instead she put her arms around him, just as he was taking a swig from the bottle. He looked at her for a moment, before the demanding kiss brought their bodies into unison. Without a word they retraced their steps, this time passing the study and entering the corridor to the bedroom.

There was no holding back the passion that had been building. Love has this way of breaking all physical barriers before it lodges quietly in the soul; as if it needs to test itself first on the corporeal, create the material bond before declaring the heart. It was good they were alone, because the presence of others might not have able to constrain their libidinal cravings for each other. For this coupling was not born of absence alone; it was the seminal outcome of deeper conjunctions.

After lovemaking they lay back, momentarily spent in their ardour He noticed she had lost her initial shyness from the first time they had made love. Both arms were cradling her head as she breathed deeply, satisfyingly. He moved to put his head on her breast close to her shoulder, near the fount of her aphrodisial must. She did not stir. Moments later she moved one arm down to caress his hair lazily.

Slowly she sat up in bed, to allow some of the fresh breeze coming through the window to waft over her body. He noticed her firm large breasts again, with the purple nipples, erect, perusing their expectance.

"Doug, I didn't finish about Bonhoeffer, yu know?"

"Finish what?"

"Only that suffering and action are only two of his dicta. The third is exile."

"Yes, he didn't expect everyone to follow him into impossible situations such as he was in. There were honourable ways to fight by withdrawing for another day. I think that's what he meant by exile."

"I think yu right. Only wanted to mek sure yu got all of it down in yu head."

"Madge, yu know, sometime I kyan' keep up with yu. Yu brains move too fast."

"Too fast for yu? Cho." And she sucked her teeth exaggeratedly to underscore the disagreement. But she was not going to make the message any plainer.

"There are things I should tell yu. Decisions I took."

"Like what?"

"I decided to leave Duncan. Get a divorce."

Doug sat up so quickly he almost knocked her off the bed. "No rawtid! When yu decide that?" He was really agitated now.

"Kyan' give yu an exact date. It was comin' for a long time. Jus' had to mek up me mind."

"Have yu told him?"

"Not yet. Certain things have to happen firs'. Doug, before I tell yu there is something I wan' to mek clear."

"Go on, nuh."

"Well, yu know I not like another woman." She was referring to M.J., of course, but did not intend to make that explicit. She continued, "I know what we feel together. For you, an' for me, this was no blin' jump-up. At the same time, I not askin' yu for nuttin. What we have, we have, an' maybe even not going to have more of. Yu understand?"

"Yes. Of course."

"Because what I goin' tell yu next is serious, an' between yu an' me. Awright?"

By now his heart was pounding again, not knowing what to expect, but somehow, in his post-lovemaking lassitude, he was not too overly concerned.

"Yu know I have a sister in Toronto?"

"No, yu never mentioned it."

"Well, last December I decided to take out papers. She is going to sponsor Michael an' myself." He sucked in some air, looking dismayed.

"Yu mean yu goin' emigrate to Canada?"

"Exactly."

"But sis, how yu goin' support yuself?"

"Not to worry. I'm a capable little so and so." She laughed. "Probably I look for a job teaching."

"Raas." He couldn't help himself; neither did she chastise him.

"Food for thought, nuh?"

"Not food. A damn feast, if yu ask me. Can I ask yu. Why?"

"Yu know the answer already. I don' want to be stuck in this little forever land, watching it swim from one shore to the other, can' find a place to land. Insecurity. Michael future. All of those things." She had her legs drawn up, her arms around them, with her head resting on one side, not pensively, but with a slightly embarrassed yet determined expression.

Doug did not know how to respond. The thought of not having Madge there worried him. No. It was not worry. There was something else. As they sat there looking at each other, he had a moment to ponder. What would her decision mean for him? For them?

They had been crossing deserts until now; barren places where soil and sand prohibit growth, with little water. Yet something had been planted; it had nourished itself over the past months, and a sturdy plant had taken shape. Its roots were deep. Its flowers had not appeared yet, but the buds were discernible.

At this juncture something else had occurred. How to explain, to imagine it? Whatever the "it," they had crossed a threshold. There was, could be, no retreat. No going back. No avoiding. No denying. Whatever their decisions, something incomprehensible, bewildering in its ferocious intensity had taken place, had caught them, unawares, but implacably, in its grasp.

Their urgent, displaced love-making was one thing. That had been invaded, captured by another feeling, another meaning, to them yet only dim with possibilities—but omni-present from this moment.

Chapter XVII
Ganja Tragedy

The weekend after Madge's visit and her irrepressible disclosures Doug had decided to go into town. He had not seen the family for a few weeks. His mother, especially, was in need of his company. He left late that afternoon, as the sun was beginning to end its diurnal course, so that he would arrive just before supper.

Coincidentally James had also just arrived. They met almost going up the stairs, the one with rucksack, the other with legal briefcase.

"Wha' happen, big man?"

"Jus' in for the weekend," Doug explained.

"Give me a moment an' we tek a waters. It's been a long, raas week."

Christine appeared. After her, his mother and the two children. Friday was free of extra lessons, besides having their dad for a short while—uncle, too.

"How yu feeling, Mama.?"

"No too bad, son. After all that excitement, especially around the season. Yu know how it is." She was fanning vigorously to try to exterminate the day's stubborn remaining heat.

James appeared. They sat quietly on the corner of the veranda, sipping drinks before dinner.

"Any changes?" Doug asked.

"None, if yu mean our conversation."

"Told her yet?"

James grimaced slightly. "No. Still trying to wrap up some deals, negotiate. I don' wan' to sound a move before everything is ready. Moving is one thing, but moving without some security is out of the question." He grinned at Doug as he said it. "Yu know I not reckless like yu. Besides we have pickney dem. Have to think about school and all those things. Anyway, just time. Things movin' along nicely."

Doug knew his brother well. When he said "nicely", that meant "well." He would be close to wrapping up some contract soon, probably a lucrative one at that. Only after that was secure would he begin the application procedure. Everything at the right time. Quite the opposite to Doug, who would apply to move first, then put things into place after. Two siblings, but entirely different *modus vivendi*.

Dinner was served. During dinner it was the children who dominated. James junior wanted Uncle Doug to take them to Morgan's harbour again. Jennifer didn't care. She only wanted some ice-cream. A compromise was reached. They would go for some ice-cream after dinner. But just then the telephone rang.

"Maas Doug," Imogene called. "For you, sar."

"Doug, hear yu in town." It was M.J. How she came to know so quickly was ever a mystery for him.

So she accompanied them to Manor Plaza, where they gorged themselves on fistfuls of mango and guava ice-cream. Doug drove them home, then went over to M.J's for a bit. They sat on the balcony sipping drinks, attempting conversation; but it would not come. He was not interested in her office problems; neither was she in the school or politics. Words just wouldn't come. He offered to take her to the movies the next night.

Lawrence of Arabia with Peter O'Toole and Omar Sharif was playing at the Regal. They decided on the eight-thirty show. Afterwards they stopped at the Terra Nova for drinks. The conversation was still awkward, halting. Doug tried discussing the film, O'Toole's brilliant evocation of the spirit of Lawrence, his idealism, his competence, and subsequent betrayal by the British government. He tried the link to contemporary problems of imperialism: nothing worked. She was not interested, seemingly wrapped up in her own thoughts.

Finally she spoke, as he was taking a rest from the discussion of modern imperialism. "Doug, I want to ask yu something. Yu know when yu came back how elated I was. I thought that finally, especially after that wonderful first weekend at Strawberry Fields, that we were going to evolve into something. But I hardly ever see yu. It's almost as if yu don't want to see me."

"I know," he answered slowly. "I'm truly sorry, M.J. But work seemed to just capture me. And I wasn't too resistant. But I had a feeling that you wanted more from me."

"Can I ask you now, in all sincerity, whether there is even a chance of something more developing between us?" It was out in the open now. She had broached the subject. All along it had been the expectation of marrying that had caught her up in the vortex of his life. She had not taken the discussion that far, only wanting to indicate she would like to see some progression.

He took a deep breath before he began, slowly, choosing his words very carefully. "M.J. yu know how much yu always meant to me. We grew up together. It was almost inevitable that some feelings of this nature would develop between us."

"So what happened to them?" she persisted.

"I really don't know. It is so difficult to put my finger on anything. Just, it seems, these feelings didn't go anywhere after I came back?"

"But when I came out to see you the first time? What did you feel?"

"I felt the possibility, of course. I was really happy to have you with me. When we made love for the first time, I really wanted you."

"Then what happened. Did you find someone else?" There it was. The usual explanation: the other woman. But now he was caught. There was another woman, but, then again not really. Madge was only a possibility, not yet a certainty. Both she and he had a long way to proceed, if anything more definite was going to develop. But he could not confide that to M.J. It would have hurt too much. And there was the uncertainty. There was no guarantee that he and Madge, given their different plans for the future, would play a number together.

"No M.J. There is no other woman."

"Then the problems are with you?" She wouldn't let go either. She wanted to get to the bottom of the mystery. "Is that why we never seem to have any conversation?" Again he was trapped. To explain the vast gulf which separated their minds, their mental habits, their spiritual worlds, that would really hurt.

"M.J. I don't know I can give you an honest answer," he offered evasively. "But you are right. There doesn't seem to be much spark between us." He tried to be jocular, light, acknowledging the obvious without proffering an explanation.

"Then what are we going to do?"

"I don't have an honest answer for you right now," he tried.

"You mean that sometime in the future you might know more? Be more certain?"

"It's possible. I mean, who knows what the future will bring. Right now it doesn't appear as if we are going anywhere. More I can't say. And I feel a bit guilty because I know you want to get on with your life."

She tried another tack. The kind of tack women pull out when all else has been assayed and found wanting. "Yes, darling. Precisely. I have other suitors, you know. And I do want to have a family." Children. He knew.

He did know. But he also knew she was lying. She had not allowed other suitors. But he didn't let on. Perhaps it would be best if he left her in doubt. Absence and lack of interest would eventually bring the message home to her. That way he would not have to inflict instant pain. For now though, she was satisfied that she had gained the upper hand. It was best to wait and see; shock him through some honest jealousy into reacting. Really, she did not understand how close she had come to the truth. Maybe she didn't want to see it. It might be better that way.

Sunday Doug, James and the children went out to Cable Hut for a swim. They both preferred it to Morgan's harbour, anyway. The children loved splashing in the surf, running back across the sand, building castles and watching their father and uncle play football with friends.

M.J. was there, too, with other friends. She came over to Doug as he and James were having a Red Stripe by the little shack that served as bar and shower at the same time.

"Well, I didn't expect."

"Just taking the children for an outing."

"Going back today?"

"Right after lunch." He laughed. "Right after an after-lunch nap." They all laughed.

"See you next time." She reached up and kissed him on the cheek, carefully stroking his naked back with her soft hand. It had its effect.

"So yu don' look like a couple today. Problems?"

"No man. Nothing to worry about. But..." and here he paused.

"Seen." James used the Rasta expression for "understand." "But I think I get the picture," he said nodding.

Doug didn't answer. He just puckered his cheeks and finished his Red Stripe. "Time we got going?"

'Yes, master, come.'

He returned to Highgate that afternoon with the mounting questions concerning M.J. and how to handle the situation. He felt an irrepressible nostalgia about their relationship. It was so right in many ways. He even found her sexually attractive, still. Yet, that could not be all. There were those moments of awkward silences, the spiritual chasm that emerged as an impenetrable barrier of meaning. There was no bridge of desire with which it could be spanned.

Then his thoughts reverted to the one true connection he felt. The moments with Madge where they had sat quietly, not even needing to communicate verbally, just sitting there in the enjoyment of convivial contentment. Empathy rose between them as a cloud of vapour enveloping all in its path, blotting out discrepancies, erasing discordances, dissimilarities, creating new paths of harmonious concordance, of compatibility.

And when they did finally speak it was as if the ideas of the one opened possibilities the other had not yet contemplated. Conversation, the exploration of ideas, flowed so effortlessly, the conjunction of minds billowing over into the satiating beat of bodies in unison. He shuddered with delight when he thought of it: of the death to his soul its opposite would bring.

He swerved to miss a rock in the road on the climb into Highgate. He passed the railway station, the Chiang's grocery, before breaking ground over the ridge which brought the school entrance into view. He slowed, craning his neck to see up the driveway, maybe, just, maybe. But it was Sunday. He would have to wait for the morrow.

For the next few days and afternoons he was kept busy with the literacy class and the 4-H Club. Tomatoes, red peas and green pepper were reaching maturity and would have to be harvested soon. He and Madge met occasionally in the staff room, or had lunch together, but couldn't get together until the following weekend. For then they would have the house to themselves.

On the Saturday she visited him again. This time they let no conversation intervene before they made love. Again it was effortless, passionate, bespoke of the longing for more time together, and imparted to both the feelings that both lacked from other partners, feelings of completion, of love. Yet, they had not used the word, but it was felt by both that something stronger was growing within them.

The next week began as usual. Easter and the next holidays were only a few weeks away. More exams to set, and more which would have to be marked.

On the Thursday afternoon, he was informed that there was an urgent phone call for him. He walked quickly to the office wandering what it could be.

"Doug, it's me. Old man, you will have to steel yuself. There is horrible news." It was James, and Doug could tell his voice was shaking and that he was upset beyond belief.

"What's wrong. Is it mother," he asked.

"No brother. It is horrible. Anne and David. They were just found up at the house in Tulloch. Both gone."

"Gone? Yu mean...." His voice was rising now, the two secretaries stopping what they were doing at his obvious consternation and distress.

"But what about Robert and Susan? Are they all right?"

"Doug," was all James could say. His usual composure had turned into sobbing. "They, as well."

"NOOOOOOOOOO. Oh my God," he screamed, dropping the phone and doubling over his head in both hands.

One of the secretaries picked up the phone as Madge and young Barry came running out of the staffroom, startled by his scream. Mr. Johnston too, working upstairs in his office, had heard the commotion and came running down the stairs into the office.

Madge had picked up the phone. Barry had gone over to Doug and was holding him tightly around the shoulders. He was sobbing uncontrollably. Madge was listening to James, as the tears came streaming down her face. She gave the phone to Mr. Johnston who managed to communicate something to James.

Together they managed to calm Doug, who was breathing heavily, looking helplessly around the room as if he did not know what to do. Finally Mr. Johnston spoke. "Mr. Austin, come up to the office. We can sit quietly there. Come."

He took hold of Doug's arm firmly and with avuncular consolation, leading him upstairs. He motioned a word of thanks to Barry and Madge.

"This is a terrible shock, Mr. Austin, would you like me to call a doctor."

"No, thank you. I need to get over there right away. James is alone. They haven't told mother yet."

"It was your sister and brother-in-law."

"My neice and nephew, too. I must get to them," he replied, sobbing again.

"There is no problem of leaving. We will cover your classes for the time it takes. And, pardon my being practical at this moment. How will you get there? I don't think it is a good idea for you to drive."

Doug thought for a minute. Madge had now entered the room. She looked at him. They thought for a moment. "I know you are going to want to go. Let me make a suggestion," she turned to look at the headmaster. "Young Barry has two free periods this afternoon. He said he would like to drive Doug wherever he needs to go."

"I don't want to disrupt anything..."

The headmaster broke him off. "There is no question of disruption, sit." Turning to his intercom he called down to the office and asked them to ask Barry to come up.

"Mr. Ritschuk, thanks for coming. We have a request. Would you be able to go with Mr. Austin? I don't want to let him drive alone."

"Of course, anywhere. Come on Doug, let me drive you over there."

Doug thought awhile. He looked at Madge, but she just nodded yes. Mr. Johnston too, got up as if to indicate, yes, the matter is decided. Doug got up, too. He looked over at Johnston and Madge. "Thank you," he whispered softly.

They left. Before starting off, he phoned James's office hurriedly. He was also just getting ready to leave.

"James. I'm leaving. Barry Ritschuk is coming with me. But I'm not coming into Kingston. I think the best way is to cut across through Richmond and Troja then to Bog Walk. It is a paved road so that will save me an hour and a half. I will probably meet you there in two hours." He was regaining his composure. But it would be a difficult meeting.

At the school, the staff were all visibly upset. Winsome and some of the younger teachers were in tears. They had brought the little radio into the staff room, to catch the latest news. Gradually the story unfolded.

At about mid-day when David would have been home for lunch, one of the headmen had gone up to the house to get some instructions regarding the dairy cows that were to be taken for dipping the next day.

He had knocked at the back door, and receiving no answer had gone to the maid's quarters to see where everyone was. He called out over again. Finally he knocked and pushed in one of the doors, recoiling almost immediately with horror. The cook and the housemaid were both lying tied up on the narrow bed they used for taking a rest in the afternoon. Blood was already dripping through the mattress. Both had been shot in the head. Cook's face was turned towards him and he could see the bullet hole in the centre of her forehead.

He ran down the hill as fast as he could shouting and calling for help. He managed to attract the attention of some field hands. One he sent off on a bicycle to get to a phone and call the police. With the others he rushed back up to the house. The back door was firmly locked, so two of them lent their weight against it until finally the lock snapped.

There was an eerie silence inside, so they moved gingerly, not knowing what to expect. There was a trail of blood leading from the living room into one of the bedrooms.

They pushed open the door quietly after calling out. There on the floor was David. He had obviously been beaten before being dispatched with a bullet to the head. Anne was lying half clothed on the bed. She had a spreading blot of blood on her chest. Both were dead.

The men next went to examine the other bedrooms. In one, they found Robert and Susan tied together on the bed, turned towards each other as if grasping and hugging for the few last minutes of comfort. Their throats had been slit.

The men retraced their steps as quietly as they had come. One retched over the back steps. The others reached hurriedly for cigarettes, looking at each other without saying a word. Then they sat down quietly waiting, each with his own thoughts.

It was some time before the police could arrive from Bog Walk. But they were in force, led by a young sub-inspector who efficiently cordoned off the area, before phoning his report in to the station. He immediately asked for his report to be communicated to the CID (Criminal Investigation Department). Word also got out somehow to the JBC, which would put together a camera crew for the evening news.

About five-thirty in the late afternoon Doug and Barry pulled up at the house. James had arrived a few minutes earlier and was talking to the sub-inspector. Two CID inspectors had already arrived from Spanish Town, less than an hour away, and were taking fingerprints and photos. The JBC camera crew also arrived, but were confined to the front lawn. They were not allowed inside the house. But they were able to film the ambulance attendants as they removed the bodies, before taking them to the morgue at Spanish Town. An expected interview with either James or Doug was also not forthcoming. Both had been allowed in to the scene prior to the removal of the bodies, and were in no fitting mood to talk to reporters.

In the days that followed the whole island was abuzz with rumours and discussion. Speculation was rife. No one could believe that there was someone so evil as to murder two little children in cold blood. It was becoming obvious that it was either the work of a madman or madmen, or something even more sinister. There had been no robbery. Even David's expensive Rolex watch had been left on his hand. No jewellery was missing. But the police had no answer either. There was no note, such as would-be revolutionaries like to leave as a warning to others. No indication who might have been the culprits. If the police knew anything, they were keeping silent.

The funeral was held at the parish church at Half Way Tree. Two large and two small coffins rested before the altar. The church was packed. People who had no connection at all to the Austins or McCormacks were there. The explanation was simple. Jamaicans were outraged. The brutality of the crime, the murder of two innocent children sent shivers down everyone's spine.

Jamaicans as a whole have a very keen sense of justice. There are usually no mitigating circumstances. In this particular case, not at all. Right is right; and wrong is wrong. And wrong has no colour. Two little children and their parents had been murdered. That was all. There was no apparent motive, nor could there be one for such a horror. Justice needed to find the perpetrators and try them.

Their mother had not been able to attend the funeral. It was M.J. who broke the news to her slowly. She was so overcome that she had to be taken to the hospital and given tranquilizers. Her sobs would be heard for weeks.

Doug also had to explain, as best he could to James junior and Jennifer. It was not an easy task. But M.J. was at his side throughout. It was not only because of Doug. Anne had been like a sister to her. They had grown up side by side, scraped knees together, discussed boys, grown through puberty with their secret confidences, had attended university together.

Doug had to get back to school. The staff there did all they could to show him their solidarity. His pupils were marvellous. Even the most recalcitrant ones tried their best to behave now and again and curb their mischievous sides. He was comforted, too, by his friend Stanley, by his political friends, especially Drowsy. Nobody condoned such wickedness.

But the mystery remained. Who had done it? The answers were slow in coming. In the next few weeks a picture began to emerge. First, and this time another shock for the family, John was arrested by the police and charged with the crime of growing and trafficking ganja. Next, it was ascertained by villagers in the area of Tulloch, that two men, unknown in the area, had been seen coming and going to David's house. They usually drove a large, black Mercedes.

Then John's trial began. And only then did the truth begin to emerge. John's lawyer would not let him acknowledge the charges. But under a skilful prosecutor, and perhaps under the weight of his brother's and sister-in-laws death, and that of the two children, he broke down on the witness stand and asked the judge permission to speak freely. It was granted.

John took the whole blame on himself. Yes, the ganja pastures the police had found had been planted under his instructions. The reason they had not been spotted earlier was because of the terrain. Behind the Great House the land rises sharply to a ridge of hills. They are covered with dense brush and trees. But behind it the land falls of sharply onto some wide plains. There, hidden from view was where they had decided to plant the ganja. The reason?

The dairy business had fallen off. Costs had risen, especially after the price of feed had increased with the removal of government subsidies. Then there was the cost of fuel. It had seriously hurt the sugar refinery which depended on cheap sources of fuel. So they had decided to do something else.

John had met some people in Miami by coincidence, who, hearing that he controlled some extensive properties in Jamaica, had made them an offer. They had quietly begun to grow and sell ganja to what appeared to be a syndicate. The whole operation was covered by the dairy business. Feed would be trucked in, and the ganja trucked out in the same trucks covered with hay. The ganja would then be transferred on other trucks in the back roads behind Bog Walk, belonging to the syndicate. Cash would be deposited in an American bank in Miami. So the Jamaican authorities were none the wiser.

This was the very reason Eustace had refused to go up to the properties any longer. He must have known something funny was going on. But out of self-preservation decided he wanted nothing to do with it. And out of loyalty, especially in case he might be wrong, he had not wanted to discuss it, even with Doug.

What had probably led to the murder were increasing demands by the syndicate. They had wanted to construct a dirt airstrip further at the back of one of the properties, to facilitate the export. David had consistently refused his brother's requests. Finally the syndicate had decided to put more pressure. David's refusal had led to the murders. And the guilty? They were more than likely living in the States and would be out of reach of the Jamaican police. John was given six years at hard labour, a demeaning but appropriate sentence considering. He would also have to live with the thought, for the rest of his life, that his complicity was the trigger for the murder of his brother and his family.

Still, it bothered many people that the criminals could not be brought to justice. The two men who had been seen on the property were described by many villagers: one was Black, the other was light-skinned. As usual, the US authorities were reluctant to track down their own, and, even so, a possible extradition for murder might have taken decades. But then there was a startling breakthrough.

It is almost impossible for good-thinking people to imagine the minds of criminals. No, not almost. Completely. Criminals think altogether differently, especially those sufficiently cold-blooded to carry out the murder of children. There is no accounting for the hubris, the heights of arrogance that cold-blooded killers can attain. They feel themselves sacrosanct, not just above, but beyond the law. And sometimes it expresses itself in funny ways. Then there is the question of conscience. Killers are thought not to have any. But is it there lurking somewhere, this idea of the values of right and wrong, which from its own necessity needs to surface every now and again?

Whatever the answers to those questions may be, one of the killers decided in his wisdom to take a holiday. He must have been working too hard. And the holiday resort of choice was Montego Bay.

Not just six weeks after the murders, the police reported calmly one day that they had arrested one of the suspected murderers at the White Witch hotel resort in Montego Bay. One evening the man, whose name now was given as one Raimundo García Ramírez, a Columbian living in Miami, had gone to the Skipper's Rest, a local bar not far from Montego Bay's market, near the area which is commonly called, "The Strip." There he had imbibed a sufficient quantity of 'whites,' and had been taken in tow by one of the area's experienced, pretty, local, beauties, who made her precarious living from male tourists willing to exchange a few hundred dollars for her pum-pum. And he must have taken a liking to her. Because after pum-pum, and again sufficiently liquored-up, he had told her about the murders, expressing some pride at his handiwork.

This little gal had listened with interest, laughing with García at the right moment, expressing her admiration, feeding his vanity as well as enough rum to ensure a deep sleep. With him snoring loudly in her little house she had then slipped out and gone straight to the police. That early morning, García woke to find a pair of handcuffs securely fastened around both hands.

Jamaican justice can be swift. There is not much horsing around with niceties such as how poor his upbringing was, or whether he had experienced violence as a child. No, for a Jamaican jury right is right, and wrong is wrong. And it took no time for them to find the latter was the case and that García was guilty. There was no recommendation for mercy. Nor did the judge hesitate. His condemnation was emphatic, as was his reaching for the black cap to pronounce the expected sentence.

García was taken immediately to Richmond prison, ironically only a few miles from Highgate. Six weeks later, appeals being unfavourable, his lifeless body at the end of a rope attested to the penance exacted from murderers. Justice had been done.

Doug's existence thereafter took on a new meaning. He was found as many weekends as he could, at his mother's side. She would not allow herself to be comforted. They all felt the pall of gloom that hung over them. M.J. was in constant attendance with the family, especially taking on the task, as Christine had her children to contend with, of sitting with his mother.

And so they saw more of each other than they might have, had things taken another course. But their relationship did not change. If anything Doug was further away from her than ever. They did not make love any more. Of conversation, too, apart from the mundane, there was nothing.

In Highgate, on the other hand, his heart found it easier to function. Madge's presence provided the bulwark against the train of events and gave him strength, sustenance and the quiet support that comes from profundity. They met secretly as often as they could. He tried to gauge the weekends when Barbara and Dave would be away, and to coordinate these with his visits home. Sometimes he would just run in on a Friday evening to sit with his mother, or to sip a rum or two and chat quietly with James.

Chapter XVIII
Epilogue

THE WEEKS FOLLOWING THE MURDERS SAW Doug in a very depressed state. He could not achieve peace in his mind. Madge did her best. She came to see him as often as she dared. At times they just sat still saying little. Their lovemaking was, well, if not perfunctory, void of the earlier passion. Not that he had lost feelings for her. Quite to the contrary. She was now his main comfort. Spiritually they remained as close, if not closer than before.

But he felt the duty of spending as much time with his mother and family as possible. It was especially hard on his mother, and also the children. He tried his best, but in the circumstances all he could provide was his presence as support.

It was on one of those visits that his Uncle Benjamin approached him. Poor man: eldest son, daughter-in-law and grandchildren murdered, second son in jail for a long period. He was now faced with the prospect of carrying on alone. It was a daunting task.

Eustace had come forward to offer his help. But he knew little of the dairy business. For that they had to rely on his father, who managed to take over the running of the herd and supervising. So one Saturday, as they were sitting on the veranda, Ben came over to see them.

'Doug,' he said in a most supplicating voice, "You know I always wanted you to join us in the business. Now that I am alone, I feel even more the need for your help." Doug's mother sat there nodding. Mary Jean who was also present said nothing, but in her heart she hoped that Doug would consider. Give up the idea of more academic work. Stay in the island with her and manage the business from which they would make a good living. With her skills in administration she would be his helpmate. And the rest would follow.

"Uncle Benjamin," Doug started, slowly, measuring his words given the delicate situation. "You know it's not easy for me to sit here and know you need help and not pitch in. As I love this family, it would be easy for me to say yes. So, believe me I would rush to help you if I could. But you've known me from a boy. I'm not at all cut out for business, managing a property, a hardware business; it would just not be me. You don't know how much I would like to help. But I would be a liability more than an asset. I wasn't cut out for it. It is as far away from my capabilities as it is from my soul."

As he spoke he dropped his head down into his hands, propping them up at his knee. M.J. was sitting across from him. He saw the look on her face. He could feel her dejection. It was not what she had wanted to hear. The air had gone out of her life, with that announcement. The hope of a young girl, an expectant young woman, bathed in the natural love of a woman for a man, a love which had grown as a sturdy plant within her soul, now lay withered, dead on the ground of possibility.

Uncle Benjamin also looked crestfallen. He had almost been begging Doug. And to get this "no" from Doug at this time especially, added further pain to his other misfortunes. But how could he have understood? He lived, the others too, in an entirely different mental world.

"In fact, I came to a decision last week," Doug continued "I haven't told the school yet, nor mentioned it to anyone else. What I am most cut out for is an academic career in my chosen area. It seems what I'm most suited for. It's what gives me the most satisfaction in life. It is what I love above all. I have to consider that first, hard as it is to say that to you. So I decided to enrol for a doctorate at Toronto, starting in September. Hopefully, later on when I'm through, there will be a university post for me somewhere." He added softly, "It is what I really need to do."

James sat there quietly. He understood his brother. He was not as upset about Doug's response as the others, but he felt for his uncle and his mother. Theirs would have been deep satisfaction had Doug decided to stay. But he knew his brother. As yet, also, he had not told the family of his own decision. That shock would come in time.

M.J. had had her inklings. Like Uncle Benjamin, she did not fully understand. But at least she had been closer to Doug, sharing, to some extent, in his life and his expectations. If his mental world were not hers, still her emotions understood ever so faintly that he was for another existence. The thought tore through her with the renewed pain she had felt that last weekend together. But at least now she knew where she stood with him.

Doug had mulled it all over in his mind after the tragedy. There had been little progress in the island: lots of words. Yes, good intentions, great plans and vision, but little else. The economy was still in the doldrums with little hope for improvement. Government successes were likely not going to appear. Doug felt he had personally overcome the racial divide at least in his own mind. In fact, it had probably just been in and of his mind, well, most of it anyway.

But could he overcome history? Not bloody likely. That one had eluded him, as it was obvious it would have. Jamaica's problems were not going to go away. It was impossible to turn around, after centuries of hegemonic dictation, even a small island, to encourage people on to a path of non-imperialistic independent venture. Perhaps it could never even be accomplished.

What about himself? Did he feel a sense of failure? Could, should he have done more?

What failure—the sense of inability to challenge or change the existing matrices of history, of property dictation? The sacredness of the latter seemed to jump out at him everywhere he turned. How could he have thought with such naivety, that he could accomplish the impossible? Madge had been right, of course.

The problem was also with revolution: to revolve, turning the wheel, standing everything on its head. That meant putting those at the bottom on top. But that was merely a change of personnel—a change of roles, not real change. Real change meant an end to the social matrix of property; the mind, the psyche had to be cleansed, altered and reconstructed in a new mode. That necessary and important element could not be understood by the masses. It had been the bane of every revolution in history. Time, only time, perhaps ages, would be needed.

And then there were the leftovers of slavery and the plantation system. Slavery had covered their lives with an amalgam of hatred. It had grown and remained like moss covers stone. Intermittently growing, hidden in interstices of thought, of possibility, it lurked in its festooned slime, impacting language, smothering good intentions. It finally encased, erased hope, even emasculated the future.

Slavery took the scrotum of history in its hands, squeezing every last drop of forward sperm out of the realm of engendering.

One couldn't war against it. Transformation was impossible. Righting the wrongs of history? Ridiculous.

Only new beginnings would suffice. But these had to be guaranteed slow germination so as to ensure voluptuous growth over ages. And so, what was one to do? One had to survive. There was the individual test of location, of immanence. One was alone in the world of emaciated history. Survival alone was the key. One was going to survive, but within the shadowy movement of the historical sundial. The seasons would arrive, depart, and recur. There was nought to hold against them.

It was at the beginning of June, not two months before the school year closed, that he came to a final decision. His family was the first to know. After he returned to school that following Monday, he went to see the head.

"How are you coping, Mr Austin. Your family?" The warmth of the condolence was obvious.

"We just have to get through Mr. Johnston. It's not easy, but we have no choice. Thanks very much for your sentiments. But, you know, I actually came to see you about another matter." He had decided to get to the matter quickly, before other, and extraneous factors brought him to hesitate.

"In fact I was expecting you, Mr. Austin. Unfortunately."

"Yes, it is unfortunate. You know how I have loved being here: yourself, the staff, the children. But it is time for me to think of other things. My own future, for example. I put it off for a while, but now it's time I made a decision."

"I think I know what's coming, Mr. Austin."

"Yes. I've decided to leave early and to start some more academic work in Toronto. I know it means breaking the contract, but really, in my heart of hearts, it would be difficult to stay and do an adequate job."

"I am truly sorry to hear that, sir. Not as though I didn't feel it was coming. But, you know, Mr. Austin, as much as I sympathize, and understand personally, mine is another role as well."

"I understand that Mr. Johnston."

The head continued. "You will have to pay all the back taxes and will forfeit the twenty percent stipend you would have had at the end of your contract."

"Yes, sir, I am aware of that."

"Let me have it in writing then, and I will start the necessary procedures."

He had one more meeting with Madge. It was two Saturdays before his departure. The school term was over. She had come up to Highgate to do some shopping. The others had departed so the big house was empty. They had it all to themselves.

"So, Maas Doug. Yu ready?"

"Depends wha' yu mean. To leave? No. To study? Maybe? To forget? Never."

She didn't press him. But this time it was she who reached for his hand pulling him towards the bedroom. This time their passion seemed to have returned. She gave herself as if no other mode with him in the world existed. He held her long and ardently as if no other woman did, could, exist. They didn't need to say anything. There were few words. Only looks. No goodbyes.

At the airport his other goodbyes were hurried and seemingly without emotion. The family was still bathed in the shock of their tragedy. He held M.J. for a moment in a long, sincere, embrace—then his mother. He threw one wistful glance over his shoulder at the airport gallery, noticing her standing at the railing, waving a small handkerchief. M.J. was beside her. James, Christine and the children stood a little back. There was also Uncle Benjamin and Aunt Mae. Before leaving home he had had a phone call from Madge. She just said "See you in Toronto. Have a safe flight." Nothing more.

As he walked across the tarmac toward the big jet he glanced down and was struck by the sun reflected from one of the little puddles that had been left on the ground after an unexpected cloud-burst. As he looked up again he realized that the sun was high in the sky signifying the arrived summer.

The seasons had come full circle again. Like a great pendulum, the earth seemed to rock back and forth from one pole to the other. And so with human affairs. One season ended while the other began, continuously through the aeons.

The sun would continue along its path and the seasons would come and go.

AUTHOR'S NOTE

AS IN MANY WORKS OF FICTION there is an element of biography. This book is no different. The author did return to Jamaica in the 1970's in a spirit of idealism and did teach at St. Mary High School in Highgate. The setting of the novel and the historical context, are, therefore, very real. There, however, biography gives way to fiction.

A propos the matter of fact and fiction, there are more than a few passages which reflect the first. Jamaica in 1972-1980, the setting for the book, was in the hands of Michael Manley and the PNP, who were trying their best to bring about social and economic change, using Democratic Socialism as the model. It was a bold, visionary, experiment, intended to break the stranglehold of colonialism, imperialism and historical racism. It is also a fact that it failed.

That that government tried to interest the Russians in a Cuban-like venture is also a fact. That whole story was revealed when a high Russian official, Alexi Leshtchouk, defected to the United States in August 1980. He stated that Manley had not only invited the Russians to come and take a look, Manley, himself, went to Moscow in April, 1979. In any case the Russians did not trust Manley's commitment to parliamentary democracy, preferring the party programme of the Workers Party of Jamaica (WPJ) led by Trevor Munroe. (Jamaica Weekly Gleaner (N.A.), December 28, 1981, pp. 23-31.) They were also apparently disinclined to finance another Cuba. This entire matter has subsequently received academic corroboration. (See Cole Blasier, *The Giant's Rival: The USSR and Latin America*, Pittsburg: University of Pittsburg Press, 1983).

There was also some rather humorous speculation that the Russians had taken a good look at Jamaicans and decided that we are such an undisciplined people that Socialism would never have been a possibility. I rather like that explanation, for if true, it is rather a compliment.

That the government must have been thinking about a "Cubanization" in 1973, however, especially after the oil shock, is purely my own conjecture. I mean, for them to have tried to implement this idea in 1978 means that there was some thought, not to speak of discussion about it before then. I am as convinced that the matter must have been broached in Cabinet before that date, as I am that there must have been a few members of Cabinet in favour of such a move. But there is no evidence to date to attest to that fact.

In addition, most of the place names are real, as is St. Mary High School, which has since evolved into one of the best secondary schools in the island. The government's Teacher Recruitment Programme which began in 1972, and which brought many qualified expatriates to the island, is also a fact.

Nevertheless, the characters all, (except for the major politicians), including the protagonist and the members of Doug's family are all composite, imaginative, constructs.

Karl B. Koth,
Winnipeg, August, 2012.

Author's Biography

THE AUTHOR WAS BORN IN KINGSTON, Jamaica. His father Bernard, was a German immigrant businessman, who fell in love with the country and stayed, marrying Beryl Campbell, of mixed Jamaican heritage, African, Luso-Jewish and Scots, not necessarily in that order.

He grew up in St. Andrew, attended Westbrook Preparatory School (Miss Butler's) and then Jamaica College, enjoying holidays in the foothills around Constant Spring, stoning mangoes and riding his bicycle around the Sandy Gully area. Spending holidays with a cousin on an estate near Bog Walk, from which there were many excursions on horseback, afforded an intimate contact with people and moulded his feelings for the land.

After leaving high school he went to Germany, ostensibly to study engineering, but ended up joining the new German Air Force, where he became an officer and flight instructor on jet aircraft.

There he married Beverly Sharp, his first wife with whom he had three children, Charles, Christopher and Natalya. He went on to pursue university studies in the United States. With BA in hand, he returned to Jamaica and inter alia taught History and English at his old school, Jamaica College.

In 1968 he and the family emigrated to Canada, where he completed a Master's degree at the University of British Columbia. The lure of Jamaica and the promise of the new Michael Manley government being too much to resist, he returned under the Teacher Recruitment Scheme, and taught History at St. Mary High School in Highgate for two years before returning to Canada.

After completing a doctorate in History at the University of Manitoba he was professor of Latin American History at Okanagan University College in British Columbia, as well as Associate Dean of Arts.

Retiring from that institution in 2004 he lived for a time in Brazil, then returned to Winnipeg where he now lives with his wife Nina and lectures in Contemporary World History at the University of Manitoba.

He is the author of *Waking the Dictator: Veracuz, the Struggle for Federalism and the Mexican Revolution, 1870-1927*, and has published short fiction and poetry in the Winnipeg Journal, *Caribe: Black Creative Writers.*

# Glossary

Is So We Labrish

Abeng – A horn made from a cow, used to summon slaves to uprisings; especially used by the Maroons

Anancy – Of West African origin, Anancy is the spider, very cunning, who usually wins every encounter. Anancy stories are a favourite with Jamaican children

Backra or buckra – A White person, or someone living in such style in the Caribbean

Banana walk – Banana fields or planted banana areas

Banggarang – A great noise or disturbance

Boonoonoonoos – Term of endearment; very pretty, wonderful

Bruckins – A lively boisterous party

Bumbo – The buttocks, especially the female pudendum, used as a swear word.

Bulla – A round flat cake, tough and reliable, made from brown sugar and flour

Busha – An overseer

Buss-ass – A beating or licking

Butu, Buttu - A low-classed person, uncouth

Bwai,bwoy – Boy, but in a derogatory sense

Chile – Child, girl, in an affectionate sense

Cho, chu – Exclamation of astonishment, anger, disagreement

Country – Anywhere in Jamaica, except the capital, Kingston

Cuffy, or cuffee – A backward or stupid person; one easily fooled

Dungle – Jungle, but the name given to the shanty-town outside Kingston whence had emerged the Reggae beat

Duppy – Ghost

Facety – Impudent, bold, rude

Fast-fast mouth – Quick talker

Fene, fenay – To faint

Fenky-fenky – Slight; puny; effeminate; fussy
Fool-fool – Simple; stupid
Fun-fun – Just for fun, make believe
Funkify – Make someone angry; speak precociously
Gal, gal dem (pl) – Girl, girls
Ganja – Marijuana
Higgler – Small buyers, usually women, who buy from farmers and sell in the market
Jinal – A crafty, tricky, person, often a crook
John Crow – A carrion
Jonkanoo – A derivative African custom; a band with masked drummers, they appear at Christmas and with various antics, tricks and noise try to inveigle money from passers-by and households.
Jump-up – A dance or party
Kwashiorkor – Children's tropical disease caused by lack of protein
Kyan – Can not
Labrish – Idle talk; gossip; chatter, usually untrustworthy
Lamps – To fool someone
Naw – No, not
Nuff – Enough
Nuttin – Nothing
Nyam – West African word for eating voraciously or roughly
Otaheite apple – Delicious fruit introduced from Polynesia in the 18th century
Pickney – Child
Pickeny dem (pl) – Children
Pocomania – A revivalist and spiritualist cult with definite African roots
Property – Jamaican slang for an estate
Pu-dong – From "put down"—a quarrel
Pum-pum – Pussy
Q flask – A pint bottle of rum; literally a quarter of an imperial quart
Raatid – An expression indicating anger, annoyance, amazement or surprise
Raas – Buttocks; but a vulgar expression showing extreme anger, contempt, impatience, scorn. It is the most widely used Jamaican swear word, and grammatically versatile.
Ring-game – A typical Jamaican country game, reminiscent of, but stylistically different from Maypole dancing. Some of the favourite ones are "Brown Girl in De Ring," "Dandy Shandy," and "Bull Inna Ring."
Rungles – Tricks
Smalls – Small change; a tip

Sore-toe – A crude torch made of stuffing a cork or some wadding into a bottle filled with kerosene oil
Teach – Affectionate form of address for a teacher
Yard – A symptomatic Jamaican word for home; it often connotes a tenement.
Ya-so – Here
Waters – A drink, or drinking as in "taking up yu waters."
Whites – White over-proofed rum
Wuk – Work